COUNTED

With the

STARS

CONNILYN COSSETTE

BETHANYHOUSE

a division of Baker Publishing Group
Minneapolis, Minnesota

© 2016 by Connilyn Cossette

Published by Bethany House Publishers
11400 Hampshire Avenue South
Bloomington, Minnesota 55438
www.bethanyhouse.com

Bethany House Publishers is a division of
Baker Publishing Group, Grand Rapids, Michigan

Printed in the United States of America

ISBN 978-0-7642-1437-0

Library of Congress Control Number: 2015956737

Scripture quotations are from the King James Version of the Bible.

This is a work of historical reconstruction; the appearances of certain historical figures
are therefore inevitable. All other characters, however, are products of the author's
imagination, and any resemblance to actual persons, living or dead, is coincidental.

Cover design by Jennifer Parker

Author is represented by The Steve Laube Agency.

17 18 19 20 21 22 23   8 7 6 5 4 3 2

To Chad, whose sacrificial love makes this possible

To Collin and Corrianna, my most precious gifts

And to my *Abba*, Yahweh, who opens my eyes

PROLOGUE

My sandals have not crossed this threshold since I was ten.

Inhaling, I focused on the Eye of Horus woven into the papyrus mat beneath my feet. After summoning an infusion of courage from its steady gaze, I lifted my chin and entered my father's chambers.

My father's braided wig lay on his desk, as if flung aside without a thought for his usual meticulous appearance. He stood with his back to me, studying a document with such intensity that my quiet entrance had gone unnoticed. Did I imagine that his hand trembled?

Intuition fluttered in my chest. Never had I seen my father so unraveled.

Appointed with vibrant tapestries and a gilded sleeping couch fit for Pharaoh, this room resurrected a long-forgotten memory of sitting beside my father as he studied trade reports and his warm hand enveloping mine.

Hoping to swallow the quiver in my voice, I cleared my throat. "Father, you sent for me?"

He startled but did not turn as he spoke. "Yes, Kiya. Come in." Scratching at the silver stubble on his head with one hand, he continued examining the document in silence.

Fidgeting with the beaded shawl I had just purchased in the market, I stroked the embroidered ibises and the silver beads that twinkled like stars along the hem. I had also been considering a lyre at a musician's stall. Roses scrolled down the body of the instrument, the petals so lifelike I could almost inhale their delicate fragrance. But before I could make any offer, Yuny, my father's servant, had skidded to a stop in front of me. His chest heaved from exertion as he repeated a curious demand from my father that I return home in haste. The stricken look on the man's wrinkled face had caused me to abandon the lyre and rush back to the villa.

My sandals, although crafted from the finest kid-leather, had not been designed for running, so now blisters plagued the sides of my feet and between my toes. Surveying the room for somewhere to sit and ease the pain, I was surprised to see my father's friend, Shefu, on a chair in the corner.

Shefu's children and I had played together when we were young, and we were frequent guests at his wife's extravagant banquets, but I had never spoken with him. A wealthy businessman, he was very tall and quite handsome, even with the touch of gray at his temples. He seemed quiet and kind—standing in sharp contrast to his wife, whom my mother avoided whenever possible.

I attempted to catch his eye and offer a smile, but his gaze was locked on the floor, and he gripped the ebony armrests with his long fingers, knuckles white.

Were he and my father discussing exports? Arguing? My father had seemed distracted for the past few days and had been even more distant than usual when he'd returned from a trip north to Avaris. But why would I be called in during a business negotiation?

"Kiya . . ." My father paused, placing the document face-down on the desk. He sat on a nearby chair, giving me the faint impression that he was sinking into the tiled floor. He gazed at his palms, as if searching there for words.

"What is it, Father? Is it Akhum? Have you heard something?" My pulse began to thrum with concern for my betrothed, who was away on a military expedition.

"No, it's not Akhum." He dragged in a quivering breath. His eyes flicked to mine but then away, as if he was afraid to meet my curious gaze.

"Shefu—" He raked his fingers across his scalp. "Shefu is here . . . to take you with him."

Panic rose in my throat as I tried to decipher his statement. "Take me where?" I looked back and forth between the two men, but neither of them would meet my eye.

My stomach hollowed, and alarm screeched in my brain. "Father? Tell me. Where is Shefu taking me?"

After a few agonizing moments of silence, my father's words broke free, flooding out in a rush. "I am ruined. My boats, all of them, sank in the Northern Sea. I did all that I could to avoid this. But everything—" He rubbed the back of his neck and swallowed hard. "Everything we own will be auctioned off to pay my obligations. I owe Shefu for the five boats I purchased last year, among other things . . ."

My father looked me straight in the eye for the first time in years. "This is the only way. To protect your mother, and Jumo, from being sold as well. I have no choice."

A blur of colors and a torrent of swirling sounds met my

senses. I staggered backward, shaking my head, blinking away the cloud of confusion that threatened my sight.

My hip knocked into a marble-topped shrine table near the doorway, causing a large cow-headed carving of Hathor to tip. She fell, clanking into another idol, which toppled into another, which in turn knocked a golden image of Ra onto the stone floor, his sun-crowned head splitting from his body and his hooked scepter scattering into pieces. The other statues followed suit, until not one god stood intact. Shards and splinters littered the tiles.

I turned from the tragedy, meaning to run, but the truth crashed over me like a wave, and my knees gave way. Arms over my head, I called for my mother, over and over, through choking sobs.

But it was Salima, my handmaid, who lifted me from the floor, her dark eyes pooling with tears, and led me back to my own room by the hand.

She removed my wig, soaked through with sweat from our excursion to the market that morning. Then she washed my face and head with cool water she had retrieved from the Nile long before I had awakened.

After she dressed me in a shift woven from fine linen but simple in design, and reapplied my kohl, Salima placed her warm brown hands on either side of my face.

Since my seventh year, Salima had bathed me, groomed me, applied kohl to my eyes, and dressed me in gowns and wigs. Although only a few years older than me, she'd endured my childish impatience and fits of temper without a shadow of bitterness ever crossing her face. And now, for the first time since my father had gifted her to me, she stared directly into my eyes with her luminous dark ones.

At times, I had glimpsed a depth of wisdom in those eyes that made me wonder what her life might have been before she became my handmaid. But I had never asked. Why had I never asked?

Salima leaned her forehead against mine and whispered something in a language I did not recognize. But the music of it washed over me, leaving behind an impossible calm and a surprising clarity.

My father had sold me.

There was no choice but to go with Shefu and serve him. What that meant I could not begin to guess. He seemed benign, but was he as good to his servants as he was to his peers? I had seen slaves in other homes, cowed and skittish, some with obvious bruises on their faces and arms. Was that to be my lot?

It did not matter. I could not let my mother and my disabled brother be separated. Jumo would not be safe anywhere but with the woman who had fought for his life from his first breath.

I straightened my back. "Salima, where is my mother?"

She looked down. "I do not know. I think your father sent her and your brother away before we left for the market."

"Do you have the gifts I purchased this morning? The ivory combs and the dyes and brushes for Jumo?"

She gestured to the reed basket at the foot of my bed.

"Please make sure they receive those." If nothing else, I could at least leave a token of my love for them.

She dipped her chin at this, my last request.

I closed my eyes, inhaling deeply, as if I could breathe in the serenity that clung to Salima along with her customary sweet-almond fragrance.

An image from earlier this morning surged into my mind— sweat sparkling on Salima's dark forehead and across her closely trimmed scalp as she shifted the heavy basket full of my purchases from one shoulder to the other.

The burn of shame welled in my eyes. "I cannot begin to tell you how . . ."

She placed her fingers on my lips and shook her head, her expression full of mercy. "No need, mistress."

The address jarred me. I was no longer her mistress. Salima would be sold as well, to feed the same yawning chasm of debt, another offering at the altar of my father's excess. I grasped her hand with the urgency of a lifeline. "Call me Kiya. Please."

Salima dropped her eyes to speak my name. "Kiya."

Abandoned on my vanity table next to us was the elegant wrap I had purchased earlier. I picked it up, allowing the silken fabric to flow across my skin like water. My practiced eye had ensured that not one flaw marred its surface as I dickered with the cloth vendor.

I folded the linen piece and pressed it into Salima's hands, insisting that it was my gift to her. To my surprise she accepted it with grace, grasping it to her chest in wordless gratitude.

She handed me a small woven basket and attempted a sad smile. "Master Shefu will be waiting."

With a nod, I turned and walked away from the room in which I had slept every night of my life, and every comfort contained therein. I followed a silent and stoic Shefu out of the white villa that had been my home since birth and into the violent sunlight, with the incomprehensible realization that my handmaid and I were now on the same footing.

1

1ST DAY OF AKHET
SEASON OF INUNDATION
1447 BC

The sound of my knock on the wooden chamber door echoed in the pit of my stomach. Shira opened the door, but the Hebrew girl refused to meet my eyes. Two streaks of fur, one black and one gray, fled the room—even the cats knew enough to escape.

"Is that Kiya?" My mistress's sharp voice raised the hair on the back of my neck. "It had better be."

Tightening my grip on the water jug I carried—my only shield—I drew a deep breath as I stepped past Shira and over the threshold.

Tekurah crossed her bedroom in four swift strides to tower over me. "Where have you been? You held up this entire household all morning."

What an exaggeration. I abandoned the temptation to try and explain the throng of people, animals, and merchant booths clogging the city today. Pushing my way through the crowds during festival preparations had proved almost impossible, especially carrying a jar full of water from the canal. Besides, Tekurah was never at a loss for reasons to reprimand me.

With practiced obedience I mumbled, "Forgive me, mistress."

My show of humility did nothing to placate her. She thrust the ebony handle of a fan toward my face while accusing me of deliberate delay. I flinched. *She might actually strike me this time.*

She threw her hands in the air. "Why do I have to put up with such a worthless slave?" She growled like one of her cats and then continued her tirade. I didn't bother to listen. I had heard all of this before and doubtless would again.

Jaw locked and mind numb, I waited for the end of her diatribe. Instead I focused on the intricacies of the painted mural on the wall. The lush scene depicted the glorious paradise of the afterlife, where gods and men traveled together in gilded boats on the sparkling blue waters of the eternal Nile. The vivid colors were striking, but they were nothing compared to my brother Jumo's masterful artwork.

Shira's posture snagged my attention. The Hebrew girl stood in front of the open window, wrapped in sunlight, head down and eyes closed—submissive as usual. Were her lips moving?

"And if you keep me waiting again"—Tekurah pointed the fan an inch from my nose—"I *will* hit you. Even the gods wouldn't fault me."

Bitter retorts bubbled up inside me, threatening to burst free. Silently, I prayed to Ra, Isis, and any other god who would listen, for the strength to keep my mouth shut. Sweat trickled in rivulets down my spine.

Tekurah drew a long breath through her nose, black eyes flashing. With another growl, she hurled the ebony fan toward the enormous bed in the center of the room, but it tangled in the sheer linen canopy and clattered to the floor. She stared at it, blinking, and then exhaled through gritted teeth. Hands on hips, she turned and stalked to her bathing chamber.

As Shira retrieved the fan, I breathed quiet thanks to the gods for such a brief scolding today. My sliding grip on the heavy earthen jug would not have held much longer.

Tekurah's bathing room was tiled floor to ceiling in white-washed stone and decorated with lush palms and splendid scenes from the Nile—hippos, crocodiles, and ibises. My skin prickled at the chill in the room. I placed the jug on the floor next to the long stone bathing bench in the center of the room and flexed my relieved fingers. Shira added a few drops of rose oil from an alabaster bottle to the water as I uncovered the drain that emptied into the gardens. A little blue-headed agama lizard startled me when I moved the stone, and then scurried back out to the safety of the courtyard. *If only I could follow.*

Every Egyptian woman labored to appear youthful—Tekurah more than most. The many face creams, balms, and ointments she insisted upon complicated an already arduous process. We spent hours tending her body, fetching potions, purchasing magic cures, and delivering offerings to Hathor, the goddess of beauty.

After Shira and I undressed her, Tekurah perched on the bathing slab, lips pursed and pointed chin high. Shira scrubbed our mistress's head with natron soda paste. Then together we sponged her body with rose-scented water and massaged sweet balms into her skin, head to toe. At least I would enjoy soft hands for a few hours. This dry season sucked the moisture from my skin. I savored the heady aroma of the imported oils. The exotic spices, pungent balsam, and sweet myrrh reminded me of Salima.

A full cycle of seasons had passed since Salima had lugged cumbersome pitchers from the river for my own baths and applied perfumed oils to my body. Now I served a mistress of my own, fetching water and bowing to her every demand. Coveting her luxuries made my labors all the more torturous.

Shira brought in Tekurah's new gown, the delicate weave almost translucent. I ached for the sumptuous glide of fine cloth over my skin. My own abrasive, unflattering tunic provoked my vanity.

I struggled to pull the dress over Tekurah's head, but she jerked away. "Let Shira do it. She is worth three of you."

Slipping her dark braid over her shoulder, Shira reddened and reached up to adjust the mangled neckline before tying a beaded belt around Tekurah's narrow waist, adding some curve to her otherwise willowy body.

Tekurah spoke the truth. Shira's skills exceeded mine. It had surprised me, when I'd first entered servitude, that a Hebrew girl held such a trusted position as body-servant to the mistress. It did not take long to see why, though. She was nimble, efficient, and hardworking. Never speaking out of turn, she served Tekurah with utter, inexplicable politeness.

I worked to emulate her in all our tasks, but sixteen years of soft living had rendered me all but useless as a servant. My strength had grown over the last year, my once-pampered muscles now sinewy, but Tekurah still insisted Shira redo almost everything I attempted.

"Mistress, which jewelry today?" Shira's voice barely broke a whisper.

"The usekh gifted by Pharaoh." Tekurah glanced at me out of the corner of her eye.

Shira bowed, eyes downcast. "I will fetch it from the treasury while Kiya attends to your wig." This was one task I performed with minimal clumsiness.

Tekurah sank onto a low stool by a mahogany vanity, her narrow face reflected in the polished silver mirror. "Make it quick. Don't forget bangles and earrings."

Shira padded out of the room, head down.

"The new wig." Tekurah snapped her fingers at me. "Now."

The large closet overflowed with chests, baskets of gowns, countless pairs of sandals, and wooden stands laden with all styles and varieties of wigs. For all the seeming lack of affection between Tekurah and Shefu, he certainly allotted her a generous share of clothing, jewels, and accessories. The Queen herself might covet such a vast assortment.

A new rosewood wig chest was tucked behind a basket. I carried it to the vanity and opened the lid, choking back a sneeze. Spiced to mask the odor of wool and human hair, the box reeked of cinnamon with such potency my eyes watered.

An exquisite hairpiece lay inside, interlaced with gold and red faience beads and braided with the elaborate plaits made popular by the First Wife of Pharaoh. I centered the wig on Tekurah's bald head. Bodies, candles, and lamps would elevate the temperature of the hall during the banquet, and the weight and heat of such an intricate headdress was staggering. Tekurah would thank the gods for her shaved head tonight.

The one mercy in my downfall was release from wearing wigs. Allowing my hair to grow freely, I escaped the burden and irritation caused by the uncomfortable fashion. I had always abhorred shaving my head, but Salima usually convinced me to at least trim it short during the blaze of the hottest months. My straight black hair brushed past my shoulders now, and I rejoiced to simply pull it back with a leather tie each morning.

By the time I adjusted the wig to Tekurah's satisfaction, Shira had returned with the jewels. Fashioned from beads of pure gold, multicolored glass, and brilliant blue lapis lazuli, the usekh collar was indeed extraordinary. A large gold amulet embossed with etchings of ibises in full flight sat suspended in the center. The neckpiece extended just past the edges of her wide shoulders. Enhanced by Tekurah's height and long neck, the collar did not overpower her as it would most other women. It galled me to admit such a thing, but Pharaoh himself would take pride in the impressive display of his gift.

Shira applied kohl to our mistress's eyes—the art still eluded me. After a few failed attempts and dangerous near misses, Tekurah forbade me to even approach her cosmetics chest. The newest trend—green malachite on the upper lids and gray galena below—accented and widened her black eyes. I loathed the almond-ash-and-water concoction I was allotted to beautify and protect my own eyes. However, after a year, I could finally apply it without stabbing myself in the eye each morning.

Tekurah did not turn, but her gaze pierced me from the distorted reflection of the silver mirror. "You will not embarrass me tonight. Clumsiness will not be tolerated."

My skin flashed cold.

The Festival of the New Year, birth day of Ra, would be the first celebration I attended as a servant, instead of one being served. Standing behind Tekurah's chair and at her mercy, my humiliation would be on full display for all the guests—many of whom I was well acquainted with.

Tekurah's cruel mouth curved into a smile.

2

Every surface in the main hall bloomed with vibrant blossoms in anticipation of the lavish banquet tonight. I wilted at the reminder that a year ago I had attended this annual celebration as a guest, enjoying the splendor of Shefu's hospitality. Now the pungent jumble of fragrances overpowered my senses, evoking queasiness instead of awe.

Tekurah had commanded that we help prepare, so Shira approached another slave to ask for direction. The tall Egyptian girl was dressed like me in a roughly woven garment, but instead of bare feet, she wore sandals with fine leather bindings. She threw a dark glance at me and then jerked her chin toward the baskets in the corner.

"Decorate tables." She dismissed us with a turn of her back and continued wrapping a garland of roses and jasmine around one of the painted cedar columns.

Shira rummaged through the baskets overflowing with lilies, henna blooms, and other exotic flowers. She selected a few blue lotus blossoms and arranged them in the center of a table with smaller flowers encircling them. She then tucked two alabaster oil lamps into the centerpiece, where they would flicker and sparkle amongst the vibrant color of the flowers. I marveled at her ability to choose flowers with complementing scents. Their careful placement would cast lovely shadows on the faces of the ladies seated around the tables.

I handed her another lotus. "Why are you a handmaid?"

"Excuse me?" Surprise flashed across her face. I rarely spoke to her.

"You should manage an entire household. Where did you learn these skills?"

Her curious expression transformed into shock as she looked over my shoulder. She dropped her eyes and bowed low. "Master."

I spun, scattering my armful of flowers across the floor as I collided with Master Shefu. My cheeks flamed.

"A word please, Kiya." He eyed the mess on the floor. "Shira will tend the flowers."

"Yes, master." I bowed and followed him into the empty corridor. Already dressed for the banquet, he wore a pleated white kilt and belted tunic, paired with simple gold cuffs and a short, tightly braided but unadorned wig. Shefu lavished his wife with finery but wore little jewelry himself.

"Tekurah and I will not attend the processional today. We must prepare for this evening. The twins are pouting." A tinge of a smile colored his voice. "I would like you to take them down to the parade route so they can have a little bit of excitement. Will you do that for me?"

"Of course, master." I dipped my head, not daring to look into his face.

For a long moment he stood silent. Then he put his hand under my chin, lifting my face to meet his eyes. "I wish things were different, Kiya. You know that. Don't you?"

My heart pounded a confused rhythm. Shefu's gentle question and familiar manner baffled me, but his deep brown eyes held nothing but kindness. I tried to conjure an answer, but no words formed. He sighed and released my chin, his shoulders seeming to droop. "Sefora and Liat are waiting for you in their quarters."

I backed away to collect the children, my mind hazy and flooded with questions.

Sefora and Liat were full of nine-year-old boundless energy. Thankfully, they did not echo their mother's disdain for me. Cheering and clapping greeted me when I entered the room.

"Kiya, can we go now? Please?" Sefora pulled on my hand, her kohl-rimmed eyes gleaming with excitement. "I don't want to miss the dancers and acrobats."

"Or the sweeties." Liat grinned and licked his lips.

Against my better judgment, anticipation swelled in my chest as we left the house and walked through the villa gate—a faint echo of my own eagerness as a child on festival days. Glad for the preoccupation, I pressed away the dread of tonight.

The city of Iunu bustled with activity. Servants scurried here and there, baskets on heads, bundles in hand. A baker with crates stacked three high on his head wound his way through the city, drawing a procession of children tantalized by the aroma of fresh bread.

I grasped Sefora and Liat's hands. "Stay close. I do not want to get separated in all the confusion."

Liat eyed the baker's parade with longing but trudged along next to me.

Shefu's magnificent home stood at the heart of the city, nearly adjacent to the Temple of the Sun. The Temple gleamed like a polished white diamond in the late-morning glow. Banners of red and purple draped from every freshly painted column and marked the processional route. Priests in brilliant white tunics, leopard-skin robes, and flashing gold jewelry streamed through the pylons and up and down the entry ramp. Merchants snaked through the mob with baskets of flower garlands, bouquets, sweet breads, and fruits. Their rhythmic invitations to buy goods harmonized with the laughter and chatter of the crowd.

My mother plied wares here, among the other merchants and tradesmen. Jumo's exquisite artwork drew attention to her stall and piqued interest in the rest of the goods. I'd searched for her earlier this morning as I returned from the canal with Tekurah's bathwater, but my quest was fruitless. Too much confusion and chaos reigned in the city on festival days. My delay yielded only the tongue-lashing from Tekurah.

The Festival of the New Year drew unparalleled crowds. As soon as Sopdet, the brightest star in the heavens, rose from her grave below the horizon, we knew Inundation would soon be upon us. People from all over the region streamed into Iunu, anxious for the celebration.

All classes of people mixed together in the melee. Powerful priests with flowing robes, wealthy merchants, pampered wives, and even common household slaves pressed in on one another— intoxicated by the arousing sights, sounds, and smells of this festival day. The children and I made our way through the crowd to catch a glimpse of the procession.

Sefora hopped around on tiptoe. "I can't see!"

Relieved Sefora had asked first, I lifted her onto my hip to watch the dancers, just as my nursemaid had done for me as a child. Although tall for her age, her willowy body was as light as a reed. Liat's love for sweets made lifting him a bit more complicated. For now, he directed his attention to the treats being passed into the crowd by the priests' attendants.

The dancers, clad in little more than beaded linen girdles tied about their hips, preceded the barge. Most were Syrians or Kushites, enslaved by conquests of the great Pharaoh. Their dark bodies gyrated to the wild pulse of the timbrels and sistrums played by temple musicians.

Ra's golden barge sparkled with jewels: brilliant blue lapis lazuli, scarlet carnelian, dark green malachite, and deepest obsidian. At the center stood the god himself. Once again the wonder of beholding the beautiful statue struck me. Seated on a golden throne, his human-shaped body and falcon head had been polished to gleaming, and his onyx eyes glittered like black fire.

Fifty priests bore the barge through the flower-strewn streets, their heads, brows, and faces shaved clean in the ancient tradition and pristine linen kilts shining in the sun. A troupe of acrobats followed, flipping, flying, and performing mystifying feats of contortion.

Cloying incense tainted the air. The pungent odor wafted from the robes of the priests and the rich fabric adorning the barge. Spying a lotus blossom on the ground, I put Sefora down and snatched up the flower, desperate to camouflage the smell. I buried my nose in its petals, but even so, a headache throbbed in my temples. I always did my best to steer clear of the Sun Temple during times of sacrifice. The sickly sweet odor poured out of the entrance during the daily offerings, and the stench permeated the courtyard day and night. Sometimes, when the breeze carried the stink through the windows of the villa, my head would pound and my eyes would swim for hours.

When the priests and their burden had passed, Sefora tugged at my hand. "Can we go down to the canal? I want to see the decorated boats."

"All right." I would take full advantage of my semi-freedom today. "But stay back from the water. There are too many people down there. Let's go, Liat."

I looked around when the boy did not answer. "Sefora, where is your brother?"

She shrugged and pushed out her bottom lip.

My heart galloped like a team of Pharaoh's stallions. I had lost Tekurah's son! Until now I had escaped being beaten by her, but this very well could be the day I experienced a cane against my back.

I grabbed Sefora's hand, dragging her with me against the crush of the crowd. I would *not* lose a second child today.

Every noisy beat of my heart drummed new fears into my mind. Why had I let go of Liat's hand? Why did I pick up that flower? How long had he been missing? Would he go back to the villa? Did Tekurah already know?

I pushed harder against the mob and received many angry glances and a few curses in response. The baker. Might Liat have gone to find him?

Nearly empty of customers, the market lay ahead, a sea of colorful linen-covered stalls. Most of the revelers had followed the procession down to the canal to watch the launch of Ra's boat into the Nile. Perhaps Liat had followed the priests passing out treats to the crowd.

I stopped, torn. Should I go back the other way?

"There he is!" Sefora pointed across the market.

Relief coursed through me. Liat was perched on a stool in the shade of a merchant's stall.

Still not releasing Sefora's hand, I hurried across the market. Before I even reached the boy, I yelled, "Where have you been?"

Liat offered only a lopsided grin and a shrug.

A dark-haired man behind the booth turned on his stool. He wore a simple sleeveless brown tunic, not a kilt like most other male slaves. He must be foreign. No Egyptian would let his beard grow in such a barbarous way.

His eyes narrowed as I approached. "Is this your child?"

Musical instruments littered the table in front of him. He held a large, hollowed-out cut of wood between his knees: the beginnings of a drum, perhaps. Tiny flecks of wood from the project he was sanding dusted his disheveled hair.

Something about the way he spoke—accusing and with a heavy accent—aggravated me. My response was equally terse as I gripped the boy to my side, my heart contracting with gratitude that he was safe. "No. But he is with me."

Liat held up a lyre. "Look, Kiya! Eben let me play this. Even taught me some notes. Want to see?"

"No, we must go." I took the lyre from him, ready to place it back on the table, when a memory washed over me from the last morning before my father sold me. This instrument, carved with intricate markings, was similar to the one I had nearly purchased before Yuny found me and summoned me back to the villa.

Although that lyre had been carved with roses, this one was decorated with swallows, their wings lifted in swift flight against the backdrop of the sun, as if they were declaring its arrival. My finger traced their progress up the smooth rosewood.

"Do you play?" The instrument maker, Eben, had stopped working to look at me.

I blinked, startled by the mixture of curiosity and disdain in the man's question, as well as the intensity of the green-gray eyes that scrutinized me.

"No." I slid my thumb across the tight gut strings, but not hard enough to elicit music from their tension. I had always wanted to learn to play the lyre. Its haunting, sweet tone reminded me of lullabies sung by my mother long ago. Now I would never have the chance to do so; every minute of my life was dictated by Tekurah.

Unlike the swallows, whose quick split-tailed flight scorned captivity, my cage was securely latched. Perhaps, like my ancestors, my soul might one day ascend on unfettered wings, becoming one with the imperishable stars, as the legends promised.

Battling the desire to strum the lyre and enjoy a moment of pleasure from its melodic vibration, I moved to place the instrument back on the table while avoiding the weight of Eben's gaze.

A large Egyptian, wiping his beefy hands on a soiled cloth, emerged from the shop behind the stall. I recognized him as the vendor I had spoken with last year regarding the rose lyre.

"Ah. I see you have chosen a beautiful instrument. There is no craftsman more skilled." He clapped Eben on the shoulder. "I would not trade Eben for all the artisans in Pharaoh's workshop."

Eben shifted in his seat and returned to sanding the drum with long, swift strokes. Had he also created the rose lyre that had caught my eye last year? I did not remember seeing him at that time, but then again, I had barely regarded Salima with more than a passing glance when I was her mistress.

A rush of longing for her quiet presence by my side seized me. Salima had been the only steadfast companion in my life not driven by greed. The look in her dark eyes as she bade me farewell that day had told me she'd considered me more than a mistress. She had loved me, in spite of my selfishness.

"Will you be purchasing today?" The shop owner's thick brows shot skyward in anticipation of a sale. "Perhaps for the young master?"

Liat's round eyes pleaded with me. If only I could purchase such a treasure—for him, or for myself.

"Thank you, no. We must return to the villa." I placed the instrument back on the table, and my hands immediately missed its weight.

The shop owner shrugged and turned away, all friendliness erased in the absence of a profitable transaction.

At my urging, Liat hopped off his stool and waved. "That was fun, Eben."

The man winked at Liat, and a corner of his full mouth

turned up the tiniest bit. I nodded at him in thanks, but he diverted his green-gray eyes back to his task and ignored my gesture with an air of dismissal.

Hopefully Tekurah would never have need of a musical instrument. I'd be glad to not have to deal with such a rude man again—no matter that the lyre he'd crafted was one of the most beautiful things I had ever held in my hands. Yet somehow, with or without the uncivilized beard, there was something about his face and his stormy eyes that intrigued me.

Wrapping both children's hands in my iron grip, I quickly walked toward the villa.

Liat tugged the other way, begging, "Can't we go down to the canal first? Please?"

"And lose you again? No. There are thousands of people down there."

Sefora added to the pleading. "We promise to stay right next to you. I swear by the sun and moon and all the stars."

I looked back and forth between the two of them, hesitating. Letting out a noisy breath, I dropped my shoulders. "Oh, all right. Only—" I cut off their loud rejoicing. "Only if you both keep what happened today quiet. Your mother will not be pleased with me. We must keep it secret. Understand?"

They nodded with wide eyes, and I prayed to the gods that the children would hold to their promise. Tekurah needed little provocation to berate me.

I jogged the trade road with the children, hoping that the pleasures of the day would overtake their memory of the few breathless minutes Liat had been lost.

Hundreds of papyrus boats glutted the wide canal. We stood at the back of the crowd but found a high spot where we could see Ra being loaded onto a huge cedar boat. The vessel sparkled with gold and shining white electrum. A hundred soldiers in full regalia stood at attention upon each shore of the canal, ready to heave the enormous boat and its precious cargo down to the Nile by rope. Children splashed in the water, laughing and wrestling, wading through the masses of floating lotuses and lilies thrown by revelers.

When the barge finally floated around a curve on the canal and toward the main body of the Nile, I told the children we must return to the villa.

Liat dragged his feet and pouted. "I wish Mother and Father were not having this banquet tonight."

"Do you not enjoy the feasts?" I squeezed his hand.

"I don't like going to bed while everyone is still having fun. And I hate wigs. Mother always makes me wear a wig when we have guests." He scratched his head at the memory. A smudge of kohl streaked up to his hairline. It would need to be reapplied when we returned. When I'd been Liat's age, Salima had to all but tie me down for my daily cosmetic regimen.

I laughed. "Well, Master Liat, in a few years you will be old enough to stay awake until the early hours of the morning as well. I know the wigs are irritating—believe me, I had my share of wearing them for parties, and I do not miss them, but"—I winked and tugged on his forelock braid—"just think of all the lovely leftover treats for tomorrow!"

A grin lit Liat's round little face.

"I adore banquets." Sefora's brown eyes twinkled. "All the ladies with their beautiful gowns, the flowers, the wonderful food, the music, the dancers . . ." She swung her arms back and forth, tripping out a little dance on her toes. "Besides"—she clapped her hands—"tonight I get to wear the gown Father bought in Thebes. I cannot wait!"

My afternoon with the children had seduced me into feeling normal, as if I retained the same footing as they did. In spite of their position—and their mother—they were sweet children. They seemed, thanks be to the gods, to take after their father,

Shefu. An attentive and affectionate parent, he lavished upon them their hearts' every desire.

Tekurah, on the other hand, was more concerned with raising her standing in society than in raising her children. She spent her days shopping for luxuries and gossiping with well-connected friends, gleaning information useful for climbing the social ladder. The children were an afterthought—a commodity to be trotted out at parties to impress the guests with their beauty, talents, and fashion.

In only a few years, Sefora would be given to the wealthiest and most powerful man Tekurah could manage. Liat would marry the daughter of someone whose power and status his mother coveted.

The two older children, Kemah and Talet, were already married. Kemah, only a year older than myself, had been given to the son of a powerful priest. Talet, the oldest son, had married the daughter of a steward in the house of Pharaoh, which gave Tekurah endless pleasure—and a direct line to court gossip.

By the time we returned to the villa, Sefora and Liat were whining for food. I reminded them to protect our secret and then led the children to the kitchen to beg for a few sweet rolls. We took their treats to the main courtyard and sat by one of the pools in the shade of the regal date palms. The children devoured the apricot and raisin bread, licking the honey off their fingers. My mouth watered at the memory of the sweet taste, and I looked away.

With a fresh coat of limestone whitewash, Shefu's sprawling villa gleamed. My family's home had been grand, but Shefu's put it to shame. Servants carrying pillows, mats, oil lamps, and flowers climbed the outer staircases, preparing the roof for guests needing an escape from the oppressive heat of the main hall. Many would sleep off the night's drinking there, enjoying what little breeze might stir up from the river in the early hours.

Shefu employed the most talented master gardeners in the city. A vast array of colors flooded the garden. Lilies floated in the courtyard pools, and the walls dripped with many varieties of grapevines and climbing roses. I entertained a fleeting notion of lingering here in the dappled shade of the palms with the children, breathing the sweet air and soaking in the divinity that inhabited the fragrances of the lovely flowers—but Tekurah waited. I slipped into the house again and fetched a pitcher of water to wash the children's hands and feet.

As I knelt to untie Sefora's sandals and rinse her feet of the day's grime, she asked, "Kiya, why do you wash our feet?"

I laughed and tweaked her big toe. "Because they are dirty."

"No, I mean, your family came to the festival last year, and the servants tended you then."

I looked up into her wide eyes, smaller versions of Shefu's kind ones. My family's misfortune, the shame of losing our position, our wealth, and our worth, the jealousy Tekurah held for my mother—I bit it all back. Instead, I offered the part of the truth she would understand. "Because the gods turned from me."

They had abandoned me. Abandoned my whole family.

The gods had ignored my mother when she begged for Jumo's healing, disregarding daily offerings to Isis and Thoth. Yamm, the god of the seas, had not prevented the waves from swallowing my father's magnificent ships. And no matter my allegiance to all the gods, slavery became my lot.

What curse had been cast upon me? Why had such black luck fallen on my path? I did not know.

I owned nothing now except the clothes on my back, a small brass mirror, and a little box of cheap cosmetics. How could I earn Ra's mercy when I could not provide the tributes he demanded? I had nothing to offer—no goat, no bull, not even a dove.

I dried Sefora's feet with a soft linen towel. When I glanced up, her whole face had crumpled into a frown.

"Now, Mistress Sefora"—I patted the top of her foot—"don't be sad today. My luck is gone, but yours is not. Remember your new gown."

Her little face brightened. "I wonder if Hattai has it ready!" She skipped off toward her bedchamber, my misery forgotten.

3

The slate cooled my bare feet as I scurried down the hallway, a welcome respite from the blazing limestone pathway in the courtyard. The few slaves I encountered averted their eyes as they passed. A reaction I was used to, but still, I bristled at the slight.

I pressed open the door to Tekurah's chamber, wincing at the squeak of the bronze hinges. Shira was slathering coconut balm over Tekurah's arms and legs.

"Where have you been?" Tekurah pushed a glossy black cat from her lap. He strutted off with a quick backward glance, as if annoyed with my tardiness as well.

Tekurah's host of cats ruled this house, second only to their mistress. Sleeping on the hard floor while a pampered feline sprawled on a goose-down cushion, and eating scraps as the cats enjoyed choice morsels from Tekurah's plate, infuriated me. Tekurah had long ago selected the cat-headed goddess Bastet as her patron divinity. She treated her pets as if they were the goddess herself—to ensure prompt acknowledgment of her prayers.

"The master asked that I take the children to the processional to keep them out of the way," I said.

Obligated to do whatever Shefu asked of me, even ahead of Tekurah's wishes, I needed no further excuse. She gaped at me for a moment before a slow, malevolent smirk stole across her face.

"No matter." She dismissed me with a flick of her wrist. "The guests will arrive soon. I must be in the main hall to greet them." She stood and swept from the room. Shira and I glanced at each other in confusion before running to follow, both of us skittering along to keep up with her long stride.

House slaves washed the feet of the early arrivals and placed perfumed wax cones on their heads. They would melt all evening, dripping and cooling, adding to the intoxicating mixture of fragrances from the abundance of flowers.

Tekurah ordered us to wait behind the head table. Turning obedient eyes to the floor, Shira and I became fixtures in the room along with the tall candle stands gracing the large, columned hall. My stomach twisted. Who would be here tonight, gawking at me?

As more guests arrived and the noise level in the room rose, I forced my breath to slow, blocked out the voices around me, and let my mind wander into a memory.

Knee-deep in the canal . . . cool mud squishing between my toes . . . breathing deeply and savoring the swirl of the water around my legs . . . the rush of the gentle current curling through my outspread fingers . . . birds in full song . . . cicadas thrumming in the whispering rushes . . . the sun's delicious rays on my upturned face, breathing Ra's life into my weary bones.

Still. At rest. Free.

A sharp laugh startled me, yanking me out of my daydream. At least forty people sat at low tables or on cushions scattered around the room, with servants at attention behind them or lurking in the shadows near the walls.

Ushered in by their nursemaids, Liat and Sefora entered the

room. I stifled a giggle at the sight of Liat's wig, perched askew on his head. He would be scratching at it all evening. His eyes grew as large as plates as he surveyed the luscious food. Sefora stood next to her father, leaning against him as he talked with another man, but she scanned the room. When she caught my glance, her eyebrows arched with excitement. I tipped my head down, and my heart sank.

I could not be a friend tonight.

Through lowered lashes, I surveyed the room for people I knew—and there were many. Old business partners, friends, even some distant relatives of my mother and father were in attendance. None looked my way. Either they refused to acknowledge a common slave, or they mercifully ignored my existence as they reveled in the privileges that I was now denied.

I was at Tekurah's mercy because of such decadence—the food, the dresses, the jewels. My father had always hosted the most extravagant of parties, our villa packed with people arrayed in their finest. And when the time came to repay his debts, he sold my freedom, not his own. Though I'd once delighted in the parties, the wigs, the cosmetics, the gold and silver, now the abundance made me ill. All the vapid people who had once filled my world, seemed to hang on my every word, now refused to meet my eye.

As the night wore on, snatches of conversation about my family and our demise reached my ears. Each time the discussion would steer that way Tekurah glanced back at me, brows high. She took each opportunity to regale her guests with tales of my incompetence. ". . . can't even figure out how to dress me . . . about strangled me with my dress earlier . . . nearly poked my eye out . . ." They all laughed, some more heartily than others, but none looked my way. I dug my nails deeper and deeper into my palms. *Cowards.*

My stomach snarled. My paltry ration of bread, a few vegetables, fish, and barley beer each day never satisfied. Rare bits of beef or game were permitted at times, but two weeks had passed since we'd enjoyed such a treat. The abundant array of roast duck, grilled beef, fish, and goose prepared with savory spices caused my mouth to water. Shefu's guests dined on the finest succulent fruits, gathered from his orchards, and drank wine from his own vineyards.

Shefu's bountiful vines produced the sweetest vintages in all of Lower Egypt. My father's boats had carried their yield as far away as Phoenicia. My tongue remembered the exquisite wine and pined for a drop of it again.

A familiar laugh interrupted my covetous fantasy, and my head snapped up to search for its source.

Now I understood Tekurah's demand that I attend tonight, as well as her strange attitude and triumphal sneer. For there, not fifteen paces from me, smiling, laughing, and unaware of my presence, sat Akhum. Tekurah must have heard my intake of breath. She turned in her seat, painted brows arched high.

Akhum's regiment must have returned in the last couple of days. I always kept diligent watch for his men about the city. An army campaign had taken him north to Canaan well over a year ago, before my downfall and only weeks before my father's boats surrendered to the waves.

My most ardent pursuer, Akhum had surpassed all other suitors who had approached my father. Handsome, regal, and from one of the wealthiest families in the city, he stood a head taller than most others in his regiment. He had showered me with jewelry, beautiful gowns, and the finest perfumes.

Head of his regiment and aspiring to a generalship like his own father, he commanded avid admiration in his soldiers. My father, of course, loved him, his power, and his influence. Akhum paid more than the usual bride-price in his determination to secure my hand. My father accommodated him by permitting the betrothal to extend until Akhum returned from the incursion in Canaan to deal with rebelling chieftains.

But when Akhum had returned from his long journey, his intended bride was a slave, not fit to tie his sandals, let alone to be his wife. The floor beneath me seemed to quake violently. Did he know about my family? What had he heard? What did he think of me now? Did he know I stood here?

He must have felt the weight of my stare, for after a few moments he turned his attention my way. At first no recognition lit his eyes, but he held my gaze, perhaps curious about the audacity of a slave gaping at him, until shock flashed across his face. My legs trembled with such violence I fought to continue standing. It took every ounce of will left in me to lock my feet in place.

A sharp command from Tekurah jolted me. "Kiya, Shira, fetch my cosmetic box and refresh my makeup, I am melting in this heat. And bring a fan, I need some air."

By the time I plowed through the door of Tekurah's room, tears blinded me. My own makeup would need to be reapplied. I found myself kneeling on the floor, sobbing and moaning, Shira hovering over me.

"Kiya . . . oh no, Kiya, what is wrong? What can I do?" The Hebrew girl smoothed my hair and patted my back.

I shook my head, unable to speak. She knelt and put her arms around my shoulders, rocking back and forth with me as I wept.

Fetching a box should not take so long. The last thing I needed tonight was an upbraiding in front of the guests—one in particular.

I shrugged off Shira's arms, avoiding her sympathetic gaze. Safe in the knowledge that Tekurah was occupied at the banquet, I used her makeup to outline my tear-swollen eyes. I replaced the pink alabaster kohl pot in the ebony box and closed the lid. The ivory inlay on top reminded me so much of a chest my mother had given me long ago that even in my anguish, I thought of her.

My mother's honey-gold eyes looked back at me in the mirror. What would she do in this situation? I had watched her in the marketplace, bartering with her old neighbors or their servants. Many former acquaintances came to her stall, driven by curiosity, or pity, or simply to revel in her downfall. My mother, however, always held her head high. She did not look at the ground. She did not hide. She plied her goods and smiled, thanking them for their business. They left, unsatisfied in their gloating.

Her blood flowed in my veins, and I would banish any thought of what my life would have been, what it should be, and hold my own head high. Tekurah would not prevail.

I picked up the cosmetic box, swallowing hard to steady my voice. "We need to go back."

"Shouldn't we wait a few more minutes?" Shira peered at me, seeming to gauge whether I might cry again.

"The last thing I need is Tekurah screaming at me tonight." I lifted my chin and hastened toward the door. But before I could cross the threshold, my foot slipped on a reed mat. I stumbled. Tekurah's treasured cosmetic box flew out of my hand.

In horror, I tried to grab at it, but my fingers found only empty air. The box cracked against the wall, and the lid broke away. Both pieces crashed to the floor, and the inlay shattered. Ivory shards and splintered ebony skidded across the tile.

What have I done?

4

My heart stuttered, then rushed loud in my ears as I braced myself against the doorway.

Shira's pale face appeared in front of me. "Shh." She put her hand over my mouth, anticipating the anguish threatening to pour out of me.

I bit my cheek hard, until I tasted blood, forcing myself to stay calm.

"Let me clean it up." She arched her brows. "Can I let go?"

I nodded, and she released me. Then, in silence, Shira retrieved a small woven box from the vanity chest, knelt down, and placed Tekurah's kohl pots, rouge, brushes, and the application stick inside. She cleaned the mess from the destroyed cosmetic box, fetched a peacock-feather fan, and then held out a hand and beckoned me to follow.

In a daze, I trailed behind her, dreading each footstep and sifting my thoughts. What could I do to lessen the blow? How could I protect myself?

Nothing. I could only endure as my mother would. Stand tall. Accept the verbal lashing. Submit to the punishment.

A graceful Syrian dancer performed for the guests in the

hall, her enormous feathered headdress swaying in rhythm with the dance of the drums and pipes. Tekurah motioned for us to hurry and bring her the box. I drew in a deep breath and moved forward, but Shira stepped in front of me, walked up to Tekurah, and handed her the little woven basket.

"What is this?" Tekurah opened the lid. "Where is my ebony box?"

I opened my mouth, but Shira spoke faster. "Mistress, I must apologize. I caught my foot on the mat and dropped your box. It is broken. I am so sorry."

Tekurah's face flushed scarlet. "You did what? That cosmetic box was a gift! How could you? You stupid slave!" Her voice spiraled louder and louder, and everyone stared at the three of us. "I would expect this out of Kiya, but you know better than to be careless with my belongings."

Tekurah glared at me. Did she know?

But the Hebrew girl stood fast, her voice calm and firm. "It was entirely my fault, mistress. It is my responsibility."

I fixed my eyes on my bare feet, avoiding curious stares, but my mind reeled. Why would Shira put herself in the way of Tekurah's wrath? Accept the inevitable punishment?

Tekurah demoted Shira to the kitchens immediately. Then, without a blink, she ordered me to reapply her cosmetics. She must have done so with trepidation after the last incident. However, adept after months of applying my own kohl, this time I refreshed her makeup with ease.

Shira must have assumed our mistress would be less severe with her. But how foolish! Standing in the way of another's chastisement—and for an Egyptian who ignored her most of the time, no less. Although confusion and guilt warred in my gut, relief washed through me as well. There would be no reason for Tekurah to shred me in front of the guests.

But still, shame gnawed at me.

Trying to evade thoughts of what Shira would endure in the kitchen, I lifted my eyes, not enough to chance crossing eye-lines with anyone, but enough to survey the guests within the immediate vicinity of Tekurah's table.

Everyone in attendance was stunning.

The women displayed the finest linens, delicately woven and brazen in their transparency. Oiled and hennaed bodies shimmered in the lamplight, competing with the golden sparkle of usekhs, bracelets, earrings, and jewels. The men, too, rivaled the women in plumage and ornamentation, their braided and beaded wigs bobbing along with conversations.

The wine and beer flowed with abandon. In response, the guests grew louder and livelier. The music and dancers followed, but barely stirred the air in the stifling room. Even with the shutters on the high windows opened to the night, not a hint of a breeze drifted through. Shefu summoned more slaves with enormous ostrich-feather fans to cool the guests. I thanked the gods again that I no longer wore a wig. My simple shift, although coarse and roughly woven, hung relatively light, unlike the oppressive jewels and heavy collars most of the men and women wore.

Next to one of the flower-wrapped pillars, I stood as much out of the lamplight as I could, yet still within earshot of Tekurah in case she beckoned. Gossip consumed her at the table, and she did not notice Akhum move from his seat.

A year on a campaign to Canaan had defined his long muscles and darkened his golden-brown skin. He was even taller than I remembered. Befitting his rank, the kilt of the decorated battalion commanders wrapped his narrow hips in pristine white pleats edged with blue embroidery. Gold cuffs encircled his biceps and wrists, and a huge fly amulet hung around his neck—the Gold of Valor. Akhum had been decorated for bravery on the battlefront. My heart swelled with undeserved pride.

Where was he going? He moved through the shadows around the periphery of the room, sliding behind the crowd of servants waiting to attend their masters. He had left behind a table of dazzling young maidens, hand-selected for sure by Tekurah to ensure his attention remained on that side of the room. She did not want him to notice me, but she wanted me to suffer, to look from afar on the life I should be enjoying and mourn.

Akhum's rich, exotic scent alerted me to his presence long before he spoke. He had secreted into the dark shadows behind me. His breath touched my hair and paralyzed me, with the exception of my trembling knees.

"I did not know, Kiya." His warm whisper caressed my ear. "Had I known I would have . . ."

I dared not even twist my neck to look at him. "There is nothing you could have done," I whispered back, willing my voice not to quaver.

"No, I won't have this." His low voice whipped out as sharply as a blade.

I sighed. "I am indentured for life."

"I will think of something."

His silken hand brushed down the length of my hair. "You are still so beautiful. Somehow even more so without the jewels and gowns . . ."

Silence took his place.

I was glad I had not faced him. I could not have endured looking into his eyes. His nearness alone brought fresh grief crashing down on me again. Dizzy and afraid to breathe, I feared losing control of the knot forming in my throat.

Did he mean what he said? Could I hope? Should I? Akhum rescued me from my misery each night in my dreams. Could the fantasy become reality? Was freedom within reach?

Tekurah had noticed Akhum's empty chair and signaled me.

She watched his return out of the corner of her eye. She looked between the two of us, back and forth, but Akhum kept his gaze averted.

She pinned me with a look meant to remind me of my place. "Fetch me different sandals. These pinch."

I backed away.

For the rest of the evening, Tekurah kept me running to her chambers to retrieve different articles: her fan, a silver mirror inlaid with emeralds Shefu had bought in Thebes, the perfume purchased at the market yesterday. She ignored the servers and ordered me to bring different platters of food or keep her cup of wine replete.

Evening stretched into night, and night lengthened into the early hours of the morning. My feet ached and my eyes stung from the smoke of the many dancing candles and the oil lamps bathing the room with light.

Akhum moved from his assigned table to sit with his parents. Their backs were turned, but from the way they were gesturing, they must have been discussing my fate. There was no way to judge where I stood on the balances.

My stomach flipping like a suffocating fish on a riverbank, I pleaded with the gods, as I had every day these past months. *Please let his father honor the betrothal.*

From time to time, wealthy Egyptian men took a bride from among the serving class. Akhum could still honor the agreement made with my father a year ago, if he so chose. But if his father forbade the union, Akhum might endanger his position with his family and Pharaoh's army. His father was a general, and without his blessing, I stood no chance.

I tried to avoid staring at their table, but again and again my attention snared on their tense conversation.

Akhum looked back at me one last time. The defeat on his face answered the question I dared not ask. Agony swallowed up my last and only hope to escape slavery. My heart shattered as the last shred of promise fell away in tatters.

Tekurah, too, witnessed the look Akhum gave me. She turned, placed her bony chin on her shoulder, and flashed a victorious smile.

5

Tekurah must have ordered Shira kept out of sight, for a month passed before I caught a glimpse of the Hebrew girl in the kitchen courtyard.

Hauling heavy pots, scrubbing dishes with sand, plucking feathers, gutting fish, endlessly kneading dough, and tending to the blazing-hot bread ovens—Shira endured all this because of me.

Her clothes now engulfed her tiny frame, and her weary face looked gaunt. She collected bowls in a basket on her hip, speaking in pleasant tones with the cooks and other slaves.

Broken down, compelled to endure a life of abject slavery, treated lower than a dog. What did she possibly have to smile about?

I refused to wait any longer. I gathered my bowl and cup in the pretext of bringing them to Shira for washing. Leaning close to her, I placed them in the basket. "I need to speak with you right away."

Her eyes darted toward the doorway and then over my shoulder. "The canal path. Dawn." She put her smile back in place and raised her voice. "Thank you, Kiya."

I nodded and slipped out of the courtyard. Tekurah awaited me, as did another upbraiding for my lateness.

Shira's absence had forced Tekurah to rely on me. Latikah, the Egyptian girl with the fine leather sandals, replaced Shira but still lacked experience with her duties. Tekurah and I had settled into a stiff, but tolerable, pattern in the last month. Without Shira to lean on, I became more competent. Although she still grasped any opportunity to shame me for anything less than perfection, silently and without fanfare Tekurah acknowledged me as head handmaid.

Much progress would be erased by my tardiness, but I did not care. Relaying my gratitude to Shira for her astounding, albeit perplexing, act of kindness was worth the loss.

Well before dawn broke and the rest of the household began to stir, I rose and rolled up my linen sleeping mat in the corner of Tekurah's bedchamber, grateful that Latikah still slept in the servants' quarters.

Allowed to bathe during my morning trips to the canal, I hoped, if Tekurah awoke before I returned, she would assume I'd left earlier only to spend more time in the river.

Few pleasures broke the endless monotony of my days, but the sunrise over the Temple numbered among them. A grand obelisk stood at the heart of the Temple courtyard. From the canal each morning I watched the sun glide to the very tip of the obelisk before launching into the sky. When the sun reached the pinnacle, it reflected against the silver electrum at the top, and dazzling white beams refracted, a signal to return before Tekurah rose from her bed.

Among all the deities, Ra held first place in my heart. The sun-god traveled across the sky each day to bring us light and fought the snake-god Apep in the underworld to push back the chaos of night. The exalted ancestor to the great Pharaoh also entertained foremost importance in our city. The enormous center of worship in Iunu put even the grand temples of Thebes to shame.

I perched cross-legged on a large rock at the head of the path—a remnant of a monument or boundary stone from ancient times—now pitted and faceless. When I'd first arrived in Shefu's household, Shira herself had pointed out this hidden path through the flax fields.

What a glorious morning. The sun still lingered low, and the breeze breathed cool on my skin. The Season of Inundation had nearly reached its zenith. The Nile had overflowed her banks and submerged the fields nearest the canal. When she returned to her path at the end of the season, rich black silt would bless Egypt's crops.

Sounds of the earth awakening surrounded me. Ibises, egrets, herons, and ducks called out in seeming joy at the bounty of fish, frogs, and turtles the high waters provided. I closed my eyes to drink in the music of the morning.

Someone called my name, and my eyes flew open. Shira appeared, smiling and waving, a huge earthen pot balanced atop her head. The skill of carrying a burden upon one's head still eluded me. I could not balance an empty jar, let alone a full one.

Uncomfortable with such familiarity between myself and a Hebrew, I offered a reluctant wave.

"Good morning!" She placed the jar on the ground. Her light green eyes glowed translucent in the golden early sunlight.

What should I say? "What were you thinking? What is wrong with you?" Or perhaps, *"Forgive me, remorse is chewing a hole in my gut"?*

I attempted a smile. "Thank you for meeting me. I've been trying to speak with you for weeks."

"Oh, they keep me in the kitchens most of the time. I sleep

in the courtyard. I cannot mingle with the other slaves outside my duties."

I looked down at my feet. That should have been my fate.

"No . . . no, Kiya." Shira closed the distance between us and clutched my hand. "Please don't feel guilty."

I looked into her eyes, determined to understand. In a rush, all my desperate questions flowed out. "Why? What possessed you? It should have been me . . . It wasn't right . . ." I shook my head and pulled away from her grasp.

"No, I did what was necessary. Tekurah was looking for some excuse to break you. Dropping that box would have provided her with the perfect opportunity. Even Shefu could have done nothing to prevent it."

True, in front of so many guests, Shefu could only stand by while Tekurah punished Shira.

"Tekurah suspects I took the blame for you. But I needed to step in to protect you from her revenge."

Her response provided more questions than answers. *Revenge?*

I brushed aside that enigma for a moment, determined to understand Shira's motives. "But why do you care? Why not stay silent and keep your well-earned position?"

Shira raised a hand to shade her eyes against the sunrise and smiled up at me, her nose wrinkling. Freckles scattered across her fair skin.

"My position matters little. Besides, the way she treats you, it's . . ." She gritted her teeth. "Unjust . . . and not even about you anyhow. I saw the opportunity to protect you."

She pitied me? This foreigner? I bristled at the thought. The gods had created Hebrews to be enslaved to Pharaoh. Did she think she held something over me? I might be a slave, but I was still an Egyptian.

She picked up her jug and rested it on her hip. "Let's keep walking so we can talk and get back in time."

Mystified, yet annoyed with her presumptions, I fell into step behind her out of habit. This narrow footpath cut across wide flax fields. The dainty blue flowers had winked in the sunlight for almost two months now, but their stalks remained green, not yellow enough for harvesting. No one collected crops here today.

Sharp stones plagued the path, but tender feet belonged to my past. Rough calluses now protected my soles. Still, I missed wearing soft leather sandals, one of many luxuries I'd taken for granted all those years. Numerous irrigation ditches cut across our trail, drawing the river's overflow to fields in desperate need of moisture in this arid land. Fertile fields, from rock and sand, were the yearly gift of Mother Nile.

As we neared the engorged canal, the glitter of sun on water made me squint. I glanced around, checking for crocodiles as we neared the edge of the river. The prospect of the lurking beasts brought to mind Shira's strange notion. "What makes you think Tekurah is vengeful toward me?"

"Don't you know how she feels about your mother?" Shira stopped and turned, brow furrowed.

"She is jealous of my mother's social connections, but that's all in the past." I fluttered a dismissive hand over my shoulder.

"Kiya, Shefu is in love with your mother. Always has been. Tekurah is jealous of his wayward affections. Her only recourse is to take it out on you." She tilted her head to one side. "You must look a lot like her."

I nodded, blinking. My mouth hung open, and my throat locked tight. The words slammed around inside my head. My mother? Shefu? What about my father? Did he know?

Shira clucked her tongue against her teeth. "I thought as much. I think she takes perverse pleasure in punishing you in place of your mother."

The world pitched and swayed, and my eyes refused to focus.

My thoughts came out in a jumble. "But . . . how do you know all this? Who . . . ? Who told you about my mother?"

She gave me a sympathetic smile. "I overheard a conversation the night before you arrived at the villa. You know Tekurah takes no pains to keep her displeasure quiet." She lifted her thin brows.

Tekurah's raving fits of fury regularly entertained the servants, and sometimes all the surrounding villas.

"I waited in the hallway as they argued. Shefu told her about the agreement with your father to purchase your indenture contract."

Heat buzzed up my spine. I could just see my father, agreeing to sell me, wiping his hands clean of his debt and his daughter—all in one act.

"She was furious. She insisted he jail your father and sell you, your brother, and your mother into slavery to recover his losses."

My stomach churned as I considered what our fate would have been, left in Tekurah's hands.

The Nile ahead of us hurried along in a swirling reddish-brown torrent. Shira and I knelt next to a filtering pool near the edge of the overfull canal, the sand helping to sift out the minerals swept along on its swift current.

I tied a linen patch over the mouth of the jar to help clear the water even more. As I submerged the vessel to fill it, I tried to reconcile thoughts of Shefu with my mother. Did she return his affections? Was this relationship long ago . . . or more recent? Shefu must have strong feelings for my mother to challenge Tekurah. He rarely raised his voice to his wife.

Shira placed her jar on the ground and leaned back on her heels. "Shefu's anger surprised me. He told her that he would never do such a malicious thing. Your father had been a friend. He told her she had no say in his business dealings."

Amused by the recollection of Tekurah's chiding, Shira lifted her chin. "He ordered her to assign you as her own handmaid and forbade her from ever laying a hand on you."

Shira tucked an errant curl of brown hair behind her ear. Her tight braid hung below her waist, and I wondered if her hair had ever been cut. "That, of course, explains why she beats you only with her words."

I did think it odd that Tekurah restrained herself with me, when never a day went by that she did not slap a house slave or two. No doubt Shira remembered the sting of Tekurah's palm as well.

"She seemed taken aback by his adamancy. She accused him of being so smitten by your mother that he could not think clearly. Shefu left the room in such a rush, I do not think he even saw me sitting by the door." She shrugged her slight shoulders. "Shall we bathe?"

I nodded. The sun pressed a dangerous point near the tip of the obelisk.

Six-foot-tall papyrus rushes guarded the pool, but even so, Shira cast a surreptitious glance around before slipping into the water. She wore her simple shift even while immersing herself.

Another new enigma.

Children played naked in the streets until age nine or ten. Slaves labored scantily clothed. Gowns fashioned from sheer linen left little to the imagination. Why would she act so strange and embarrassed?

I harbored no such discomfort about nudity. In fact, I savored the feeling of the sun and warm breeze on my skin. But Shira's obvious unease at being undressed made me feel awkward. I washed my body and hair with haste.

I shared a bit of cleansing natron from the supply Tekurah allowed, for a kitchen slave received no such ration.

Shira overflowed with gratefulness as we dressed. "How wonderful to be clean! The work in the kitchens I can endure, but I do miss Tekurah's aversion to overripe servants." Her musical laugh erased my earlier irritation with her and I found myself smiling back at her.

We dressed quickly. Twisting the water out of my hair, I gazed across the swollen canal at the submerged fields on the other side. "Thank you, Shira. I cannot ever repay you for what you did for me. I don't understand why you did it, but I thank the gods that you intervened. If Tekurah had unleashed on me . . ."

She fluttered a hand. "Oh, it doesn't matter what happens to me." She moved to stand by me on the riverbank. "But what happened that night? Why were you so distraught?"

I chewed the inside of my cheek, reluctant to share my heartache with this odd little Hebrew slave who seemed to worry more for my safety than her own.

She placed a warm hand on my arm. "Kiya, tell me, why did Tekurah insist you attend that banquet?"

Shira was nothing if not tenacious. And truth be told, I needed to tell someone. Anyone.

I released a deep breath and told her about Akhum—about our betrothal, his absence during my downfall, and his surprise at my presence that night.

"He was powerless, or perhaps unwilling, to rescue me. I am at the bottom of this pit." I sniffed, squeezing my eyes against the burn of tears. "There is no hope."

Shira wrapped a fragile arm around my waist and pulled me tight against her side, causing me to ache for my mother and brother. "No, there is always hope. As long as we have breath in our bodies, there is hope."

No graceful bowing palms shaded us here, and the tall clumps of papyrus afforded little refuge from the sun's unrelenting glare. Even the soft morning breeze did little to assuage the heat. Sweat trickled down the back of my neck as tears threatened to spill over.

Shira did not let go. I did not pull away.

Just as I realized the sun had already passed the tip of the obelisk, hundreds of birds lit into the skies in unison. Shrill cries of alarm shattered the stillness of the morning.

Shira gasped and pointed upstream with her free hand. "What is that?"

I stared, blinking, trying to comprehend the darkness spreading across the water as it rushed toward us. No longer a muddy reddish-brown, the river ran a deep, dark crimson.

Mother Nile, the Great Heart of Egypt, was bleeding.

6

Like the gush from a fatal wound, the crimson current swirled closer to us.

Dread churned in my stomach. "What is happening?"

Shira dropped her arm from my waist. "We need to get back to the villa. Everyone must know."

I bent to pick up the full jar and recoiled at my reflection in the dark water. I tipped the jar with my foot and a rush of bloody water stained the ground red.

The water we had collected from the pool had been perfectly clear only minutes ago, yet now it, too, was defiled. How could this be?

I shuddered at the thought that only minutes ago I had been immersed in the now-foul water. We dumped our tainted jugs and hurried back up the path. As we neared the city, shrieks ripped the air. Shira and I looked at each other, eyes wide, and agreed to take different routes back to the city. Red water or no, Tekurah must not know Shira and I had met today.

A guard leaned against the entry post at the front gate of the villa, his face troubled.

I stopped to catch my breath after my jog from the canal. "Is the water here in the villa changed, too?"

He bobbed his bald head. "The kitchen staff found every pot and bowl full of red water."

The hair on my neck prickled. "And the garden pools?"

He nodded again, face drawn and pinched.

"The river is tainted, too."

His kohl-rimmed eyes widened. "What curse is this?"

I gagged on my way through the gardens. The pools stood red and fetid—they even smelled like spilled blood. Yes, this had to be a curse of some sort.

Tekurah's voice echoed through the villa, her demands for a fresh cup of water no doubt audible to all the surrounding neighbors. Dread swirled through me. My already furious mistress would not be pleased with my empty water jar.

The sweet waters of the Nile had always flowed from the veins of Osiris, the god of the underworld and granter of fertile life. But two days after Shira and I had stood on its banks, bloated fish, frogs, and snakes floated along the surface of the river. The rushes and palms drooped with thirst.

The regional Nomarch had ordered teams of slaves to dig additional pools along the water's edge, although the sand did little to filter out the red color. A complicated process of linen sieves and filters, followed by boiling for hours, made the water potable again, but only barely. No matter what we did, a distinct metallic-sulfur odor remained. Drinking the repulsive result required courage. My every nauseated sip intermingled with horrendous thoughts of priests drinking sacrificial life-blood during temple rituals.

Tekurah's panic continued to boil over. Bathing in the strong-smelling water nauseated her, and the prospect of washing her body with something resembling blood made her—made all of us—cringe. She insisted evil spirits inhabited the cursed water and purchased magic potions to mix in it, attempting to ward off the bad luck. Whether or not the potions had any effect, the water reeked worse than before.

Still, to my great relief, she insisted Latikah and I bathe in the treated water. Who was I to question protection against malevolent spirits?

Everything smelled revolting—the water, the dead animals, the unwashed people. A stench of death hung over Iunu. Decaying fish and reptiles lined the banks of the swollen canals. Even a few crocodiles and hippos washed up on the shore, their carcasses stained pink. Birds vanished from the once-teeming banks of the Nile, gone to search out fresher waters.

We tried to mask the smell, rubbing myrrh balms and almond oil on our bodies. The villa overflowed with flowers of every variety, but the stench overpowered their subtle fragrances, and without fresh water they withered quickly. Incense burned in every room, causing my head to throb in relentless agony.

When the third day dawned and the water still ran red, a terrified Tekurah ventured to the temple to hear what explanation the priests offered for this curse. Throngs of people gathered outside the temple gates, demanding why Hapi, the protector of the Nile, allowed this strange curse on the land. Tekurah and I pushed our way through the crowd, straining to hear the priests assembled on the grand temple steps.

One of them wore the elaborate beaded headdress that signified the office of high priest. "Please, please." He stretched his arms wide, like an indulgent father. "Calm down."

Shouts echoed through the crowd.

"Why is this happening?"

"What did we do to deserve this?"

An elderly man standing next to me lifted his chin to call out. "How long will this last?" The chaos swallowed his voice.

"Let us assure you, this is perfectly natural." The priest stood with hands spread wide, as if trying to push back the surging emotion of the crowd.

The mob roiled, voices rising like a tide.

"Natural? I've never seen it before."

"This is a curse!"

"Hapi is angry!"

"Osiris is stricken!"

The man next to me lifted his voice again. "I've seen fifty-two inundations. Never seen the river turn to blood."

The high priest's face belied nothing but serenity. "We have offered many sacrifices to Hapi and consulted the oracles—"

The swell of voices rose again, many accusing the priests of inaction.

"Let me assure you." He shouted above the melee, his expression losing its careful composition. "Our gods are pleased. It is a natural occurrence. Unusual, but natural. Our histories bear witness to red waters and tides from time to time."

Tekurah pushed around me to speak to the elderly man. "My husband says every branch of the river, every canal, is affected—is this true?"

He leaned forward on his walking stick, scratching his grizzled chin. "I've heard the same. All the way to the Northern Sea."

"Haven't there been red waters before, when red dirt washed down the river from Kush?"

"Not like this, such a dark stain. And not mid-inundation." His silver brows furrowed. "This has not happened before . . . at least, not in my lifetime."

"The priests have no answers, husband."

Tekurah washed down succulent bites of roasted beef with wine. My mouth watered as I eyed the scraps of meat she had pushed aside.

"What answer can they give? They don't know the minds of the gods." Shefu wiped his mouth with a linen cloth. He glanced at me with a pained look, then pushed away his plate.

"But surely, the oracles . . ." She placed her hand on his.

He pursed his lips and shook his head. "I don't want to hear talk of oracles." He slid his hand away.

Tekurah shrank back in her seat, looking around, no doubt to make sure no one overheard his blasphemy. She must have forgotten I stood at attention behind her chair.

"I don't know why this is happening. But I am concerned about our crops." Shefu stood to leave. "With inundation at its highest point, I worry that the silt deposits will not be healthy for the farmland. Thankfully the grapes have already been harvested."

The annual blessings from the Nile made our fertile land the envy of the world. The lush vegetation and bountiful crops supplied Egypt with food. We exported goods to all the surrounding nations. If even unflappable Shefu was anxious, then the situation must indeed be grim.

Shira placed her empty jug on the ground and hugged me. Unused to such displays of affection, I stood immobile, arms pinned to my sides by her boisterous embrace.

"It has been so long since we talked." She hoisted the jug back to her hip. "Filtering and boiling became my full-time occupation these last few days."

"Thanks to Hapi, the water is finally running clearer." *Praise the gods, they heard our pleas.*

People pressed into the temple courtyards all day long again—this time to offer sacrifices in gratitude for a lifted curse.

Her brow pinched. "My brother said it would only last the week."

"Your brother?"

"He came the other day. We only had a few moments, but it was good to hear from home." A tender smile graced her lips.

"He is allowed to see you?" Jealousy shot through me. I managed only a few stolen minutes in the market with my older brother, Jumo, every few weeks.

"Oh, goodness no, I meet him the same way I am meeting you. He hides here in the rushes." She trailed a free hand through the tall stalks along the path. "He comes every seventh day of the week. He knew I would be curious about the river and the excitement among our people."

"How does he get away from his master?"

"He is not a slave." She lifted a shoulder. "Well, not like I am anyhow. My brother is owned by his master, but he is given unusual freedoms. He is allowed to come and go at will and is paid a small wage. On the seventh day, the *shabbat*, his master allows him rest."

I stumbled and then stopped walking. "Why?"

"There is such a thing, you know, as Egyptians who have compassion." She winked, and one corner of her full mouth lifted. "My brother's master even secured my position in Shefu's household."

"He did?"

A shadow crossed her face. "I had just begun working on the looms. Finally old enough to work alongside my mother, when I was . . . attacked."

"By whom?"

"An overseer." Her downcast eyes seemed ancient—they told the rest of the story. "My brother begged his master to find a safer place for me. Akensouris is a friend of Shefu." She lifted her chin. "Shefu is a good man. He's been kind to both of us."

"You and your brother?"

"No, you and me. He's protected us both. Me, from an evil man, and you, from perhaps an even worse fate."

Considering that fate, I walked forward again. "What did you mean about excitement among your people?"

"Oh, that!" She slipped her free arm through mine. "It is so exciting! We have been waiting so long. Hundreds of years. I think the time has finally come. The signs have been building for a long while."

"Signs?"

"Yes, a great number of our people have been turning back to the God of Our Fathers—crying out for rescue. Almost as many have turned away, given up. And many doubt that Elohim even hears us. But he does, and he sent a Deliverer!"

"Who is Elohim?"

"Oh . . . I forget who I am speaking with." She clamped her hand to her mouth and then spoke through her fingers. "You are Egyptian . . . maybe I shouldn't tell you."

She paused and looked deep into my eyes, brow furrowed. Then, after a few still moments, she broke into peals of laughter that echoed across the canal. A gray heron, one of the few birds to brave a return to the Nile, startled out of the rushes, lifted on majestic wings, and flapped away.

"You should see your face. I'm teasing." She giggled again.

Was every Hebrew peculiar like this girl?

Shira composed herself and sat down on a flat rock near the watering hole. Few souls stirred this early, and the sun tarried low on the horizon.

"I will tell you what I can, but I may have to finish another day." She patted the rock, beckoning me to sit, and although still a bit unsettled by her mocking, I sank down beside her.

"Elohim, the Strong One, is how we call upon our God," she said. "The God of Our Fathers—Avraham, Yitzhak, and Yaakov. We also address him as Adonai, or Lord."

"But what is his name?"

"We call him by many terms."

"How can you ensure answered prayers if you cannot name him?"

"He hears." She closed her eyes and drew a deep breath through her nose, as though drawing divinity from the very air around her.

She opened her eyes and gestured to the water. "When the river changed, that was Moses—our Deliverer. The rumor my brother heard is that Moses met Pharaoh that very morning. When he struck the water with a staff, it turned blood-red."

"Why would Pharaoh do such a thing to the Nile?"

"No, Moses struck the water to show Pharaoh who is the highest god."

"Pharaoh is the highest god, descendent of Ra, creator of life." I spouted the creed without hesitation.

"Pharaoh is not the highest god, and Moses will prove it to him." She stared into my eyes with an unfathomable expression.

Words escaped me. This strange girl had blasphemed Pharaoh without a blink. She could be tied to a pole in the public square and scourged, or worse.

"I know that this is confusing. It goes against everything you have been taught. But I tell you, my friend, it is truth." She laid her small hand on my arm. "To help you understand I must start from the beginning. Do you want to hear?"

I did. For some inexplicable reason, I thirsted to know more. I gestured for her to continue.

"You see," she began, "my people, the children of Avraham,

Yitzhak, and Yaakov, we are sojourners here in your land. Over four hundred years ago, a prophecy ensured deliverance from our wanderings. We will return one day to our own land."

Slipping easily into the story of her heritage, she told me how the Hebrews—once a free and proud people—came out of the land of Canaan during a time of famine and were protected by one of their own disguised as an overseer of Egypt, second in command to Pharaoh himself.

Preposterous. No pharaoh would allow Hebrews to hold such power.

"The Pharaoh invited our people to live in Egypt and gave us fertile land to settle in and raise herds. Elohim blessed us and we prospered." Shira's eyes shone with a fearsome hope. She was intelligent, witty, and wise—well beyond her years. My perception of Shira tilted, and then shifted. This was no ordinary slave girl.

"How did you become slaves?"

"After many years, a new Pharaoh rose to power who did not know our forefathers and did not respect the invitation given by the former rulers of Egypt. Our numbers multiplied. He feared an uprising, so he enslaved us."

"How did Pharaoh enslave such a numerous people? Why didn't you rise up, as he feared?" It seemed my opinion of Pharaoh had shifted as well.

"He began very slowly. First he offered loans and burdened them with heavy taxation. Then he allowed the people to sell themselves into indentured servitude to pay those tax debts. Deceived into volunteering for work crews to prove their loyalty to Egypt, many stepped willingly into shackles. After a few years, volunteering turned into forcible conscription, and within a decade he had enslaved the entire Hebrew population."

"They sold *themselves* into slavery," I whispered, not wanting to interrupt her story.

She nodded and released a heavy sigh. "Our men serve on the work crews, making bricks, digging canals, building the huge store cities of the Delta, building palaces, fortresses, and of course, monuments for the Pharaoh. Our women do what they can to help: bringing food and water to the men, working linen and weaving baskets, or serving Egyptians in their homes and businesses, as I do."

Forced, like me, into slavery and daily humiliation. However, I endured only personal shame and pain, whereas Pharaoh had enslaved their entire race. I leaned back on my palms and watched a lone high cloud meander across the barren sky.

"They subjugated us in every way. Except one." Shira's voice grew strong as the brilliant sun rose behind her. "Our families. Our numbers grew rapidly. The harder Pharaoh and the Egyptian people worked us, the larger our families grew. They hoped to break our spirit, but instead, they made us more resilient." The ferocity of her words startled me. "We are bound to one another through our covenant with Elohim. He preserved us . . . prospered us in spite of Pharaoh's oppression and the faithlessness of many."

Disembodied voices, of fishermen casting nets far downstream, echoed across the water.

"We should hurry. It won't be long before others come to wash." She bent to fill her jar with sweet, clean water.

"If your God is preserving your people, then why are you still enslaved?" I attempted, without success, to keep the sarcasm out of my voice.

Shira winked. "I am getting to that."

"About eighty years ago . . ." Her voice dropped into a sorrowful tone. "Pharaoh made a law that all Hebrew male babies were to be exterminated. The guild of midwives was ordered to kill the little ones while their mothers still stood on the birthing bricks."

I stared at her. I must have misunderstood. In Egypt, children were highly valued and cherished—pampered even. I could not imagine anyone, let alone Pharaoh, the son of the creator-god, insisting on the destruction of thousands of healthy infants.

Shira said that many of the midwives complied out of fear for their own lives. Thousands of infants were exposed to the elements. However, many midwives refused to take the lives of the Hebrew babies, among them, two leaders of the midwives' guild, Shifrah and Puah.

"These brave women deceived Pharaoh," she said. They told the overseers that in contrast to the Egyptian women, who were pampered and soft, the Hebrew women were strong from daily heavy labor, and the babies delivered quickly. They insisted that the babies were secreted away before the midwives arrived at the birthing huts.

"What happened to them?" The midwives' disobedience relieved me, but a twinge of guilt for my inward rebellion against my king stabbed at me.

Shira beamed. "Elohim protected them, and Pharaoh did not punish the midwives. In fact, both their families grew large and powerful. Our people venerate Shifrah and Puah to this day."

Awe filled me. What courage those women must have had to defy the most powerful god-man in the world.

"However"—she frowned—"after the midwives failed in their mission to eradicate our precious babies, Pharaoh became enraged and ordered all of Egypt to take care of the Hebrew problem. He decreed that any Egyptian who came in contact with a male Hebrew child must report it immediately."

The faces of my parents' friends came to mind—traitors, every one. Perhaps their parents or grandparents had participated in this injustice as well.

"The priests and the overseers said the Hebrews planned to revolt: they must be controlled or they would take over the country, stealing Egyptian wealth. Fear and suspicion flourished. Thousands upon thousands of precious baby boys were ripped from their mothers' arms and thrown into the Nile."

Bile swam in my throat. The image of babies, shrieking, sinking to the bottom of the Nile, flooded my mind. I scrubbed the last of the stench from my hair, suddenly needing to get out of the pool. Neither of us spoke as we climbed onto the bank, dressed, and collected our jars to head back to the villa.

Even though I knew little of politics, and even less of governing a nation, Pharaoh's destruction of the very workforce that helped build his own legacy seemed irrational. Pharaoh employed the world's mightiest standing army, heavily equipped and more than capable of quelling any rebellion that might have reared its head.

The Hebrews had no more hope of freedom than I did. The law demanded obedience to my masters, and if I ran, my mother and brother would bear the brunt of my rebellion against Tekurah. They would be punished in my stead, perhaps even sold to satisfy the remainder of the debt. Even with the assistance of all the gods, no chance remained—for myself or the Hebrews.

"This Deliverer you mentioned . . ."

She looked over her shoulder. "Moses."

"That is an Egyptian name." We neared the point on the path where we must separate to avoid suspicion, but my curiosity about this mysterious man slowed my pace.

"Moses is Hebrew. In our language he is Mosheh, but a daughter of Pharaoh himself raised him in the royal household." A hint of smugness heightened her voice.

A Hebrew raised as a prince? Why would Pharaoh allow such a thing in his own palace?

Before I could ask any more questions, Latikah appeared, coming toward us on the path, expertly balancing an empty jug on her head. Our mistress must have sent her to collect water for a second washing. I pressed ahead of Shira, pretending that I had only passed her on the way, knowing she would understand.

I steeled myself for another furious reprimand, half hoping Tekurah would demote me to the kitchens as well. Shira's stories, of her people and her God, were like wild honey. They had the curious effect of making me hunger for more, and I did not want to wait long for another taste.

7

Shira waited for me by the ancient boundary stone, but she was not alone. A man stood with her, his back toward me. My pulse spiked as I tripped to a stop. Had our secret meeting place been discovered?

Shira caught sight of me over the man's shoulder and waved, a broad smile across her face. She gestured for me to join them.

The man, dressed in a simple brown slave garment tied with an embroidered leather belt, turned as I approached. His dark hair, whipped by a breeze from the canal, obscured his face for a moment, until he brushed it away with long fingers.

Oh no. It was the man with whom I had found Liat in the marketplace during the festival. What was he doing with Shira?

Shira must have sensed my trepidation. She met me halfway. "I am so glad to see you." She hugged me again and I half returned the embrace. "Come, meet my brother, Eben." Her face emanated unmistakable pride.

Her brother? How could such a sullen man be related to Shira, whose baffling optimism radiated like the sun?

Shira linked her arm in mine and towed me toward him. His

unkempt hair, now clear of sawdust, was darker than hers, but sure enough, they shared identical green-gray eyes.

"Eben, this is my friend Kiya. I am so pleased you two can finally meet." Without giving him a chance to respond, she turned to me. "He came to tell me all that is happening with our people. I have so much to share with you!" She squeezed my arm.

I chanced a quick smile at Eben. "Hello again."

He dipped his bearded chin but did not speak. A muscle worked in his jaw as he fixed me in his gaze.

Shira looked back and forth between us. "You know each other?"

"Yes, we met in the market once." Thinking to offer a gesture of goodwill, I added, "Thank you again for your help with Liat."

Although he stood not much taller than I, Eben's chin tilted up and he glowered down his narrow nose at me, but said nothing.

Desperate to escape the scrutiny in his penetrating gaze, I forced an excuse. "Tekurah is suspicious after our run-in with Latikah. I must hurry today. You talk with your brother. I'll see you another time."

Such a lie. My worries had been misplaced yesterday. Curiously, my mistress had given me no more than a demand to bathe her immediately, as if her desperation to be clean washed her mind of my delay.

Slipping from Shira's grasp, I hastened down the path, relying on the papyrus rushes and date palms to veil my retreat. Even so, I felt Eben's dark glare boring into my back.

Shira caught up with me, breathless. "I am so sorry."

I sniffed, blinking away traitorous tears and chiding myself for reacting. Why should the opinion of one Hebrew upset me so much?

"What for?" I attempted a carefree smile.

"Eben . . . Oh Kiya, he was so rude to you. I cannot understand why . . ." Her voice trembled.

I straightened my shoulders and huffed out a noisy breath. "That doesn't bother me. I put up with Tekurah screaming at me every day. You think I cannot handle the evil eye from some slave?" I brushed away her concerns with a flip of my hand.

"I know. But he is my big brother, and you are my only friend. I just hoped you might get along. Unrealistic expectations, I suppose. He still—" Her voice faltered. "He blames all Egyptians for my father's death."

Although curious about her father, I was anxious to change the subject. "I really should get back before Tekurah misses me. I don't have time to bathe today. But I am impatient for the end of your story about this mysterious Hebrew prince. Let's fill our pots and get back to the villa." I wiggled my fingers at her. "You can spin your tale as we go."

Shira beamed, all disappointment swallowed by pleasure at my interest in her stories. "Where was I?"

"The Deliverer?"

"Mosheh." Her voice swelled with reverence reserved for gods and kings. "Mosheh was born during those black days, when crocodiles in the Nile still devoured our babies and weeping mothers vowed to give birth to ten more sons to replace those who had been murdered. Mosheh's mother, Yocheved, devised a plan. She succeeded in hiding him from the Egyptian overseers and corrupt Hebrew supervisors for three months."

"You mean some of your own people spied for Pharaoh?"

"Gold is a powerful persuader, even among my own, and many have turned from the God of Our Fathers."

A sharp laugh startled us. Someone was coming up the path. We slipped into the tall rushes near the edge of the canal, squatting there among the feathery plumes of grass and shoulder-high weeds. A group of three slaves, two of whom were from Shefu's household, undressed and waded into the water to bathe.

"That was close," Shira whispered, her eyes glimmering with mischief, as if she enjoyed our childish game of hide-and-seek.

"We will have to wait," I whispered back.

She nodded. "Won't Tekurah be looking for you?"

I flushed, caught in my lie. "Actually, Tekurah was up nearly until dawn at a banquet. She will sleep for hours." I yawned, having only dozed for a couple of hours myself.

Shira pursed her lips and arched her brows. "So you just needed an excuse to get away from my brother?"

I deflected. "Tell me the rest of your story. But keep your voice down, it may carry across the water."

She stared at me a moment, settled into a cross-legged position, and then continued in a low tone. "Yocheved was a wise woman, full of the audacity all mothers summon when forced to fight for their children. She formed a basket of papyrus reeds, made it watertight, then placed her precious treasure inside and set it afloat on the Nile."

Shira brushed at a yellow-and-black-striped spider that had taken up residence on her tunic, and she continued. "The baby's sister, Miryam, guarded the little boat, hiding in the rushes." She smiled and winked. "Just like we are doing now."

I peered through the tall grasses at the glint of sun off the river, imagining the young girl watching her brother float down the river in his makeshift ark. I almost expected the little papyrus boat to glide by.

"Yocheved knew Pharaoh's daughter bathed and swam each morning in the river. This royal daughter was widely known to be compassionate—as well as stubborn. But most importantly, Pharaoh cherished this beloved daughter, the only child of his favorite wife."

This sounded familiar. I had grown up with tales of a princess who became a regent in the land. She held power unrivaled by most women in a world ruled by men. Could it be the same woman?

"Yocheved counted on the princess finding her baby and prayed Pharaoh's daughter would have mercy on her child. And, of course, Elohim heard the devoted mother's prayer."

I interrupted. "What tribute did she offer?"

"Tribute?"

"Yes, how did she make Elohim protect her baby?"

Shira cocked her head. "She just had faith."

"Faith?"

She smiled. "She knew Elohim had a special purpose for the child. He was . . . different in some way. The tales handed down speak of his quiet nature, an unnatural calmness to the child. Yocheved was able to hide him for three months because he was so quiet. She called him Toviah, which means 'goodness' in my language."

Jumo flashed through my mind. Unable to speak with clarity as a child due to his afflictions, my brother reserved his precious words only for his family, yet somehow drew people like honey. No one was immune to his sweetness.

Shira said the princess found the baby, fell in love with him, and determined to adopt him as her own. Miryam emerged from her hiding place among the rushes. She offered to find a wet nurse from among one of the Hebrew women. So the baby was nursed and raised until he was weaned by Yocheved herself. The princess provided food and clothing and extra goods for the family in exchange for the care of the little boy.

"So you see"—Shira raised her chin—"not only did Elohim protect Moses, as he was named by the princess, but the family was blessed for their faith. Raised in Pharaoh's own household, educated at Pharaoh's own expense, adopted by the willful princess—Mosheh enjoyed the full rights of a true royal son."

"Did Mosheh know who he was? A Hebrew?"

Shira nodded. "He did. Being raised at the breast of Yocheved, a woman of strength and courage, he was steeped in the stories of our people. Although raised as a royal prince, in line for the throne, his status as an adopted son lay heavy on his heart. And because he was an adopted son, he pushed himself even harder to be worthy of his royal title. He studied and practiced the arts of war with more diligence than any other royal son and grew to be a great general in Pharaoh's army."

I wrinkled my brow, wondering if Akhum had ever served under the Hebrew. "I have never heard of a general named Moses."

"No one really knows what happened, but forty years ago, he vanished. Rumors floated around that he killed an Egyptian overseer." She raised a brow. "I highly doubt that. But, all of a sudden, he was gone. There was no word from him, even to Yocheved. She died before setting eyes on her beloved son again."

What an implausible tale. A Hebrew baby floating down a river in a basket, saved by a princess at the perfect moment, raised by the very Pharaoh who sought to have him killed? The longer I listened to Shira, the less I believed her dubious little story.

"And then, a few weeks ago, Eben told me Mosheh returned." She paused as if to gauge my reaction.

Startled, I arched my brows.

"He returned from Midian, where he had lived as a shepherd and where Elohim appeared to him on a mountain and told him to return to Egypt—to deliver our people. Here in Iunu we hear only rumors. Mosheh lives among his brothers in Goshen, but we hope to hear from the elders soon whether what we've heard is true." The gleam in her eyes told me she needed no such confirmation. Shira believed every word.

"Did Mosheh take a carving of your Elohim with him on his flight?"

She waved a hand. "No, our God is not limited in such a way. We do not worship idols. In the days of our forefathers, He talked with them, met with them in various ways, through dreams and visions. At times Elohim even appeared as a man and walked with them."

This poor girl was delusional. True, Pharaoh personified the ancestor gods, but only a high priest entertained any sort of interaction with those gods. Perhaps her forefathers served as high priests, schooled in the magic arts, as this Mosheh must be.

Shira pointed at the river. "The Nile turned crimson to show Pharaoh that the Deliverer is here and that Elohim will bring us out of slavery and pay him back—blood for blood."

I restrained a shiver. "Listen. I know that you wish, as I do, that someone might whisk you away from this life. Up until the night of that festival, I hoped Akhum might free me. But this"—I touched the pot on the ground next to me—"this is our reality. And the sooner you accept that, the sooner you will stop believing such foolishness. The Nile changing was a natural thing, the priests said this happens every hundred years or so."

"If it was a natural occurrence, how do you explain that it happened at the height of inundation? Most of the silt came down the river a month before. How did it happen at the precise hour Mosheh hit the water with his staff? Can the priests explain that?" She lifted her brows, lips pursed.

The other women had left the canal, and Shira and I were free to leave the green prison of tall grasses that had protected us, but I felt compelled to keep her from raising her hopes too high.

"Maybe your Mosheh is a powerful sorcerer. You said he was educated in Pharaoh's household . . ."

She nodded.

"Then he might have been taught the arts of divine persuasion. Besides, if your god-without-a-name is powerful enough to threaten Pharaoh the Almighty, why has nothing else happened since then? It's been a week. The river runs clear. And I am fairly sure Pharaoh did not release you. Or am I mistaken?"

"Eben says that Elohim is not finished yet." A frown settled on her lips. "This is only the beginning."

8

Torch in hand and skin crawling, I walked between two enormous statues of our Pharaoh at the grand entrance to the Temple of Iunu. I searched for something but knew not what. Somehow, though, I sensed it lay deep at the center of the holiest chamber.

Blackness hemmed me in, augmenting the lonely silence and my fear of the dark.

Passing through one deserted courtyard into another, I came to a cavernous hall. My footsteps echoed off the endless lotus and papyrus columns. I held the torch high and tipped my head back, taking in the beautiful etchings that stretched from the floor into the dark reaches above me. The ceiling seemed to be only an endless black sky. The darkness pressed down upon me, heavy with the weight of spirits that roamed this temple in the darkest hours of the night.

Statues of lesser gods guarded the holy sanctuary before me, their faces obscured by the liquid vision of dreams. I stepped past the thick bronze doors and into the chamber, grasping the torch in front of my chest, a burning shield against whatever lay ahead.

Ra loomed large in the room, his golden body burnished to gleaming by the ministrations of the priests. Wilted lotus flowers encircled the base upon which his throne stood, and food offerings lay rotting at his feet. I raised my torch higher to take in his face and his obsidian eyes. But his eyes were not black—they gleamed red! Dripping red. The smell of the bleeding Nile met my senses, and I choked. Hapi, Osiris, and Isis—all the gods hemorrhaged bright red blood from their eyes, ears, and noses.

A shriek ripped me from deepest sleep. *Was I screaming?* The smell of the cursed river had plagued my nightmares for days.

But it was not my own scream that awakened me. Tekurah stood atop her sleeping couch, shedding her bedclothes. "Get it off! Get it off!"

"What is it, mistress?" I sat up on my mat and rubbed my eyes, never surprised at Tekurah's ravings.

"Something just crawled across my face. And then something else moved against my hand. Get it out! Now!" She tumbled off the bed, tangled in a flurry of nightclothes and sheets, ranting at me. With all her noise, Shefu's men would burst through the door at any moment, swords drawn.

The oil lamp on the table burned low. Tekurah had fallen asleep early last night, and I risked a reprimand by keeping it lit. So many nightmares plagued me lately, I could not bear the pitch-black one more night. I retrieved the clay bowl, thankful that the wick had lasted so long. Something brushed my foot on the way. A cat's tail perhaps?

I pulled back the linen cover on Tekurah's bed and gasped.

Not just one or two, but twenty or more little frogs nestled in Tekurah's bedclothes.

I lifted the light higher. Hundreds of tiny frogs blanketed the floor. Tekurah hyperventilated, pleading with me to do something. What could I do? Frogs crept everywhere.

I rushed to the corner to retrieve a straw broom, recoiling

whenever I stepped on a frog with my bare feet. I attempted to sweep the tiny creatures out the doorway. However, the weak pre-dawn light illuminated a hallway that swarmed with frogs as well.

Tekurah stood on top of a stool in the middle of the room, petrified, pointing out each frog she saw and urging me to hurry. The frogs terrified me, too, but the luxury of standing on a stool, ordering a slave about, belonged to her.

Latikah came from the servants' sleeping quarters to help, but as many frogs as we found and scooped out the windows and into the hallway, more took their places. Where were those cats when they were actually needed?

"This is useless, mistress. We have been working for hours, but they just keep coming. We are fighting a losing battle." I wiped sweat from my face with the back of my hand, another vain gesture.

"Go get Shefu," she commanded. "Latikah will keep at it."

I took my broom, swiping at the tiny beasts before each step. Some of them clung to the straw, and I was forced to shake them off every few steps. By this time, I'd given up being scared of the frogs. Now every time one jumped at me, I gritted my teeth and lashed out with angry force, only to face more of them scuttling my way.

A sea of tiny, green and brown creatures swarmed the hall-way, hopping wildly. I swept my way to Shefu's quarters and knocked on his door. One of his handservants, Lefar, answered.

"Mistress Tekurah requests the presence of Master Shefu in her quarters." I bowed my head.

Shefu appeared in the doorway. "What, pray tell, does she expect me to do? The same curse plagues us here."

"She's terrified, master. She's been on a stool for hours."

He covered his eyes with a hand. "All right." He groaned. "Lefar, bring your broom."

Lefar and I swept a path back to Tekurah's room.

Using the broom I'd given her to defend against the on-slaught, Tekurah swiped at the frogs that hopped high enough to reach her feet on the low stool.

"Do something!" she screeched as Shefu entered.

He slid the little monsters aside with each step and approached her. "What would you have me do, Tekurah?"

"Get more slaves in here to clear out my quarters!"

He shook his head. "All the servants in the household are using every broom, shovel, and basket on our property to clear out the frogs. The entire city is besieged. I can no more control this plague than you can."

"Then go to the temple and make a sacrifice to Heket, the frog goddess. Anything to stop this horror." She slapped at more of the creatures with her weapon.

"The priests are already sacrificing to her, Wife. I went to the temple court before dawn as we became inundated. They are incanting and consulting the oracles, to no avail." He rubbed an eyebrow with two fingers. "Strangely, I think somehow it has made it worse. Even more frogs have come pouring into the city over the last couple of hours."

"Well, do something!" She lifted her arms. "Please!"

Shefu shrugged his shoulders, shook his head, and left the room, swiping the frogs aside with his sandals.

Tekurah stood on the stool, arms outstretched, staring at the empty doorway. When she finally dropped her arms, her shoulders slumped and her black eyes were rimmed with tears. Was it fear of the frogs? Frustration with Shefu? Did his apathy wound her? I held no tenderness for Tekurah, but her reaction confused me. My mistress seemed lost, pathetic.

It took only a couple of heartbeats for her to snap back to her normal posture. "Why have you stopped sweeping? Keep working. I don't care how many frogs there are in this city. There will be none in my room by the end of the day."

Tekurah could not order about the frogs as easily as her servants. We worked all day, but nothing staunched the flow of the tiny creatures. The entire household worked to remove them, to no avail.

The tiny frogs slipped in through cracks and doors. Normally the ibises and herons kept the frog population well under control, but many of them had flown away when the Nile turned sour and so many fish died. The few birds remaining were completely overwhelmed by the teeming multitude of croaking little pests. The villa pool overflowed with them. They blanketed the floors in the bedchambers, the storage rooms, even the kitchen courtyard. The kitchen slaves kept a close eye on the bread, but even so, the little frogs crawled into the ovens and were baked inside the loaves.

I woke, stiff and unrefreshed, as I had for a week. Sleep eluded me—and Tekurah—for days. She screeched at me every so often to shake out her covers when she felt frogs creeping around on her bed. No matter how tightly I wrapped the linens around Tekurah, or myself for that matter, they wormed their way in. My skin crawled every time one brushed my face when I lay on my pallet. So I leaned against the wall in the corner, propped on a three-legged stool, trying to sleep, if only for a couple of hours, until Tekurah's next tantrum.

The first thing that struck me was silence. The incessant croaking had ceased. I looked down and gasped. Hundreds of tiny frogs lay dead or dying on the tiles. *Did the priests' spells finally work?*

"Ugh. What is that horrid stench?" Tekurah sat up on her bed with a hand clamped over her nose. When she saw the frogs, her eyes went wide. "They are dead?"

I nodded.

"Then why are you still sitting there?" She removed her hand from her nose and swirled it in the air. "Go get Latikah, and get to cleaning."

Latikah and I scoured the room, scooping up tiny carcasses with shards of pottery to deposit on burn piles outside the villa gates. Burning only strengthened the death stench of the frogs. I soaked a linen cloth in rosewater to tie about my face, attempting to mask the smell, but nothing helped. With every breath, I gagged at the taste of rot on my tongue.

After inspecting her room to ensure not one frog remained, Tekurah ordered us to help clear the rest of the villa with the other slaves.

Assigned by the steward to clean the family sanctuary, I trudged with my frog-collecting basket toward the small out-building that lay in the western corner of the property. Gardeners raked together more burning piles in the center of the gardens as I passed. My linen cloth needed another soak of rosewater; the decay, ash, and burning flesh smell assaulted me once again, and I jogged the rest of the way, trying to avoid a deep breath. A voice—singing? humming?—met my ears as I tripped on the threshold entering the sanctuary. Not the most respectful way to enter, but at least the incense in here masked the reek.

Oh no. Incense. My vision blurred, and lights flashed.

"Hello there. Come to help?" Shira's crouched form swam in front of my eyes.

"Mmm." I closed my eyes. Needles seemed to be digging into them.

Shira's face seemed to float out of nowhere, flashing blue, red, and yellow lights. "What is wrong?" Her hands gripped my wrists.

"The smoke. It gives me . . ." I shook my head against pain-wrought confusion. "Headaches."

"Oh. Let's get you out into the fresh air." She dragged me by the wrists out the back doorway of the sanctuary. I barely registered the gold and silver idols nestled in alcoves all about the room. Were they leering at me? Whispering curses?

Behind a tall rosebush, I leaned against the side of the house, head between my knees. I tried to suck in fresh air and managed only decay-infested breaths. At least my vision began to clear after a few minutes. Shira disappeared and then came back, looking over her shoulder with a mug of fresh water from the kitchen. I downed the refreshment.

"Better?" Shira's concerned face hovered, clear now, in front of me.

"Yes, thank you. But we need to clean the sanctuary."

She waved a hand at me. "All done. You didn't even need to come in."

"You did it all?"

She nodded. "I work fast when I sing." A smile dimpled her cheek.

"That was you singing?"

She looked over my shoulder. "The idols in there . . . they . . . Well, I was singing to keep my mind off them staring at me. There is evil in that room." A slight shudder jerked her shoulders.

My defenses shot up. She dared accuse my gods of malevolence?

"You said your God brought about the bloody waters. Isn't that evil?" I threw the accusation at her like a dagger.

She ignored the thrust. "And the frogs."

"Oh, he cursed us with the frogs, too, did he?"

She winced.

Annoyed with her silence, I pressed harder. "What kind of god does such things?"

She looked down at her hands and then to the north, where

her family lived in the Hebrew quarter. "I don't know the mind of Elohim. I wish I did."

She sighed. "But I know there is a reason for everything he does, and even if my human mind can't wrap itself around his plan, I will follow. All I know is what my father told me from the time I was a tiny girl. Elohim will rescue us, and as we suffer under the hand of Pharaoh, he is building us, preparing us for something."

"For what?"

"For something we cannot even imagine." Her strange green-gray eyes searched mine for a long moment. "Perhaps he is preparing you, too."

9

The bites on the back of my neck burned like fire. Although they were healing now, I could not stop scratching; even thinking about the lice set me to ferociously itching again. Our hair, our eyelashes, our skin, our clothes: everything had crawled with tiny vermin for days. Cows, goats, dogs in the street—even Tekurah's precious cats—had incessantly scratched and rolled in the dirt, trying to assuage the itch. At times I wished I could roll in the dust, too.

We washed every bit of cloth in the villa in scalding-hot water, but nothing staved off the infestation. I had spent the last week alternating my time between sponging Tekurah's lice-ridden body with vinegar, applying aloe and natron to sooth her sores, and shaving her body and head daily.

Out of sheer vanity, I had refused to shave my own head. Instead, I coated my scalp and hair with olive oil. Tekurah was so miserable she did not even complain that I had used her oils—instead she asked me to apply some to her scalp as well.

Tekurah had sent me to the market today for a stronger ointment for her slow-healing sores. Since I came alone for once, I decided to chance a visit to my mother.

Palpable relief and a jubilant air hung over the city. The insects that had seemed to appear from the very dirt under our feet finally had vanished. Strangely, it seemed to happen overnight, as if someone had simply spoken a word and made them disappear.

After dodging donkeys, rambunctious children, and the pushing and shoving of customers who were packed shoulder to shoulder, I found myself pressed against a table laden with platters of indigo, saffron, vivid red carmine, henna, and dyes and pigments of every hue. If only the copper deben I carried in the satchel around my waist were my own to trade, I would buy every color for Jumo to mix into vibrant new paints. This stall boasted powdered malachite, the perfect green for depicting feathery papyrus plants—or for stormy green eyes.

Would Eben be here today? The instrument shop was not far away from where I stood. An almost irresistible urge to search it out twisted through me, nearly forcing my path to veer the opposite direction from my mother's stall. Perhaps for Shira's sake I should try to make peace. But the image of Eben's glare lingered in my mind, and I shook off the idea.

My father must have recently returned from his latest excursion up the Nile with many goods, for my mother's stall seemed well-stocked. My father never stayed in town long, and never came to the marketplace. He faced only the slap of the river waters against his boat, never the sting of shame in the market.

Customers crowded around my mother's booth, bartering loudly, demanding her attention. One man offered three fresh fish for a small stack of linens. My mother caught sight of me, and a broad smile lit her face even as she shook her head and countered his ridiculous offer. The man left a few minutes later, lighter by four fish and a turquoise bracelet. Nailah drove a hard bargain.

Tekurah was attractive, elegant, and carried herself well, but she held nothing over the magnificent beauty of my mother. As the jewel in my father's crown, my mother once enjoyed status as one of the most popular women of Iunu. My father had always indulged her with the latest fashions and finest jewelry he could obtain.

But my mother did not need gifts from Pharaoh, the sheerest of linens, queenly fashions, or expensive cosmetics to be beautiful. Regal by nature, she bore herself with elegance—even now as she traded wares in the marketplace.

When the last customer finished his purchase, she pulled me into a fierce embrace. Tears glinted in her honey-gold eyes. Mine were the same shade, and just as wet.

Safe in my mother's arms, if only for a moment, I burrowed my face into her thick black hair, drinking in its almond-oil scent, trying to ignore the accusations that bubbled to the surface.

"My girl. My girl." She tightened her grip for a moment, and I wondered if conflict was raging inside her as well. Would she finally tell me why—here and now?

How could I account for a mother who seemed to love me so much yet allowed my freedom to be sold in exchange for her own? Had she known? Why had she not come to my rescue? Where was she that day? And what of Shefu? So many swirling questions jumbled inside my head that I could not untangle any of them. Besides, I lacked the courage to ask—I feared the answers.

She released me abruptly to refold a stack of linens toppled by hurried customers. I straightened my shoulders and expertly pressed down the desire to beg for answers; it was not the time or the place for such conversations.

"I don't have much time, Mother . . . only enough to say hello. Where is Jumo?" Usually he was here with her, painting and studying the people passing by.

Jumo's pots, painted with vivid flowers, and his brilliant papyrus wall-hangings enticed customers to my mother's stall. Trained by no master, he simply practiced and perfected his craft on old pottery shards and spare scraps of well-worn papyrus.

"He was tired today, and his bites are still healing. I made him stay at home." She scratched absentmindedly at the wounds on her own arms.

"Were you both affected severely?"

"Weren't we all? That Hebrew sorcerer is torturing us. He brought on the blood and the frogs—and now lice."

A large woman with a wig dyed a bright henna-orange pawed through a pile of woven mats. She overheard our conversation and interjected, "Pharaoh's priests have more magic. The plagues went away, didn't they?"

My mother nodded. "But my husband just returned from Avaris this morning. The city is ablaze with rumors. He told me the sorcerer wouldn't lift the affliction until Pharaoh gave in to his demands."

"Which demands?" asked the woman.

"That he let the Hebrew slaves go worship their god in the desert," my mother scoffed.

So Eben's information had been correct. Mosheh had indeed demanded the Hebrews' release.

"And why, if this Moses is so powerful, were all the Hebrews bitten by the lice as well?" The vitriol in the woman's voice struck me. "The frogs hopped in their homes, too. The Hebrews strained their water right alongside the rest of us."

My mother laughed and winked. "Perhaps their slave-god can't tell the difference between a Hebrew and an Egyptian."

Someone jostled me from behind and, still unsettled from the direction of my mother's conversation with the rude woman, I glared at the perpetrator, but then startled when I recognized her face.

Shira? With her hair covered with a brown headscarf, kohl-lined eyes, and her face half hidden behind a veil? Without blinking, Shira mumbled an apology. Then, so slightly only I would notice, she tipped her head toward the north end of the market. Eben's stall.

I nodded as if to accept her regrets and turned back to my mother. "I must head back to the villa. Tekurah's sores need tending."

My mother winced but kissed my cheek. "Come again soon. It's been far too long."

"I will do my best. Give Jumo my love."

I threaded my way through the buzzing, chattering crowd. Pungent spices mingled together with the tang of raw meat hanging in the butcher stalls and the acrid smell of unwashed animals and bodies. Jangling bells and the clang of metal from a blacksmith shop nearby composed a chaotic harmony. Two men seated on low stools argued over a heated game of Senet as barbers shaved their heads.

There, at the far end of the marketplace, the musical instrument stall nestled in a gap between two-story buildings. Only this time, another slave, a Kushite, sat behind the table. Eben was nowhere in sight.

A hand gripped my elbow. "Come, let's walk fast. I must get back." Shira's brittle tone shocked me.

"Why are you dressed like that? And your eyes—?"

"It's the only way I can brave the market. Hebrews are not welcome here anymore."

I stumbled on an uneven cobblestone, twisting my ankle, but she pulled me along.

"Shira, what is wrong?"

"Things have gone from bad to worse for my people." Her voice trembled. "Pharaoh is furious over Mosheh's threats. To punish Mosheh and turn the people against him, Pharaoh ordered that no more straw be delivered to the brickmakers. They have to scavenge in the fields to find enough to strengthen the bricks."

"Won't that slow down progress?" Our Pharaoh seemed to be on a pursuit to surpass the glory of any other king before him, and extensive building projects were underway all over Egypt.

"It will. But he told the overseers that the quota of bricks is not to be lessened. Their burden is twice what it was before."

"Are your people angry at Mosheh?" *Some Deliverer.*

She glanced at me. "Many are. The increase of hardships, along with the abuse, is difficult to bear."

"Abuse?"

She pressed her lips into a harsh line, her brows gathering. "I have to disguise myself to come here. Five men have been beaten in the marketplace in the past few days. Eben is forced to stay out of sight in Akensouris's workshop."

"Why?"

"Many blame us for these plagues or mock us for worshiping our invisible god." Shira looked north toward the Hebrew quarter.

"Can you blame them?" I blurted without thinking.

Tears of hurt welled in Shira's eyes. I had not meant to wound her, but I spoke the truth of my heart.

"Perhaps not." She dropped her gaze, and her hand fell from my arm. "But as my friend, could you not have the least bit of compassion?"

She trudged away from me, shoulders dropped, heading back to the villa.

I should have hurried to catch up with her, apologized. My heart wanted to, but my feet seemed like iron weights.

She was right. I should have compassion for her people. I had been sold into slavery through no fault of my own. Mosheh, and his sorcery, were responsible for the heavy burdens of his people, just as my father was for mine.

Shira, and all the Hebrews, trusted in a nameless, merciless god of slaves. A god just as unwilling, or powerless, to free them as Akhum had been for me.

The Lord of the Two Lands held the power in Egypt. His mighty name commanded fear throughout the earth. How could anyone believe in an invisible god? Pharaoh was here among us; it was he who would protect us from any threat that could possibly come at Egypt. He, the Divine One, would call upon Ra, upon Osiris, upon all the gods who had made our country great among the nations and would put Mosheh, a mere mortal, in his place.

Yes, strange occurrences plagued Egypt, but I was not convinced they were supernatural. An unusual inundation, the frogs fleeing the Nile after the fish died and their food sources were destroyed, their natural enemies the birds having also fled. And with millions of rotting carcasses of frogs and fish came the bugs. These were natural events.

Had it really been all that serious? Like the woman in the market had said, we dug wells along the Nile and survived the red waters, the frogs died, the lice vanished. And along with us, the Hebrews suffered as well—Shira's skin was as dotted with sores as mine.

I was sorry her people were burdened more. I did not wish them to carry a heavier load, but their God wielded no more power to relieve their afflictions than I did to alleviate my own.

Besides, how could a powerful god who loved them, as Shira insisted he did, let them live in slavery and watch them suffer?

Tekurah stroked the golden cat in her lap and gazed into the tranquil garden pool. Clusters of fruit hung heavy from the date palms that shaded us from the vicious afternoon sun—further evidence that the country flourished again. I stirred the still, dry air with a white ostrich-feather fan, grateful it cooled me as well. White lilies dipped and swayed to the rhythm of Tekurah's foot swirling in the water.

"I am so glad things have returned to normal." She pulled her foot out of the pool and lay back on the heels of her palms. "There will be a bountiful harvest in a few weeks."

"Yes, mistress." Her placid tone and unexpected conversation alarmed me. "Master Shefu is blessed of the gods."

"That he is." She tilted her head to peer at me. "Thankfully, he is not such a fool as your father, losing everything in one huge gamble."

She was baiting me. She must be bored, in need of entertainment on this quiet day. Little did she know, I agreed wholeheartedly with her assessment.

"As you say, mistress." I dipped my head toward her, forcing a disinterested tone.

"And your mother, Nailah. An even bigger fool for marrying such a dolt."

She knew how to get under my skin, this vengeful, jealous woman. I bit my cheek to restrain myself from responding.

Pure evil dripped from her smile. "And now that Akhum is married to my niece, Hapturah, he has been saved from a similar fate." Her brows arched.

Blood iced in my veins as my heart contracted. Until now, I had kept reminders of Akhum at bay. Each time he flickered through my thoughts, I whispered a prayer to Bastet to wipe my mind clean of such memories.

And now, at Tekurah's malicious revelation, every whisper, every caress, every promise rushed back. I dropped the fan. Hitting the edge of the stone ledge, it toppled into the pool with a muted splash.

The last cherished shard of my life, the man with whom I shared my secrets, whispered with late in the night, kissed under the stars in my mother's garden—this man now shared his life with another. I would never know love, or feel the shelter of a man who would protect me from this life of slavery and share my burdens. I was alone.

Like Tekurah.

Somehow as my heart shattered, I saw my mistress for who she was—bitter, lonely, broken—abandoned inside her marriage. Shefu protected her and her children, provided for their every need, but he neither gave her affection nor shared his heart with her. According to Shira, he loved my own mother.

This woman did not know the tenderness and gentleness of her husband's love. Perhaps she still hoped to capture his heart. She watched him covertly at meals. Her eyes followed him as he talked with his children, laughing with them, teasing them. Shefu spoke only of household matters with his wife, if at all.

Unloved, unwanted, and with a heart void of anything but resentment, it was no wonder she lashed out with such violence. Everything in me wanted to lash out as well, but I would not give her the satisfaction.

Instead, I fished the fan out of the pool, shook the water out of the feathers, and resumed fanning.

Her hooded eyes studied me. I braced for more provocation, but she kept her lips pursed and said nothing.

The golden cat startled and ran off. Tekurah's hands remained upturned in her lap for a few moments. Then she stood, brushed cat hair and dust from her dress, and strode into the house without a backward glance.

⁓

"What is that?" Tekurah pointed her bony finger to the north as we left the marketplace the next morning.

I squinted. At first it appeared only as a shadow of low hills along the eastern horizon. But the black cloud swelled and billowed, stretching higher and higher, spreading like pooled ink across the sky.

"We'd better get inside." A heavy basket filled with perfume, cosmetics, and gifts for the children bumped against my hip, but I picked up my pace. I turned to glance at the cloud. It raced toward us at breakneck speed, a huge, grasping monster of black silhouetted against the bright blue sky. We were only a few blocks from the villa. Tekurah lagged for a moment, watching the dark swirls, but soon caught up, and then outpaced me.

We ran past the temple gates. Lined up on the porch in front of the pylon, the priests stood petrified, mouths agape.

"What evil is this?" Tekurah yelled over her shoulder as we neared the gates to the villa.

I attempted to match her long stride and hoped she wouldn't notice the perfume that had jostled out of the basket back near the gates of the temple.

Before we made it to the front door, the cloud overtook us. But it was no storm cloud. Within ten paces of the entry, a massive swarm of huge flies enveloped us. They swirled, biting, latching onto our skin, refusing to let go, ignoring our vigorous swats and thrashings.

The rest of the contents of the basket landed on the ground, and we ran shrieking into the house. I slammed the door behind me, swatting at the flies. They clung to my eyelids, behind my ears, tangled in my hair. Their merciless bites stung like the fire of a thousand scorpions, burning away the notion that these scourges, and whatever was causing them, were anything but natural. How much more would we have to endure?

10

Shira would never miss her weekly meeting with Eben. It had been days since I had seen her, and I was so eager to apologize for my hurtful words that I would brave crossing paths with her brother.

Before any light threaded through the darkness on the seventh day of the week, I rose, triple-checking to ensure Tekurah's breath remained slow and even. With hands outstretched to feel a safe path through the pitch-black room, I padded to the door, hoping to avoid stubbing a toe or stumbling over a cat on my way.

A rainstorm had swept through during the night. The morning smelled fresh and crisp—a welcome change from the stagnant air that had settled over the city the last few months. The winds cleared the remainder of the horrid flies from the land.

We had spent seven days trapped inside the villa, locked inside windowless rooms, stuffing every crack and crevice with cloth, trying to evade the flies. Even worse than the bites from the flies were the headaches I endured from the constant burning of lavender and lemongrass in the household braziers, which did little to ward off the insects.

I shivered, my eyes burning at the memory, and quickened my pace toward the canal, savoring the cool, moist earth beneath my bare feet.

After filling my jug, I curled up cross-legged on my favorite rock until dawn feathered across the horizon. The clouds from last night's storm rested in the eastern sky, and the sunrise shattered through them, creating bright oranges and pinks. Captivated by the splendor, I did not see Eben until he stood in front of me.

He stopped, ten paces away, clearly surprised that I, and not his sister, waited for him.

My surprise echoed his. *Where is she?*

I had not seen Shira since that afternoon in the market. Perhaps she was still avoiding me, but it was not like her to be late to a meeting with Eben.

The weak predawn light obscured Eben's face. A stray breeze ruffled his dark hair. Did the man never visit a barber?

"Where is she?" His voice sliced through the stillness.

My defenses rose, and when my hands began to shake, I grasped them in my lap to hide them. "I don't know."

He moved closer. "Where . . . is . . . she?"

Suppressing the instinct to retreat, I unfolded my legs and stood, leaving the water jug on the rock. "I have no idea. I thought she would be here this morning."

He moved within a few paces. "Why are you here?" He pointed a long finger at me.

I lifted my chin, but my stomach flipped. He glared at me, contempt narrowing his eyes to dark slits.

I crossed my arms. "She is my friend."

He huffed out a scornful breath. "Friend?"

"After what she did for me, she became my friend." *My only one.*

He flinched. "What did she do?"

Shira hadn't told him. Of course not. She would never take credit for her kindnesses.

"Months ago, she took the blame for something I did and was relegated to the kitchens." Did the weak light hide the flush on my skin?

"Why would she do that?"

I shrugged. "Honestly, I have no idea. But you know your sister better than I do. She had her reasons."

He clenched his fists and spoke through gritted teeth. "And you did not speak up?"

I saw myself then, in the mirror of Eben's accusing eyes. It was true. I should have confessed after I'd smashed the box. But cowardice and pride had kept me from accepting the punishment. I had allowed Shira to stand in the way of Tekurah's wrath.

A thousand excuses came to mind, but none held any weight.

"And now my sister is missing, and you"—he aimed a condemning finger at me again—"her so-called friend, have no idea where she is?"

I winced. "She *is* my friend. And I am worried about her."

"You'd best ask your mistress. Her spy has been following Shira for quite some time."

"I've never seen anyone following her." I surveyed my memories. All the times we'd met at the river Shira never mentioned anything. And I had seen no one lurking about.

The sun pushed higher into the sky, and shadows no longer guarded Eben's face. His eyes released me, and his gaze lifted over my shoulder, toward the Nile. The brilliant sun at his back outlined his body, illuminating gold in his dark brown hair. His beard, and its foreignness, momentarily fascinated me. Clean-shaven men surrounded me. But the beard fit Eben, lent a certain strength to his face. He was not striking like Akhum. No kohl accented his eyes. But I felt myself drawn to the planes of his face, his narrow nose, a small scar at the top of one high cheekbone, the line of his lips pressed together in aggravation.

"Perhaps you ought to look around yourself sometime. You people only care about yourselves and your own comfort."

I startled at the venom in his tone. *"You people?"*

"Yes, you Egyptians. With your self-centered prancing about." He twirled his hand in the air.

"You don't know me. You have no idea about my life and who, or what, I care about." My own fists clenched tight, finger-nails slicing my palms.

"I know enough. I've had my fill of this country and her people. Egypt deserves what's coming." He folded his arms with a haughty jerk of his chin.

"And that is . . . ?" I stepped forward in challenge.

He mirrored my movement. "Vengeance."

"By whom? An army of slaves?"

"Aided by Yahweh."

For some reason, I shrank back when Eben pronounced this name. My pulse raced, and my breath shallowed. Surprise flashed across his face at my reaction.

When the strange emotion released its grip on my throat, I sputtered out, "Who is that?"

His curious gaze swept over my face. "Our God."

"Shira said your god has no name."

"An elder from Goshen arrived this week to tell us what has transpired there—since all we have heard was rumors. Yahweh gave Mosheh his name as a sign, among others." Pride leaked into his voice, and he stood taller. "The name in our tongue means that he always has been and always will be the Almighty God."

"How mighty is a god who cannot deliver his people from slavery?"

He folded his arms across his chest and shifted his stance. "He will."

"So the last two hundred years your god was, what, asleep?" A caustic laugh slipped past my lips.

"Yahweh does things in his own time. He is preparing us."

Shira's odd statement, that her god might be preparing me for something, brushed through my thoughts. "For what?"

Standing at eye level with a man was strange to me, especially in such close proximity. I was taller than Shira, but all the men I knew—my father, Shefu, Akhum, even Jumo—towered over me. Eben's ability to stare straight into my eyes unnerved me.

Defiance hardened his features as he brought his face closer to mine. "We will soon be ready to take back what has been stolen: our freedom, our wealth, our pride. Egypt will pay."

His fierce words tore into my heart. My galloping pulse, caused by Eben's proximity, was drowned out by their echo. When he looked at me, he saw only an enemy.

"You forget you are not the only one who has lost such things." I turned my back on him to conceal the insistent tears that stung my eyes, snatched my jug, and rushed up the path.

Entering Tekurah's room carrying a large water pot on my hip, without making noise, was no easy feat. I had cracked another vessel once in this same doorway in the past. I nudged the door open with my elbow, willing the leather hinges not to squeak and breathing freely again when they did not.

My stealth went unrewarded. Tekurah was awake.

She perched, head down, on the edge of her bed, with one hand on each of the cats sprawled on either side of her. The black and gray cats basked in the golden sunlight spilling across the white linen spread.

"I've been sitting here, without my head handmaid, for the last half of an hour."

My stomach twisted. "I apologize, mistress."

She still did not look at me. "That is all you have to say? You are sorry?"

I racked my brain for a suitable excuse, fear shredding through my veins at her strange response. "There were many other servants at the canal this morning. I was forced to wait my turn."

She flew off her bed, dislodging the cats, to tower over me. "You. Lie."

I drew back, afraid again that she might finally resort to violence—her claws seemed quite unsheathed today. "No . . . mistress."

Her face contorted in anger. "I knew something was going on. Do you have a lover you've been meeting?"

"No."

"Then who?"

"No one." I looked straight into her eyes, desperate to protect Shira and, against instinct, Eben as well.

She glared back, waiting, studying me as if she could lift the truth from my brain. Like a bird caught in the hypnotic gaze of one of her cats, I was ensnared.

"Tell me," she said through gritted teeth.

"There is nothing to tell. If I have been late, it's only been from walking slowly or waiting on others to fill their jugs. It won't happen again, mistress. I will walk faster. I swear. I swear upon Bastet."

Her body relaxed, and she lifted her chin, looking down her nose at me. "You are right. It will not happen again. You will be here before I wake each morning or I swear by all the gods in the sky, you will feel the end of a whipping cane."

I shivered.

"And have no doubt, I will ensure that not even Shefu will have anything to say about it." She touched the corner of one kohl-rimmed eye. "I have been watching. I will watch even more closely."

I ate my afternoon meal without tasting a bite. I picked at the whitefish stew in my bowl, usually a welcome change from my daily fare. The delicious aroma tantalized me a little, but dread soured my stomach.

Most of the household servants gulped down their meals and ran to attend their duties. A few lazed around the courtyard, stretching out their last precious minutes of false freedom. Two men behind me argued about fowling and fishing. The women clumped in small groups, laughing, gossiping. None of them spoke to me. None glanced in my direction.

Another quarter of an hour passed before the courtyard started to empty. I would be late, but I must know what had happened to Shira.

When only Hashma, the head cook, and a few weary kitchen slaves remained, I stood.

Most of the servants in Shefu's household acted less than cordial to me. Being new to slavery and a former-master-turned-slave branded me as an outcast. Most of them had been born into bondage, some in this very household. Therefore, no one trusted me. Besides, friendship with me, or even kindness, might bring about wrath from Tekurah. I was a pariah. No longer on equal footing with masters and mistresses and rejected by the servants that bowed before them.

Hashma, however, did not follow the rules. She treated me as an equal. As dark and exotic as my Salima, she worked tirelessly, with a tattered headscarf barely containing her wildly coiled hair. Her wide face gleamed with perspiration from laboring in the courtyard all day. Her voice boomed with authority, yet compassion exuded from her every pore.

And Hashma knew everything that went on inside this villa.

She ordered the kitchen girls to scrub the pots with sand and to boil water for rinsing. Then she knelt, with a heavy breath, in front of the still-smoldering bread oven to scrape ashes with a clay shard into a flat-sided pot.

"Hashma, may I speak with you?" I glanced over my shoulder.

She looked up, and her eyes flickered, but she smiled and nodded.

"I have not seen Shira for days now. Is she all right?" My voice was soft, for her ears alone.

The warmth on her face faded.

"What happened?" My heart picked up its pace. "Where is she?"

She looked past me and pasted on a bright smile. Someone stood behind me. "Thank you, Latikah, you can put down the tray there on the table."

"Mistress Tekurah says to hurry up, Kiya." Latikah's tone dripped acid.

"Thank you. I am on my way." I did not turn, for my expression would give away my panic.

Hashma cleaned the oven in silence. The seconds stretched long, but I set my jaw, determined not to leave without an answer.

"You must be more careful." Her words suddenly flew out in a hiss, but her eyes held on her task.

"Careful?"

"You are putting me in danger." She glanced again over her shoulder.

I forced an even tone. "Where is Shira?"

"The storeroom."

"Which one? How do I get there?"

"She is chained in the wine storeroom, guarded."

I covered a gasp with my palm.

Hashma still did not look up. "Tekurah had her followed down to the canal a couple weeks ago. She had been meeting someone there. I do not know who. The other person had already slipped through the tall grasses and disappeared."

"Who followed Shira?"

She leaned back on her knees and shrugged her wide shoulders. "Tekurah was furious and accused the poor girl of trying to escape or plotting treachery against the family. She did not imprison her then, but she was gone the morning after the flies left."

I dropped my head and groaned. "It was me."

"You?"

"It was me, meeting her. We heard a noise while we were talking one morning. I slipped into the rushes and escaped." Once again Shira endured my punishment. I closed my eyes and Eben's livid face loomed.

"Tekurah is determined to finish what she started with that one over the cosmetic box. She knows you were friends."

"Some friend I am."

Hashma stood with a quick look around and then patted my shoulder. "It's all right, dear one. I took her some food last night. She is in good spirits." She pursed her full lips, brows drawn, her wise eyes bloodshot and rheumy. "I wish Master Shefu knew. He would not stand for it."

With Shefu gone on business to Thebes for the past week, Tekurah ruled the villa unfettered.

I chewed a thumbnail. *What can I do?*

Hashma peered at me, divining my thoughts. "An armed guard stands watch. You won't be able to get in."

How strange. Why would such a tiny bird need to be under lock and key?

"Can you supply me with some food to take down there?"

"I cannot." She dropped her voice low. "A whipping would surely follow."

Reaching forward, I grabbed at her hand, pleading. "Then say nothing, just leave a tray of food on the table there, near the door, and go about your duties. I will steal it. No one will suspect you were in any way involved."

"I hate to see that little girl suffer." She let out a long sigh, shaking her head. "All right. But you be careful. You are stepping into an adder's nest." She pointed a callused finger at me.

"I will brave the venom. I owe it to her."

11

I will be taking Latikah to the market today. There are chores for you." Tekurah primped in the mirror, inspecting the carnelian collar I had just tied around her neck.

Latikah looked down, toying with a thin silver bangle on her wrist.

Dipping my head, I feigned acquiescence so neither of them would notice my relief.

Tekurah listed a full day's worth of chores to accomplish in the next couple of hours and then strode out of the room. Latikah gave me a satisfied smile over her shoulder before following. Let her rejoice in her prize. Little did she know how grateful I was for my cleaning duties today.

With inordinate speed, I reorganized Tekurah's linens and wigs in the closet, changed the linens on her sleeping couch, scrubbed down the tiles in the shower room, and dusted every surface in the chamber. Then, stealing down the hallway to the kitchen, I prayed I might avoid crossing paths with anyone who would report my wanderings to Tekurah. A large, blue faience water clock stood on the table in the vestibule, dripping steadily. I looked inside, relieved that the water level was higher than

I'd expected—less time had passed during my furious cleaning than I had thought. I kissed my fingers and tapped them on the well-worn bronze feet of Bes as I slipped by his form in the corridor. I welcomed any divine intervention today, even from a grotesque and leering minor god.

A bowl of food and a mug of beer waited on the table. *Thank the gods for Hashma.* I snatched up the offerings after a quick glance for watchful eyes and put swift distance between myself and the kitchen. I could not allow Hashma to be implicated if my plan went awry.

A guard sat on the top step of the short stairway leading to the cellar door. He slumped against the wall, eyes closed. Egyptian by the look of him, he was young, maybe twenty, but broad-shouldered and muscular. A short sword lay across his knees. Again I wondered why Shira would need an armed guard.

Too nervous to play up charm, I forced a note of authority into my voice. "I have food for the Hebrew."

He opened one eye, then two, and cocked his head. "You are not the one they sent before."

"No, she is sick. And I need to return to my duties as soon as possible." I gestured to the door with a commanding expression. Would he be fooled?

He brushed a slow, appreciative gaze from my hair, down to my feet, and back up to my face. Perhaps flirtation might have been more effective. Too late for that now. I widened my stance.

A corner of his mouth lifted, and he winked, obviously not deterred by my show of dominance. He rose. "Well, be quick about it." He clomped down the wooden stairs. The iron bolt clanked as he pushed it aside and then opened the door. A small oil lamp burned on a shelf above the lintel. He handed it to me, offered another suggestive grin, then returned to his post at the top of the stairs.

I closed the door with my foot, balancing the tray in one hand

and the lamp in the other. My eyes took their time adjusting to the pitch-black. Racks of Shefu's precious wine cooled here in the cellar. But it was the darkness, not the cold, that made me shiver. The feeble glow of the lamp led my way. A small mercy.

"Shira?" My whisper seemed like a shout in the dank stillness.

A small, rough voice reached out from some dark corner. "Kiya?"

"Where are you?" I held the light higher, but the flame barely cast a shadow.

"I'm tied to the wall."

I followed the direction of the disembodied voice to her child-like form curled against the back wall of the cellar. Her drawn face contorted as the weak lamplight made her blink. She covered her eyes with one hand. After many days here, shrouded in darkness, the weakest light must burn like the sun.

I put the lamp on the ground and handed her the tray. Sitting cross-legged in front of my captive friend, my heart bled as she devoured the fish and bread Hashma had provided. She drained every last drop of barley beer. Poor girl, surrounded by amphorae of the finest wines in the country yet tied to a wall, dying of thirst.

I kept my voice soft, not wanting to alert the guard. "What happened?"

"Latikah caught us, or me, after our last meeting by the river before the flies came."

Latikah. Threads I'd failed to weave together earlier revealed their design. The fine sandals, the silver bracelet—Tekurah's castoffs. Rewards for surveillance. *I should have known.*

"But why are you still here for such a small offense?"

"I have spent this time trying to figure it out. I wondered if she was setting a trap for you. Which may yet be true, you should not stay long."

She could be right. Perhaps the shopping trip was only a ruse.

"But I think it's because I am Hebrew."

"She knows that."

She nodded. "But ever since Mosheh declared these strokes against the country, hostility has grown. They think we are causing the plagues."

"I've heard the talk in the market. It's ridiculous. Your Mosheh may be a sorcerer, but the rest of you are harmless."

"That is true. This is not our doing. In fact, it's not even Mosheh's doing. He is just a vessel, a prophet." She paused. "I think, though, that *this* may be the reason Tekurah locked me down here." She held out her arms, and I leaned close to see in the dim light of the lamp.

Sores still healed all over my body, many of the bites infected and oozing with puss, but the flesh on Shira's arms was smooth, untouched.

My breath hitched in my throat. "You were not bitten?"

"No. I pretended to scratch, hoping no one would notice. But not one fly bit me. Tekurah must have discerned my pretense and decided that the superstitions were true. I think she imprisoned me to protect herself."

My mind reeled back to my conversation with Eben the day before. No sores had marred his face or arms either. Had the flies affected none of the Hebrews?

The guard banged on the door, and I jumped.

"What's taking so long in there? You need to be done. Now."

I called out so he would not look inside and catch me sitting knee to knee with Shira. "She's almost finished. I need to return this tray to the kitchen. A few moments more."

"Hurry up, girl," I added for his benefit.

Shira giggled. "So sorry, mistress, I am a slow eater." She nodded toward the bowl that she had all but licked clean.

Locked in a cellar, guarded and chained to the wall, and laughing—I would never understand this girl.

Now in a rush, I outlined my plans for her escape.

She tried to smother a smile. "I'm sorry, it seems quite impossible." But her eyes danced in the weak lamplight.

"Well, I don't care if you think it's humorous, I am going to try. I do not care what Tekurah does."

Her amusement vanished. "Don't underestimate her, Kiya. She is dangerous."

"Perhaps, but Shefu seems willing to protect me from her wrath. When he returns, I will try to get you out of here." I gathered the bowl and cup. "In the meantime, I will do my best to bring you food every day and show the guard I am harmless." I winked at her and fluttered my eyelashes. She grinned.

I stood and looked at her forlorn figure on the ground. "I wish I didn't have to leave you here."

"I'm all right." She waved her hand at me. "At least I'm not scrubbing pots with sand all day. I can feel my fingertips again."

"I'll be back tomorrow."

I looked back at her one more time before my exit left her shrouded in darkness. She was so small: a tiny, harmless bird. Who could fear her, no matter what the rumors suggested?

12

Tekurah kept me running for days, nerves raw, preparing for Shefu's return. I scoured her rooms from top to bottom, laundered every linen, scrubbed every inch, and beat the dust out of every tapestry and floor mat while imagining Shira wasting away in the storeroom.

On the sixth day of the week, Latikah and I slathered Tekurah's entire body with a fragrant mixture of coconut oil and myrrh—one of the only duties I enjoyed. The delicious smell lingered on my own hands and arms, which remained supple for hours. I shaved her entire body, scalp to toe. I stained her fingernails and toenails with orange henna, adorned her eyes with malachite and galena, and tinted her lips and cheeks with red ochre.

When Tekurah was satisfied with her face, Latikah placed a wig on her head, one of braided curls, with tiny silver beads interspersed every couple of inches. Whenever Tekurah moved her head, the beads plinked together, giving the illusion of a hundred little bells. I wondered if she would tire of the jangling noise, but she seemed pleased with her latest purchase and admired it again and again from different angles in the mirror.

All afternoon Tekurah startled every time someone came through the door or she heard a voice in the hallway. She barked orders at us, demanding we tidy her spotless room, reapply her makeup, and fetch any number of odds and ends.

Tekurah ran out of redundant tasks for Latikah and me, so she took to shrilling orders at the kitchen staff, the gardeners, and anyone else unfortunate enough to cross her path.

Liat and Sefora waited in the gardens, avoiding their mother's tongue and playing in the shade of the date palms. Their joyful cries alerted us to their father's arrival. Tekurah ordered Latikah to tell Hashma that the master would need supper and then rushed to the door to welcome him home, anxious, I assumed, to press him for news from Pharaoh's palace in Avaris.

The Pharaoh passed much of his time there among the lush green and the cool breezes of the Delta. All the important trade routes from the Mediterranean came through Avaris. I doubted Shefu had time, while negotiating trades, to pay attention to what the First Wife wore, but Tekurah seemed certain he would have all manner of information at hand.

Manit and Lefar, Shefu's Kushite servants, entered first with his traveling baskets. When Shefu came into the house, both his children tagged along, begging for the treats and presents they knew would be tucked among his clothing.

"Give me a few minutes, children. I have just returned." Shefu removed his sandals and dipped his feet in the laver by the door without waiting for the servants to wash his feet.

Shefu never used a sharp tongue with his children. They stood blinking teary eyes and even inched closer to Tekurah.

"Husband, I am anxious for news of our son and his wife. Did you find them well?" She was unfazed by his mood.

Shefu threw down his sandals. "I said, I need some time. I will give you your fill of gossip later." He stalked out of the entry hall toward his quarters.

Tekurah, never one to be patient, followed Shefu. As was my duty, I followed her. She entered his quarters without knocking, and I stood next to the doorway to wait—perhaps a bit closer than necessary. Their voices drifted through the gaps in the door.

"Husband, what is wrong? What has you in such a state?"

"I knew you would harass me until I gave you an answer." Shefu breathed a ragged sigh. "Manit, Lefar, please leave the unpacking until later. I would speak with my wife a moment."

The door swung open, and I shrank back. The two tall slaves saw me standing there, and I raised my brows. Lefar shrugged with a smirk and walked down the hallway toward the kitchen. Manit walked the opposite way, shaking his head. I slid closer to the doorway with my back pressed to the wall.

"What is wrong? Has something happened to Talet?" Concern for her firstborn pinched her voice.

"No, Talet and Lathia are fine. Their baby is due any day now."

"Then what is troubling you so much? Is it the business?"

"Yes and no. The business will be affected. But even more troubling is that Egypt is under attack."

Tekurah gasped. "Who? The Amalekites? Not the Canaanites. Pharaoh has kept a firm hand over them for these past few years."

"No, no, it's not an outside nation threatening us."

"I don't understand."

"Are you blind? Are you deaf? You've heard the rumors, the stories about the Hebrew Moses and his god. Were you sleeping when we were under siege by biting flies? Have you forgotten the blood in the Nile? The frogs? The lice?"

Tekurah barked a laugh. "Shefu. Pharaoh is more powerful than some slave-god."

"I was there. I heard Moses with my own ears." Shefu's voice softened.

Eager for gossip, she pressed him. "You did? What was he like? Does he seem like a powerful sorcerer? What did he say?"

"He didn't speak. At least not much. Another Hebrew speaks for him. I do not know the man's name, but he certainly projects great authority. Moses only said one thing. That all our livestock would die."

"How is that possible?"

"How does the Nile turn entirely to blood on the command of such a man?"

A tremble weakened her voice. "What did Pharaoh say?"

"He was livid. He vowed to never let the Hebrews set one foot outside Egypt. Said he would not be bullied by some unknown slave-god who—"

She talked over him. "As he should not."

"Perhaps."

"Do you doubt Pharaoh?" Her voice dropped so low I almost missed her words.

"I don't know, Wife, I don't know. But I fear this may only be the beginning."

They must have walked into another chamber, for I heard no more of their conversation. When Tekurah exited a few minutes later, she did not see me. Soft-footed, I followed and slipped into her room behind her, hoping she would think I had been waiting there all the time.

To my surprise, she was so deep in thought that when she turned and saw me she startled.

"What are you doing skulking there?" she snapped.

"Just waiting for your direction, mistress." I dipped my head.

"Direction. You want my direction?" Her voice smoothed as she stared across the room at the paradise-decorated wall.

She blinked, slowly, but did not look at me. "Fine. Go get my meal; I will be eating in my quarters. Then go sit in the hall until I'm ready to give you more . . . direction."

I fled the room. Tekurah's many personalities were well known to me. But this one—calm, deep in thought—I had not yet met. This one could be the most dangerous of all.

Tekurah did not beckon me into her room all evening, so I sat in the hall, studying the intricate blue-and-red mosaic patterns on the floor around me, considering the fruits of my eavesdropping.

Something truly unprecedented was happening to our country. Shefu had said Pharaoh was angry at Mosheh, but could there be fear underneath the bluster?

Perhaps Pharaoh feared this Hebrew god.

Perhaps we all should fear this god.

I rose well before the dawn. Tekurah had tossed and turned far into the night; she would sleep late. I had thought all the gods were against me, but some divinity must be my ally.

A hush enveloped the entire city. Usually as I walked to the canal before the sun rose, the sounds of the morning greeted me—the hum of insects in the brush, the racket of birds and animals stirring to life before the first touch of light exploded into the eastern sky.

But this day there was nothing, only eerie silence. The hair on the back of my neck stood on end.

I quickened my pace, heading to my rock by the head of the path, hoping I would not have to wait long for Shira's brother.

But he waited there for *me* today. He must have received the message I sent through Hashma.

Back turned, he stood as still as the morning, only his disheveled hair ruffling in the cool breeze. He was not tall, but slight did not define him. He built fine instruments, his shoulders solid from hewing wood, and his bare arms, though lean, were well formed.

"Thank you for coming." I shrank at the sound of my voice, too loud for this lifeless day.

He looked over his shoulder. "Why are you doing this?"

This man refused to return pleasantries. My reticence at raising my voice vanished. "I told you why. She is my friend. I can't stand to see her imprisoned. Our mistress is hateful. I'm afraid she will hurt Shira."

He turned. The haze of predawn light obscured his face, but during the long pause, he seemed to be searching mine. "What is your plan?"

"Be ready to meet her in the front garden at sunset."

"How will I get past the guard at the gate?"

"Here"—I pulled a parcel out of my empty water jar and handed it to him—"Tekurah is expecting this wig to be delivered today. I did not tell her it arrived yesterday, a fortunate mix-up. Tell the guard you are from the wigmaker and your master insists you deliver it to Tekurah's maid."

"And how will you get her out of the house? Your message said she is being held captive." Eben raked his dark hair back with one hand.

"She is. But the guard wants . . ." I stopped.

"I don't have any silver, if that's what you are planning."

"No. He wants . . . me." I looked away. The sky blushed pink as dawn pushed the last of the night away.

Why was he so silent?

When I finally gathered the courage to look at him, he shook his head, rubbing a hand down his bearded cheek with a groan. "This is dangerous."

"She's worth it."

He stepped closer, looking straight into my eyes. I drew in a sharp breath but forced myself not to step back and to return his gaze. He pressed his lips together and glanced at mine. My pulse rushed in my ears, and my chest squeezed like a vice.

"Yes . . . yes, she is." His voice was tender, almost sweet. Then his intense gaze tore away from me suddenly, flicking behind me toward the rushes. Was Latikah spying again? "Don't. Move." The urgency in the order froze me.

He whispered. "There is a cobra on the path behind you."

My arms and legs went numb as I imagined the hooded black-and-yellow-banded serpent sinking its fangs into my heel. The deadly creature was aggressive and quick. I had learned early in my servitude to be aware at all times when passing through the fields, especially on unseasonably warm days like today.

Eben's hand went to his belt, and he pulled an ivory-handled dagger from a leather sheath. With one deft motion, the knife hissed through the air and past my shoulder, taking my breath with it.

"There." He blew out a sigh.

I peeked over my shoulder and then whirled, stunned and panting at the release of my fear. The snake lay dead, the dagger protruding from its twisted body, ten paces from where I stood.

My pulse still raced as I turned on Eben in surprise. "How did you hit it from so far away?"

He shrugged, but his lips quirked. Pride? Or amusement at my disbelief? "Years of practice."

"But . . . y-you are a musician," I stammered.

The storm gathered in his eyes again. "I am also the son of a murdered father. Justice demands blood for blood, and I will not let my family go unprotected."

The sun came up at his back as I studied his face. Why was he still standing so close? My heart fluttered a strange rhythm, and a temptation to close the gap between us pulled at me.

He swayed closer, his eyes dark, and then he hesitated, as though he had something more to say, but instead he brushed past me to retrieve his dagger and then walked away. I watched until he disappeared around a bend in the trail.

As I neared Tekurah's chamber, the head steward flew around a corner. He knocked me against the wall, sloshing water out of my jug, and was gone before I could react. Where was he rushing off to?

I entered the room, dripping wet and equipped with excuses for arriving late and with only half of her bath water. Tekurah was pacing the floor.

"I don't have time for a bath today. Dress me immediately."

Setting the jar by the door and relieved that she seemed not to notice my late arrival, I chanced a question. "May I ask, what is the commotion with the steward?"

"The animals are dead."

"Dead? Which animals?"

"All of them. Every single cow, pig, ram, and goat is lying in the fields, rotting." Her tone was even and deadly.

Mosheh.

"The steward ran all the way in from Shefu's fields south of town. All of our livestock is destroyed." She spun her hand in the air, motioning for me to dress her quickly. "I have things I need to do. Get on with it."

When I'd finished dressing her and applying her cosmetics, she ordered me to go to the marketplace alone to buy a handful of items.

Shefu's house was not the only one in upheaval. Iunu boiled with chaos. Crowds pressed all around the temple. The courtyards overflowed again, everyone shouting at once.

"I've lost everything!"

"Why are the gods cursing us?"

"Where is Pharaoh? Why isn't he protecting us?"

"Why is this happening?"

Jostled by the swarm at the temple gates, I pressed through the river of people rushing to join the chaotic scene.

A nearly deserted market greeted me. Only a few brave customers and vendors spoke in hushed tones around their stalls.

Liat and Sefora's new sandals were ready, and I dropped off an usekh that needed mending with a Syrian craftsman known for his excellent handiwork. Next I had to find beeswax, almond oil, and kohl. Since the marketplace was so barren, I could visit my mother's stall without being spotted by anyone who might report back to Tekurah. In spite of the strange and ominous cloud darkening this day, rays of hope broke through the gloom at the thought of seeing my mother and brother.

Wooden stalls shaded by linen canopies lined the streets, laden with a colorful array of fruits and vegetables, platters of spices that burned my eyes as I passed, and stacks of linen, wool, and flax.

When I found her, my mother was deep in conversation with an idol merchant in the adjacent stall.

". . . and the Hebrews are to blame." The man waved a tiny soapstone figure of Osiris in rhythm with his sharp words. "None of their animals died. Not an ox, a lamb, or a goat. Only our livestock decay in the fields today."

The Hebrews' fault. None of their animals died? How was it possible that our livestock would be singled out? And what would be the consequences of such a pointed and mystical distinction between Hebrews and Egyptians?

My stomach dropped like a stone. *Shira. I have to get to Shira.*

My mother called my name, but I was already running. I pushed through the crowd, screamed at people in my way. My toe jammed against a wayward stone, but I didn't stop. No wonder Tekurah had sent me out on an errand alone. The memory of her strange behavior this morning urged me to move faster. What was she planning?

The guard at the entry gate beckoned me, holding up a parcel that looked like the undelivered wig I had given Eben the day before. I ignored him and ran into the house, the heavy reed basket bumping along, bruising my hip. I cut across the kitchen courtyard, turned the corner, and ran down the hallway to the cellar stairs.

No guard.

I was too late. What had Tekurah done? Had Shira flogged? *Oh, please not that. She is so fragile.* The door to the cellar stood open.

"Shira? Are you here?" I called into the blackness.

No answer.

"Shira?"

"Well, hello there. Come back to see me?" a voice said behind me.

Shocked, I nearly dropped the basket. The guard, key in hand, had returned to lock the door.

"I am looking for Shira. Where has she been taken?"

"She's gone."

"Gone where?"

He shrugged. "The mistress came and told her to go. Even gave her a written release from service."

My head spun. I blinked my eyes and leaned against the wall. "Tekurah?"

"She told her to go back to her home and never come back."

"But why?" None of this made sense. If Tekurah blamed the Hebrews, and therefore Shira, for the plagues, why would she tell her to go instead of punishing her?

"I do not know." He lowered his voice. "But between the two of us, she sounded afraid. No . . . terrified. She wouldn't even come close to the girl."

13

Magic terrified my mistress. Twice daily she prayed in the household sanctuary—not out of religious fervor or devotion, but as protection from curses. And, like many Egyptians, if her desires went unheeded, she threatened her gods with desecration of likenesses or withdrawal of sacrifices. A fickle lot, the gods at times ignored even the most fervent of pleas. When offerings did not suffice, occasionally threats were offered instead.

And never were more threats heard by Bastet than when Tekurah was covered in boils.

"Bring the statue of my goddess." Blisters ravaged her throat, so the command was only a rough whisper.

Crossing the floor with tender lumps on the soles of my feet was like walking across fire. Each slow, deliberate step aggravated the boils in my armpits, my groin, even under my eyelids.

Thankfully, Tekurah kept a figure of Bastet on her cosmetics table only a few paces from my bedroll. Wincing with every step, I brought it to her, and then, loath to return to my mat, I sat on the floor next to her bed, trying to hold my body still, measuring torture with each chafing movement.

"Twenty years of allegiance, Bastet," Tekurah rasped. "Daily homage. My house filled with your likeness. I treat your children, my cats, with respect. Don't you hear? Heal me!"

I studied the figure she addressed, the body of a woman with a desert-cat head. Was this goddess listening? Was she ignoring Tekurah? Were any of the gods listening? All the healing gods—Isis, Imhotep, Thoth—how could they allow everyone in this country to suffer these agonizing boils?

Everyone, from the lowest slave to the Pharaoh himself, Shefu said, was beleaguered with horrible boils, some more afflicted than others. The priests suffered the most, with painful, oozing sores enveloping them.

Tekurah commanded that I escort her daily to the temple to beg, plead, and bargain with the gods. We hobbled there, out of sheer necessity leaning on one another, relying on each other for warmth against the chill, and grateful the temple stood only two blocks away. Abscessing boils covered the worshippers lying prostrate in the outer courtyards. The incense-laden air lifted their moaned supplications into the heavens, where the gods resided among the stars. Or did their pleas simply vanish into nothing?

Herbal remedies helped little. The priests offered incantations day and night to Isis and all the healing gods. But for days, everyone suffered horrific agony.

Everyone but the Hebrews.

When they proved untouched by the boils, it confirmed the rumors. Mosheh the sorcerer was at the heart of these plagues.

Any Hebrews brave enough to venture out of their quarter were accosted in the streets. Some Egyptians threatened the gods in desperation, but most saved their more malicious warnings for the foreign slaves.

My first instinct was to beg the gods for mercy. Intimidation of the deities seemed futile. Then I remembered that during the lice and fly infestations, those who relied upon the divinities, who wore amulets and burned incense in every corner of their homes, seemed most afflicted. I avoided the sanctuary, ignored the statuary, and the boils on my body were smaller and less numerous than most others in the household.

Tekurah noticed too.

"Did that Hebrew slave give you a spell? An incantation? Tell me what it is!" She pulled at my tunic, her grasp sending shattering pain radiating down my arm.

"No, mistress. I have not spoken to Shira for many months."

"Liar! I had you watched. I know you were"—she ground her teeth—"friends with that slave."

I looked her in the eye, something I never did.

"We were friends. But she is gone, and I have no contact with her. She gave me no incantation."

Or did she? Was I less affected because of my friendship with her? Had some sort of bewitchment rubbed off on me? I doubted it. The one thing Shira had shared with me were the stories of her people. She had entertained me with stories of foreign slaves with a faceless god who forbade them to deal in magic, curses, or dealings with the spirit world, or even associate with those who did so.

Now all Egyptians lay on their beds, moaning and crying out to deaf gods. And the Hebrews had escaped unscathed.

Thunder shook the house and the ground beneath our feet. Pottery tipped off shelves and shattered as crashing booms layered one behind another.

Hail began to fall, pattering soft on the cedar roof between each enormous rumble of thunder. Soon the tap of ice on wood gave way to a steady *thunk, thunk, thunk*. I balanced on a stool to peek out one of the high windows in Tekurah's bathing chamber. Dark clouds roiled. Chunks of frozen rain the size of my fist—jagged, spiked, and fierce—fell from the sky. One flew through the window and slammed into the wall next to me. I tumbled off the stool and fell hard onto the tile.

Tekurah watched me, wide-eyed, naked and shivering on her bathing slab.

Lightning coupled with the thunder. An explosion ripped through the heavens, brilliant and constant, illuminating the room like a thousand candles. Another flash split the sky, and before I could cover my eyes, the lightning struck nearby, the jolt vibrating the ground.

Shouts drew me into the hallway, which reeked of smoke. I grabbed the empty water jar by the door and ran toward the commotion.

Shefu stood, stricken, in the open doorway at the back of the villa, his fists at his temples. Furious flames licked the sky. The treasury was on fire.

The shed, which stood apart from this villa, housed the master's greatest valuables and was guarded by four of Shefu's most trusted men—men rewarded well enough to ensure they would not lust after the gold housed inside.

"Master, what can I do?" Would he even hear me in the uproar?

He looked over his shoulder, hollow-eyed. "Nothing can be done. The fire is too wild." He turned back to watch the flames.

"Will it threaten the house?"

He shook his head.

"I will get more water." I ran to fetch some from the garden pool.

When I opened the front door, my knees went weak. The storm had torn through the city with unparalleled speed and fury; astounding devastation lay in its wake.

Shefu's beautiful gardens were destroyed. Enormous chunks

of ice had crushed the flower beds, stripped the palm branches, and ripped the climbing vines from the walls of the house. Ice covered the ground ankle-high.

A scream of agony jolted me from my surprised paralysis, and I ran, undeterred by the misery of my still-tender feet, toward the sound.

Tekurah knelt on the ground near Shefu, hands in the air, moaning and sobbing. All her jewels, her many collars, her bracelets, her earrings—everything was gone. The fire burned so hot that her riches would be reduced to fine puddles of gold and silver.

Bites from flies, the burning itch of lice, and the misery of boils—all these my proud mistress could endure, but the loss of her finery broke her.

Shefu was shrewd. He doubtless retained other places in which he spread out his store of gold. But this storm-of-all-storms would strike a great blow.

Shefu returned from surveying his fields, his shoulders low and face drawn.

"The barley is gone. The flax is destroyed," he told Tekurah.

"All of it?"

He pinched the bridge of his nose between his forefinger and his thumb. "Our only hope is the wheat and spelt."

"They weren't ruined by the storm?"

"No, they aren't quite ready for harvest, and their stalks are still flexible. They were bent by the storm, but not broken."

Livestock decimated and crops destroyed—Egypt, the fertile Black Land that exported goods to every surrounding nation, would be forced to import food so her people would not starve.

Thunder, lightning, and hail remained our constant companions for days. The treasury fire was only one of many Shefu's men were forced to extinguish around the villa.

Mere hours of respite passed between new surges of seething clouds and angry clashes of thunder. Funnel clouds tore through the country. I saw three with my own eyes, tall spindles of swirling destruction reaching down from a fuming green-black sky to a stricken land.

As fast as the hail melted, ice covered the ground again, ensuring the hearty plants that survived the initial deluge of flying ice were sufficiently beaten down.

Few buildings remained untouched. Most people lived in mud-brick homes with rush roofs that stood little chance against the fire from the sky. My mother's house, on the edge of the city . . . was it destroyed as well?

The rich fared no better. Fine Lebanese cedar-plank roofs smoldered for days. Shefu's villa was no exception. The main hall now braved the open sky.

Miraculously, the fire had not spread to more of the house, only the treasury and the main hall were destroyed. Sefora and Liat's quarters had started to burn, but Shefu's men were quick to douse the flames. The children now slept in Tekurah's quarters. She attempted to be maternal, but her need for private space and jealousy over the attention of their father caused her to peck at them at every turn.

So, despite having their own nursemaids, Sefora and Liat both clung to me. I constantly reminded them I was not free to entertain them, and every time I watched them wander off, shoulders slumped, I wished more than anything I could simply be a playmate, or an older sister.

When the locust swarm blocked out the sun, it was not Tekurah that the children ran to for comfort, but their father. Once he left to survey the destruction after unyielding hours of millions upon millions of bugs covering every surface of Egypt, they turned to me to alleviate their fears.

The relentless locusts gave us no reprieve. They clung to

everything—walls, trees, our hair, our clothing. Every surface swarmed with them. Their constant humming grated my every nerve. The ground roiled like a living, breathing thing. When I retrieved water, I held my breath as I slipped through the doors. Latikah closed the door tight behind me and stuffed thick linens in the cracks.

More than ever, I missed my fine sandals. Locusts covered the ground, dead and alive. I attempted to pick my way through without stepping on any, but it became an exercise in futility. Eventually I just ran, wincing and bracing for the *crunch crunch* at my every step.

The few remaining birds that had braved the storms fled when the locusts came, so instead of the call of birds, the assault of millions of tiny jaws, feeding on any green left after the hailstorms, filled the air.

There was no trail to the canal left. All the vegetation near the water was broken down, burned, or consumed. The feathery white stalks of plume grass whispering in the sunlight were no more. Only dead and dying clumps of brown remained.

I picked my way through the remains of the flax fields. The little blue flowers that had danced here in the breezes off the canal were long gone. Dead stalks tore at my bare legs.

The canal appeared in front of me, no longer bordered by tall papyrus and elephant grasses dancing with the current. The water now caressed only dirt and rocks as it swept upstream. The starkness of its missing and broken vegetation struck me then. I sat in the dirt on the riverbank and cried.

Where were the gods? Hapi had not protected the Nile, Heket had not controlled the frogs, Geb had not staunched the flow of lice, Kehpri did nothing to keep the flies from the land, Ptah and Hathor ignored the pleas to protect our livestock, sacrifices to Isis seemed to only aggravate the boils, and Set seemed to have no control over the angry storms and failed to protect our crops. We would starve—all the gold in the land could not prevent widespread death from the famine and disease that would now ensue.

Had the gods fled Egypt with the birds, or was this Hebrew god, this Yahweh, more powerful than all of them? Did he have such power over the world that even the storms and the beasts obeyed his command?

He was attacking each of our gods, one by one. This was no natural occurrence as the priests had assured us when the Nile had turned to blood. These were pointed, powerful attacks on the deities of our country. Each assault was more destructive than the last. How much more could we endure? If Pharaoh did not let the Hebrews go, I feared there would be nothing left of the Black Land at all. It was as if all of creation were being undone by Shira's god.

If Shira were here, I could ask her more about this destructive god of hers. I missed her, but I hoped she was safe with her family. I was desperate for my own.

If I die now, will Osiris even greet me on the other side? I shook the strange thought out of my head. I would not die. I refused to let my mother or my brother die. I would do anything necessary to protect the only light left in my life.

14

Blackness consumed everything. I blinked my eyes and swallowed hard against the fear that wrapped its tentacles around my throat, squeezing tighter with every moment my sight betrayed me. I could not see my own hand in front of my face.

How many days had it been? Without even a hint of light anywhere, there was no way to tell. Each time I fell into the depths of sleep I awoke with a start, dizzy and disoriented, locked in a frigid, timeless, endless night.

Darkness clung to me, wrapping me in a shroud of confusion. The air pressed thick on every side, as if I were trapped under the dark waters of the Nile. No candle would burn, no lamp would light, for the flames could not catch a breath.

How much longer would we endure this torture? Would the sun ever rise again?

Tekurah stirred on her bed and ordered that I bring more food and water. No matter that I had stumbled my way to the kitchen four times before in this blackness, the terror of venturing into the hallway seized me once again. I forced myself to inhale with long, slow breaths until the rushing pulse in my ears quieted.

I rose from the prison of my pallet, wrapped my woolen blanket around my body, and shuffled across the room, hands outstretched and feet cautious. Although my mistress was bound to her bed, she insisted that I continue serving her in the dark. Bruises covered my shins and hips from other excursions, unseen yet tender and layering one upon another after each unfortunate collision with furnishings. The temptation to refuse her demands grew stronger with each black minute, and I was glad she could not see the rebellion upon my face.

My fear of the dark had lingered with me from earliest childhood. Older children had spun stories of spirits of the dead who wandered the world with their heads on backward, amplifying my night terrors. Now, enveloped by the object of my greatest fears, my mind conjured horrors.

Visions of lights flashed and then were gone. Images of the idols that inhabited the alcoves along this corridor flashed through my mind, their sightless eyes staring at me as they uttered wordless curses. I squeezed my eyes tight, but the silent whispers continued. Glowing red eyes leered; slithering serpents and icy, grasping claws ripped at my imagination.

My fingers and toes were numb. The useless braziers lining this hall refused to ignite. My teeth chattered from fear and a deep, bone-aching cold.

The scuffle of sandaled feet on the tiles startled me and I turned, frustrated that my eyes could not discern even a shape nearby.

"Who is there?" I whispered over the pounding of my heart.

"Latikah. Is that Kiya?" The fear in her voice surprised me.

"Yes. Where are you going?"

She did not answer. Perhaps she had walked away. I took

a couple of steps, my hand on the wall guiding my slow trek toward the kitchen.

"I cannot take one more minute of this blackness. I can't. I can't. I'm losing my mind." The rush of her words told me she was close to letting go of her precarious hold on sanity.

I understood. I was straining to clutch that lifeline as well. But Latikah had betrayed me and sold Shira for trinkets.

My instinct was to continue down the hallway, leave her to be swallowed up in her fears. However, the image of Shira pushing to stand in front of me and taking my punishment upon herself overruled my inclination toward vengeance. Yielding, I exhaled and moved toward Latikah's voice.

"I am coming toward you. Reach out your hand."

"Where are you?" Her voice trembled.

Our fingers collided, and she grabbed ahold of my arm, yanking it as if she were drowning. "I'm so scared, Kiya. I have to go. I need to get out of this house."

"There is nowhere to go. Outside is just as dark as in here." Each time I ventured to the kitchen courtyard, I expected to see some light, any light, but the void outside was as heavy as inside the house—as though all the good in the entire land had been extinguished along with the light. No stars pierced the night. No torches lit the courtyard. The air hung thick with a menacing silence broken only by the moans and shrieks of terrified men, women, and children begging Ra to return from the underworld.

Latikah began to whimper, and her hand shook. "I have to go. I have to. I can't breathe. The walls are closing in on me, but I can't see them." She gasped again and again, short and shallow, as if she truly could not draw enough air.

Anxious to complete my task, I told her to sit with her back against the wall and wait for me to return with some water. She complied, but her rapid pants echoed behind me as I clung to the wall, groping past woven tapestries on my way toward the kitchen courtyard.

Knowing I was in the main vestibule, I was forced to let go of the safety of my wall and brave the open space to reach the other side of the room. I counted my steps, remembering it took only ten before—I slammed into the table in the center of the room, having misjudged or miscounted the space, and a horrific crash echoed down the hallways. I must have toppled the water clock that stood on that tabletop. Startled by the sound, a cat hissed close to my feet, and a tail grazed my shin. The animal did not go far but stayed nearby, yowling at me. Even animals were helpless in this pitch-black, their mournful cries constant since the plague had begun.

There was nothing I could do about the disaster I had caused. Getting on my hands and knees would be useless. I could not see to clean the mess. I continued my blind journey to the kitchen, where Hashma had left jars of water and the last of the food she had scavenged on a table near the door. The ovens would not light, so the only bread left was stale, but it would soothe the bite of hunger for awhile at least.

After I groped my way back to Tekurah's room, Latikah did not answer my call. She must have calmed down enough to return to the servants' quarters at the back of the house. Although I felt no friendship with her after what she had done, hearing my own fears echoed in her voice tugged at my compassion. I lay back on my mat, once again happily fettered to my bed, nested in my blankets and waiting for oblivion to take me under its wing. Yet I was unable to forget the desperate panic in Latikah's voice as she clung to me. Perhaps I should have stayed with her until she calmed.

What mysterious force held the sun-god captive in the underworld for so long? Certainly something stronger than Ra, the Almighty, should be feared. Perhaps Shira's god did wield more power than all the gods in Egypt, as she had insisted. He'd bested the gods of the Nile, the gods of the land, the gods of the sky. Perhaps this god-of-slaves would deliver the Hebrews after all. If he had more authority than all the gods of Egypt, did that mean he was superior to Pharaoh? The Morning Sun, Incarnation of Horus, Son of Osiris? Perhaps Yahweh was even supreme to Osiris, the Lord of the Afterlife himself?

Did he have authority over death, too?

15

After the fearful dark of those eternal three days, without even a pinprick of light in the sky, I yearned for the stars. Desperate to reassure myself that the oppressive blackness had not returned, I had stolen outside each night for a week as soon as Tekurah's breathing slowed. A compulsion to study the swirling patterns in the sky and the dance of the gods in the heavens each night gripped me.

Tonight, I wandered around the barren ground that no longer resembled a garden, bereft of all its blossoms, vines, and palm branches. What a waste. Once the jewel of my master's villa, its smell intoxicating and its colors dazzling, the garden was now an empty courtyard with a brackish pool at the center.

Latikah's body had been found there the first morning the sun had risen, floating facedown in the icy green water. She must have given in to the torment, tried to escape, and ended up falling into the pool. Unable to see and tangled in lily pads, most likely disoriented, she had drowned.

I shivered and looked away from the image the pool conjured in my mind. Poor girl. No matter what she had done to me or Shira, no one deserved that sort of lonely death. Why had I not stayed with her that night? Perhaps I could have prevented her sad demise.

A warm breeze caressed my face, promising a welcome change in the season, yet my bones seemed to ache with a cold that refused to go away.

Perching cross-legged on the cool stone ledge surrounding the pool, I leaned back on my arms to distract myself by looking at the stars. The glittering sky stretched over me, whispering of the grandeur of the universe and my smallness, my insignificance. Loneliness, for my mother, my brother, even Shira, swelled in me. If only I could speak to her, or Eben, to hear more about what was happening with Mosheh and Pharaoh. But now that Shira was free, Eben would have no more to do with me.

Since the morning he had turned away from me, I had done my best to expel him from my mind. But tonight, with a heart battered by despair and the sky filled with stars, I allowed my thoughts to linger on his face and the enigma in his expressions.

Although he was just another Hebrew slave, his bitterness affected me, and when he had drawn close, his stormy green eyes locked on mine, I must admit, I'd wished him closer. Disappointment had spiked through me when he stepped away.

"What do you see up there?" said a voice in the darkness.

I stood, scraping my leg on the sharp ledge as I did so. My quick intake of breath was as much from the injury as the realization of who stood in the garden. I could not see him in the shadows, but there was no mistaking his voice.

No words would form. I stood with my mouth agape as Akhum drew closer through the night. Blood rushed so loudly in my ears that I strained to understand his words.

"I could not stay away any longer." Akhum reached for my hand and pulled me toward him.

I could not speak. His dark eyes reflected the moonlight. Although the moon waxed less than full, it illuminated the garden.

I swallowed and managed to rasp, "Why are you here?"

"I told you I'd find a way."

"A way?"

"For us to be together. All of these strange things happening in our country, all the suffering around me, all I could think of . . . was you."

I blinked for a moment, my mind chasing thoughts that refused to bind together. "But . . . you are married."

"Kiya, I want you. I need you close to me." A sultry edge pressed through his voice.

"How . . . ? You . . . What do you mean?"

He drew me close and wrapped his arm around my waist. The sweet, warm-spice smell of him enticed several intimate memories to surface.

"I have more than enough to purchase your contract. I have a house in Thebes waiting for you."

A thousand questions buzzed in my brain. He wanted me? Away from Tekurah? A house? What of his wife? His father? Eben?

The most important question bubbled over first. "What about my family?"

"They are welcome to come with you." His lips brushed my ear, sending heat surging through my skin.

"All of them?"

"Well, your father travels now most of the time, correct? And your mother can trade her wares in any market."

I nodded.

"Listen, I will provide all you need. I just want you. I need you near me."

He brushed the backs of his silken fingers down my jawline and then traced my lips with his thumb. A shudder swept through me, and my questions floated away.

He grinned.

After all the dreams of Akhum, the impossible fantasies I'd entertained, here he stood, offering my life back. My thoughts spun wildly—a home, my family close, food and clothes, freed from the yoke of menial labor, *and* a new life with Akhum. Dizziness overtook me, and I swayed.

He kissed me.

I didn't care if Tekurah or Shefu or Pharaoh came into the courtyard. Akhum loved me and was going to buy my freedom.

Or was he? I pulled back. "You are going to purchase my contract?"

"Yes." And his lips again claimed mine.

I pulled away. "And I will be free?"

He winced.

"I won't be free?" I slid from his grasp.

His voice dropped low. "The only way my father agreed to let me have you is as my concubine."

"Concubine? You want me to be your slave?" The blood rushed in my head again, but this time it throbbed, blurring my vision.

"Lower your voice." He glanced around the garden. "I bribed the guard at the gate to turn a blind eye, but if Shefu finds us here . . ."

He came forward again and smoothed my hair. "Don't be angry, little Kiya. My sweet. My darling."

This man who once paid an exorbitant bride-price for me, who had prized me so highly, now wanted me to serve him? I had wasted almost two years of my life enslaved to Tekurah, serving her hand and foot, and now Akhum wanted me to do the same for him, but worse. Menial labor was not all I would endure. My body would not be my own as a concubine, not a wife of equal standing. I would be used and cast aside at his pleasure.

"No." I shook my head vehemently.

"What do you mean, no?"

"I won't let you own my body."

"I already own your body. You gave it to me . . . willingly, I might add." He narrowed his eyes and flashed a crooked smile.

I winced at the reminder, surprised at the whispered guilt those memories raised in my mind, yet somehow the arrogance in his tone fractured his hold over me.

"Yes, I did. But . . . I don't know how to explain so you will understand." I pulled farther away, folding my arms across my middle. "I have no freedom. Every movement is dictated, and if all I have left is my body, then I will not let anyone, not even you, take that from me."

Anger flashed across his face, something I had never seen before.

"You would turn me down? After all I have done to convince my father?"

I put my hand on his arm. "Forgive me, Akhum. I don't mean to hurt you. But . . . my perspective has changed."

He shook me off. "You ungrateful slave. Why have I wasted my time? My money?"

I jerked back, shocked at his fury and hateful words.

"How can you say that to me? I was almost your wife."

He snorted. "Well, you are only a slave now."

"Perhaps I am, but I am a slave who will keep her heart intact."

He sneered. "No one else will want your precious heart. You are only fit as a concubine now . . . if that."

Eben's face flashed again through my mind. Akhum was right; no one could ever see me as pure.

"It doesn't matter, Akhum. I won't sell my body to you or anyone else."

A cruel smile spread across his beautiful face. "I can still

purchase the contract, you know. And then I can do whatever
I want with you."

"Shefu won't sell me." At least I hoped for my mother's sake
he wouldn't. "But go ahead and try." I turned around, pushing
my feet toward the villa door, my heart still pounding in my ears.

A low curse knifed my back as I stepped inside, drawing as
much blood as he'd intended.

16

Angry tears blurred my vision, and the dark hallway swam in front of me. All this time I had dreamed of Akhum sweeping in, rescuing me from this oblivion. Wasted, wasted months.

The last futile vestige of hope separated from me completely, revealing the truth of my situation. I was Tekurah's slave, nothing more. Akhum saw me as I truly was: property, a commodity. Perhaps I had always been little more than a concubine in his mind. An expensive one, perhaps, for the bride-price was steep, but a woman to satiate only his body, not his soul.

Isis and Bastet—the goddesses I had offered sacrifices to from the time I'd begun my first flow, who promised enraptured love, enduring love—had abandoned me, betrayed me.

My chest ached after enduring the abuse of my furiously thrashing heart. As I forced my breath to slow and willed my pulse to calm its wild pattern, a thought suddenly screamed inside my mind.

Would slavery with him be better than no love at all? I had hoped and prayed for a way to be free, to protect my mother and brother—had I just turned down the answer? Should I have gone with him, endured the chains to obtain protection? I hesitated, rocking back on my heels.

I made the wrong choice. Spurned the only way to protect my family. Nausea welled in my throat. Akhum's stride was twice my own, but perhaps I could still catch up.

I turned to run—and slammed full force into someone.

The person fell back and something shattered: a vase, perhaps? Although too dark to distinguish any features, it didn't take long to know who blocked my path.

"You stupid slave! You can't go a day without breaking something!"

Tekurah.

She grabbed me by the hair. How could she even see? Bastet must bless her with eyes for the dark.

"Where are you going?" Her even tone told me she was not surprised to find me here.

"Nowhere." Akhum was a thousand miles away now.

"He doesn't want you." Her smile was audible in the blackness. She had seen us in the garden. And like one of her cats, she had been waiting to pounce.

My voice came out in a squeak. "Yes he does."

"No, he wants a concubine." She had heard the entire conversation.

She pulled me closer by my hair. Her breath smelled of sleep. I must have woken her when I stole from the room. "He has a wife, a well-connected one, one who is giving birth to his first child in a few months."

She laughed at my quick intake of breath.

"Oh, you didn't know that, did you?" She clicked her tongue against her teeth. "Yes, stupid girl. He only wants you because his wife is large with child. He hasn't been pining over you these last months, just been driven, as any man, by his lust."

Of course. He was a commander in Pharaoh's army, I was a

slave. I would be only a useful tool, no more beloved than his horse . . . perhaps even less so.

I stood straighter. "Thank you."

She stammered, "For what?"

"If I'd followed him, I would have suffered a worse fate than staying here with you."

No reply.

"You are right. He doesn't want me. I was deluding myself."

She drew a quick breath through her nose. For some reason, my acquiescence had infuriated her. I tried to draw back, but her grip on my hair tightened.

For the first time, she hit me.

In the pitch-black I could not see when the next blow was coming, or the next, and I tripped over my own feet trying to pull away. Even when I lay on the floor, she would not abate. I knew better than to cry out, nothing could save me. Shefu had slipped out of the villa two days ago on business. If I screamed, it would only be worse.

I tried to protect my face, but her nails ripped down my right cheek. I bit my lip, hard, to prevent a cry of pain. I refused to let her have the victory of my submission.

She kicked me, clawed me, pulled my hair, and ripped my shift. Her grunts of exertion changed to laughter as she unleashed maniacal fury.

When she finally stopped, I lay on the floor, my hands spread over my face, praying to Bes, whose statue stood somewhere guarding this black hallway.

When I finished praying to Bes, I prayed to Ra, I prayed to Isis, I prayed to Bastet—I prayed to every god my mind could conjure.

But even as I pleaded, I knew nothing would happen. Nothing could. The gods were silent to me. They did not hear a worthless slave with nothing to offer. They cared nothing for my bleeding heart and body.

Where was Tekurah? I dared not look up but kept my face shielded for another attack. A torch lit the hall. The glow seeped through the cracks between my fingers.

"Mistress?" It was the voice of Manit, Shefu's servant.

I peeked through my fingers. Tekurah stood with her back to me, leaning over a marble-topped table, the statue of Bes in pieces around her feet.

The man cleared his throat.

"Mistress. Are you all right?"

She whirled around, kicking the largest piece of the statue as she did. It clamored against the wall and shattered further.

Tekurah did not look at him. "Take this slave to the cellar and lock her up. She tried to escape. She will be punished tomorrow."

Deep inside, something in me snapped.

I raised my head. It pounded in agony, but I put my hands under my shoulders and lifted my bruised and bleeding body off the floor.

My head swam, but I stood in front of Tekurah. My swollen lip throbbed and cracked open. I pulled in a painful breath. "I have done nothing to you, Tekurah. You hate me for my mother's sake. I do not deserve your wrath. Whatever you do to my body, you won't steal my soul. You can beat me, lash me, tie me to a stake. You will never break me into pieces like you want to do."

Manit was incredulous, his eyes as large as boulders as he looked from Tekurah back to me.

Tekurah hissed, "You are—"

"No." I steeled myself. "I am not done. I see the way you look at Shefu, at your children. You want them to love you, but they don't. How could anyone love such a bitter woman? You treat everyone around you like a slave and expect love from them? Ha! It will never happen. You think I am the one unwanted? Maybe Akhum only wants me to keep his bed warm, but I have a mother and brother who love me deeply. You think I am the one in chains? Look at yourself in your fancy silver mirror and think again."

I turned to Shefu's servant. "I am ready."

He took my arm, gently and without meeting my eye. I leaned on him as we walked down the hallway, the torchlight following us, leaving our mistress in the dark.

For all I knew, three mornings came and went—it was nothing but black in the cellar. Yet after enduring the thick darkness of the plague, it seemed not nearly as frightening. I enjoyed blissful, deep sleep—an extravagant freedom—even chained to the wall.

When I awoke and attempted to stretch, I kicked a tray of food that lay next to me. Fish, bread, and warm, watery beer: the usual fare. I savored each bite, chewing slowly—something else I had not been allowed in such a long time, always in a rush to accomplish some task or another for Tekurah.

Only a few weeks before, Shira had sat eating in the darkness in this very spot, shackled by these same chains. Somehow being bound here made me feel close to her.

I laid my head on my knees, forgetting my scratched and bruised face. I hissed in a breath at the sting of pain. Instead, I placed my left cheek, somehow left unscathed, against my knees and closed my eyes.

Tekurah had accused me of escaping. She would cling to that story—it was the only way Shefu might forgive her. She would have me flogged publicly, before Shefu could return to prevent it. He was usually gone on business for many days. Hashma had told me yesterday he'd sailed north to Avaris, hoping to salvage what he could of his trading empire, since the entire economy of Egypt lay in ruins.

However, only one servant traveled with him. Perhaps he planned to stay only a brief time and then return.

No, that was too much to hope for, and there was no god to plead to.

Was there?

Would Shira's God listen to an Egyptian? How would I even pray to him, with no image to conjure in my mind, no temple to turn my face toward? No tribute. No offering. How could I possibly make him do what I needed him to do?

I spoke out loud, feeling foolish praying to a foreign, faceless god, but desperate enough to try.

"God of the Hebrews." Fear prevented me from speaking his name. "I am trapped. If you can hear me like Shira says you can, release me from this pit. I have nothing to give you, but if you will show me mercy, I will find something to sacrifice, somehow."

Silence.

What did I expect? A flash of light? My chains to fall away? The door to swing open wide? Nothing came back to me but the sound of my labored breathing and the press of darkness and cold on all sides. I shivered. I curled up with my back to the wall and my arms around my knees.

I fell asleep again, feeling a bit like a traitor to my gods and my country, and ridiculous for attempting to pray to Shira's invisible god.

17

The long hours of sleep in the storeroom allowed me the luxury of dreaming. I slipped quietly in and out of the world of shadows and lights, disjointed colors and faces. I saw Shira, Eben, Akhum, and Tekurah arguing over me, fighting over whom I should serve. The Nile rose and fell, black, red, and then sparkling gold. A mountain stood high above me, a swirling rainbow of smoke rising high above, an earthquake shaking the ground and a crack appearing between my feet.

The door to my prison slammed open and light flooded in, blinding me.

"Kiya," someone called out, voice thick with concern. "Where are you?"

Shefu stood silhouetted in the doorway.

"Here." My throat burned.

A torch hovered over me.

"Manit, bring me the key to the chains." Shefu crouched next to me and put a gentle hand on my swollen face. "Kiya. Oh, I'm so sorry."

Manit unchained me, shifting his eyes away. He needn't feel guilty. This was all Tekurah's doing.

"Here, drink." Shefu brought a cup of water to my cracked lips. Placing his hand on the back of my head, he held the cup as I drank, as if I were an infant.

"More?"

I shook my head.

"How long has she been down here?"

Manit shuffled his feet. "Since the night before last. I sent for you right away."

Shefu rubbed his eyebrow with a free hand. The other still curled around me, cradling my neck.

"Go get Lefar. I have errands you both need to do. Hurry!"

Manit turned and disappeared up the stairway.

Shefu's dark eyes sparkled in the torchlight. Tears? Or anger?

"Can you walk?"

"I don't know."

I tried to stand, but my legs wobbled. My sore ribs screamed, and when Shefu put an arm around my waist to steady me, a whimper escaped.

"What did she do to you?" His voice broke.

Suddenly he bent and put his hands behind my knees, lifting me into his arms.

The pain and anger on his face confused and terrified me. Through Shira, I knew he'd given Tekurah orders not to lay a hand on me for my mother's sake, but why was he so distraught?

He carried me to his own quarters.

His chambers were richly appointed, but sparse compared to Tekurah's lavish suite. A bed with embroidered linens stood in the corner, a few clothing baskets at its foot. Paintings hung on the walls, one with ducks and geese hiding among the rushes in a pond and one of the pyramids at Giza, with the sun framing them from behind. Apart from these decorations, only a tall oil lamp, a low couch, and a large desk underneath the high window, covered with parchments and notes written on broken pottery shards, filled the space. Lefar served not only as his handservant, but his personal scribe as well. I imagined Shefu standing in the center of this room, dictating letters to tradesmen.

Shefu placed me on the couch, then found a linen cloth in his bath chamber and dipped it in a jar of water standing on a pedestal by the door. He washed my face with tender strokes, wincing when I reacted to the sharp stabs of pain that even his gentle touch provoked.

His voice was so quiet at first, I wasn't sure if he'd addressed me. ". . . how she could have done this, after I told her not to lay a hand on you? Foolish woman. She knew. She must have known or she would not have defied me so."

My fractured mind attempted to piece together his meaning.

He continued, "But you have to go now. If you stayed . . . no. You have to go. For Jumo."

"Jumo?" I pushed myself up on my elbows, wounds forgotten.

"Lay back down." He pressed me gently back to the soft cushions. "Yes, Jumo. You have to go tonight to save your brother."

"Save him? From what?"

"The Hebrew God." Shefu sat on the edge of the bed, his head in his hands.

"Master, you are not making any sense. Is Jumo in danger?"

His head snapped up, and he looked into my eyes. "Don't call me *master*."

Utter confusion must have been plastered across my face. His features softened as he watched me react to his command. He patted my hand.

"It's all right. Just call me Shefu."

"All right . . . Shefu. Is my brother in danger?"

"Yes. I can't explain it all. I wish I understood myself. I was there when Moses, the leader of the Hebrew slaves, sent a messenger to Pharaoh. The God of the Hebrews will kill every firstborn Egyptian male. Tonight. Every one."

I could not breathe. No. Shefu was mistaken, or lying, or delusional . . .

"You have to go. You have to save him."

"Where would I go?" The room seemed to spin.

"To the Hebrews. Your friend Shira. I don't understand how or why, but their God protects them, and Jumo's only chance is to take refuge among them. Do whatever you can to get in the midst of them. You must save his life."

"But . . . I . . . how?" I didn't even know where Shira lived.

A knock on the door startled me, and Manit and Lefar swept into the room. I could barely distinguish the difference between the two tall, dark Kushites. *They must be brothers. Who is first-born? But they aren't Egyptian, maybe they will be spared . . .* My thoughts refused to move in a straight line.

Shefu burst into action, giving the men quick orders to fetch different items—a donkey, linens, clothing, and my meager belongings. Shefu sat at his desk, cleared a spot at the center, and laid down a fresh parchment. He wrote with a beautiful quill, made from the feather of a peacock, dipping the tip again and again into the inkpot, squinting as he concentrated.

He stood, walked to the side of the bed, and handed me the papyrus document.

Many women were ignorant of reading. I was not one of them. My mother had insisted I be taught to read and write, as her own mother had done. My father had grumbled but paid tutors to teach me. Many women in Pharaoh's court were not so well educated.

The declaration on the parchment shocked me. I read it several times before I understood the meaning of the words.

A bill of release. Shefu had released me from indentured servitude. I was pardoned and all debts satisfied.

"I am sorry that I ever did this, Kiya. My only thought was to protect you and your family. If you were sold elsewhere, and separated, I would never have forgiven myself. Jofare agreed . . . I mean, your father agreed to do this to satisfy his debts, and I wanted to watch over you, but it became more complicated than I expected." His words tumbled out in a confusing jumble.

I put up a hand. "No. Master . . . Shefu . . . I don't fault you. My father is the one who enslaved his own flesh and blood."

Shefu looked at the floor.

His stricken expression confused me. "I know you tried to protect me. Tekurah was determined to break me one way or the other."

I read through the document again, internalizing it, believing it. I caressed the rough parchment, and tears overflowed.

"I'm free," I whispered.

"Yes, my beautiful girl. You are free. You can go home to your mother."

"But how am I going to convince her to go? To bring Jumo?"

He pursed his lips, rubbing his temple for a moment, then put up a finger and walked out the door.

Confused, I waited, reading the parchment over and over again.

Ten minutes later, he came back in, carrying a large pouch.

"The sun is starting to go down. You need to hurry." He reached in the pouch and brought out a beautiful necklace, fashioned from pure gold and brilliant blue lapis lazuli.

"This will convince your mother. Give it to her. Tell her Shefu says she must go. She will understand."

Unclasping the necklace, he held it out. "Do you mind?"

I shook my head.

He placed the necklace around my neck and fastened it. Then he smoothed my hair and kissed my forehead. He grasped me by the shoulders and gazed into my eyes for a long moment.

"Please, I need to hear it from your lips. Do you forgive me?"

I nodded again, still unsure why he needed my forgiveness, why he seemed so desperate for it. "Yes."

"Then go. Tell your mother . . . No, she knows that I—" He brushed a trembling hand over his face. "Just get Jumo to safety. Beg the Hebrews for mercy. Perhaps these will help." He handed me the bag.

I looked inside and gasped. Gold and silver glimmered. These must be what remained of Tekurah's jewels. "No, she will be furious. I can't take these."

"They are mine to give. She has no say—especially after what she did. You leave her to me." He pushed back the bag I tried to press into his hands. "Consider this payment for all you have endured. I owe you much more than this."

"But . . ."

"Do you want to save your brother?" Authority rang in his voice.

"Yes."

"Then do as I say. Hurry, you only have an hour or so before the sun goes down, and you must be inside with the Hebrews by midnight."

"Midnight?"

"The message relayed to Pharaoh said this judgment would come at midnight."

A thrill of fear spread through me.

"Here are Manit and Lefar with fresh clothing. I wish I could dress you in fine linen to send you on your way, but it is best that you move through town without raising suspicion. There would be no time for you to explain where you are going or why."

He stood at the door, gazing at me with such a look of tenderness that my throat tightened. He must see Nailah in my face. He turned his back and disappeared without another word.

After I dressed, tucked the necklace into my shift, and tied my sandals to my feet, Manit led me to the front gate. A little brown donkey waited, tied to a post, laden with two baskets on either side.

Manit untied the donkey, wished me the gods' protection on my journey, and disappeared into the house, never once looking into my eyes.

I blinked into the golden evening light. The guard at the gate ignored me.

The sun slipped farther into the west. My mother's house was all the way across town from Shefu's villa, so I needed to move quickly.

I tucked the jewel pouch and my priceless document of freedom into the basket among rich linens. I stifled the temptation to stroke the soft fabrics. The baskets also held food and jugs of beer and water.

Shefu, it seemed, anticipated a longer journey than just across the city of Iunu.

18

Tales that should never be told to children, legends of dark spirits roaming the blackness on the hunt for souls to devour—these stories had always fueled my fear of the dark.

Tonight the myths were real. The awareness that something lurked out there, something that truly would consume, pulsed through my body and pushed me forward. The whole of Egypt must sense the foreboding. No dogs barked. No birdsong greeted the twilight. Not the slightest breeze whispered through the broken trees.

The sandals Shefu had returned to me chafed, the papyrus scraping against my callused feet. The bondage of the straps was disconcerting after so many months of going barefoot. There was no time to remove them, so I pressed on. My little brown companion followed so close his muzzle bumped against my back whenever my pace slackened. The donkey, too, must sense the urgency.

How would I convince my mother to follow me? Would the bauble I wore around my neck persuade her to drop everything and flee?

Without a doubt, Jumo would agree to go. Although I was his younger sister, he trusted me implicitly. My mother adored Jumo, and for his safety, she must trust in the unknown and flee. She had only to understand the immediacy and the danger that lay ahead this night.

I wound through the city streets, hunting for my mother's house. Many months had passed since Tekurah had allowed a visit, and never at night. Homes, many burned-out by the storms and fires, haunted the streets like dark-eyed specters. I hoped my mother's stood intact. I searched for familiar landmarks, but in the waning light, nothing looked as I remembered.

Deserted streets met my every turn. All of the houses in this quarter of the city were so similar: mud and brick, a few venting windows at the top of the walls, most of them two stories . . . differentiating between them might be next to impossible. Pressing down panic and wishing I had a god to pray to, I turned the next corner.

Throwing a glance over my shoulder at the sunset, I gauged the time left to convince my mother to abandon everything she knew. Ra's boat hung low over the western horizon, silhouetting the pyramids in the distance.

I breathed a sigh of relief when I recognized my mother's house. How I had found my way through the tangled maze was a mystery. Somehow my feet led me to her doorstep. The decoration around the doorway, painted by my brother's gifted hand, marked the mud-brick home as theirs.

Standing on the doorstep, I drew a deep breath and prayed for calm from whatever god would deign to listen. The donkey nuzzled my elbow with a whiskered chin as I knocked. No answer. I knocked again. Whispers floated through the thin wooden door.

"Mother"—I knocked again—"it's me. Open the door."

The door swung open, and my mother appeared, her black

hair swinging free and her eyes wide with surprise. Her gaze took in my frazzled appearance and the donkey behind my back.

"Kiya, what are you doing?" She gasped. "What happened to you?" She reached to lay a gentle palm on my injured cheek.

I craned my neck to peer around her. "Is Father here?"

"No, he left a week ago to trade downriver. It will be weeks before he will return."

Or not at all.

A shiver snaked up my back, and I sensed eyes peering out of doorways. I must have knocked louder on the door than I'd realized. "I have to get out of the street." I tied the donkey to the door handle and slipped inside, scanning the street before closing the door behind me.

"Ya-ya!" Jumo rose from the low couch on the back wall of the living area and limped toward me, his long arms held wide. "Why . . . you . . . here?"

My brother's unruly legs and staggering gait prevented him from moving about unaided. His affected speech garbled and strained to convey his thoughts. However, though his legs and tongue were uncontrollable, his artist's hands were deft and his mind keen. He missed nothing.

As he took in my bruises and my swollen face, his warm brown eyes rounded, full of alarm. Ignoring the burn of my ribs, I wrapped my arms around him. I hadn't seen him in months, long before I'd met Shira. His thick black curls were unruly as usual; my head barely touched his shoulder now. Was he still growing? At nineteen?

My older brother squeezed me tightly, a reminder of the urgency of my mission. I pulled back to look at him—the affection exuding from his eyes caused my heart to constrict.

"Mother, we must leave . . . now," I said over my shoulder.

"Leave?" My mother's beautiful face contorted in confusion. "Kiya, did you escape? Is that why . . . ?"

I shook my head and dropped my arms from Jumo's waist. "No, but if we do not go, Jumo will die, tonight, within hours."

She sank onto a low stool, looking from me to Jumo and back again. "Ridiculous." She breathed the word. "Jumo is fine. Why would you say such an awful thing?"

"It's the truth. I am here to save my brother's life, and I must leave here within the next hour, with Jumo and with you, if you are willing."

How do I make her understand?

"Listen to me. I know this is confusing and frightening, but I wouldn't have come if it wasn't real. Shefu himself sent me here. He released me from service after Tekurah did this." I gestured to my face. "He gave me the donkey and said you must listen to me and go."

I removed the necklace Shefu had tied around my neck and placed it in my mother's hand. That hand immediately began to tremble, and I knew the veracity of my words was proven. She looked up at me, face blanched and golden eyes brimming with tears.

"Where can we go?" she whispered.

"We will go with the Hebrews and leave Egypt." I startled myself with this statement. I hadn't considered we would leave the country, but it only made sense. If the Hebrews were leaving like Shira had said, we would go with them. There was nothing here for us anymore. Shefu must mean for us to go too, for all the goods he'd sent with me.

She pulled her arms tight across her middle.

"The slaves? Why?" She shook her head as if to dislodge the strange idea.

"The Hebrews are leaving, and if we do not hurry, it will be too late."

"Too late for what?"

I sighed and glanced at my brother, who seemed to be gathering his brushes and inks. As anticipated, he was more than ready to leave with me, no explanation necessary.

"Mother, you know the havoc unleashed upon this country . . ."

"That the Hebrews have heaped upon us . . ." She jutted her chin.

"No. Pharaoh caused this."

Her eyes went wide and darted to the window. "Kiya, hush. How could you speak against Pharaoh? It is blasphemy."

The discussion was spiraling into an argument. I did not have time to quarrel.

"Mother"—I knelt before her and grasped the hand that held the necklace—"Jumo is in severe danger. If we do not refuge with the Hebrews tonight, he will die. Something worse is coming tonight. Please, pack with haste and come with me."

She looked at the necklace, a delicate lapis-beaded chain with a golden pendant in the shape of Hathor, the goddess of love and beauty. A tender look floated across my mother's features, and as confusing as it was, I was grateful for it: it was my greatest ally at the moment.

"Shefu says that we have to leave, that for the sake of Jumo, you must believe me. This danger, Shefu heard about it with his own ears in the court of Pharaoh."

She looked up sharply. "What did he hear?"

I lowered my voice and leaned in close. "Tonight the Hebrew God will kill all the firstborn sons of Egypt."

My mother gasped, and her face went ashen. Her mouth hung open as her golden eyes searched mine. Then she looked past me and surveyed her little home, which seemed to have somehow sustained little damage in the violent storms.

For a moment, I worried she might faint, but then she rose to her feet. "Let's pack as much food as we can. Who knows how long our journey will be?"

My brother hobbled into the room, struggling with a large basket—his own clothing and supplies, packed while I was busy persuading my mother.

"Jumo." My mother opened a small ebony chest and handed him a pouch. "Go next door to Meritabah's home and ask to buy their wagon. Tell her we need it for a journey. She will be confused, but she owes me a favor. This should more than cover the cost."

Jumo nodded. He shuffled to retrieve a crutch leaning against the wall and opened the door. I was relieved to see my little friend still tied to the door latch, laden with his treasures. Jumo pushed the donkey out of the way before hobbling off into the dusk on his mission.

My mother darted in and out of the room, gathering clothing into baskets, rummaging through her cosmetic chest, and talking to herself, listing articles she would need. Her change in attitude astounded me. She must have complete faith in Shefu.

How close had they been? And how long ago?

My mother was beautiful. No, exquisite. No doubt many men had been in love with her. And although humbled to the position of a lowly merchant in the marketplace, her beauty remained unparalleled.

Her ebony hair shone in the lamplight. As a child, I'd always hated when she wore wigs. There was no wig beautiful enough to match the luster of her hair. Her shapely form was the envy of all Egyptian women, even after bearing two children. Unconsciously graceful, with a voice like honey, my mother was a goddess, and I practically worshipped her.

She had always been so far above me—untouchable, unknowable. Would I ever truly understand her? Why had she married my father? Who was foremost in her heart? How could she let me be sold? Was I not worthy of her love, her protection? Was her freedom more precious than mine?

Lost in my silent conflict, I startled when she spoke.

"Kiya, Jumo is back. Go pack as much bread and food as you can. There are jugs of beer and water in the storeroom."

We hitched my donkey to the front of the small wagon and packed baskets full of clothing and food in the bed, along with the jugs. When one more item would threaten an avalanche, I helped Jumo mount the black donkey Meritabah had insisted on including in the price of the wagon. Where had she even acquired such an animal? Perhaps, like Shefu had done, her family had purchased it from the Hebrews, whose livestock had survived.

How could such a thing even happen? That an Egyptian-owned sheep or cow or horse would die, but the Hebrews' stock would remain unscathed? I had once heard my mother joke about the slave-god not knowing the difference between Hebrews and Egyptians, but it was very apparent that he did. Would Jumo truly be safe tonight, even among the Hebrews?

I had little choice but to hope.

19

I knocked on the door of the one-story hovel, my stomach curling with apprehension. Had the neighbor down the street directed us to the right door? Even if it was the correct home, would we still be turned away? Shira's family may not be as kind as she had been to me. Eben's disdain for Egyptians was more than evident; perhaps their mother was of the same mindset.

Voices overlapped on the other side of the door before it opened, spilling lamplight across my face and into the street.

Eben filled the doorway. "What are you doing here?" His face was awash with surprise and confusion. His wide eyes traveled over my injured face, and I fought the urge to recoil from his perusal.

"Who is it?" Shira's voice from somewhere behind her brother flooded me with relief, and my shoulders relaxed. She would fight for me.

Suddenly, her bright face was in the doorway. "Kiya! You came!" She squeezed past her glowering brother and grabbed my hand, trying to pull me inside.

"Wait, Shira." I glanced behind me. "My mother and brother are with me."

"Oh!" She clapped her hands together. "I prayed and prayed that you would come—for Jumo's sake." She stepped over the threshold and gestured to my mother. "*Baruch haba*, welcome, come inside. We will find a place for all of you. Eben, please take their animals around back, inside the shelter."

"Shira, we can't . . ." Eben shook his head, brow furrowed. The torchlight illuminated the conflict flickering in his eyes.

She turned on him, fists on her narrow hips. "Eben, if our father were here, you know he would not turn anyone away. I will not either. Would you keep Kiya's brother—her *firstborn* brother—unprotected this night?"

Eben looked past me at Jumo sitting on the donkey, and after a moment, his stony expression melted. Jumo shifted his crutches across the donkey's neck.

"Please, just take their animals around back and come back inside. There is only a little over an hour until midnight." She did not wait for his answer but instructed me to bring Jumo and my mother into the house. For such a seemingly fragile little girl, I sensed she had an iron will when it came to her loved ones—and tonight I was grateful for that loyalty and that I was counted as such.

Jumo slid off the donkey without assistance but hobbled up to the doorway, overdramatizing his limp and winking at me as he passed. I bit my cheek to restrain a smirk and followed him into the house.

The doorway was painted red—to ward off evil spirits perhaps? My sleeve brushed against the smear before I realized it was still wet and dripping. I cringed. Was it blood?

Many bodies filled the small room. They were all dressed as if ready to depart, mantles across shoulders and wearing their sandals inside the house. These Hebrews were strange indeed.

"*Ima,*" Shira said to a woman standing by the curtained doorway between the living and sleeping quarters, "this is my friend Kiya, her mother Nailah, and her brother, Jumo. They are taking refuge with us tonight."

"Kiya!" Shira's jaw dropped. "Your face!"

My hand went to my cheek, and I flushed. "I am sure it looks worse than it is."

Her eyes shimmered with tears. "Did Tekurah . . . ?"

"I am fine. Truly."

She peered at me, hands on hips. "You will tell me tomorrow." Her tone assured me I had little choice.

Shira's mother offered a generous smile, cutting the tension. "You are welcome in our home. Shira has told me much about you. Adonai brought you to our door this night."

Shira's mother was not much taller than Shira. She wore a tightly wrapped linen headscarf, but a few escaped wisps confirmed that Eben had inherited his hair color from his mother. Her eyes were almost as dark as Tekurah's, but warmth exuded from their depths; in fact, they shone as if lit from within. Something told me, however, that her eyes would snap black if she was crossed. Although a tiny woman, strength radiated from her, the reflection of which I had seen in Shira.

She put out her hands to grasp my mother's. "My name is Zerah. I apologize that I have nothing to offer you, we have already packed our stores. And the remainder of the meal was burned."

"Oh, no, thank you." My mother glanced at me. "We ate before we left home."

My stomach murmured a contradiction, but I said nothing. My mother sat on the wooden crate Zerah offered, wrapped her arms about her middle, and stared at the floor.

Blood painted on doorways, burning the leftover food—what strange customs these people have.

Eben came in through the back door and slunk to the opposite side of the room, then sat down, leaning his head back against the wall. Although he seemed to be avoiding looking my way, I caught him a few times watching me from the corner of his eye.

Wishing I could turn away and hide the evidence of Tekurah's cruelty without drawing attention, I raised my chin instead, determined to portray strength, even if Eben's occasional glances made me feel like tucking my head between my knees.

Zerah introduced us to the others seated on the floor, on low stools, and on overturned baskets and pots around the room. They included Shira's two younger sisters, Shoshana, whom I knew from Shira's stories to be nine, and Zayna, who was six; an uncle and aunt; as well as another family with very small twin boys and a couple from next door. The young wife was heavy with child. She and her husband glared openly at us, reminding me of the other slaves in Shefu's home, who saw me as an interloper. I fit in among those slaves no better than I did these Hebrews.

Would their God single us out here? Or would we somehow blend in, be counted as one of them, and therefore saved from whatever horrors were yet to come?

20

Although his eyes remained closed and the back of his head against the wall, Eben's long, tapered fingers tapped against his thigh, an indication that his relaxed pose was merely pretense.

Fear seized my heart, and my breath quickened. What would happen at midnight? Was Eben waiting for some signal to take up arms against Egypt tonight? Would it be the sword lying on the floor next to him that spilled the blood of our firstborns— of my brother? Eben had made it clear that he was anxious to avenge his father—had I led Jumo into the enemy's hands?

As if he could feel my gaze on him, Eben's eyelids fluttered open. Instead of the anger and bitterness I had expected to see, his expression portrayed only confusion and curiosity.

Intensity vibrated in the air, causing a flurry of nerves to swirl in my stomach and dispelling the idea that Eben would hurt my brother. Afraid that someone might notice the screaming tension between the two of us, I looked away, grateful that the lamplight was dwindling and no one would see the effects of my overheated face.

As I worked to avoid glancing toward him again, minutes

dwindled away and silence settled over the house. No one slept, except for the youngest children. I strained my ears, listening. I felt the entire land of Egypt was doing the same, waiting, listening, fearing that a night of desolation lay ahead of us—one more terrifying than three days of darkest night.

When the lamplight flickered low, casting dimmer shadows on the wall, Zerah's strong voice startled me. "Sing something, dear one."

I did not know who she was addressing, but there was no mistaking the voice that cut through the silence. I had never heard Shira sing. She sometimes hummed wordless tunes while we attended to our water pots or bathed in the sunshine at the river, but now her clear, sweet voice filled the room. She sang a verse by herself and then others joined in, their voices growing stronger with each line.

They sang in their own language, a beautiful, lyrical tongue, a tongue I had no knowledge of. When I had heard the language in the marketplace, it seemed foreign and awkward to my Egyptian ears. But as Shira's voice rose and spun higher, I understood the beauty, the complicated dips and swells of the words swirling together to form a poetry beyond anything I had ever before experienced.

There was no need to understand the words. Every syllable rang with clear meaning. It was the song of her people, desperate for their God, crying out to him in their bondage: the plaintive cry from a broken heart, from a nation of broken hearts. The cry rose in one verse and fell in another, as the tide of hope grew and receded. Over two hundred years of bitter bondage had seen the rise and fall of the Hebrews' hope, time and again.

The last verse, however, was full of joy—a strange irony on this night. More than once, the name of Mosheh wove its way into the fabric of the lyrics. I expected the melody to end on a melancholy note, to echo the fear and dread around us, but it was full and high and sweet. The other voices faded as Shira held the last note.

It hung there, resonating in the darkness.

When this last note of Shira's masterful song faded, no one moved or spoke. Everyone, it seemed, felt as I did, that the spell would be broken by the slightest of whispers, as if any movement would be an affront to the magic Shira's voice wrapped around us.

I thought she had begun singing again when a sound met my ears. But the voice was not from inside this house. Instead a high-pitched keening rang out in the distance, the shrill wail rending the silence. The hair prickled on the back of my neck.

The sound was all too recognizable.

Death.

The lone voice remained solitary for only a moment, then others joined its lament, and then still more. Soon a cacophony of lamentation surrounded us on all sides, as though the entire land of Egypt grieved with one loud voice.

Most jarring were the shrieks from homes shockingly close to Shira's. The sounds of mourning were familiar. I had always hated the dreadful ululating of the professional mourners as they led the processions of the dead to their resting places—but this was different. The wailing and shrieking made my bones ache with icy horror.

My mother's frozen hand slipped into mine and, as the sound grew, she trembled more and more. Or was it my own hand shaking? My whole body tensed to flee, but there was nowhere to go. Death surrounded us on all sides. Would anyone survive this unimaginable terror?

A loud knock thudded on the door. We all jolted, eyes wide, but no one moved to open it.

Had Pharaoh sent his army to kill the Hebrews? Had I doomed not only Jumo but my mother and myself by putting our lot in with these foreigners? My heart lurched and flailed, and nausea rose in my throat.

Another knock . . . and then pounding. "Open up, you have to leave!"

Eben stood, tucking the short sword into his belt but keeping a grip on the hilt. His hand paused on the latch a moment before he opened the door.

A small group of Egyptians surrounded the doorway, two men and five women. Tears and kohl streamed down their faces. The men were on their knees, and two of the women lay prostrate in the dirt in front of the threshold.

One of the men crawled forward and pushed a large bundle at Eben's feet. "Please. Take this—take it and go. We cannot endure any more. We will all die if you Hebrews do not leave our land."

Eben did not move to pick up the bundle. "What has happened?"

"They are all dead. You killed them all." He sobbed, gripping his chest. "My son. My only . . ."

"All of your firstborn are dead," Eben said. It was not a question.

"Every one, every house. Even the firstborn of the animals are gone, and our slaves. Not even infants were spared . . ." The man's voice quavered and broke.

"Please." The woman who stood at the back of the group spoke up. "You have to go, all of you. Egypt cannot survive any more of your sorcery." She caught sight of me and my family, behind Eben. Without blinking, her expression transformed from sorrow to malice. "Go, and take the traitors with you." She spat on the ground, muttered a dark curse, and turned her back on us.

21

"What will we do?" My mother's whisper tickled my ear. "Will they kill us?"

Eben's sword sliced through my thoughts, but I had every confidence in Shira. "No. We will go with them, as Zerah offered."

My mother's eyes widened, and she leaned closer to me. "With these Hebrews? Why? Can't we just settle in another town? Where no one knows us?"

"If we stay here, everyone will know that we took refuge with the Hebrews, Mother. You saw how that woman reacted. Just the fact that Jumo survived tonight—we will be deemed conspirators."

She was silent, conflict playing across her features. "But we could go somewhere else. Where no one knows us. Start over."

Shaking his head, my brother reached out and patted her hand. "No . . . we . . . go."

Her eyes tightened as she looked at him, but then her shoulders sloped, and she nodded. She would deny Jumo nothing. She knew as well as I did that there was no other choice but to go. We had no home. No gods. No country. We must place our fate in the hands of a faceless god that I still was not convinced even existed, except in the minds of slaves.

A new commotion in the narrow street caused Eben to step outside, and we waited in silence for minutes that seemed like hours, all eyes on the wooden door. When it swung open, a rush of chill night air rushed in with Eben.

"It's time," he said. "We are going."

A flurry of commotion swirled around us. The neighbors and the couple with their twin boys left. The boys slept against their parents' shoulders, blissfully unaware of their brush with death. Shira and her mother scurried about, packing the last of their meager belongings into baskets. My mother, Jumo, and I stood helpless in the middle of the room. My heart felt like an anchored boat being tossed about in the middle of a rushing river as I watched Shira's family, liberty now within reach after hundreds of years. I felt the pull, the call of freedom, yet I felt moored to Iunu, even in her destruction.

But I would not stay. I could not. There was nothing for me in this town but chains. And shame.

When the last of their family's meager belongings had been packed into their cart, Eben pulled our donkeys around to the front of the house. Both animals were skittish from the turmoil in the street. Hundreds of Hebrews were doing the same as Shira's family, loading their wagons and pushcarts. Some with bright faces and laughter, others in silent solemnity.

I had never seen this many Hebrews before tonight, and the differences among them shocked me. I had expected most of them to look like Shira and Eben, but many women wore painted eyes, and many men sported clean-shaven faces. There were numerous stooped backs, some crisscrossed with the markings of whips, echoes of the brick teams charged to build the magnificence of Iunu for Pharaoh's sake. Until Shira had told me of this heavy burden of her people, I had barely considered how many slaves it had taken to build my beautiful city, or their misery in the hot sun each day under the cruel oversight of their masters.

Jumo pulled himself onto the black donkey, and I waited, nervously shifting from foot to foot. My mother leaned against my brown donkey, as if needing something to hold her up as she surveyed the chaotic scene around us.

Just as our caravan began to move away from Shira's home, a wagon, pulled by a magnificent horse, skidded to a stop in front of us.

"Eben!" a voice called out.

Akensouris, the man I recognized as Eben's master from the music shop, jumped down from the wagon. He enveloped Eben in a hug. "Thank you. Thank you, my friend," he said, kissing Eben's cheeks. "Without your warning and instructions, my little son would be dead. I owe you his life—and mine."

Shira's low voice whispered in my ear. "My brother told Akensouris how to protect his family. He has been good to us for many years."

"What protected you . . . us?"

She pointed at the doorway behind us. The torchlight illuminated a glimmer across the lintel, on both sides of the doorway and across the threshold that I had passed over now twice. "We killed a lamb and painted its blood around the doorway."

A threshold sacrifice, like the one held every year in Osiris's honor when a pig was slaughtered at every door in Egypt. A chill crept up the skin of my arms. "Did that keep the Spirits of Death away?"

Her eyes tightened. "Because we cut a covenant with Yahweh, one marked by the spilling of innocent blood, we were spared from the judgment."

The conversation between Eben and his master caught my attention, an argument over whether Eben should take the magnificent black horse and the wagon. Akensouris was insistent that it was a small sacrifice for what Eben had done to save him and his son. He vowed to serve Eben's god the rest of his days and teach his children to do so as well.

After the man walked away, having won the debate, the wagon was revealed to contain gold, jewels, and stacks of linens, along with food, clothing, and many beautiful instruments, made, I assumed, by Eben himself.

Years of slavery, both Eben's and his father's, paid for in full.

Before the shroud of night lifted, we were on the move. A large group—hundreds in front of us and perhaps a thousand behind—merged on the northeasterly trade road. A large contingent of foreign slaves, Syrians, Semites, and Kushites mingled among the Hebrews, all seizing this opportunity to escape their shackles. Many of these fugitives would no doubt disappear once they were free of the most populated areas and return to their homelands.

A few Egyptians traveled among this throng. Some seemed to be part of Hebrew households, perhaps joined by marriage. Some traveled alone. A couple of them noticed me staring, mirrored curiosity in their kohl-rimmed eyes.

So many dead. If all firstborn sons in the land were indeed annihilated, how could Egypt ever recover? Millions of men and boys had vanished into the underworld. Priests, soldiers, government officials, fathers, brothers, sons, infants—wiped out in one malevolent breath. What kind of a deity would do such a thing?

My father was among those millions this morning, without a doubt. On his boat far down the Nile, my father, the firstborn son in his family, breathed no more. Did he know what was coming? Did he fall asleep in peace? Or did fear for Jumo fill his last thoughts? Had he even thought of me since he'd signed my life away?

I had avoided thoughts of him since the day he turned his back on me and left me devastated on the floor, but now memories welled up, unbidden.

Only once had I been allowed to go on a trading run, aboard one of his graceful river boats. Anxious to experience the places I had visited only in my father's stories, I pleaded, cajoled, and used all my ten-year-old charms on him until he could do nothing but comply from sheer exhaustion.

We traveled only to Thebes—my mother would allow me to go no farther. But the sight of the grand palace, even through childish eyes, was unforgettable. The giant temples guarded by towering granite gods and past Pharaohs, the buzz and hum of trade in the never-ending marketplace, the towering limestone cliffs that launched Ra into the morning sky—I drank it in, grateful that my imagination did not do the grand city justice. It was so much more.

My father's strong hand enveloped mine as he navigated the maze of stalls and tradesmen hawking their wares. Older than my mother, silver already streaked his brows and neatly trimmed black hair, but he was tall and handsome in his daughter's eyes. I waited patiently as he dickered, always getting the best trades for the wines, linens, and other goods we brought from Iunu. Never raising his voice and with gentle care to keep their pride intact, he haggled with the tradesmen. As young as I was, I understood my father was talented as a trader, and pride swelled in my little breast as I watched him that day.

That evening, my father and I sat together on the boat, our feet dangling over the side, watching the sun blaze red, orange, and purple across the horizon. He told me of the tombs there on the western bank, of Pharaohs and Queens cradled within, enjoying the pleasures of the afterlife and the riches buried with them.

"But how can someone take things with them into the after-life, Father? Don't you become a spirit? Your ka parted from your body?"

"I don't know, sweet one. I have often wondered it myself." He shrugged, looking off into the distance. "I guess we must trust the priests, and thereby, the gods."

The water glittered, reflecting the vibrant palette of the sun-set.

"How can I believe something that I cannot see?" I rubbed my temple with two fingers.

He did not answer. Instead he studied my face intently until the strangest expression flitted across his features; it seemed to be a mixture of shock, surprise, and anger.

With an abrupt move, he stood and told me to lie down in the tent on the deck and go to sleep. Confused and seized with an anxiety I could not comprehend, I complied. I listened to the lap of the water against the hull for a long time, thinking of the spirits that roamed the western desert without their gold and silver and wondering why my father had seemed so upset. Finally, rocked in the gentle cradle of Mother Nile, I fell asleep.

Never again did my father take me with him.

He blamed me, I had decided, that my mother had almost died when she carried me. If not for skilled midwives, she would have, but my mother would never again bear a child. Jumo would be unable to care for our parents in their old age, and no other male heirs would be born to carry on my father's name. The disappointment behind his eyes had been palpable, and it grew with each year, as did his relentless drive for more riches.

Did my mother know he was now gone? She'd made the choice to leave with the suspicion she might not see him again. And with the death knell of Egypt's firstborn still hanging in the air, it was confirmed. With surreptitious glances, I watched her as we walked. Her dry eyes were enigmatic. I could not tell if they held sorrow or relief in their depths.

My heart was strangely absent of grief. In truth, I had grieved the loss of my father since that trip to Thebes. In that at least, today was no different than any other day. But I wondered: did my father enter the afterlife with a light heart? Or did Osiris find that his misdeeds outweighed his goodness? Could a man who sold his daughter be counted among those who deserved the pleasures of the afterlife? For that matter, what of a daughter who did not grieve her own father?

Annihilation covered the land. Carcasses of hundreds of animals bloated in the sun. Most were nearly rotted away, destroyed during the plague of the beasts, but many lay along the road, their breath stolen only a few hours ago, glassy eyes staring into the void.

Gone were the lovely date palm branches that used to line this road. Their wasted trunks stood like ghostly sentinels now, guarding a ravaged city. What the hail and fire hadn't destroyed, the locusts had finished. Only bleakness and desolation met my eyes.

My heart ached for the beauty and the lushness of my home from only a few months before. The former jewel and envy of the world, Egypt was no more. Barren now, she lay naked, stripped of her beauty, her children, her pride, and her power—the entire world witness to her violation and despair.

She was a desert, her golden-green fields now gray and desiccated. Tumbleweeds and sand already encroached upon my beautiful Iunu. The city of Ra, the city of jeweled gods and of the golden temple, now was only a city of despair, home to defeated deities and defeated people.

We walked for hours without rest, traveling the trade route running alongside a wide canal, thousands of feet churning up a haze of dust. I pulled a linen cloth from the wagon bed to drape over my head and keep the grit out of my mouth and nose.

As the road climbed, the ghosts of palm trees destroyed by hail and locusts became more and more sparse. Only hardy scrub brush and the occasional skeleton of a yew tree ushered us out of the Valley of the Nile.

When we reached the top of the ridge that offered our final view of the river, I slowed my steps and looked over my shoulder at the beautiful land that was no longer beautiful, nor bountiful. All that was left of my home was a wasteland, stripped of her green trees, her thriving farms, and the spirit of the people who worshipped her once-fertile soil.

The destruction made my stomach turn. What good could come of destroying Egypt? What kind of pernicious deity would ruin my home and my people? And here I was, at his mercy, stumbling along with this ragtag group of slaves, fleeing to the-gods-only-knew-where.

For the sake of my brother and my mother, I kept my face composed. The farther we traveled from Iunu, the smaller my mother looked. She seemed to be shrinking along with the outline of the pyramids in the distance, and I refused to add to her fears with my indecision.

I shrugged off my home, the Black Land, turned my face toward the road ahead, and placed one sandal in front of the other into the Red Land, the unknown.

22

A teeming mass of people, animals, makeshift tents, and belongings stretched out around us on the shore of an enormous lake. After a few failed attempts, Shira and I had finally succeeded in creating a crude tent from two linen sheets, some rocks, and the side of our wagon.

Shira shaded her eyes with one hand, a slow smile spreading across her face as she took in the sight of the massive congregation. "We came in seventy strong."

"Excuse me?" I swatted at a lazy fly buzzing near my ear and cringed at the memory of hundreds of bites.

"When Yaakov and his sons came to Egypt, there were but seventy in their group. Adonai multiplied us—well, just look around you." She waved her hand in an arc. "I wonder if Pharaoh himself is even aware truly how many people have exited his kingdom."

"I thought Pharaoh killed your sons? How is this possible if there are so few Hebrew men?"

Shira laughed. "You underestimate our women, Kiya."

172

I wrenched my eyes from the throng to look at her. "What do you mean?"

"You remember the story I told you of the midwives?"

How could I forget?

"Well, I told you the midwives rebelled and that even many Egyptians were unwilling to turn in the newborn boys. But, even so, Pharaoh sent his guards to search houses, randomly checking for babies of any age. Each time a precious little one was taken and thrown into the Nile, the stronger the will of the women became. They vowed to give birth to ten children in place of those they had lost."

The pain of losing a little one to such a gruesome death was unimaginable, but the drive to protect my brother had allowed me a glimpse into the strength of their hearts. I would have vowed the same.

"They became adept at hiding the babies. Some even took refuge in the limestone caves, among the tombs of the dead, until their children were weaned. The Egyptians thought the wails came from spirits of the dead." Shira smirked. "Once the little ones were of an age where they could be put to work—as young as four or five—Pharaoh's guards ignored them, figuring they were worth more alive than dead."

I pictured children younger than Shoshana and Zayna toiling in the sun, and acid burned my throat.

"When that Pharaoh died, his successor did not have the same bloodlust, so the extermination law was not enforced much anymore. He decided we were sufficiently subdued and was ambitious enough to know that it was foolish to kill more of his workforce."

What would Egypt do now, with the majority of that work-force gone? Who would build roads, temples, and cities? Who would dig the canals?

"From time to time, if whispers of rebellion arose, the guards would be sent out again to destroy babies, but it became rare over the years."

I looked again at the millions surrounding me. "A quarter of Egypt must be camping here on this shore."

"Possibly. And just think, after the Night of Death, how decimated that population is to begin with." She shook her head, and tears glistened on her lashes.

"Does that make you sad? The destruction of the land that enslaved you? Killed your people?" I could not believe it did.

She sniffed. "Yes, it does. Egypt was a beautiful land. It is the land of my birth. Everything I have ever known was there. Just like you."

I hadn't considered that. Shira was as much a child of Egypt as I was.

"And I have known many good and kind Egyptians, like Shefu and Akensouris." She patted Jumo's donkey. "Many treated Hebrews with respect, as more than chattel to be bought and sold. My heart is heavy with the thought of their sadness, their hopelessness, and their desperation."

I had forgotten about Shefu. Was he a firstborn? If not, today he would be grieving alongside Tekurah over the death of Talet. A stab of empathy surprised me at the thought of my former mistress weeping for her firstborn son. No matter the selfishness of the woman, no mother should outlive her child.

The depth and dreamlessness of my sleep caused disorientation for a few moments when I awoke. The sun had dipped only a little deeper into the west, but my sleep refreshed me, as if I had slept a whole night uninterrupted.

The sand molded to my body, its soft warmth cradling me—such a contrast to Tekurah's tiled floor. And waking next to my mother . . . maybe I was dreaming . . . but no, she smiled and caressed my face.

"My girl," she murmured, her voice still wrapped in sleep. "I missed you."

My mother had been my world before the day that world crumbled. Every minute I had been in Tekurah's house I had ached with missing her. But I could not speak it now. My mouth could not form the words.

Where was my mother that day, the day my father sold me? She never said good-bye, did not call my name, did not run after me. There must have been some explanation, some reason she could condone it—her love for me had always been written on her face. My splintered heart could not put one together with the other.

And the relationship with Shefu? Did she know the price I had paid for his love—the humiliation, the abuse?

She trailed a soft finger across the bruise over my eyebrow, and I winced. Her eyes held questions, but I knew she feared the answers as well.

"I think I will go see what I can do to help Shira and Zerah." I kept my voice low, remembering the linen walls around me.

She dropped her hand from my face.

I rummaged through a basket in the tent to find clean clothing, for I wore the same rugged slave garment Shefu had outfitted me with. I took one of my mother's, the kalasaris of a tradeswoman, and pulled it over my head, tying it closed with a strip of blue cloth. It may not be a fine linen gown, but I sighed as I let the soft material ripple around my shoulders.

A smile hovered on my mother's mouth. "I wondered if you were ever going to get rid of that hideous shift," she said with a wink.

I shrugged.

"I wish we could wear some of the fine linens we are carting around in the wagon." She sighed and lay back on the ground.

I snorted out a laugh.

"What?" She cocked her head.

"I just pictured the two of us in Tekurah's gowns, jewels, and wigs, tromping around the desert, leading our donkeys."

She joined in my hushed laughter until tears ran down our faces. Yet even our laughter seemed strained, on edge. Only a day away from the death of so many, my heart was too tender to voice the questions that needed answers, and I knew she felt the same. I would wait. But not much longer.

When I emerged from the tent, our campsite was deserted except for Shira and her elderly uncle, who huddled against a wagon wheel, weaving a rope from grasses he must have collected from the waterside. He gripped a great knot of strands between his toes as he braided. Already a good length of rope looped on the ground next to him.

He did not look up.

"*Boker tov,* Princess. Sleep well?" Shira winked.

I ignored her teasing. "Where is everyone?"

"Eben and Jumo have gone to trade for food. My mother and sisters are bathing at the canal. Shall we join them?"

"Yes, please. I need to be clean." I sniffed my hair. It reeked of donkey and sand. "Tekurah wouldn't even allow me in her presence." We both laughed.

I peeked in the tent to see if my mother wanted to come with us, but her eyes were closed. She looked peaceful for the first time since I'd knocked on her door—I could not bring myself to disturb her.

Shira and I headed down to the canal. As we wove our way through the camps, the immensity of the mass of people overwhelmed me. I hoped Shira remembered how to get back to our wagons, for I was completely lost. Everyone jumbled together in a chaotic mess.

We followed another group of women that seemed to be heading toward the same purpose, winding their way through the melee toward the water.

Children splashed about, enjoying the coolness. Their mothers called out to stay close and watch for crocodiles. I shivered.

Crocodiles, those silent, swift hunters, were well known in canals such as these. I hoped there were grates protecting this stretch from the giant killers.

Many of the women bathed in the nude, as I did, but some were discreet like Shira, wearing a shift in the water. I didn't see Zerah or the girls, but among this massive population, it would be hard to find anyone.

A small group of women gathered on the banks, their washed garments lying about them on the shore, drying in the midday sun. Shira approached them and in her strange melodic tongue, asked a question.

They all seemed to have an opinion about what she inquired—voices overlapped, growing louder. An argument broke out between two of them, and more than a few regarded me with open hostility.

Shira pleaded with them in her gentle voice, and to my amazement they stopped quarreling.

What an effect this girl had on people.

Something in her spirit soothed, calmed. Even Tekurah seemed more docile when in Shira's care. She was like honey: everyone was drawn to her—myself included.

My mother was awake and helping Zerah and the girls prepare a meal when we returned.

"And where have you been?" Zerah pointed a large wooden spoon at us. A quiver ran through my chest, but she smiled.

"It's good you made it in time. Eben and Jumo were about to steal your portion."

Jumo and Eben sat cross-legged on the ground next to each other, eating out of clay bowls. Jumo grinned at me, his mouth full, and shrugged. I made a face at him before I realized Eben's eyes were on me as well. I turned my head quickly, hoping he missed the flush in my cheeks.

"What do we have to eat?" Shira peeked into the pot in the middle of the fire. "Mmm, smells lovely."

"Eben found someone willing to trade some ibex for a gold necklace from one of the Egyptian packs."

"Ibex? Don't we have plenty of cattle or sheep for meat?" Shira filled a bowl and handed it to me.

There were thousands of sheep, cattle, and goats milling around the basin near the lake—surely enough to feed even this multitude.

"We must be careful not to overuse our resources," Eben said.

My mother sat down across from me. "It's only an eleven- or twelve-day walk to Canaan, is it not?"

Eben nodded. "It is."

"Then surely we wouldn't use all the animals in that time, would we?"

"Possibly not." He lifted a shoulder. "But if everyone eats whatever they want, and the journey takes longer than expected, we will be without meat at all. There must be some restraint, or there will be anarchy."

"Some of the women at the canal said we may not head for Canaan."

Eben raised a brow. "Where else would we go?"

"Some say we will go back." Shira broke off a piece of flatbread. "That we will invade Egypt."

"Why would you do that? How would slaves invade the most powerful country in the world?" My mother's golden eyes were wide and troubled.

I placed my hand on her arm. "Mosheh was a general as a young man, Mother, in Pharaoh's own army."

Zerah nodded. "The Kushites, the Syrians, the Canaanites, they all feared him. Many tribes gave up without a fight when his army invaded their villages. There was talk that he was a contender for the throne at one point . . . until he disappeared."

I glanced at a few of the Hebrews gathered around their own cook fires, seeing tattered clothes and the markings of years of sun on their weathered faces. Most of them had not fared as well as Shira's family during their years of captivity.

Here they were, following a leader they had probably never seen, trusting that he would take them to a freedom they had never known. Instead of sheep, Mosheh now led a shabby army of slaves, blindly following him into this forsaken desert.

As if he could hear my thoughts, Eben said, "We may look like slaves, but we have been hardened by our service. And many of us have been training, for months, to prepare for whatever may come."

Zerah glared at her son with what seemed to be frustration. Had she not known Eben had been developing military skills?

Ignoring her, he continued, "Regardless of whether we turn back or go forward, there will be conflict." He pointed to the northeast. "If we go up the Way of Horus to Canaan, there are garrisons all along the road. It's most likely we will take another route."

How long would we wander out here in the wilderness? We could very well run out of food. The beer was already running low, and the grain we carried would stretch only so far. Was this sorcerer Mosheh able to conjure bread out of rocks? Fresh water from air?

The fear that my family, led by me, faced more death and destruction pulled at me, weighing me down. In Egypt we would be traitors, but at least there we had Pharaoh to protect us.

Yet, Pharaoh hadn't really protected us, had he? The Lord of the Two Lands was powerless to keep his people from starvation, economic ruin, and pestilence . . . or from death.

Maybe the Hebrew God, with all his power to destroy, might be the best protection for my family, but would he still deign to protect us, as strangers among his people?

The dark glances from the women on the shore tugged at my thoughts. They didn't want me here. I was their enemy, their slavemaster, their oppressor. A traitor among my own people and a foreigner among theirs. Tekurah may have had the power to hurt my body, but this God the Hebrews served—what kind of a master would he be?

Before Shira and I finished our ibex stew, loud shouts echoed all around. We stood to see what had caused the commotion.

Young men walked through the camp, yelling as they went, calling heads of families to a meeting. They were instructed to move to the closest banner. Fifty or so makeshift banners lifted on the points of spears, hoisted aloft by men standing on wagons. These banners were spread throughout the multitude. Symbols decorated each banner—symbols that made no sense to me. Two banners stood in our vicinity, on one a coiled snake and on the other, a lion's head.

Eben was the head of his family. Some discussion followed whether Jumo should go, since he was Egyptian, but Eben insisted that he should.

Eben's obvious disdain for all Egyptians didn't seem to extend to Jumo. Of course, no one resisted my brother's charms, but somehow Eben didn't seem to fit into that category in my mind. The two men walked off together, Jumo hobbling deftly on his crutches. Thinking of Jumo as a man was foreign to me. He was my older brother, two years my senior, yet I had spent so much of my childhood protecting him. Now that my father was gone, he was indeed the head of our family—disabled or not.

My mother whispered in my ear before retreating to the shelter of our tent. "No matter where we go, we should not just be sitting here."

She was right. We should flee as fast as possible away from Pharaoh and his chariots, the most feared army in the world. As the shadows stretched long across the sand, millions of pairs of eyes kept diligent watch on the horizon. Each time a breeze stirred up dust in the west, my heart quickened.

Shira's uncle and his wife had kept to themselves, sitting with us only when we ate a meal. Otherwise, she stayed inside their shelter, and he sat with his back to a wagon wheel, weaving grasses into baskets and ropes. I wondered if he felt a little useless not being the head of a family and simply needed something to occupy his time and hands.

I whispered into Shira's ear. "Are your uncle and aunt childless?"

"They are. There were a few babes, but none ever took a breath outside the womb."

"But even so, is he not the head of the family? As the eldest male?"

"Oh, no. He is my mother's brother."

"He has no authority?"

"No. An older brother lives in Goshen. He bears the authority in my mother's family. She is of the tribe of Ephraim."

"Tell me about your father." I needed a distraction from the eternity of waiting for Eben and Jumo to return with news.

"I was only ten when he died. I have scattered memories since he was gone so much working for Akensouris, but I loved him so much. His stories, his loyalty to Yahweh, shaped who I am. Eben, however, was already apprenticed at the instrument shop with him at twelve years old. He was very close to my father, which is why his heart is still so shattered."

Unbidden compassion flooded through me at the thought of Eben's pain. "What happened?"

"Several years ago, there were rumblings again of a rebellion against the Pharaoh. Many of our people prayed fervently for the Deliverer to come, for Elohim to rescue us. A few men decided that they could not wait for a Deliverer that would never come. There was a failed attempt at escape by about three hundred people. They made it as far as this very canal, in fact." She pointed to where we had bathed earlier. "Pharaoh's chariots were faster than slaves on foot. They say the water ran crimson for days."

I shuddered. The shrieks of three hundred men, women, and children, pleading for mercy, seized my imagination. What would possess them to attempt the impossible? They were no match for the might of Pharaoh.

Shira lifted the question from my mind. "It was desperation that drove them. Those who attempted to escape had been driven to it by the whip of the overseers. They figured they were dead already under the heavy hand of the Pharaoh. Most of our men don't live past thirty-five or forty. They were laden with such extreme labors, bodies broken by years of carrying bricks and rocks to build the storehouses and palaces. Many women were violated by overseers, and their children were forced to labor as soon as they were weaned. How could they not dream of freedom or try to reach for it at any cost?"

I understood that desire all too well. "But your father was not among those who tried to escape, was he?"

"Oh, no, my father believed the Deliverer would come. He had been told of Mosheh's departure all those years before and was certain that he would return." Pride in her father shone on her face, but it faded quickly. "It was shortly after the massacre that Pharaoh decided to teach our people a lesson. He ordered his soldiers to cull one thousand men from each tribe and execute them publicly." She closed her eyes against the simmering tears.

"They weren't given the dignity of a quick death." The bitter voice startled me, and I jerked my head around.

Eben loomed behind me, his green-gray eyes reflecting the embers of the cook fire. "They were tied to stakes and whipped, one hundred lashes apiece, although most of them didn't make it to forty." He glared at me, fists clenched, loathing on his face.

"And you Egyptians stood by while my father was shredded by the spiked scourges of the soldiers. Some even cheered as they tore the life from his broken body."

"I was not there." I clenched my own fists, willing myself to remain calm.

A wave of emotion stole across his face, and then was gone. "It makes no difference."

23

A slight breeze fluttered the linen tent, casting transient shadows around me as I turned, again and again, trying to find a comfortable position on my mat.

My mother and I lay side by side in the tent. Her back was to me. She had not stirred for a long while.

This is foolish. Why am I dancing around demanding answers?

Sitting up, I steeled myself for the long-overdue conversation. If I could confront Tekurah, I must have the courage to speak to my mother.

"How could you do it?" I whispered softly, half hoping she would not hear me.

She startled me by turning over.

My heart raced.

"Shefu came to me," she whispered back. "It was his idea."

"But I thought Father . . ."

"No, Kiya, your father did not want to sell you."

I slowed my breath, not wanting to miss a word.

"We knew we were trapped. There was no other way to pay back our debts than to sell ourselves into servitude. Your father, myself, you, and Jumo." Sorrow edged her voice. "The debt was greater than even I knew."

"How could you not know? Everyone in town knew Father insisted on the finest of everything. His ships, jewels, our home."

"I knew that, but I assumed he was bringing in a fortune, and I had no concept of any such dealings or the cost associated with them. I didn't even know that he'd asked a loan of Shefu for the ships."

"You didn't know? Why didn't he tell you?"

"Your father did his best to hide his failings from me. It must have galled him to ask Shefu, of all people, for a loan. He must have figured that the return on the investment would pay Shefu back before I ever suspected."

"It was his greed that did this, subjected us to this misery."

"Yes, it was. But it was mine as well. I may not have known the cost or understood the burden of debt we were under, but I spent the gold. The gowns, the wigs, the jewels . . . we are both to blame. And for that, my beautiful daughter, I am so sorry." She placed a warm hand on my cheek. I resisted the urge to pull away, but still I winced.

"When Shefu came to me, offering to pay off our debts, to shield us from slavery to some unknown master who knows where, to protect our family from being permanently ripped apart, I jumped at the chance. You have such strength, my precious girl; I knew you would emerge on the other side of this in victory. Shefu promised to protect you, to ensure that no harm would come to you. It was either allow us all to be sold or put you under Shefu's care and trust him—as I always have."

I let her confession hang there. Sink in for a few moments. She must have known what my next question would be.

"Shefu. Tell me. I need to know."

She expelled a long, slow breath.

"Ah, Shefu. I loved him as a little girl. Our fathers were friends from childhood, and our families were close, but his mother was ambitious. She forbade us from marrying. My father had been a wise businessman but had nowhere near the clout that Tekurah's father did, as a high priest in the temple of Ra."

She reached up to caress the lapis necklace tied about her neck, tears glittering in the corners of her eyes. "He was my first love. My heart's desire. Everything I knew was wrapped up in Shefu. Without him, I was lost. And he, as well, was heartbroken. He vowed he would never love another. As did I."

"You didn't love my father?"

"I did. Well, in a way, I loved him. He adored me and pampered me, treated me like a queen. But not the way I loved Shefu. Shefu was my morning sun and my evening star."

"Tekurah always knew?"

She closed her eyes. "No. I am sure she had heard rumors of affection between me and Shefu, but he never told her."

"Then how did she find out? She surely knows. I dealt with the results of her knowledge every day."

Her expression was tortured. "I know, my dear. I'm so sorry. I was told how awful she was to you. I was helpless to do anything, but I knew you were strong. I knew you would endure."

"Yes." My tone was brittle as anger began to burn in my chest. "I endured. I endured daily humiliation, shame on every level, and complete lack of dignity."

Her eyes welled with tears, and her chin wobbled. "Please. My beautiful girl. Forgive my weakness. When I came home that day and you were already gone, I should have gone after you. Begged Shefu to reconsider. My heart splintered into a thousand pieces that day. If it weren't for Jumo, I would have come. I promise. I would have come."

What would I have done, in her place? Caught between love for her son and love for her daughter. I knew the answer. Jumo would not have survived slavery, and there was nothing I would not do to save him, even now.

A thought struck me. "But Tekurah—why was she so vengeful? It was not simple jealousy, Mother. The way she beat me that day . . . there must be another reason."

My mother was silent, her lips trembling.

"Mother, what happened?"

She pressed her eyes shut again, lashes fluttering on her cheeks, drawing a few quiet, ragged breaths before she spoke.

"Every day, sometimes twice a day, I gave offerings to Tawaret, believing that the goddess would protect me and my baby. But when Jumo was born, he was so small. So still. It wasn't until the midwife laid him at my breast that I even believed he lived."

A gentle smile played on her lips. "He looked up at me with those huge, dark eyes, and I was smitten. When we saw how rigid his little arms and legs were . . ." Acid leaked into her tone. "Even some of my closest friends suggested we should just let him pass and try again."

A spike of hot anger shot through me. What if my precious brother, with all his talent and goodness, had not been allowed to live? How many other beautiful children were wasted, exposed to the elements for the sin of being born unwanted or sickly? How many artists? How many brilliant minds?

"Jofare and I agreed that Jumo must live, that we would make sure he thrived, and we would beg the gods to heal him. When he was almost two and still had not walked, or even crawled, your father and I took him to the temple. We paid for spells, incantations, healing balms, anything the priests and priestesses recommended. Nothing worked. My heart was broken."

She stopped. Gauging my reaction? Gathering courage? "Your father was away on a trading run, as he was much in those days. I think perhaps it was his escape from the grief and disappointment. And Shefu . . ."

"You had an affair." My tone was flat.

She winced. "Yes. In a moment of weakness, I sent him a message. I was desperate for comfort from someone who loved me. And he came, to be a listening ear. I was so lonely and hurt, frustrated with the gods for not healing my little boy. And angry that your father chose to be away when I needed someone close. When Shefu held me in his arms, the love that I harbored deep in my heart rushed back, and we gave in to our desire for each other."

It was as I had expected. All of it. No wonder Tekurah was so harsh and vengeful. Not only a woman unloved by her husband, she had been betrayed and made a fool. If I had been in her position I would have been just as bitter, I had no doubt.

My mother looked at me, brows pinched, face wet with tears. "He loved you, though. As his own."

"Shefu?"

"No, Jofare."

I couldn't speak, my mouth could not form words.

"Shefu is your father, Kiya. It is why I knew I could trust him with you. That he would protect you and ensure your safety."

Spots of light flashed before my eyes, as if I'd been struck by temple incense again. My head swirled.

"But your father—Jofare, that is—I don't think he ever knew. If he did, he said nothing. Tekurah, though, she probably suspected our relationship from the beginning. Knowing her, she may have had spies following Shefu. When you were born, you looked so much like me, I hoped no one would suspect my infidelity. But Shefu is there too, his strength, his intelligence. Sometimes when you would gaze up at me with a certain look in your eye, I would catch my breath. You are so like him in some ways."

That must have been what my father, what Jofare, saw that day on his boat in Thebes. Something in my face proved that I was not his own. He saw his friend Shefu in my expression. As I am sure his wife did as well.

"I wonder why Tekurah never exposed you."

"Tekurah is shrewd, Kiya. She knew that exposing us would only make her look foolish. Instead, she held it over Shefu's head. With the information, she ensured her every heart's desire would be fulfilled."

"Does Jumo know?" My heart skipped a beat. Jumo was not my full brother.

"No, I doubt it. Although you and I know that Jumo sees much more than anyone else. It's possible he has caught a glimpse. But even if he did know, it wouldn't change his immense love for you."

Sefora and Liat. They were my half siblings. The yearning I'd felt toward them, that I could gather them to me like an older sister, must have been understanding beyond my own comprehension. And I would never see my little brother and little sister again.

I dug my toes into the sand, desperate to feel the strength of the bedrock buried beneath.

My heart throbbed with the weight of the secrets she had unloaded on me and the lack of solid foundation upon which to stand. My gods were not all-powerful. My father was not my father. My master was not my master. And my mother was only human, not the goddess I had lifted her up to be.

Everything I knew, built my every belief upon, drifted away like dust in the breeze. I floated, unbound to the earth, unsure of where my destiny lay, grasping at false memories and inherited lies.

24

I patted my little donkey's brown neck as he munched a stray tuft of grass. He pivoted his head and butted my arm, his white muzzle nipping at my sleeve playfully, long whiskers tickling my skin. "Well, little friend, you had a day and a half of rest. I wonder how much farther your faithful legs will take us." I scratched his cheek and he pressed against me, white-lined eyes rolling back in pleasure. He blinked long lashes slowly and watched me as if he understood every word.

Leaning down, I whispered, "Do you speak Egyptian? Or Hebrew?" He twitched the ear, slapping my face with the long appendage. I laughed and left him to finish his last meal before we departed. Eben and Jumo had brought back news that we were to pack and be ready to move before sunset, but that was all we knew.

I found Shira packing cook pots and supplies in her wagon and offered to help. "How do we know which banner to assemble under?" I asked.

"We are of the tribe of Levi." Her wide smile radiated pride in her heritage.

"How do slaves even know what tribe they belong to after

four hundred years, especially being scattered all over the country?" I handed her a basket of clay mugs, and she pressed it into the corner of the wagon bed.

"Well, the tribes are broken into clans, with a head over each clan, and clans are broken into households, and then finally individual families, and the family authority passes to the firstborn sons." She handed me the end of a sheet to fold. "In the last two hundred years since being enslaved by Pharaoh, there has been some confusion over which family belongs with which clan due to intermarriage, but every family holds fast to the knowledge of which tribe they are descended from. It's passed from father to son with great pride. You'll see . . . everyone knows their tribe."

When our belongings were loaded, donkeys and Eben's black horse watered, and the girls perched atop the overfull wagon beds, we followed the river of vehicles and people streaming toward the clumps of banners spread out across the flat, sandy plain.

The ensuing confusion would have been comical if it hadn't been so frustrating. After hours of maneuvering, our little party found our way to the banners of the Levite tribe. The hastily painted symbol on the white banners seemed to be some sort of fish or sea serpent, but the design was difficult to distinguish in the waning sunset.

Once all of the tribes were gathered, with wagons and livestock interspersed, we waited for more hours. Would a ram's horn signal the march eastward?

The last brilliant-red Egyptian sunset I would see, possibly for the rest of my life, faded into twilight and then melted behind the western hills.

No shofar announced our departure. As soon as a few brave stars opened their eyes to the dusk, our signal arose in the east. Perched atop the mountain of belongings, Shoshana bounced her legs against the side of the wagon, impatient, as we all were, to leave the lakeside. "Look there." She pointed to a small bluish glow at the edge of the horizon. "What is that?"

Soon everyone looked toward the east. Shouts of "Look!" and "There it is!" muted into awed silence as the shimmering orb grew higher and floated toward us. Blue-white light began to leap and dance and then, stretching toward the heavens, it swelled into a towering pillar of swirling brilliance. Its glow lit the evening like the sun itself. The Hebrew God had sent a pillar of light to guide us.

Most people fell to their knees; some covered their heads with their hands or clothes. Others knelt not out of holy reverence, but in sheer terror, my mother among them. I restrained myself, with everything in me, not to follow suit. Would this terrible god-of-the-slaves continue his campaign of destruction of our people even here, out in the wilderness? My knees shook. I glanced at Jumo, expecting my fear to be mirrored in his expression, but to my surprise, the blue light illuminated a look of inexplicable peace on his face.

Jumo had witnessed the devastating effects of the Hebrew god's wrath upon our country, the broken lives, broken people, the death and destruction left in his wake. What reason would he possibly have for such contentment while witnessing a manifestation of this god's power?

This fearful display terrified me. I needed to get away from it, all of it. It was my fault we were in the wilderness. We couldn't go back to Egypt, that much was clear, but there must be somewhere we could go and begin a new life far away from this fearsome god and his strange people.

Shira came to stand with me and slipped her hand into mine.

"Isn't it beautiful?" Her whisper was full of awe.

I nodded my assent, but a shiver slithered up my back.

She stood transfixed. "It's like we are on the edge of something. Something wonderful."

Or something terrible.

"Look." She pointed at the swirling pillar of blue fire. "It stopped moving. I wonder if that is near where Mosheh and Aharon are."

"Aharon?"

"His brother. Haven't I told you that Aharon speaks for Mosheh?"

"Can't he speak for himself?"

She shrugged. "Mosheh has some sort of trouble speaking clearly. Aharon simply helps him vocalize what Yahweh reveals."

"Why would your god choose a prophet that can't speak?" I regretted the sharp accusation as soon as it flew past my lips.

She ignored my rudeness. "I don't know. But sometimes it seems to me like Yahweh chooses to work through the most unlikely of people."

"What do you mean?"

She looked into my eyes. "Our forefather Avraham was the son of an idolmaker, too old to have children, yet Yahweh blessed him with the child of promise. Yaakov stole the birthright from his brother, and yet he is the father of our people."

She turned back to the flaming cloud. "Perhaps Adonai chose Mosheh to show us all this is not about Mosheh, but about Yahweh."

The companies of Hebrew tribes worked to situate themselves in columns in front of the pillar of fire. The effort was anything but smooth. In fact, it was a disaster, millions of people jockeying to keep themselves and their livestock in lines hundreds wide. People mixed with bleating sheep, thousands of cattle, every shape and size of wagon, pushcart, and oxcart. Even the strange irony of a few chariots drawn by fine white horses driven by bedraggled slaves stood out among the throng.

Most were on foot, the majority of them unshod, although some sported beaded and gilded sandals to match their recently inherited fine linen clothing and golden jewelry.

The blue fire burned so bright we snuffed our useless torches in the dirt. Shira went to walk with her family, and I pushed the torch into the cart behind Jumo's donkey. Jumo, still silent, faced the swirling light, his silhouette clear against the brightness.

The mass ahead of us finally shuffled forward, so I tapped the donkey on his hindquarters. He responded with a jolt, perhaps as spellbound as Jumo by the phenomenon. The cart jerked forward, and a back wheel slammed against a large rock partially buried in the sand. One of the spokes shattered, and the wheel broke free of the axle.

My mother and I tried to grab the cart before it toppled, but we were too late. Our baskets and clay pots tumbled onto the ground, spilling linens, clothing, and food into the dirt. Jumo slid off the donkey and tried to help right the cart—to no avail. Shira's family was ahead of us and unaware of our predicament. I called to them, but the maelstrom of shouts and animal noises swallowed my voice. We might lose them in the crowd, and once they were lost, we would not find them again for a long while.

"Let's try again to lift the cart, Mother. Jumo, can you get the wheel?"

Jumo limped to the wheel while my mother and I attempted to lift the cart. Hundreds of people streamed about us, gawking, but none offered help.

I pressed my feet against the rock that waylaid us and pushed at the cart with my back. To my great surprise, it moved.

Astonished, I looked around. An Egyptian held up our cart as Jumo pushed the wheel back onto the axle. The man instructed Jumo to press rocks and sand around the wheel to hold it in place while he retrieved a spare one from his own wagon.

The man turned to me with a wide smile. "Weren't you traveling with friends? Perhaps you should alert them."

"Hmm? Oh . . . yes." I turned to my mother. "I'll be right back."

It took me a while to catch up to Shira's family, but luckily they had stopped already, wondering what had happened to us.

"I will help, Ima." Eben handed the lead rope of the black horse to his mother and gestured with a flourish. "Lead the way."

Pushing against the relentless stream of bodies, animals, and vehicles was nearly impossible. Eben moved ahead of me, snaking through the mob. I restrained the temptation to grasp the back of his tunic for fear I would lose him in the chaos.

The Egyptian had already fitted his spare wheel to our cart. He was tall, almost as tall as Akhum. He dressed in plainer clothing, just a simple linen kilt, but was nearly as handsome as Akhum as well, with short-cropped black hair and wide shoulders.

"Thank you so much, Sayaad. I don't know what we would have done had you not stopped," my mother was saying. "Kiya, I'm so glad you made it back. I was worried about you. Sayaad has been so wonderful fixing the cart for us."

"It was nothing at all, my lady." He bowed low. "As head of my master's stables, I was more than once charged with repairing broken wheels."

"You are a slave?" I blurted.

He laughed and tipped his head toward me. "Yes, I *was* a slave. But we are all free now, are we not?" He glanced at Eben, who stiffened beside me. "I had better get back to my own wagon. Are you all right to move on?" Sayaad gestured to the east.

"Yes—"

Eben interrupted with a cold "We are fine, thank you" and then shocked me by wrapping his long fingers around my arm and turning me back toward the cart.

He released me as if his hand were on fire. "Jumo, do you need help mounting the donkey?"

Jumo shook his head, expertly pulled his unruly body onto the donkey, and swung one leg over its back. I handed him his crutches. A strange little smile played about his lips.

My wide eyes and raised palms questioned him, but he just shook his head with a smirk and turned his face toward the light.

25

fter a long night following the unearthly blue fire eastward, I was almost grateful for the year and a half of hard work under Tekurah's hand. No longer was I a soft maiden with tender feet and weak muscles—my body was hard and strong, my feet callused and sure. Everyone around me, with the exception of a few stray Egyptians, had lived a life of harsh servitude. Our bodies were prepared for days of grueling marching in the wilderness.

As the sunlight grew stronger, the fire at the head of the multitude transformed. It became an enormous column of cloud, shimmering an unearthly bluish-white as it roiled and swirled across the landscape. I was glad to be far back in the throng and away from the towering, ghostly column.

The trade road stretched out endlessly to the east. A few hills lay to the south of us, but as far as the eye could see in all other directions, the land was barren. No streams, no trees; only a few squat shrubs broke the monotony of the view.

When the Cloud finally stopped during the heat of the day, we prepared a quick repast of the flatbread from last night's supper, some of the last of the water we carried in our wagons, and salted meat from Zerah's stores. We set up our shelters quickly and rested, knowing that sundown was only a few hours away and the Cloud may not wait for twilight to start moving again.

I woke after three or four hours of satisfying rest and lay on my mat for a while, listening to the overlap of voices and languages: men arguing, women gossiping, the joyous sounds of children scampering about, playing games of stick-throwing, chase, and hide-and-seek. The sounds of free people enjoying their life without shackles. I envied them. A tether seemed to be latched somewhere under my ribcage. I felt the pull of it more and more with each step I took away from my homeland. The enormous cloud hovered to the east of us. I turned my back to it.

Stretching, I came out of our little shelter, leaving my mother to sleep and therefore avoiding the brittle tension between us. Although I understood the reason for her choices, my heart still ached from the revelation of lies, secrets, and betrayal. I had wanted to hear that she fought for me, that she tried to follow me, or rescue me, that my father was the only one to blame. But with her admission, my mother had destroyed the image of perfection I had built in my mind.

Jumo emerged from the tent he shared with Eben with his usual big smile. When would he shave that beard shadowing his face? I didn't like it.

He tousled my hair and put his arm around my neck. "Nice . . . day. Paint . . . for . . . you?"

Only Jumo could act as if racing through the desert, fleeing from a vicious army, was completely normal.

I laughed. "Please do paint for me. It will keep my mind off this." I gestured around me. "It's been so long since I have watched you work."

He smiled and asked for his box of paints and brushes. The

box, carved with intricate swoops and swirls and scenes of foreign gods, was a gift from my father from a voyage in the Northern Sea, and was Jumo's greatest treasure.

Our father, though disappointed in Jumo's affliction, had been as charmed by his sweet spirit as the rest of us and had doted on him. Did Jumo grieve for him? I was afraid to ask for fear of revealing my new knowledge about the man I had called Master.

I fished the box out from under a pile of goatskins given to us by Shira's family, whose laden-down wagons overflowed with gifts pushed at them by desperate Egyptians. My poor little donkey pulled this wagon along the bumpy trade road, carrying all the spoils of Egypt. He lay in the sand now, legs folded underneath him, enjoying his rest. I ran my fingers up his prickly mane and he huffed at me. His white-tipped ears twitched, but he kept his eyes closed.

I gave the box to Jumo and settled on a nearby overturned basket, a piece of scavenged flatbread in my hands, ready to watch the magic of my brother with a paintbrush in his hand.

Sitting on the ground, he tossed his crutches to the side and winced as he crossed his unruly legs with his hands.

He began with a large jar, empty of the precious last of the beer we'd brought with us. I wondered if we might have time to make more—we still had a few loaves of barley bread tucked in the wagon bed. We should be able to let it ferment, even on the move.

Forced to hold one arm steady with the other, his movements at first seemed awkward, but once Jumo's brush touched the jar, it flew. I had forgotten just how transporting it was to watch him work. When Jumo painted, his disabilities vanished.

He decorated the upper rim with blue lotus flowers—so life-like I could almost breathe in their intoxicating scent. Then he painted a scene of three people, walking together, donkeys plodding along behind, pulling overflowing carts, an illustration of this sojourn from our homeland. Looking closer at the faces of the people, I recognized the three of us. My mother and I walked with downcast faces, but Jumo's enormous smile blazed, even in still life.

No matter that I did my best to paint myself glad about our escape, to protect him from the crippling grief that overcame me at times—he knew. Jumo watched. He listened. Perhaps being unable to verbalize easily made him more aware of his surroundings—more perceptive than the rest of us.

"Jumo . . ."

His rich brown eyes locked on mine with sudden intensity. "I . . . had . . . dream. Go . . . with . . . Hebrews."

I gasped and held his gaze. I whispered, "You had a dream that we should go with the Hebrews?"

He nodded, slow and firm.

"Before the Night of Death?"

He dipped his chin again.

He'd come so willingly, without a word. I had assumed that he simply trusted me, but Jumo had experienced some sort of mystic vision.

"This dream, what—?"

"Shalom, good morning!" Shira came up behind me, cutting off my questions.

"Or . . . well, good afternoon. Isn't it a lovely day?" she trilled, seemingly, like Jumo, oblivious to the prospect of Pharaoh's army hurdling over the western ridge at any moment. When she saw the magnificent artwork Jumo had created on the jar, she caught her breath. "Oh! Jumo! Did you paint this?"

He grinned at her, never too humble to enjoy someone discovering his talent for the first time.

She crouched on the ground next to the jar. "May I? Is it dry?"

When he nodded, she traced the flowers around the rim with

a delicate finger, entranced by their beauty. "As if one could reach out and pick it . . . extraordinary."

"Jumo is a natural artist, never taught by a master." I didn't even try to resist gloating. I beamed at my brother. "His art was the main draw to my mother's market stall."

"I can certainly see why, don't you, Eben?" Shira looked over my shoulder.

There he was, lurking again, glowering.

"Yes." His eyes locked on mine for a brief moment, then flicked back to his sister. "Jumo shared some of his other drawings with me. They are well done."

I blinked, stunned. I knew Eben and Jumo were tentmates, but had they become friends? Although they were the same age, I did not see them as compatible in any way. They were in different realms—Jumo with his effortless, warm spirit; Eben, abrasive and bitter. What could they possibly have in common?

"Well . . . done? You . . . wish . . . you . . . could . . . paint . . . like . . . me!" Jumo threw back his head and laughed loudly.

Eben's face transformed, and his green eyes softened.

A fissure had started inside me the day he killed the cobra to protect me, lengthened whenever he held me in his gaze, and widened when I heard of his pain at his father's death. But at the genuine smile on his face, warm melodic laugh, and his obvious affection for my brother, it became a gaping need that threw me into complete disarray. My resolution to part ways with the Hebrews and their fearsome god wavered.

However, I worried the chasm between us was too wide to bridge.

26

Sayaad strode into our campsite with the carcasses of two gray geese hanging from his large fists. "Good day!" He handed the geese to my mother with a bow. "These girls have not laid since we've been traveling, so I thought I would share."

"Oh my, thank you, Sayaad." My mother tipped her head in gratitude. "Won't you join us?"

"I will!" He grinned, and then winked at me. "I must admit that may have been my true motive."

I raised my brows and turned away.

"I've been searching for you for the three days we have been camped here," he said.

She gestured for him to sit. "Please then, do stay. Kiya and I are working on the meal."

I scrutinized Sayaad out of the corner of my eye as he sat down on an overturned crate nearby, arms crossed and long legs stretched toward me. Obviously he was a man used to working outside, with skin burnished bronze and thick kohl protecting his eyes. Broad-shouldered like Akhum, he was strong and carried himself with the aura of one aware of his masculine appeal. But unlike my betrothed, his eyes were an intense blue, like lapis stone. I had never seen the like in any Egyptian. Against his dark skin, they glowed, almost like the pillar of fire in the desert night.

"Sayaad, are you from Iunu, as we are?" My mother placed the geese on our makeshift table fashioned from a plank and two overturned clay pots, then sat cross-legged in the sand.

"No, I came from a small town farther up the Nile, on a small branch."

"You were near Avaris?" She plucked goose feathers and placed them in the basket.

I knelt, picked up the other goose, and began tugging feathers too, glad of the occupation for my hands.

"No, a bit farther west. My master was a vintner. The soil there was perfect for wine."

My mouth watered at the memory of Shefu's crisp wine on my tongue. I glanced at my mother. Her eyes stayed on the goose, but she swallowed hard.

"So why are you here?" I chanced a look at those blue eyes.

They pierced my own for a moment. "I couldn't stay away."

Tingles whispered up my spine, causing me to stammer. "Uh . . . uh . . . no, I mean, how did you come to be among the Hebrews?"

A smirk pulled at his lips. I could tell he enjoyed throwing me off-center. "My master was a firstborn son and died on the Night of Death. His wife was too grief-stricken to care that most of the slaves in the household disappeared the next morning and so"—he shrugged—"I left too."

"What made you decide to join this journey?"

"We heard the tales of the Hebrews fleeing Egypt. I figured one escape was as good as any other. So I came with a group of other refugees from my master's household. A small group on foot had little problem catching up with millions of men, women, children, and animals." He circled his hand in the air.

"Why not go home to your own family?" I tried to keep my eyes on the goose, instead of his smooth, clean jaw, the cleft in his chin, and the strength of his bared chest.

"My family is gone. Dead, long ago."

I caught my breath, although the truth did not surprise me. Death was everywhere, it seemed. It surrounded us like a mist. "I'm so sorry."

He shrugged and brushed away my apology. "It was long ago, I only know Egypt now."

This did surprise me, although a slight accent slipped through his fluency. "You are not Egyptian?"

"My mother was. We lived in a small village in Moabite territory. I was kidnapped by slave traders and brought to Egypt after my village was destroyed by marauders."

"How old were you?"

"Ten."

"So young." My mother shook her head, tongue clucking against her teeth.

"Old enough." He chuckled.

I glanced at him. "Old enough for what?"

"To remember where I came from and plan to escape when I had the chance." He bobbed his head. "And so, here I am."

Sayaad told us of his master's vineyards, obviously proud of his own part in their production. "My master was the richest vintner in the Lower Delta region. Of course, my fellow slaves and I made sure to collect our fair share before we left."

"Did his wife give you treasures like many of the other Egyptian masters?" I asked.

Sayaad shrugged and raised his eyebrows. He wore thick gold bands on both well-muscled arms, two gold chains about his neck, and leather sandals that rivaled any of Shefu's. "More or less."

I placed the unleavened bread on a flat rock heated by the fire. Adept now at flattening the lumps of dough and stretching them across the surface, I waited until brown bubbles appeared and then flipped them over with a stick. Our ration of flour was running low, so these circles were smaller than the last time.

My mother roasted the geese on a makeshift spit, without spices or herbs. The fat dripped and hissed into the fire, teasing my clenching stomach as we waited for the others to return. Zerah and the girls had gone to fetch more water from a nearby spring, and Eben and Jumo were at a meeting with the elders. Again.

It seemed all the elders did was assemble and, as Jumo relayed to me, argue. Each day the chaos around us became more pronounced. Millions of slaves in the desert without a clear destination was a volatile situation. Arguments broke out—a goat stolen, someone's cow trampling through another family's campsite, spilled water stores—and many voices clamored for justice. The few tribal elders gathering each day were unprepared to deal with the demands of such a vast crowd. A crowd becoming increasingly restless as days wore on.

The inevitable could only be ignored for so long. Millions of Pharaoh's slaves wandered in the desert, carting around untold amounts of gold, silver, and jewels on the backs of worn-out donkeys and oxen. He considered us his property. He may have lost one battle, but Pharaoh never lost a war. He would come. I could almost feel his breath on my neck.

As we waited for the geese to cook, Sayaad told us how he had traveled with his master on a number of overland trading runs to Canaan and Phoenicia. These eastern wastelands we walked through now, still considered part of Egypt, were familiar to him.

"If we continue along this road, the Way of the Wilderness, it will take us into Etham. To reach Canaan we will have to change direction soon." He gestured to the northwest.

I remembered the stories my father had told of his travels and knew the road he spoke of. "If we are trying to reach the land of Canaan, why did we not take the northern trade route directly out of Egypt?"

Sayaad arched one brow, perhaps surprised at my knowledge.

"Mosheh might be leading us away from the Canaanite outposts, avoiding confrontation," my mother said.

Sayaad shrugged. "Possibly . . . but our numbers would more than overwhelm any outpost." He shook his head. "I would venture to guess that any outpost that lay in wait for this multitude would be empty by the time we arrived."

Most of the men in this company were former slaves, but they were well-armed, thanks to the Egyptians who'd ushered us out of the country with any gift they could lay hands on. Swords, bows, chariots, armor—at least half the men held some sort of weapon in their possession. Whether they were able to use them to any effect was another matter. Sayaad pointed out that only a handful of trained soldiers or mercenaries traveled among the throng.

"If an army came against us, overwhelming numbers or not, these slaves would have no chance of winning at hand-to-hand combat." He scowled, looking off toward the shadowy hills in the west, as if expecting Pharaoh's soldiers to plow across the horizon at any moment.

As well they might. I shivered.

"If we continue traveling along the Way of the Wilderness . . . it travels south toward the sea and then around the tip of it toward Midian. I have never been along this way." Sayaad rubbed his jaw. "I wonder what could possibly possess Mosheh to lead us this way."

"If you haven't noticed, Mosheh is following the Cloud."

I whipped my head around. Eben stood directly behind me, glaring at Sayaad. I hadn't heard him or Jumo as they returned.

"Perhaps, but if Mosheh is the great sorcerer he is rumored to be, he must be directing the Cloud in some way." Sayaad gave Eben a permissive smile.

"You know little of our God." Eben walked out of the campsite, Jumo trailing behind as usual. Even Jumo refused to look at me.

Sayaad laughed. "What was that about?"

"He hates us."

"You and me?" He smirked. He liked the sound of that.

"Egyptians in general."

Even as I said it, however, I knew it wasn't true. Eben's shattered heart had opened to Jumo. I had even caught glimpses of him softening toward me, unless my hopeful imagination deceived me.

"Ah." Sayaad leaned forward, elbows on knees and fingers bridged under his chin. "And what do you think of this . . . Yahweh? Are you convinced of his power?"

"How could you not be? He destroyed our entire country."

"So you have decided to devote yourself to the Hebrews' God?" His brows lifted over those brilliant blue eyes.

"No." Yahweh may be real, but his unbridled power frightened me.

"Why did you come on this journey, if not to follow Yahweh?"

"To save my brother and to be free. So far no deity has done anything except ignore my prayers. I don't need another deaf god."

27

I see you still have not learned how to balance a jug." Shira's teasing laughter echoed off the narrow canyon walls.

"Perhaps not, but at least the water I fetch today will be for my own use, instead of Tekurah's." I wrinkled my nose at Shira and adjusted my grasp on the earthen vessel against my hip.

The narrow canyon cradled lush green between its meandering halls that had been smoothed by eons of yearly floods. The early rains had done their work, leaving behind a trail of verdant plant life. The distant mountains still retained their caps of snow, which meant that there would be many runoff streams threading their way through these foothills. A gift to the millions, desperate for water.

Eben and Jumo walked ahead of us, picking their way through the wadi, leading us to a stream they had scouted not far from our camp.

I hoped no one else had yet found this stream, as I was anxious to avoid any more pointed stares from the other Hebrews. Very few of them regarded me with anything other than open suspicion, and I was grateful that Shira's family had somehow accepted us into their clan.

My mother and Zerah, both widowed now, had become quick friends in spite of their obvious differences. Zerah had taken my mother under her capable wing, and as a result, my mother already seemed stronger.

Eben, too, had embraced a member of my family—Jumo limped behind him wherever he went, whether he was attending meetings with the elders or negotiating trades with other travelers for food and other essentials.

Jumo had spent the majority of his life cast to the side. Playmates were scarce for a boy with uncontrollable legs and a twisted tongue. The other children mocked him cruelly, and I was always quick to his defense. Even as a tiny child of three or four, it infuriated me when someone called him a name or parodied his affected speech. I would fly at them, scolding and chasing them away. When it came to Jumo, fear did not shadow me.

Ahead of us, Eben walked with a steady pace, not slowing for Jumo on his crutches but picking out the most even ground he could, accommodating my brother without condescension. I had watched the two of them across the campfire last night, laughing together. Eben listened intently to Jumo, not a hint of impatience on his face as my brother faltered through the jumble of his words. For the first time, another man treated Jumo as something other than broken.

So why did it bother me so much?

"There, do you hear it?" Shira's voice was nearly swallowed by the mournful coo of a startled dove in an acacia nearby. She cocked her head. "The water is near."

I had expected a trickling stream, but the rushing water pummeled the rocks as it descended from a ridge more than fifteen cubits high. Eben and Jumo crouched next to the large pool gathered at the bottom, scooping water over their heads with their hands.

Standing, Eben shook his head like a stray dog, droplets spraying everywhere. He turned, dripping and laughing, his wild hair clinging to his face, eyes dancing with amusement. Water trickled down his nose, tracing a path across his full lips and off his beard. The urge to swipe back the sodden tangles with my hand unnerved me. I looked away, feigning interest in one of the oleanders that had pushed its way out of a crevice in the rock, determined to flout its pink blossoms in the desert heat.

"Paradise!" Shira clasped her hands to her chest as she surveyed the moss-slicked rocks and the emerald pool at the foot of the waterfall. "I can't wait to jump in."

The same desire called to me, and I slipped off my sandals, eager to wade into the cool water.

Eben and Jumo left us to scout the area nearby, giving us privacy. However, Eben assured us that they were within earshot should there be any trouble. Shira and I washed in the pool, scrubbing the grit from our hair and faces and floating on our backs in the green water.

We then lay on the shore in the sun, allowing our clothes to dry as Shira entertained me with more stories of her people— Yosef and his brothers' betrayal; Yaakov and Rachel, whose love endured fourteen years of forced labor. I folded my arms behind my head and watched the sparse clouds glide south, feeling somehow connected to these foreign people from long ago.

Then Eben's face hovered over me, blocking out the early-morning sun I had been enjoying. "If I was a leopard stalking you, both of you would already be dead." Frustration was clear in his voice.

I made a face at him. "At least I would die clean."

Humor replaced annoyance in his expression, and one eyebrow

lifted high. "I do not think the beast would care how much you smelled like a donkey if he could get a taste of your lovely neck."

His eyes widened, as if shocked he had said such a thing, and he quickly turned to his sister. "There is a stand of acacias a bit higher up." He pointed back the way he and Jumo had returned from. "Jumo isn't able to climb the rocks. Can you come with me and help me drag the trees back after I cut them down? I'd like to bring back some tent poles for Ima."

Standing, I stretched my back. "I'll go. Let Shira rest, she's too little to drag trees around anyhow." I waved a hand at my brother, who leaned against his crutches nearby. "Jumo can stay here with her."

Eben looked back and forth between Jumo and me, then shrugged and handed my brother his short sword. "All right." He pointed a commanding finger at Shira. "Pay attention. And scream if you need me."

A surprising flicker of fear crossed Shira's face, but she remained silent. Remembering the attack she had endured back in Egypt, I understood her reticence at being alone with a man, but Jumo? I had serious doubts that he even had any idea how to use the sword that now hung limply from his hand.

Scrambling up the steep slope behind Eben, I considered his quick deflection after his comment about my neck earlier. I had sensed a spark of something in the air between us, but he still seemed uncomfortable around me, as if my presence was disconcerting to him. Perhaps I was still a constant reminder of his father's death.

The small stand of acacias was tucked against the hillside, a few sturdy saplings elbowing in among the mature trees. Grateful for the shade, I slipped beneath the spread of one of the larger ones, but not before checking for coiled serpents among its tangled branches that might also be benefiting from the dappled shade. Eben was right to be angry with me for not being cautious; this was dangerous country, stalked by wild beasts and venomous snakes.

Eben removed the small hatchet he had carried in his belt and set to work on one of the taller saplings, which stood only a handspan above his head. I watched him as he struck the tree in smooth, rhythmic strokes, thinking of his kindness to my brother and the protective, fatherly way he interacted with Zayna and Shoshana. They adored him. Not a meal went by when one or the other wasn't in his lap. He patiently endured their endless questions, incessant chatter, and demands for his attention. How well he had stepped into the role of father for the girls, who had probably never known their own. Zerah must have been newly pregnant with Zayna when her husband had been killed.

A sharp cry from Eben sent me scrambling out from my protective cover.

"What is it?"

He hissed in a breath through clenched teeth, trying to survey the damage. "Didn't move fast enough. Thorns sliced my arm on the way down."

"Here, let me." I stepped close to look at the jagged path the thorns had slashed down his bicep and around the inside of his arm. Gently, I removed a couple of thorn tips that had broken off and embedded in his skin. One scratch was particularly deep, and I winced as I ran a finger down the length of it. "This will need salve."

He stiffened, his muscles tensing beneath my touch. When I looked up, he was staring at me, a pained expression on his face, and his eyes turned darkest jade. The little crescent scar at the top of his cheekbone stood out against his sun-burnished skin, distracting me. Where had it come from? A fight?

Caught in the snare of whatever was pulling me toward him, I allowed myself to gaze back at him, to consider crossing the divide and drawing his wounded arm around my waist.

Akhum's face suddenly loomed in my mind, repeating the accusation he had flung at me that night in the garden. *No one will want your precious heart.*

I released Eben's wrist and stepped back, my pulse rushing like a flood. Grasping for something to say, I stumbled over my words. "Thank the gods you moved as fast as you did, those thorns can do terrible damage."

"And which god do you give thanks to?"

Eben's razor-sharp question caught me off guard. I stared at him, unable to give him any answer. My gods had little power. Their weakness, or apathy, had been proven by months of allowing Egypt to suffer under the destructive hand of Yahweh. And as I told Sayaad, I could not truthfully say I followed Eben's God, for what care did Yahweh have for me? My feet may have been following the Cloud, but only until I found another way to freedom.

"None of them. It is only a habit to say such a thing."

He lifted a brow. "You come with us, but you have no loyalty to Yahweh?"

"My loyalty is to my brother. It is for him that I am here. The gods care nothing for him, or for me."

A drop of water splashed against my cheek.

Eben looked up at the sky and then over my shoulder. "We have to go. Now."

I lifted my hand to shade my eyes, squinting at the lone cloud above us. "It should pass quickly."

"No." He pointed behind me. "It's raining south of here. In the mountains. The wadi could fill at any moment."

Understanding rushed at me full force. Rain in the mountains meant runoff, and water funneling through these narrow canyons could create sudden floods.

Leaving the saplings behind, we skidded down the rocky hillside, a current of stones tumbling down behind us.

Shira was sitting on a rock at the edge of the pool, toes dangling in the water. Jumo was in the pool fully clothed, floating on his back. Jumo was a wonderful swimmer. The laws of his handicap did not apply there, it seemed. He floated freely, his awkward limbs made graceful by the buoyancy of the water.

I called to him, gesturing furiously for him to return to shore, but before his feet touched the ground, the water tumbling over the rocks above turned muddy.

"Get to higher ground!" Eben's urgent command was laced with panic.

We followed him, back the way he and I had come only a few moments before. Eben led the way, with Shira close behind, and I followed Jumo, who used his crutches to propel himself forward with as much speed as he could muster across the uneven ground.

Hearing the crash of water behind me, I picked up my pace but slipped on a loose stone, and my ankle turned, my sandal strap breaking. I cried out at the pain, pitching forward and scraping my hands and knees on the ground.

Muddy water swirled around me, rushing forward and deepening with alarming speed. Eben gripped me around the waist and hefted me to my feet, yelling that I needed to climb—fast! He pressed me toward the steep bank behind Shira, and I stumbled up the slope, using crevices in the rocks and stray roots to keep my balance.

Looking back, I realized that Eben and Jumo were not behind me, and horror coiled in my chest. The water was rushing past, at least a cubit or more high, pushing branches, stones, and debris in its muddy wake.

Skidding back down the slope, I screamed their names. Then I saw them, struggling against the current. Jumo, his crutches washed away, had fallen, his head barely above the water.

My heart flew to my throat. I watched in helpless, wordless

panic as Eben reached out to Jumo, gripping an acacia bush to keep his balance.

Together, the two men fought the flood as they moved toward me, the water eddying around their knees, determination on their faces.

I reached out a hand to grasp Jumo's as they came close and yanked him up onto the bank, then did the same for Eben. We scrambled back up to where Shira sat perched on a ledge.

Her eyes widened as she took in the appearance of her brother and Jumo, who were covered in mud and bleeding from multiple scrapes. "What happened?"

Jumo grinned. "He . . . saved . . . me."

Eben shrugged, a self-deprecating smirk on his face. "That's the last time, though. You lost my sword." He cradled his thorn-shredded hand against his shoulder.

Jumo threw back his head, his laughter echoing off the smooth-faced cliffs around us, and Eben and Shira joined in.

I did not. It suddenly struck me how perilous this journey would be. If the deadly storms, lack of food, or wild animals did not kill us, then Pharaoh surely would.

There was no other choice but to go back to Egypt. My mother, brother, and I must find a way to return. There would be plenty of cities where no one would know us. We would simply lie and say that Jumo was a second-born son. But how could we survive on our own in the wilderness? And now that I had talked them into going with the Hebrews, how could I change Jumo's and my mother's minds?

Ra, the eternal sun, glared overhead—his disdain made clear by the intensity of his heat against my face. Although tempted to plead with him for a way back to my homeland, three days of night weighted the argument against his power. I would have to find help somewhere else.

28

Sayaad returned the next day, offering us a small goat that had been butchered and was ready to prepare for our supper.

"Where have you been?" teased my mother. "There was so much leftover food last night I had to force Jumo to have a second helping."

As if anything had to force Jumo to eat more—he ate like one of Pharaoh's stallions.

My mother's countenance had changed drastically in the past few days, after I had finally confronted her about her role in my enslavement, as if a great weight had been lifted from her shoulders. I wished I felt the same, but with each step I took away from Egypt, my burden seemed to grow heavier. The Black Land called to me, beckoning me to return.

"Mistress Nailah, I do apologize." Sayaad bowed low yet trained his brilliant blue eyes on her. "I was kept from your company by a friend. We were discussing our current . . . uh . . . situation."

"Situation?" She frowned.

"As you well know, we are heading southward and not, as

we had expected, northeast. My friend and I, along with many others, are debating why Mosheh would be heading farther into the wilderness and toward the sea, instead of toward Canaan."

He echoed my own unspoken concerns. Pharaoh knew where we were—no doubt there were spies among the throng. The Cloud had stayed here in this place for three days. At night, it billowed high, sparking blue and purple bolts of fire. During the day, it remained in place yet roiled like a violent storm was sheathed within its column. Why had it not moved?

Talk of some sloughing away from the group, heading back to Egypt or outposts, ran rampant. Our king was no simpleton. His entire workforce wandered around in the wilderness, squandering their freedom. The numerous outposts with signal fires could relay information directly to Pharaoh. Soon his footsteps would be heard behind us.

My family and I must leave, and soon, or our blood would stain the sand alongside that of the Hebrews.

"This Mosheh that we are following, you say he was some great general?" Sayaad directed his gaze at me.

"According to Shira, he led many campaigns into Syria, Kush, and Canaan." I waved a hand. "But those were just stories from long ago."

"The Hebrew girl also said that he spent the last forty years tending sheep in Midian, correct?"

I shrugged, a bit uncomfortable with his label of Shira. "That is what she was told."

"Well, if he ever was a leader in Egypt, which I very much doubt, maybe all that time in the wastelands robbed him of his military savvy. He is, what, around eighty now?" Sayaad frowned. "Perhaps it is a senile old fool we are following."

My mother's eyes grew wide. "What will we do? Pharaoh's army will come, won't they?"

"Possibly," he said. "I can't imagine he would leave his entire workforce out here in the desert with herds of valuable live-stock, not to mention half the gold of Egypt, without a plan to take it back."

"He hasn't pursued us so far."

"No, he hasn't, but we know Pharaoh, unlike Mosheh, actu-ally is a military genius. And yes, he may be smarting from the thrashing he took from Mosheh, but Pharaoh is a cobra. He knows his prey. He will wait until we are at our weakest before striking. It is his way."

"What should we do?" asked my mother.

"I'm not sure yet. I've been talking with a few other Egyptians I have been traveling with. We are working on a plan."

"A plan to leave the Hebrews?" I asked, my voice low and my heart thumping wildly.

His smirk told me it was true.

Was this my answer? Were the gods answering my unspoken prayer in the form of Sayaad?

Zerah called to my mother, asking her opinion on something she was weaving. Sayaad and I were left alone at the cook fire. Intrigued by the plan, I pressed him. "Where would we go? We cannot return to Iunu."

"We can go somewhere new, somewhere no one ever knew you," he said. "All of Egypt is rebuilding. I doubt anyone would even question where you are from. The land of Goshen was untouched during the plagues and now is practically empty."

The way so far had been fairly easy, a gentle slope rising from the Valley of the Nile. It would not take much for us to travel back the same way; in fact, it would be downhill. We could possibly trade for food; Sayaad seemed skilled enough at that. I eyed the goat roasting over the fire.

Across the campsite, Eben's skillful hands crafted a new instrument as he spoke with Jumo. He had returned to the acacia grove with his uncle to retrieve the saplings he had cut down before the flood. They gleaned several tent poles from the wood, and now Eben was using the excess for a lyre. He continued smoothing it with a rough stone and talking with my brother. Seeming to sense my eyes on him, he met my gaze and trapped it for the briefest of moments. His eyes flitted to Sayaad, whose back was turned toward him, then returned to his task, disgust on his face.

I brushed away the surge of emotion threatening to change the path of my still-forming decision. This overpowering draw toward a Hebrew who hated me, hated everything I represented, was foolish and unrequited. We must go back to Egypt—it was the only way to protect my brother and undo the unwise decision I had made.

"What would happen if we met the army on the way back?" I asked. "They would deem us traitors and slaughter us."

"I'm fairly sure that if we told them we were from one of the turquoise mines nearby, fleeing for fear of the Hebrew multitude, they would probably leave us alone. We all look Egyptian. We may have to travel westward through the hills, though, to make it seem as though we are coming north on a different route."

Thoughts of Pharaoh's chariots chasing us down terrified me. It seemed safer out in the open, traveling in a small company, than among this multitude that invited his wrath.

I was certainly no stranger to hard work now; my mother was a skilled merchant, and my brother an artist of the highest caliber. Perhaps we could find some small village in the Delta, use some of the gold our donkey carried, and set up a trade booth.

Sayaad leaned closer to me, his gaze warm. He placed a hand on my arm, his thumb rubbing circles into my skin. "You don't have to decide now. My friends are still working out the details. It is not time to leave just yet."

The contrast between his inviting tone and Eben's abrasiveness was stark. Here was a handsome man, so like Akhum in many ways, yet without the political entanglements that had cost me so dearly. And his desire for me was more than evident.

My mind whirred with ideas and plans. Egypt had been knocked down, but she would rise again, wouldn't she? Pharaoh was Pharaoh after all. He would bring her back to glory, and certainly with the Hebrews gone there would be plenty of opportunities for employment.

I could almost feel the Nile's sweet waters around my ankles.

29

The reflection of the blue fire on the walls of the canyons stole my breath. When the sun had disappeared in the west last night, the column had risen into the sky and stretched out above us like a canopy, lighting our way and casting everything around us in a pale shade of azure. Myriad stars twinkled now through the luminescent veil above.

Yet the beauty of our covering did not change our plight. We were at a standstill. After wandering in a circle, and then turning south again, we were now trapped in a narrow canyon with impatient feet and frazzled nerves. More than a few arguments broke out around us as we waited for the bottleneck ahead of us to clear. The racket from millions of feet, mouths, and animals was deafening. Every sound reverberated off the walls, amplifying the cacophony.

Since entering this maze of wadis a couple of days ago, my own nerves had been in shards. My eyes were almost always on the sky, watching for clouds to gather again as they had that day at the waterfall. Each puff of white against the blue sent shockwaves of fear through my veins. The images of Jumo nearly drowning surfaced, again and again, in my brain.

I shivered in spite of the heat radiating from the limestone cliffs and the crush of bodies around me. These wadis had been formed by the flow of thousands of years of water runoff, and the striated formations loomed high above our heads. We were imprisoned by our escape route. Pharaoh behind us; the threat of flood all around.

Where was Sayaad? How could we possibly slip away now? I had taken stock of the food and drink left in our wagon, and it was dwindling. We needed to leave soon, or not at all.

As determined as I was to return to Egypt with Sayaad, guilt nagged at me at the thought of Shira and her kindness to me and my family. I had noticed that many of the Hebrews refused to even speak with Shira or her family. They were harboring an enemy. Perhaps our leaving was best for them as well. Eben certainly would be glad of it, I was sure.

As the sunrise finally slipped its eager fingers through the cracks between the canyon walls, the people in front of us began to move, startling me from my contemplation. I tripped on an unseen stone, and my knees buckled.

Arms slipped around my waist, preventing me from falling to the ground.

Eben's voice was in my ear. "Are you all right?"

I pulled away, surprised at the concern in his tone, the tingle of his breath on my skin, and the pressure deep inside my chest.

"Kiya . . ."

I attempted a smile. "Just tired."

"No. You are not."

Taken aback, I snapped at him, "I've been walking all night. Of course I am tired."

"I've never seen your step falter in all the days we've been walking."

Blinking at him, I was struck dumb by this astute observance of my behavior.

I needed to say something. The conflict raging in my head and heart needed release. If Eben would listen, his ears were as good as any.

"I don't belong here," I said.

"And where do you belong? In Egypt?"

"Egypt is my home."

"A home that chewed you up and spat you out."

I fumbled around inside my head, searching for a response. Suddenly, I was pressed against him by the tide of people impatient to push around us.

His voice touched my ear again. "None of us has a home anymore. We are all wandering. All as lost as you."

"Sayaad said we could go with him, head back to another part of Egypt, where no one knows us. We can start over. The whole country will be rebuilding. I can start a new life, a free life. Or perhaps our family can start anew in his village in Moab," I said.

"Sayaad is not as he seems." He glared at me, his eyes gray and blazing.

"Why do you hate him? He's not full-blooded Egyptian. You have no cause."

"Do I not?"

"What possible reason do you have?"

"Enough. I have seen Sayaad"—the name sounded bitter on his tongue—"in his camp with three of his Egyptian friends. They are up to something. I have heard of gold disappearing from wagons in the night. Many suspect your friend and his company. There is talk of spies among us as well, reporting back to Pharaoh."

"And you automatically assume they are correct? Your people mistrust any outsiders. They have given me my fair share of their opinions about my own heritage. I cannot drink from a stream or bathe among the women without hearing insults hurled my way. Of course Sayaad would be a suspect, even though he has been nothing but kind to my family."

Eben was so close to me. Every point where his skin touched mine was on fire. My hand trembled with the desire to slip inside his. I dug my nails into my palms to still them. There was no use entertaining such thoughts.

"Is that so?" he said.

"Yes."

He looked up at Jumo pointedly. "Are you sure of that?"

Confused, I looked at my brother, who, mindless of the melee going on around him, rode with eyes fixed on the fire canopy that was becoming more and more opaque as the sun rose—lavender now, through the haze of the cloud. Had Jumo had some sort of interaction with Sayaad that I was unaware of?

"Regardless, it's none of your concern where I go or where I settle." I flipped my hand.

His gaze penetrated mine. "I am greatly concerned."

The pressure in my chest tightened again, trapping my breath. Could he mean that it *did* matter to him? That *I* mattered to him? Or was he merely thinking about his friendship with Jumo, or concerned that Shira might be upset if I left?

I could not prevent the tremble in my voice when I spoke, so I looked down. "Why would you be concerned for my family?"

He was quiet for a few moments. I chanced a look at him. His gaze brushed over my hair, my face, lingered on my lips.

"For my sister's sake, of course." His tone was gentle—and so intimate, my heart ached.

I nodded, speechless.

"She would be heartbroken if you left." He looked away from me, toward the dawn.

Eben and I passed the rest of the walk in silence, but he did not leave my side.

30

The ocean sparkled the same shade of turquoise that was mined somewhere near here in the mountains. In the brilliant sunlight, the water glittered as if millions of diamonds floated on its smooth surface.

Even after a week of camping here on this expansive beach, I found myself drawn again and again to wondering at the sapphire depths that stretched out endlessly to the south. Some sort of sea animal leaped out of the water, a silver shimmer against the blue.

"I found you." Sayaad's voice behind me caused me to jolt, dropping the rock I had been using to scrub my laundry before I had been distracted by the beauty around me.

He laughed at my startled expression, one brow lifting in amusement. "Salt water is probably not the best thing for washing."

"Better than dirty linens. All that remains of the fresh water needs to be saved for drinking."

He pursed his lips, acquiescing with a slight bow of his head. "True."

"Where have you been?" My question slipped out sharper than I'd meant it to.

"I apologize that I have been away. I had . . ." He glanced at Shira, who stood next to me, knee-high in the water. "I had things to attend to."

His eyes twinkled with secrets, and I knew he meant he was preparing for our departure. A stab of nerves jabbed my belly, a sharp reminder that I had yet to discuss parting with the Hebrews with my mother or brother.

For the six days we had spent on this beach, baking in the sun like bricks, rumors had swirled around us. Pharaoh was on his way. Even now, an army of Hebrews was stationed at the mouth of the wadi, their untrained hands at the ready with Egyptian swords, waiting for the chariots to thunder into view. The longer we stayed here with our backs to the sea, like rats trapped as the serpent closed in, the more distraught my mother seemed to be. It would not take much to convince her to leave, I was sure.

Shira leaned close to me. "We should return to camp."

The waver in her voice surprised me.

"Why? We are not finished."

She glanced back toward our campsite, trepidation across her features, pointedly avoiding Sayaad's line of vision. "Ima will be looking for us to help with the meal."

I had never seen Shira so unsettled. She looked as though she was about to flee across the sand. Realization dawned in my mind. I had only seen Shira around her brother and mine, both of whom were harmless to her—a sharp distinction from Sayaad, who possibly resembled the overseer who had attacked her.

"Perhaps you can walk us back?" I asked Sayaad.

He bowed, his eyes trained on mine. "It would be my pleasure."

Shira walked ahead of us, a bundle of wet linens perched atop her head.

"She's a skittish thing." Sayaad winked. "You'd think I was going to bite." He bared his teeth, white against his dark skin.

Ignoring his light mood, I pressed him. "Is everything in place?"

"Still anxious to get away from these Hebrews, I see."

Glancing at Shira, my heart flipped. "I am anxious to keep my brother and my mother safe. Wherever that leads me."

He slipped his hand around my wrist, tugging me to a stop. "Look over there." He pointed toward the Egyptian fortress nestled against the cliff, a silent witness to the horde that swarmed this beach. "Do you see the path there?"

I nodded. Pharaoh would be well warned that we were gathered here, like fowl in the marshes of the Nile, waiting for the hunter to collect the prize caught in his traps.

"That is where we will go. And soon."

My stomach lurched. "How can we get by the guards in the fortress?"

A smirk lifted his cheek. "Let us just say, the guards will be looking the other way."

Had he bribed the soldiers there? Or was there something to Eben's accusation that Sayaad could be spying for Pharaoh? A shock of cold burned through my veins.

"Now, don't look so worried, my lotus flower." His tone lowered. "I will make sure that you are safe."

"And my family."

He smiled, his blue eyes catching the reflection of the brilliant water behind me. "Of course."

Our little caravan of wagons was circled with a few others, the livestock Shira's family owned corralled in the center. A few goats and three sheep milled around inside the circle, getting in our way as Shira and I prepared what little food was left. Fortunately, Zerah had managed to ration out whatever vegetables her little garden had yielded early in the season, so combined with food gathered from others camped about our little circle, there was a small feast to enjoy this evening. There was no beer—only water saved in skin-bags and jugs from the mountain springs along our journey through the wadis.

With the bread and meat prepared—and the beans, leeks, and onions boiled in water—we sat around the fire to eat our meal. My mother surprised everyone by bringing out a jar of Shefu's wine she had found tucked at the bottom of a basket. She said she'd discovered it the first night but had saved it for a special occasion. Sweeter and more delicious than ever, Shefu's wine made our dinner a celebration. My mother certainly knew how to keep secrets.

Shira's younger sisters sat on either side of her, giggling. Shoshana leaned against Shira's shoulder, stroking her arm. Zayna jumped up to braid Shira's hair as soon as she emptied her own bowl. Zayna was a tiny little bird, smaller than most girls her age, and so quiet. She'd never spoken more than a few words, at least to me. Shoshana, the bolder of the two, had asked me a thousand questions over the past few days.

Both girls worshipped Eben, and it was plain that he adored them as well. Stern like a father, he kept watch over them and rebuked when they strayed out of sight to play with other children. But after every afternoon meal, he would hold one of them on his lap as Shira sang, and they bickered over this privilege every time.

The sun slid behind the hills, the sound of music drifting from campsites all around. Whenever Shira sang around our meal fires, a hush fell over the nearby sites; we were not the only ones who enjoyed her sweet voice. But tonight there was shouting and loud singing all around us, and many were dancing as well.

Here we were, sitting on a beach, waiting for Pharaoh and

his army to plow through the wadi and destroy us, and we were celebrating? These people were truly the strangest I had ever met.

"Eben, you must play for us!" Shoshana pleaded.

"Yes, Brother, please bring out your instruments," Shira said.

He hesitated, but both Zayna and Shoshana begged him with expectant faces. He rose and rummaged through the supply crates. "Get your reed pipe, Shira," he said over his shoulder.

"Just wait until you hear my brother play," Shira whispered in my ear as she passed me. "My father taught him well."

Eben came back into the firelight, a lyre and lute in hand. Jumo, too, had fetched a drum from his tent, animal hide stretched over a frame of the finest rosewood, which I knew could only have come from far to the south, from countries I barely knew existed.

Eben began slowly, the soft melody compelling me to quiet my breathing to hear each note. The gentle tune echoed what I'd felt since my sandals had touched the road leading away from my home. Each strain reflected the anguish of a broken heart. A heart like mine.

I could not endure another note. Tears burned, threatening to spill. Thankfully, the song began to change—to grow in complexity and in speed.

The music spun out of Eben's lute like a whirlwind, and his fingers moved so fast on the strings, I could not follow. I was transfixed by them.

When the rhythm steadied, Jumo, whom to my knowledge had never touched a drum, followed the beat with effortless skill. Shoshana and Zayna jumped up to dance, little-girl laughter spiraling with them around the crackling fire. Shira watched the girls for a few moments and then joined in, playing her reed pipe in joyous harmony with her brother's swirling melody.

How could she play and dance at the same time? She motioned

with her hand for me to join her. I smiled but shook my head. I loved to dance and had not done so in a long time, but I wanted to watch Eben play.

My mother, Zerah, and the rest of our little tribe clapped along. For the first time since leaving her home that dark night, my mother laughed with abandon. A few other families had joined our circle, and some of the women danced too, spinning in the firelight, garments and head scarves twirling about them like many colored birds in flight. Belts and anklets with gold coins and tiny metal beads jingled a festive counter-rhythm.

But my eyes were pulled to Eben across the fire. I could not help myself. I was astounded. His long, graceful fingers moved like a hummingbird's wings across the strings.

The music intensified, and the dancers retreated to their seats one by one, fanning themselves. Soon only Shira and the girls danced—twirling, laughing, and swinging their arms around and around. Jumo drummed like a madman, eyes closed, completely absorbed in his newfound skill. I found myself clapping along and laughing at the children challenging one another to dance faster and faster.

When the breathless song came to an end, I was heartbroken; I ached for it to go on and on. Shoshana and Zayna collapsed on the ground next to me, gasping for breath and giggling.

After a few empty moments, Eben picked up the lyre and strummed the strings softly, just as masterful on this instrument as on the last. Shira sang, weaving her clear, bright voice in a wordless harmony with the lyre.

I closed my eyes, letting the music wash over me, draw me into its depths, and sink into my bones.

And then, Eben began to sing.

My eyes flew open.

Since the night we'd begun our journey, only Shira had sung. Sometimes her sisters joined in, but never Eben.

If I had been transfixed watching his fingers fly across his instrument, I was transformed by his voice. In a soft tenor, he began a melody that captivated me from the first note. I understood nothing, since he sang in his native tongue, but I watched his lips form each word. I allowed myself to study his mouth unhindered under the guise of discerning the meaning of the song.

A lament met my ears, the cry of slaves to their god, begging for mercy, pleading to be heard and freed from their captivity. My heart had sung that song every day, but my gods were silent. Their hearts had sung that song, and their God had heard.

Tears dripped down my cheeks, and the firelight swam in front of me. I wiped my face with the back of my hand, glad that I had neglected decorating my eyes with kohl lately. Then I realized Eben watched me. The flames flickered in his eyes. Eyes that held no anger, no reproach. He returned my gaze, intense and searching.

An eternity passed, and the multitude seemed to disappear, leaving Eben and I alone by the fire. The crackle of the flames and his music and my heart beating a wild rhythm locked us in a motionless dance with a resonance that vibrated deeper than the notes his skillful fingers played. It seemed as though he was singing for me alone.

Like one of the potions the priestesses in the temple claimed would bind a lover to you—if the right words were spoken—Eben's music cast a spell, wound its way through me, and caused every nerve in my body to sing.

Too soon, the song ended, and his attention pulled away as his sisters clamored for more dancing music.

He obliged, playing joyful songs until the embers burned low and most of the family, including my mother and Zerah, had retired to their bedrolls. When Shira tired of dancing, she came and sat beside me, put her arm around my shoulders, and absentmindedly drew her fingers through my hair. I had never known sister-love. I leaned against her, enjoying her closeness. If only the differences between us could be wiped away. If only this were not the last night I would be among this family I had come to love. If only my heart did not scream to return to my homeland with such ferocity.

My decision to go with Sayaad swung wildly between assurance and doubt. I must keep my family safe, for no one else would. It was on my shoulders alone. I could not stay here and watch those I loved die of thirst in the desert or be crushed beneath the wheels of Pharaoh's chariots. The only way was to go back with Sayaad.

Eben did not look at me again. And I was glad—for the music, and the man, still resonated deep inside my soul, shaking my resolve like an earthquake. The memory of his gaze burned long after the embers of the campfire went cold.

31

24TH DAY OUT OF EGYPT

The sun-disk peered at me over the misty eastern hills across the water. The outline of the distant ridge stood jagged against the pale morning sky.

I sat on the shore, arms folded across my knees. Sleep clouded my eyes, a remnant of my restless night. My head ached, and the rising sun seemed to refract off the waters more like knives than diamonds today. I had slipped out of my tent, driven by a desperate need to meet the sunrise, just as I used to at the Nile.

The brush of the waves against the shore had called to me for hours, their gentle rise and fall an invitation to come and dig my toes in the sand, to trade the toss and turn upon my sleeping mat for the push and pull of the sea. Yet the still morning brought no answers, no direction.

"A restful sound, is it not?"

The unfamiliar voice that broke the silence matched a stranger's face. An older man stood next to me like a tall pillar, with his hands behind his back, as if he had always been there, a fixture on this beach, among the time-worn stones that dotted the shoreline. Although his beard was threaded with silver, his face seemed almost ageless, and his brown eyes were lined like one who had spent a lifetime in the sun and aged with cares I could only guess at. One of the Hebrews who had slaved to carry bricks for Pharaoh, no doubt.

He was a stranger, but I sensed he was no threat to me, and I turned again to face the sea. "It is."

In silence we watched as the sunrise unfurled in the east, spreading varicolored wings along the horizon.

"What's over there?" I whispered, as much to myself as the man who stood beside me.

"The land . . . of the Midianites." His cheek quirked, as if a memory had struck him. "And a beautiful bird . . . that dances on the wind." He spoke slowly, each word chosen with great care, reminding me of the cadence of Jumo's speech with strangers who did not understand his mangled words.

I inhaled, for one moment imagining the freedom that winged creatures must feel with the wind beneath their feathers, allowing the breezes to push them higher and higher until the earth below them fell away.

"Where . . . where do you . . . hail from?" He searched my face intently, his warm smile dispelling any suspicion I had after his abrupt appearance.

"Iunu."

"Ah . . . I know it well. The city of . . . the sun."

A wave of longing for my home crashed over me, and tears burned my eyes.

"You want . . . to return." His plain statement cut through any pretense I might have considered using.

I nodded.

"Do you not . . . want . . . to be free?"

"But I am not free."

He raised his brow, a signal for me to explain. His face was so kind, and his grandfatherly concern so apparent, that I was helpless to stop myself from continuing.

"I have traded slavery to my mistress back in Egypt for slavery to this Yahweh, this destructive god who cares nothing for me or my family." I scooped a handful of sand in my palm, then let it trickle out in a slow stream through my fingers. "And now I have a chance to return, and I have to take it. I must. I cannot just sit here and watch my brother and mother die."

The man did not answer. He stood in silence so long I decided that he had nothing more to say to me. I stood and wiped the sand from my tunic, preparing to go.

"Yahweh is . . . not Pharaoh. He is . . . not . . . not a slavemaster. He came . . . for his children . . . trapped in slavery, to . . . set us free . . . and he protects us, even now." He pointed to the Cloud at the end of the beach, hovering there like a watchful father eyeing his children.

"But I am not one of his people, why would he protect me?"

The man turned to me, his eyes burning with passion. "He c-c-created you . . . he knows you . . . and will . . . m-m-make himself known to you." As his tongue tangled with the unwieldy words, spoken too quickly to temper the stutter, understanding dawned in my mind.

Mosheh.

Shira had told me of his speech impediment and how his brother Aharon spoke for him. The realization must have shown on my face because Mosheh smiled and nodded, acknowledging his identity. My own tongue was too knotted to reply.

He placed a large hand on my shoulder. "Ask him . . . to . . . reveal himself." He squeezed gently, gave me a conspiratorial wink, and then walked away, back toward the Cloud that hovered near the southern end of the beach.

Sayaad came that afternoon, without his usual offering for my mother. He sat with us by the fire for a few moments making small talk, but he kept crossing and uncrossing his arms and glancing toward the gaping wadi entrance, where hundreds of men took turns standing guard against the inevitable.

Eben had taken his turn just that morning, joining the fruitless effort with only a short sword and a dagger and leather armor to protect his body. I steeled my mind against the terrible images conjured by the thought of Eben standing against Pharaoh and his merciless army. An army that no doubt would include the man I had meant to marry.

Akhum, a second-born son, would be bearing down upon us at any moment, bent on our destruction. I could see it in my mind: Akhum and Eben locked in battle, bloody and bruised, and it confused me that it was only Eben's outcome I cared for. I blinked the mirage away as I brought my thoughts back to the handsome man next to me, the one who had offered to whisk my family and me away from the destruction hurtling toward us.

But right now Sayaad was on edge. He shook his head as he gazed into the fire, as though talking to himself.

"What is wrong?" I asked.

"These Hebrews and their foolishness about a faceless god." He rolled his eyes. "I just can't bear any more. How can you endure such ridiculousness?"

I considered his assessment and shrugged. "I saw what I saw in Egypt."

He waved a dismissive hand. "Natural causes, all explainable."

"Perhaps. But the Hebrews don't seem to question it." I leaned forward with my arms folded across my knees, thinking of the conversation I'd had with Mosheh, when he'd told me to ask Yahweh to reveal himself. Would he? I glanced toward the Cloud, which had been sparking bolts of blue fire all day, as if in rebuke for my disbelief and my desire to put distance between it and my family. How would Yahweh manifest himself to me? A burning bush like Shira had told me Yahweh used to appear to Mosheh?

"How do you explain the Cloud?" I pointed toward the subject of my thoughts.

He swiped a hand in the air. "Sorcery. I have no doubt Pharaoh's priests have the same power. It's just a little smoke."

The flippant statement seemed to contradict the reality. I could not imagine such a huge, fiery cloud conjured from mere human means.

"Fools." He snorted.

"Well, going along with these fools was the only way I could save my brother, so if I have to play along and pretend to follow their imaginary god, I'll do it."

As soon as the words were out of my mouth, I knew them to be untrue. And then I saw Shira out of the corner of my eye, standing at the door of her tent, her stricken face pale as she locked gazes with me, her usual sisterly smile replaced by an expression of haunted betrayal.

Before I could lurch to my feet and follow her, to correct the hateful words that had spewed from my mouth, she turned and fled the campsite. I felt the blood drain from my face. I had wounded the only person who had sacrificed herself for me.

Sayaad suddenly wrapped his fingers around my wrist and whispered into my ear. "Come with me."

"Where?"

"Let's go for a walk down by the water." He smiled and tipped his head toward the shore.

Although I was tempted to refuse and go apologize to Shira, his sky-blue eyes, hypnotic in their intensity, beckoned me to follow.

We wound our way through the camps to the shoreline. The water was so still, it barely rippled along the edge. How clear it was—the coral swirled patterns of green and brown on the sea floor as far out into the water as I could see.

I took off my sandals to walk in the water and let the sand seep through my toes.

Sayaad strode north with his hands grasped firmly behind his back.

Trying to keep pace with his long legs, I stumbled along next to him. "Where are we going?"

Sayaad stopped and grasped my hand, yanking me to a stop. He unleashed the full power of his piercing blue eyes on me. "Let's go. Now."

"What?" I said. "Go where?"

He jerked his chin toward the garrison. "There is a small trail there along the edge of the sea. It leads to a wider road that threads its way back north and meets with the Way of the Wilderness again."

My mouth hung open.

"We have to go now. The army will be here before the sun sets tonight."

"They're almost here?" My voice pitched high. "How do you know?"

He raised a brow. "My friends have been in close contact with the army. We've been appraised of their progress."

The terrible truth of his statement landed on my chest like a thousand bricks. "You *are* a spy, just like Eben said."

His lip quirked. "You didn't really believe I was going to throw in my lot with these crazy slaves, did you?" He barked a laugh. "Pharaoh has offered a healthy reward for information on this horde. He has been waiting for just the right time to claim his property."

"Let's go." He pulled me forward.

"No." I tugged, resisting his lead. "I can't go now. I have to get my mother and Jumo. I haven't even told them we are leaving."

He shook his head. "No time. We have to escape right now."

"No!" I said, louder. I stopped walking and tried to free myself from his grasp. "I won't leave without my family."

"They will just slow us down." He pulled my arm again.

"I am not going anywhere without my mother and my brother. Let me go." He was squeezing my hand now, and try as I might, I could not slip from his grasp.

He yanked me close and grabbed my other arm. His upper lip curled, and his eyes sparked, cold and dangerous. "You are coming with me. I will not have wasted my time for nothing."

"What do you mean?" I asked, still struggling to pull away.

"You think I've spent my days at your campfire for my health? No, my beauty. I have been planning this from the start, since I saw you that night with a broken wagon wheel. You are mine, and you are coming with me."

Eben was right, Sayaad was not who he seemed. He talked sweetly to my mother and offered flattering words to me, and like the fool I was, I'd believed he was a kind former slave, wanting nothing but to help my family. But all he wanted was to own me, just like Akhum. And looking into his eyes, I saw that he did not plan on giving me a choice. I would be taken into slavery once again, to satisfy Sayaad's lust.

He gripped my arms so tightly, my hands started to go numb. "Please," I whimpered. "Let me go." Tears stung my eyes.

His face curved into an awful smile. "Never, my lovely lotus blossom."

"Release her." Eben's voice came from behind us.

Sayaad's head snapped around. "Leave us alone."

"I will not. Let Kiya go." Eben circled around us, the fierce determination on his face causing my heart to surge high into my throat.

"We are leaving, Kiya and I." Sayaad pulled again.

I dug my toes into the sand. "No, I am not going anywhere with you!"

"There, the lady has spoken. She has no intention of leaving with you, Sayaad." Eben moved closer. "Now, let her go."

The two men glared at each other, neither one backing down.

Keeping his grip on my left arm, Sayaad drew a short sword from a scabbard tucked invisibly into his kilt. He held the blade to my throat, and I stopped struggling.

"I am not about to lose my prize. I have waited too patiently to lose now."

Eben widened his stance. "Why would you destroy your prize? She is no good to you dead."

Sayaad shrugged. "True. But at least I know you won't have her. I've seen the way you look at her. Your own lust rivals my own." His laughter curled my stomach.

"You know nothing," Eben growled. "Let her go."

Sayaad leaned to whisper in my ear, all the while keeping his eyes trained on Eben. "I'd rather watch your blood sink into this sand than know that this Hebrew dog has you."

Silver flashed through the air. Sayaad roared and dropped his hand from my arm to grab his own, taking two steps backward. Eben's dagger was buried deep in Sayaad's bicep, and blood snaked down his arm, dripping to the sand.

In his surprise at Eben's attack, Sayaad had dropped his sword. Eben grabbed me and picked up the sword in one move.

"Now, leave." Eben gestured toward the fortress with the sword.

Sayaad bled profusely, the hilt of Eben's dagger still protruding from his arm. With one last murderous look at us, he turned and jogged away.

Eben stood silently with the sword by his side and watched until Sayaad disappeared around the edge of the fortress.

Relief and mortification battled inside me, making my body

shake uncontrollably. Not only had I been duped and flattered into following after Sayaad. But Eben, of all people, had to come to my rescue.

His voice still held a sharp edge from the confrontation with Sayaad. "Let's go back to the camp."

I swallowed the sob that threatened to escape.

He held my arm with a firm but gentle grip as we walked, and every so often, he looked behind us, making sure Sayaad had not decided to pursue us after all.

How long had he been following Sayaad and me? Why? He had warned me . . . he must have sensed Sayaad's plan.

But what had Sayaad said about the way Eben looked at me? Could it be true? No, Sayaad was evil, trying to get a rise out of Eben. Everything he said was a lie.

But a small part of me—or perhaps not so small—hoped there might be a grain of truth to the twisted accusation. Did Eben watch me covertly, like I watched him?

Eben was not striking or commanding like Akhum or Sayaad—and that barbaric beard and his strange green-gray eyes were so foreign. No fine linens adorned his hips, no kohl intensified his gaze, no perfumed oils glistened on his skin, but his strength and talents and his love for his family—even his friendship with my brother—attracted me. Against my will, he drew me. He had saved me now, twice.

He was silent. He did not ask if I was unharmed. He did not ask why I had followed Sayaad. He did not even chide me for my foolishness.

If only he would chide me. Or yell at me. Or look at me.

Eben did not release my arm until we neared our campsite. When he let go and walked away, without a word, the absence of his strong hand on my arm stung worse than Sayaad's bruising grip. He left me to enter the campsite and face the inevitable questions alone.

Before the sun had completely disappeared in the west, the shofarim blew. Usually when the ram's horns sounded, the hair on the back of my neck stood on end. But this time, even my blood seemed to freeze in my veins. Pharaoh's army was upon us.

In my mind's eye, I saw them: hundreds of chariots, thousands of infantry, and Pharaoh the Almighty leading the charge. All with the gleam of vengeance—for lost sons, fathers, brothers, friends—in their eyes. The second- and third-born men of Egypt were on their way with swords at their sides and hatred in their hearts.

Chaos broke out on the beach. Many people ran to the edge of the water, as if to swim to safety. Some left everything on the sand and tore up the beach, attempting to follow the trail by the garrison. Some knelt or lay prostrate on the ground, calling out to Yahweh. Louder, though, were cries of "We are going to die!" and "Mosheh, why did you bring us here?" At the southern end of the beach, near Mosheh's tent, screaming and shouting echoed across the water, as if a rebellion against him were imminent. Would they try to kill Mosheh and use his death to barter mercy with Pharaoh?

Anger stirred in me at the foolish behavior. There was no rescue from death. Shira's god and his Deliverer had led us to the sea to be drowned—or butchered. Such a god cared nothing for his people, and even less about me.

Besides, we all knew this confrontation would happen. We had dreaded it every moment since we'd left Egypt.

Pharaoh would not surrender easily. He was the Lord of Two Lands, the powerful god-man of Egypt. If he let the Hebrew slaves bully him into submission, he would never wield the same power over the surrounding nations.

Borne on the wings of revenge for his firstborn son, he came to recapture his labor force and bring back the wealth stolen from his land. All gold was Pharaoh's. It made no difference that it was pressed into Hebrew hands by the insistent ones of the Egyptian people.

Shofarim resounded again, reverberating and sending echoes across the water as the sun slipped beyond the hills at the western edge of the beach and the glowing Cloud, previously settled on the shore, now began to move.

It swirled and grew, then lifted into the air. We craned our necks skyward as it floated silently, spreading out again into a great glowing canopy overhead. One end of the Cloud gathered into a swirling, towering cyclone of light at the mouth of the canyon; the rest formed an iridescent tent over the whole beach.

The swirling Cloud blocked Pharaoh's exit out of the wadi.

32

How long could the Cloud hold off Pharaoh? We had no way of escape. We would perish here on this beach, pressed in between the mountains and the sea. Or we would be brought back to Egypt, bound, broken, and enslaved again—possibly executed publicly for the crime of treason. My mother's hand was ice in mine, but to my left, Jumo's grip was warm. I blinked away the horrific image of my brother tied to a whipping pole, paying for my choices.

A wind rose out of the east. A strong, cold wind. As it blew, the temperature dropped like a stone cast into the sea.

We must find shelter. I tried to yell to my mother above the roar of the storm, but my words dissipated into the rush of air, and my frozen lips refused to continue the effort.

I pulled them both with me, and soon my mother, Jumo, and I were huddled by the wagon wheel, using every blanket, linen, and piece of clothing we could find to wrap our bodies. Even a couple of stray goats pressed against us, and I was so grateful for the extra warmth that I did not push them away.

My fingers were stiff and numb. I had never been so cold in my entire life. Even in the dead of the coldest season in

Egypt, I had worn sandals with only a simple mantle to protect against the chill. But this wind sliced deep into my bones. Even Eben's black horse, Shoah, lay on the sand, head down, groaning against the painful wind and huffing great puffs of frozen breath. I hoped Shira's family was together by their own wagon swathed in Zerah's beautiful wool blankets. I tried to press away the sudden desire to be huddled with Eben, wrapped in the safety of his arms.

Overhead, the canopy of light shimmered. Although it was cold underneath its cover, most of the freezing wind seemed to be passing over it—howling and screaming above us. A barrier of light buffered us from the worst of the storm.

The wind blew for what seemed like hours. I fell asleep at some point; my head drooped on Jumo's shoulder.

When he nudged me awake, the wind had abated. I stood up, stretching the sleep and the cramp of the prolonged position from my body.

Turning toward the east, I gasped, my disbelief in the God of the Hebrews utterly obliterated.

The sea was frozen.

Heaps of ice jutted out of the waters, forming walls similar to those of the wadi behind us. A path threaded through the icy canyon. What had been an azure-blue sea was now a gently sloping path passing through its depths.

Yahweh had created a way to cross to Midian and escape from Pharaoh.

Mouths and eyes hung open. Again the Hebrews were on their knees, this time worshipping the God who controlled even the wind and seas.

Jumo looked out at the water with a serene half-smile on his face, as if towering walls of ice were a normal occurrence. As if it were just as he'd expected.

My mother gripped her head, fear evident on her tear-stained face. "Daughter," she whispered, "are we going to walk through that?"

"I believe so. There seems to be no other way to leave this beach."

"But what if it is a trap? We would be crushed by the water."

"Why would their God lead them out here, protect them, and then destroy them in the sea? That does not make sense." My reassuring words were a balm to my own fearful soul. Yahweh would bring them through, I felt sure of it now, and if we wanted to be free, we must follow as well.

Zerah came up behind us and put her arm around my mother's waist. She barely came to my mother's shoulder, but as she looked at the miracle Yahweh had performed, she stood tall.

"Nailah, you will see. Adonai has made us a way; he is leading us to freedom. Until we cross those waters, we are still in Egypt."

It was true. Even on this beach, we were still in the territory of the king. And although held back by a Cloud of swirling light, he was surely ready to claim his subjects.

"Pack up your things quickly. The group is already on the move," Zerah said.

We did so, packing the makeshift linen tent, already knocked down from the powerful wind, and the few belongings scattered about the campsite, loading them back into the cart without ceremony.

The moon, although no longer full, glowed bright, but the Cloud overpowered it, lighting the beach like midday.

The tribe of Levi formed itself into a group. Days of packing and unpacking camp sped the process, and this time, forming into a military-type array was achieved fairly quickly. We followed the group to the wide mouth of the frozen sea-path that seemed to be swallowing the entire company whole.

Although not visible against the black sky, opposite us on the other shore was a long mountain range hours away in the distance. A long night stretched ahead of us, a treacherous and frightening walk through the midst of a sea split by a mighty wind.

We followed the group as it spread out. Shira's family, with their two wagons, walked to the left of us. We all stepped onto the seabed together. My sandals touched ground that had been underwater until a couple of hours ago, and my heart leapt within my chest. Never before in my entire life had I set foot outside the land of my birth.

My course was set. I had chosen to follow the Hebrews and their God and take my family on the path though the midst of the waters, wherever it may lead.

Strange as it was, frightening and dangerous, it was the right path. A path marked with a few patches of coral, rocks slick with icy seaweed, and even some unfortunate fish unlucky enough to be uncovered by the wind and left to drown in the air.

If I had followed Sayaad, I would have been his prisoner. If I had stayed with Tekurah, I would have been bound for life. If I had never been sold by my father, I would have been enslaved to his decisions and then to Akhum. But here at the bottom of the sea, freedom beckoned, pulling me farther away from my chains. The tether that had seemed to bind me to Egypt had been severed by the breath of Yahweh.

The water heaped up on either side of us, but the ground under my feet was dry. The icy wind had done its work and prevented the ground from pooling into mud.

Breathtaking walls of frozen sea, taller than most buildings in Egypt, taller even than the mighty temple of Iunu, stood in shimmering splendor along the path through the depths. The blue light canopied over us, casting light across our path and reflecting off the ice in an ethereal dance. Had the Cloud abandoned its guard post at the mouth of the wadi? I glanced over my shoulder, stomach curling. No, there it stood in the west, sparking bolts of fire, containing a vast army while spreading its comforting light over our path like an eagle's wings sheltering her young.

How thick were these ice walls, to hold back the pressure of these depths? What frightening power this God, this Yahweh, possessed—the strength to part the sea. He was more powerful than Pharaoh, who stood helpless, trapped behind a pillar of light and cloud. More powerful than the sea and the winds. Each of the gods of Egypt had crumbled beneath his crushing might. A faceless, invisible god had defeated them all.

We pushed wordlessly through the sea, only the stubborn bray of donkeys and oxen mixing with the crunch of millions of footsteps reverberated against the glassy blue-green walls.

My mother walked next to me, silent, gripping the lead rope of Jumo's donkey with whitened fingers. Shira's family still moved along next to us, and Eben sat tall on the wagon seat, driving his black horse, somber concentration creasing his brow. His glance, quick but sharp, lashed at me. The sting of it cut deep, and I looked away. I deserved the wound. My folly had almost been my undoing. Without Eben's intervention, Sayaad would have stolen me, away from my mother and brother, away from Shira and her family. Away from the path through the sea.

Eben could shoot dark looks at me for the rest of my life, but I was grateful to him. How could I ever repay him? Would he ever look at me with anything other than contempt or anger in his eyes again?

The night he sang—was it only last night?—something had passed between us, something I did not understand, but craved, more than anything I had ever desired from Akhum. Had my foolishness severed the connection that had seemed to vibrate between us across the firelight?

Cold, and weary to the bone, I stepped onto a beach not nearly as wide as the one behind us, but long and narrow. The tribes branched out along the shore.

The Levites headed to the north end of the beach, still following the ever-present banners that led our way and kept us organized by tribe.

The sun breached the hills to the east. When its light hit the ice walls, they sparkled like cut crystal. I shaded my eyes from the brilliance.

A shofar blast rang out across the beach. Some of the men must have climbed up on the hill behind us to keep watch across the water. The harrowing signal from the ram's horn was not a signal of safety, but one that told us Pharaoh was on his way. As soon as the echo of it died away, the Cloud lifted from the mountains on the beach we had just evacuated, towering thousands of feet into the air and then winding its way across the sea. It passed overhead and settled itself over the top of the hills behind us.

Now unfettered, Pharaoh would not hesitate. He had the fastest chariots in the world—and the mightiest army. It may be decimated by the loss of thousands of firstborn soldiers, generals, commanders, but all of those remaining were trained to obey Pharaoh's every word, on pain of death. They were coming . . . walls of ice notwithstanding.

There was no panic this time, just horrified silence. There was nothing to do but wait. The exit from this beach was not nearly as wide as the wadi that led onto the beach we had previously camped on. There was no way that millions of people, animals, wagons, and carts would have any chance of making it off the beach before the army arrived. We were defenseless, our backs against the mountains.

All around me men armed themselves. Even Jumo pulled a short sword from the wagon.

The sun rose higher overhead, and the air warmed. My hair tumbled loose in the sea-salt breeze.

Word came down from the lookouts on the hills that the army was almost halfway across the sea floor. A crack reverberated across the waters and echoed off the hills. The ice splintered and crashed into the divide. A tidal wave surged quickly toward us, flooding the path through the sea, hurtling toward the beach at a breakneck pace. It spilled over itself, splashing high into the air as the ice walls disintegrated in the warmth of the sun.

The army of Egypt—hundreds of chariots and thousands of men—were swept away. Almost in the blink of an eye, the might of Egypt, along with the man I had almost married, was gone.

33

Rivers of unreachable reflections danced before me, sliding across the deserted horizon before melting into nothing. I rubbed my eyes and blinked against the glare. "We should have stayed by the sea. At least a couple more days."

Shira nodded her head, but her eyes were on her sisters. They lay tucked among the linens and animal hides, sleeping in spite of the bump and rattle of the wagon bed.

"The sight of water, even salt water, would be a comfort." I licked my lips. It did little to wet them.

Shoshana and Zayna's usual chatter had been stilled by thirst. They had ceased complaining about the lack of water hours ago and simply given in to their exhaustion.

The hills around us were dead. Brown. Barren.

Cracks and fissures crisscrossed the valley floor like millions of gaping mouths begging for rain. Not one plant thrived. Here and there, a lonely cactus pushed courageous plumage out of the parched ground, but even the hardiest of desert flora listed, sucked to the marrow by the angry blaze of the sun.

Listless as well, I put one foot in front of the other by rote.

Rushed along by the river of bodies around me, there was little choice.

At least my sandals survived. The leather straps should have unraveled long ago with the constant friction of walking. Curious . . . Since the night I'd braved the silent streets of Iunu, I had not endured so much as a blister. Tired and sore feet were my constant companions, but they were not raw and bleeding as they should be. Who knew why? But thank the gods . . . Or perhaps . . . thank Yahweh. Walking across blazing sand and rocks without my sandals would be torturous.

I rubbed my temple. The headaches I had endured from the incense at the Sun Temple were nothing compared to these. Each hour without water the pain throbbed worse. Colors and lights flitted across my sight, sometimes blinding, sometimes just floating like oil on water around the edges of my vision.

I wore a linen veil over my hair, hoping to deflect some of the searing heat. I pulled it farther down over my eyes, trying to block out the sun that aggravated the ache in my head. Ra must be punishing me for my traitorous escape. He was sucking me as dry as the desert in retribution, and I shriveled under his furious glare.

My skin was dehydrated and ravaged. I fantasized about Tekurah's ointments and lotions. What I would not give to be massaging them into my mistress's limbs, if only to feel the lavish coolness on my hands.

Two days past the crossing of the sea and not a drop of water in sight. Every pot, every jar, every skin-bag was empty. On the Egyptian side of the sea, streams and waterfalls trickled down from the mountains, but on the Midianite side, only dusty riverbeds and cracked earth could be found.

Rumors passed back through the multitude that Mosheh was leading us to a source of water, but all I could see was dirt, spindly desert shrubs, and menacing mountains all around.

Before we had crossed the sea, Zerah's strong voice often rang out as we walked, commanding the girls to stay close or to keep the goats corralled. But now, silence hung over her like a shroud. Watching her youngest daughters waste away in the overpowering heat of the desert was too much for even the strongest of hearts. She walked ahead of the wagon, her shoulders and head down, veil pulled low.

Up until yesterday, the cries of infants had mixed with the voices of the millions, but no longer. Every so often a thin wail could be heard, but usually not for long.

One frantic young mother had come to Zerah while we set up camp yesterday. Her breast milk had dried, and the baby lay listless in her arms. She begged for milk from one of our goats. Zerah sent her away empty-handed. Nothing could be done. The one goat we had left was dry as well, her kid long since traded for food along the way.

A few lone clouds passed overhead, too high and light to be of any use.

Although my hair trapped the heat against my head, causing sweat to trickle down the back of my neck, I refused to cut it short. Vain though it may be, the relentless sun would not rob me of my last vestige of beauty. Papyrus-soled sandals, a simple shift, and a headscarf were all I had to clothe myself with. Many of the Hebrews were willing to trade the jewels and fine clothing they'd received from the Egyptians, but I had nothing to offer for them.

My hair was my only decoration, other than kohl to protect my eyes from the glare of the sun. Even as a slave in Tekurah's house, I had been clean, my Nile-washed hair shining, my skin supple from the remnants of the oils I used on Tekurah. Here my desiccated and weary body was as wasted as the land about me.

Shouts echoed through the crowd, indistinguishable at first, but growing clearer as voices volleyed the word back and forth.

"Water."

"Water?"

"Water!"

Whistles and cheers shot up, reverberating off the hills around us. A startled child cried out, a welcome sound after two days without infant protests.

Shoshana lifted her head above the rim of the wagon weakly and moved her lips as if to ask what was happening. Shira smoothed her sister's dark hair and motioned for her to lie back down.

The pace of the multitude quickened. Then suddenly, everyone was pushing. Clamoring. Demanding the water those ahead must already be enjoying. The fragile cords holding civility together instantly severed, and tempers flared like flames in a sudden gush of wind. Cheers of exult sharpened into insults as traveling companions forced ahead of one another to rush toward the promise of water.

The stall ahead of us broke. I grabbed the bridle of the donkey Jumo was riding. This final push toward the water might be dangerous. As soon as the Levite section of the long column of people passed the mouth of the canyon, everyone went wild. A half mile away there was a stretch of low trees. A plant standing higher than my waist had not been seen for three days, and anyone could guess that the trees spread out before us signified water.

All the organization of the tribes was instantly for naught. Anyone who could began running. Wagons bounced and jerked toward the trees, dust swirling like streaming brown banners behind. Even Zerah gave in, desperate as she was for the little girls to drink. I did not hesitate when she ordered us all to pick up the pace.

My mother trailed behind. I called to her, "Mother, hurry! We need to get there before the water is gone."

Zerah reached out and grabbed her hand. I was leading Jumo's donkey, and Shira was fighting to keep up with her sisters in the wagon pulled by Eben's black horse.

I tripped over a stone and jerked the poor donkey's head down as I lost my balance. I thought Jumo might slide right down the donkey's neck, but he held fast to the mane.

"Let . . . go!" he yelled.

"No, I have to hold on, or I might lose you." I gripped the rope tighter.

"You . . . pull . . . too . . . hard." His face was a blend of annoyance, frustration, and compassion.

"Oh." I dropped the rope, brushing my hand on my shift.

I had been guiding Jumo's donkey, or *my* little donkey, as I thought of him, since we'd left Egypt. Why was Jumo suddenly frustrated with me?

I did not have time to contemplate my brother's sudden flare of temper. We were falling behind; the black horse and its passengers sped ahead of us.

Everyone was running. It didn't take long to reach the mass of people pushing and shoving toward the stream. But before we reached the water, shouts lifted along its banks.

"What is this?"

"We are going to die!"

"Mosheh!"

"We can't drink this!"

I pushed in behind Shira. "Why can't we drink the water?"

She shrugged. "There must be something wrong with it. Look at the trees."

There were many palms and acacia lining both sides of the water, but they looked sickly, wilted—still green but certainly not thriving.

Eventually the word was passed back to us. The water was bitter. Undrinkable.

"No!" Zerah's hands covered her face.

Shoshana and Zayna. How much longer could they last?

"Could we go farther upstream? Maybe the waters are clearer there?" my mother offered.

"I don't know." Eben's shoulders hung low, and fear darkened his face for the first time since I had met him. He was helpless to do anything for his sisters. The despondency in his eyes made my stomach ache.

We waited. There was nothing else to do but wait.

Would we bury these sweet girls in the desert? Never hear their eager voices again badgering Eben for a song or their mother for the privilege of playing with other children in adjoining camps? After all these days of traveling together, the girls had lost their initial shyness of me, and now they chattered to me as much as Shira ever did, playing with my hair, braiding it, and twisting it into knots—they seemed quite taken with my thick black hair—and arguing over who would sit next to me at the fire. Shoshana and Zayna accepted me readily into their family, as children do, without prejudice or forethought. I had left Sefora and Liat, my brother and sister, back in Egypt, and now I would lose these precious girls I had grown to love as sisters.

Jumo brushed his hand down my hair and then pulled me closer. I laid my head against his leg and cried.

He whispered something. I looked up, having missed the words. To my astonishment, a tiny smile hovered on the corners of his lips. I questioned him with raised brows, and his smile grew more pronounced.

We heard shouts and the shofarim again. A group of men walked down the length of the stream, telling us all to move back. They ordered that the children and those most needful of water be brought to the stream's edge but told us that no one should set foot in the stream until the horns blew again.

We did as we were told. If anything, slaves were used to taking orders. We moved back. Eben and Zerah lifted the girls from the wagon and took them to the water's edge. Hundreds of children lined the stream, as well as many elderly leaning on the arms of their concerned family members.

More waiting. What could possibly be happening? Would Mosheh's magical staff heal the waters like it had wounded the Nile?

I saw some of the children pointing upstream. I strained my neck and stood on my toes but could see nothing.

The shofarim blew, and the children plunged into the water, drinking. Drinking!

My heart sang at the melee and joyful shouting from the children. *The water must be clean!* Splashing and singing and people cheering echoed all around us.

After a few minutes, the call sounded again, and Eben, Zerah, and the girls returned—Shoshana and Zayna with brilliance in their eyes. They were still weak—but smiling and sopping wet.

The rest of us took turns entering the stream, slaking our thirst and filling our goatskin bags, most taking a couple jars full of water back to their family livestock. The shepherds of the large herds migrated downstream to prevent the animals from muddying the now sweet and pure water.

"What did you see in the stream?" I asked Shoshana when we returned to the wagons. She was sitting up again in the bed, propped against a basket.

"Sticks."

"Sticks?"

"Yes, there were tree limbs floating down the stream. At first I thought they were snakes, but they didn't seem alive. I was much happier to see sticks." She wrinkled her nose.

How could tree limbs sweeten the water? Maybe it was a

special type of wood that Mosheh knew of? Maybe his magical staff was made of this very wood?

That night, around the campfire, Zerah held both Shoshana and Zayna on either side of her, close to her chest. The sheen of her tears glittered in the firelight. How grateful she must be for their salvation. Yet such uncertainty still lay before us.

But tonight she held her girls, and my heart sang the same praises that were on Eben's lips. Shira and Eben sang together, a new song. I was beginning to understand some of the Hebrew language. It surrounded me day and night.

The song they sang was about the stars and a story told from long ago. I wanted to ask more about the story, but I sensed Shira was still tender from my hurtful words. She did not sit by me anymore like she had on the other side of the sea—so I held my tongue.

Jumo whispered into Eben's ear.

"Look above you," Eben said.

We craned our necks to see.

The fire burned low, and the heavens were clear and full. Millions of twinkling stars peered back through the black fabric of the sky, whispering stories from eons of watching humankind.

"Elohim, the Creator," said Eben, "sowed the stars in the sky with his very words. In Egypt we heard the tales of the stars, the stories of Egyptian gods and their movements above. But the true story is much more ancient than the Egypt of old. It is not Nut who makes the stars twinkle in the heavens, but their Creator. Elohim tells a story in star pictures that will resonate through the ages, unrolling like a great scroll overhead, telling us the path of Avraham's sons. We are walking that path now, and the story will continue long after our journey ends."

Shira was not the only gifted storyteller in their family. I held my breath, afraid to miss one word of Eben's tale. Shira had told me much of Avraham and the promises Yahweh made to him over four hundred years ago. She had told me of the prophecies of Mosheh and how the Hebrews would be led out of Egypt, but she'd neglected to tell me the end of the tale.

Eben looked around the fire, letting his eyes rest on me a bit, beckoning me further in. "When our first ancestors HaAdam and Chavah lusted in the garden after the fruit of the Tree of the Knowledge of Good and Evil, they were cursed, along with the serpent that tempted them to sin. Fellowship with Elohim was broken, and man was sent out of the beautiful garden Elohim had planted with his own hands to delight his children. The heart of Elohim was broken, and he desired to heal the rift between himself and his creation, for not only was man cursed, but the entire universe resonated with the evil unleashed there."

My understanding of creation was so drastically different— so many gods took credit for building the world and certainly none had done so to bring delight to mankind. I had never heard of a god wanting to have fellowship with men, to cherish them like children. As if he were an adoring father.

"But Elohim knows the end from the beginning, and he had already arranged a plan to bring us back together. Instead of killing HaAdam and Chavah as they deserved, in an act of pure grace, he made them leave the garden, so they would not live forever and eat of the Tree of Life in their sinful state. He made the first of the sacrifices with his own hand, spilled the first blood to cover their shame and spoke of a Coming One who would defeat HaSatan, the adversary, and his followers. It is this story that is written in the stars, and it is this story that the Egyptians changed and replaced with gods of their own making."

He pointed to the eastern horizon. "There is the constellation known to Egypt as the woman Shes-Nu with her desired son in her lap, but in our language she is Bethulah, the virgin waiting for the Promised One. In her right hand she holds the bright star Tsemech, the Branch, for out of Avraham's sons will come a Branch who will rejoin the people to Elohim. Another star in Bethulah is Bezah, the despised, but in Hebrew we call it Asmeath, or sin offering, for the shedding of blood is necessary, as it was in the Garden. An innocent—a perfect sacrifice must be made to pay the penalty for our sin. It covers our shame, if only for a time, for it must be repeated time and time again."

All my life, I had been told that animals must be sacrificed to appease the gods, to please them and coerce them to answer our prayers. But this god called Elohim, or Yahweh as I now knew him, asked for sacrifice not to please himself or to be appeased, but as a gift to his people, to cover their sins.

Eben's rich voice filled me with longing and warmed me, even in the cool of the desert evening. I could listen to him tell stories all night. He looked up at the stars as he spoke, pointing to the constellations along the horizon and above our heads. The stars were as familiar to me as my own family members, reared as I was on the stories of the gods and their movements in the heavens, but Eben's words changed my realities. The tales Egypt had assigned to the stars seemed almost absurd compared to the depth of meaning that Elohim designed when he placed them in the sky.

"Smat, as the Egyptians call him, or the one who rules—we call him Bo, for he comes to tread underfoot the Adversary with a sickle and spear in his hand. Then there is Tulku, the sacred mound of your creation myth." He gestured to me and I flinched, strangely resentful that he'd included me as a purveyor of those legends. "Tulku in Hebrew is called Mozahaim, the scales which weigh our deeds and show us wanting. There is a price to be paid now, a ransom to be bought. Each time a sacrifice is given and blood is spilled, it is a reminder that we owe a debt to the Righteous One and that one day, a greater sacrifice will be made."

The fire burned out, leaving only glowing embers. Shoshana slept curled against her mother's shoulder, and Zayna lay cradled in Eben's arms, long ago lulled to sleep by his soft words.

I should not be jealous of a little girl, but I wanted more stories from Eben's lips about the stars. I ached to lie against his chest and enjoy the resonance of his words against my cheek. After two years of longing for nothing more than freedom, at this moment, I wished more than anything to be locked in Eben's arms.

34

I t's like being followed around for days with wagons full of freshly baked bread at your back and being forbidden from touching it." Shira released an exasperated groan.

Even perennially optimistic Shira could not stave off the frustration of consuming hunger. "There are thousands of cows and sheep swirling around us all the time." She threw down the knife she had been using to scrape the meager flesh off a leg bone.

Eben and some of the other men had managed to encircle a weakened oryx and bring it down. Once it had been divided among the men involved, all that was left to feed our whole group was a leg.

It might have been better to have nothing.

After three days of no food, my empty stomach had stopped complaining. Fatigue and weakness told my mind that my body was hungry, but my stomach did not protest. After tasting the meat, even such a meager portion, the pain of hunger would roar back to life. Once again it would be my constant travel companion.

Shira took the meat she'd removed from the bone and placed

it in a pot of water, already scalding from sitting in the midst of the flames. The broth might help satiate and trick our minds into believing our stomachs were full, at least for an hour or two. I ached for a few vegetables—some leeks or cabbage to add to the thin broth.

"Perhaps the children might have some luck looking for small reptiles among the rocks," I said.

Disgust marred her delicate features. "No! Yahweh does not want us eating reptiles."

"Why not?"

"I don't know, but we've always been told that it's forbidden."

She sat on the ground and stared into the campfire, arms folded across her knees, her face void of any emotion. Was she dreaming of food like I was?

When I was thirsty, before Mosheh turned the bitter waters sweet, all I could think of was water. But there was plenty now— every jug, every skin-bag filled at the stream—and although it was rationed, I did not ache for it as before.

Therefore, free to dwell on the gnaw of my stomach, I fantasized about the banquets I had enjoyed in my parents' villa . . . was it really all that long ago? Roasted beef, goose, and fish fresh from the Nile, accompanied by the choicest baked apples laden with cinnamon, spiced pears, fresh cucumbers, tomatoes, onions, garlic—and fresh breads of every variety, warm from the ovens and stuffed with apricots, raisins, and dates. By the third day away from the edge of the now-sweet springs and without a full meal, my daydreaming turned to more meager fare. Even the plates of plain bread and a small fish accompanied by watery beer in Tekurah's home seemed like a paradise lost.

Zerah and Eben had already used the goats and sheep for food, the last animal sacrificed on the edge of the bitter stream to celebrate the miracle and the salvation of the girls. There was no more meat left among us, only what could be hunted in the desert.

Millions of people tromping through the hunting grounds did little to help the men forage for food. They were forced to travel out a few miles, away from the main group, to find animals not frightened away by the large human contingent. Eben traded as many wares as possible for food and grains, but we were not the only ones scraping the bottom of our reserves.

Shoshana sidled up to me. "I'm hungry, Kiya."

"Me, too, sweetness." I petted her hair, so like Eben's with its dark waves. Was his as soft as Shoshana's?

"Why won't Mosheh let us use the rest of the animals for meat?"

"There are just too many of us. If we all started butchering animals with abandon, there wouldn't be any left."

"Oh." She wrinkled her nose. "I guess Mosheh knows what he's doing."

I shrugged my shoulders. "I certainly hope so; this group is not going to last much longer without meat. There is going to be rebellion."

She nodded slowly, her large brown eyes too aged for her small face. "My aunt and uncle are saying we should have never left Egypt, where the rivers were full of fish and fowl. My aunt even said it would have been better to die there than out here in the wilderness, where our bodies will be food for the jackals."

"At least someone will be eating," I said, then clamped my hand over my mouth, my eyes wide at the carelessness of my words.

Shoshana's little-girl laugh suddenly echoed off the rocks around us on the hillside.

I let loose, and we laughed together until my sides hurt. Morbid as it was, it felt good to smile again. When we finally calmed down and wiped the tears out of our eyes, she laid her head against my arm.

"I'm still hungry, though," she said.

"Me, too." I tapped my chin. "How about we do something else to keep our minds off food?"

"What can we do?" she asked, interest piqued.

"You know, I am impressed with how you can play the lyre."

"Do you want to learn?" Her eyes twinkled.

"Do you think you can teach me?"

"Eben says I will be a great teacher."

"Well then." I spread my arms wide. "Here is your first student."

We perched on an enormous boulder on the edge of camp. I had never played a musical instrument before, and I was as eager to learn as she was to teach. We spent the entire afternoon playing the lyre. By the time Shira came to find us, my fingers were numb and it was dusk, but I played Shira a simple tune while Shoshana sang.

Shira smiled gently. "That is one of my favorite lullabies. Our mother sang that to us every night when we were little."

"It is lovely. What do the words mean?" I had picked up some Hebrew words, but many still eluded me.

"It says: As the stars in the sky, as the sand on the sea, so I will make your people, if you will follow only me."

I put the lyre down on the rock beside me. The sun was slipping behind the curtain of dusk. One or two bright stars to the north already blinked the sleep out of their eyes, soon to be joined by millions of their brothers. And around us, campfires and torches were bursting into bright existence against the dusk. Stars in the sky. That term certainly seemed to fit the teeming mass of people and tents and animals.

"That was the promise given to Avraham, the father of our people," Shira said.

There were millions here; I could imagine that after generations, they possibly could rival the number of stars in the heavens. Especially if others, like us, joined in.

Would I ever be counted as one of the stars? Perhaps if Eben—?

No. How could I even think such a thing? I was drawn to Eben, pulled by a force that left me breathless at times. But he still considered me his enemy, didn't he? He stayed away, across the fire from me, never sitting too near, never walking too close.

Yet at night, through the flickering curtain of the campfire, our eyes met again and again. A brief glance, then one more, and each time, the glances became longer, more lingering, each of us attempting to pretend that we weren't watching the other. The silent dance we performed each night intoxicated me, and I could barely wait for the sun to go down, to drink in more.

He said nothing to me outside of the mundane travel conversation, but even small talk made my stomach flutter. I assigned a thousand deeper meanings to every simple word and every brief glance.

His friendship with Jumo had grown stronger. They were almost inseparable. It bothered me sometimes, but then guilt tugged at me. How could I begrudge my brother a friendship?

Most of my life I had been my brother's only friend, his champion, his protector. I knew him like no other person. He loved me, but now it seemed like he preferred Eben's company to mine. Since Eben was almost pointed in his avoidance of me, Jumo followed suit. Whether it was purposeful or not did not matter. I was jealous—and it was not only Jumo's attention I coveted.

A bird flew over me, swooping low, missing my head by mere inches. Then another twittered as it passed to the left, streaking by in a flurry of brown and white. I twisted my body around on the boulder and gasped.

When the flies and locusts had invaded Egypt, I had watched them swarm across the horizon, but the sight of millions of birds in one enormous flock swooping down into the valley around us was indescribable.

Shira, Shoshana, and I lay flat on the rock, covering our heads with our hands, but peeking out through tangled hair and trembling fingers.

A bird landed in front of us, hitting the ground so hard feathers sprayed high into the air. They were mottled brown-and-white quail, and all of them—there must be millions—were wildly spiraling to their deaths all over the camp. People shielded themselves with jars or baskets, or hid beneath wagons.

Some quail managed to slow their descent and hovered low before alighting on any available perch. Birds covered the ground. Many people braved the onslaught to grab as many as they could carry, stuffing carcasses into the baskets and jars they had been using as shields.

When the invasion stopped and mothers were assured no more missiles would be careening out of the sky, children emerged from their hiding places and, squealing with delight, began to net as many quail as they could with their linens and blankets.

The invaders were already being defeathered and roasted over thousands upon thousands of campfires as we picked our way through camp. The rich smell wafted all around, teasing a loud growl from my dormant stomach.

When our bellies were full almost to overflowing, and another evening of Eben and I avoiding glances above the pop and spark of glowing embers of the dying campfire was finished, my mother asked me about Eben.

Usually she fell asleep long before me, but tonight she was

restless. The stars twinkled through the flap of the tent, and I was considering them once again when she spoke in a hushed voice.

"What is between the two of you?" she asked.

My mother was intuitive; I should have guessed she would notice. There was no cause to deny it.

"Truthfully, I am not sure," I whispered, avoiding her eye even in the dark.

"Has he approached you?"

"No."

"And why not?" She seemed curiously offended.

"We have been wandering around aimlessly starving to death—is it really the time for such a thing?"

"Perhaps not." Her tone cooled.

"And I am not . . ."

"You are not what?"

"I am not Hebrew."

"What does that matter?" I could almost hear her glare in the blackness.

"Shira says that Yahweh wants them to only marry their own."

She snorted. "For what reason?"

"She said it has something to do with other gods."

"Is Yahweh afraid of other gods?" she asked.

"No, we've all seen how powerful he is. I don't think it's fear."

"What then?"

"The way Shira describes it is that Yahweh refuses to let his people follow any other gods. With intermarriage comes intermixing of gods."

"Isn't it foolish to just have one god? What if that one fails? It's only smart to protect yourself by worshipping as many gods as one can afford."

"Well, we haven't been able to afford many sacrifices in the last couple of years, Mother, do you really think any of them are protecting you anymore?"

"I'm not sure." Even in the dark, I could see she was holding Shefu's necklace and stroking it with her thumb. Hathor, the goddess of love, was ever present around her neck.

"Shira's god brought us out of Egypt and through the Red Sea, gave us fresh water, and quail stacked knee-high—what more do you need?" I asked.

"Some bread would be nice."

We giggled quietly in the dark, and I was glad that it felt natural and free to be laughing with my mother. Somehow it seemed as though the journey through the sea had washed my heart of bitterness toward her and filled the empty places with a soothing tranquility. Strange that although we still wandered in a desert of uncertainty, I had never felt more at home.

The cries of children ripped through my dream. My heart was racing before my eyes opened. Shouts surrounded our tent.

"What is it? What is it?"

My mother's head appeared through the opening of the tent, bringing with her a gush of brilliant sunlight. Joy spread across her face in juxtaposition to the loud cries all around.

"Kiya! Wake up! You must come see! He did it!"

"Who did what?" I blinked against the glare of the morning sun.

"Come." She beckoned wildly. "Come see for yourself."

I wrapped my light wool blanket around my shoulders but shivered at the chill in the desert air when I emerged from the tent.

It was snowing.

Delicate white flakes fluttered all around me. It was pure delight that caused the children all over the camp to scream.

They were chasing the snowflakes, tongues out, gathering hand-fuls to toss at each other. Their wild play had stirred the flakes into the air.

But the sky was a pure, deep blue. Not a cloud hovered above us or capped the mountains that embraced the valley.

This could not be snow. It was cool this morning, as it was every morning in the desert, but certainly not cold enough to freeze.

It was not only the children who gathered handfuls of the flakes. Everyone had a basket or a jar or a linen bag they were filling with the snow—or whatever it was.

My mother seemed to be truly enjoying the melee. Her eyes danced as Shoshana and Zayna flew by, shrieks of laughter trailing behind.

"What is going on, Mother?"

"Yahweh did it."

"Excuse me?"

"Yahweh provided bread." She turned her brilliant smile to me. "I asked for bread, and he provided." Her face was an echo of Jumo's as he watched the Cloud every day, a mixture of awe and peace. Peace that I had never seen in her countenance. What was the word Shira used? *Shalom.*

A few flakes landed on the blanket around my shoulders. I took a pinch and placed them on my tongue.

Sweet. Delicious. It was like the best of honey and spices all mixed together. It melted on my tongue with a smooth, velvety texture. Craving more, I bent down to scoop it up, for it was thick on the ground. When I smashed a handful between my palms, it stuck together, forming a flat round.

"What is it?" I took another bite. It was warm as sunshine and smooth as butter going down my throat.

"No one knows, but we've been told that Mosheh said Yah-weh sent it and that Yahweh is going to send it to us every day. Every day! Can you believe it? We won't be hungry anymore."

We gathered as much of the sweet substance as we could, and we were told that there would be a limit to how much we could gather, but that each day more would appear.

It was hard to believe, but the next morning we awoke again to a field of white outside our tent doors. And the morning after that, and again the next day.

No one knew what to call the delicious substance, so we called it *manna*. It was beyond earthly description and could be baked into bread better than any Egyptian sweet roll. I didn't even miss the nuts and fruits that were usually folded into such a delicacy.

No honey was needed to sweeten it, no spices to heighten the aromas, no salt to liven the taste; it was everything we needed to eat. It filled me up and satisfied every craving. I was never so full of energy, and I noticed that everyone around me looked healthier than ever before. Their eyes were bright, their skin glowed. It was so good to see my mother looking vigorous again, her golden eyes snapping with fire. Zayna and Shoshana filled out again, their once-emaciated frames filled with child-like softness again. Gone were the sharp cheekbones and dark circles under their eyes.

A few greedy people found the reason for Mosheh's warning: anyone who collected more than his share was greeted with a pot of maggots in the morning. Therefore, we were all careful to take only what we could eat each day—except for the sixth day, before Shabbat, when two days' portions were allowed. To our great surprise, the manna collected before rest days stayed pure and fresh through the next evening.

Shira and I spent the days trying to invent new ways to cook the manna. We found it thickened stews made from either the leftover dried meat of the quail or the odd desert animal Eben ran across with the hunting teams.

A few days after the manna arrived, Eben returned from

one such hunting excursion with a quarter of a mountain goat wrapped in a thin blanket slung across his shoulders and disturbing news on his lips.

"We saw a scouting party not far off," he told me after laying down the meat on the makeshift table I had cleared.

"Scouts? From Egypt?" My stomach sunk.

"No, I don't think so. They did not look Egyptian. Maybe a local tribe of Midianites."

"Are the Midianites hostile?"

"Not particularly. I'm sure they are just keeping an eye on us to make sure we are the ones who aren't hostile."

He asked for a cloth to wipe his hands and brushed my palm as he took it from me, throwing my path of thought into disarray.

"Oh" was all I could say. I tried to say more, but no sound came out of my mouth. This was the closest I had been to him since that day on the beach.

I dropped my eyes to gather my wits. What were we talking about? I busied myself by sharpening a knife on a stone. When he said nothing more, I looked up to find him watching me with those stormy green eyes, a small crooked smile on his face.

"What?" I asked.

"You look . . ." He paused.

I raised my brows "I look . . . ?"

"Healthier."

"I look healthier?"

He looked down quickly, then a look of confidence, or perhaps release, crossed his face.

"You look beautiful." He held me in his gaze, locking me there, breathless, speechless. The multitude around us dissolved. We were alone.

He stepped closer, without a glance around to see if we were being watched. We were, without a doubt, but I did not care.

"Shoshana tells me she taught you to play the lyre."

Blood rushed to my cheeks. "A bit, yes, but I am not very good. She's a much better teacher than I am a student."

"May I pick up where she left off and teach you more?"

"If you don't care that your ears may be sore after a few minutes with me." I laughed.

"Oh now, I doubt that. Shoshana said you are a quick learner." His playful smile made my heart stutter.

"Oh, did she now?"

He nodded. "And she said you can sing, too."

I laughed. "That little girl is exaggerating."

"Shoshana never lies . . . at least, not to me." He cocked a brow.

He was right, Shoshana worshipped at Eben's feet. I could not imagine her telling him even a half truth.

"I'd best change my tunic from the hunt. But tomorrow—" His eyes twinkled, teasing as he leaned in and handed back the cloth and running a covert finger down the inside of my wrist as he did. "You and I will have our first lesson."

Leaving me trembling in exquisite confusion, he turned and disappeared into his tent.

My mother sat cross-legged across the campsite with Zerah, carding wool gathered from the flocks of the Levite tribe. There was a question in her raised brows.

Attempting to appear unaffected, I shrugged my shoulders. I no more understood Eben's change of attitude than she. She shook her head as she resumed brushing the wool back and forth, tugging at the unruly strands with a little smile on her face.

I tried, without success, to avoid thoughts of Eben by trimming the meat, but all I could think of was the thrill of finally receiving a smile from his lips, meant only for me. I relived the conversation over and over in my mind as I worked.

Midianites. Eben had never finished telling me about the scouts they had seen this afternoon. Were they simply curious about where we were going? Or perhaps now that we were no longer hounded by Pharaoh, the desert tribes that inhabited this lonely wilderness meant to take up the pursuit.

A shiver feathered across my skin. Had we escaped one danger only to be led directly into the waiting arms of another?

35

Eben placed an extraordinary instrument in my hands. My mouth gaped, and I tried to refuse the offering. "No, I can use the lyre Shoshana taught me with."

"I made it for you." He pressed it back, his voice low and rough. His searching eyes and gentle hands on mine caused my thoughts to crash into one other, fanning the sparks of attraction into a wildfire.

I had seen him working on the lyre for days, smoothing the wood with constant strokes of a rough stone, carefully steaming the wood above the fire and shaping it with skilled hands. His brow furrowed in concentration as he carved intricate etchings into the body of the instrument. I never dreamed the beautiful lyre was meant for me.

"Jumo painted it. He insisted it needed some color." Eben shifted his stance. Was he not sure I would like it?

"Thank you," I whispered. "It is the most exquisite gift I have ever received."

His lips twitched with a self-conscious smile. "Glad you like it. I remembered how you seemed to appreciate the one in the market that day."

My mind darted back to the festival, when Eben and I had met. I caressed the swallows he had carved into the body of the lyre, the ones that symbolized freedom and new love. A delicate vine trailed around the entire length of the wood, blue lotus flowers blooming along its path. As his hands had crafted this magnificent work of art, he had thought of me?

I strummed a few notes. Such a sweet sound emanated from the twisted-gut strings. A strange dichotomy—beauty born from death.

Jumo had laughed when I gagged at the sight of Eben stretching the entrails of the last goat back at the bitter-turned-sweet stream, twisting them and preparing them to dry in the sun. Now I heard the fruits of his labor and understood the reason for his method.

I followed Eben, the lyre folded in my arms and my mind buzzing. Two feathery ghaf trees nestled against the foot of the hill at the edge of the camps, providing some early-afternoon shade. A miracle, since foraging for wood was another constant in the desert.

We sat in the shade, away from the hum of voices that surrounded us all the time. Until removed from the noise, I had not realized how desperately I coveted silence.

I breathed in, eyes closed, listening to the breeze brush through the leaves above me and remembering my still mornings near the Nile.

"What are you thinking of?" Eben's voice drew me back to the present.

My eyes fluttered open. "Home."

A shadow crossed his expression. "You regret not going with Sayaad?"

"No!" I shook my head. "Never. There is no place I would rather be than here with you." I sucked in a breath, shocked by my own boldness. Would he get up and walk away from me? Turn his back? I steeled myself for the pain that would follow.

Instead, Eben leaned back against the trunk of the tree, his gaze locked on my face. The silence stretched long between us, shimmering in the air and vibrating like a note plucked from a string and growing louder with each moment. Neither of us seemed willing to break the spell.

His dark brown hair, in disarray as usual, danced about in the breeze. It was getting so long, almost to his shoulders. Should I offer to cut it for him? How could I, without giving away the depth of my attraction to him?

The beard that had once seemed so foreign to me was now one of my favorite things about him. I imagined trailing my fingers through that beard and pressing my lips to his. My cheeks flamed. Hopefully the sun had browned my skin enough that he did not notice.

I love him.

The thought startled me.

The contrast to Akhum, and Sayaad, was evident. Eben was loyal, brave, fiercely protective of his family—and mine, for that matter. His whole demeanor had changed toward me, as if what had happened on that beach had an effect opposite of the one I had predicted. I wanted to spend every moment with this Hebrew slave; this foreign man with his foreign ways fascinated me, and I was more than willing to be drawn into his world.

When Akhum had granted me his attention three years ago, I had been excited, heady at the thought of a man, especially one as powerful and handsome as Akhum, showing me favor. Bringing me expensive gifts, flattering me with praise, parading me through town on his arm—he had done it all to impress me, and those around me. And when he asked, I willingly gave myself to him, so sure of his love and his intent to make me his wife.

How would Eben feel if he knew about my intimacy with

Akhum? Fear seized me at the thought, surprised me with its force. He looked at me now with warmth in his eyes. If I told him, would disdain fill them once again?

I looked away, desperate to avoid him seeing the truth on my face. Shame coursed through me, and tears blurred my vision.

No one will want your precious heart. Akhum's vicious words reached out to me from his grave at the bottom of the sea.

But Eben's hand was suddenly on my face, stroking my cheek with his thumb. I leaned into the sensation, my lips tingling with anticipation and my pulse pounding out a quickening rhythm. My gaze flitted over his shoulder, to the nearest tents, only a few paces away. There was no privacy here, among the millions.

His lips parted, as if to say something, but then a smile lifted their corners. He took his hand away, and his brow lifted in a teasing manner. He was playing with me, testing my response to him, and my eager acceptance of his caress had told him what he wanted to know. I was hungry for more.

I narrowed my gaze. "I thought we were here to play the lyre."

He laughed, and my heart thrilled at the sound of it, as if its musical tones were created only for me.

"That we are." He winked. "For now."

I rolled my eyes at him but was glad of the lighthearted banter—such a contrast to the tension that had filled the chasm between us before we crossed the sea.

Eben leaned back against his tree. "Play me a song that Shoshana taught you."

I hesitated for a moment, unsure about performing in front of him. But the reassuring smile he offered tempered my fears.

My fingers trembled as I plucked the strings, yet I managed to push through the nerves.

"Very good. I am impressed. I told you Shoshana would never lie."

He took the lyre from my hands and played a simple tune,

then handed it back so I could mimic him. We repeated this process back and forth for a long while, and his broad smile was confirmation that he was pleased with my progress. I reveled in his approval.

I stopped to massage my fingers. "I don't think I can play anymore."

He reached for my hand, holding it palm up in his own. My heart skittered around inside my chest as he touched my fingertips. "Yes, you will need to work up those calluses, until they are no longer tender."

I flipped my hand over and smoothed it over his palm. "You mean like yours?"

He sighed, a drawn-out sound of contentment. "Unless you spend your days practicing with a sword, then no, just the tips of your fingers." He matched his own fingertips with mine, and even that tiny contact filled my stomach with flutters.

"So that is where you go every morning? To practice?"

He nodded. "Jumo and I meet with the other Levites to learn new skills and go through exercises."

"My brother is learning to fight?"

"Of course he is. We must all be able to protect ourselves and our loved ones."

I shifted, unsettled by the image of my brother engaged in combat. "Who teaches you?"

"There are a few men among us who served in Pharaoh's army. A few Egyptians, two Syrians, and even a few Hebrews who found a way to elevate themselves into a regiment. They are working to teach us what we need to know."

I raised my brows.

"Yes, it's nearly as foolish as it sounds. A few soldiers working to mold thousands of slaves into warriors." He released my hand to scratch his forehead. "It was almost laughable for the few first days because most of these men have spent their lives hauling mud bricks. They are strong, but most have no idea how to fight."

He shook his head, as if he were locked in an internal debate.

"One thing is to our benefit, however," he said.

"What is that?"

"We all certainly know how to follow orders." A bitter laugh escaped his lips.

Ignoring his sarcasm, I pointed at his empty leather holster. "How did you come to be so good with a dagger?"

"My father gave it to me shortly before . . . before he was killed. Someone traded it for one of his beautiful instruments."

And yet Eben had sacrificed that gift to save me from Sayaad. "Did he teach you to use it?"

He shook his head. "I taught myself, spending hour upon hour practicing. It was my only solace after his death. Somehow I would repay the Egyptians for what they did."

I looked down at my hands, feeling a vicarious stab of guilt for those of my heritage who had committed such an atrocity.

"I don't blame you anymore." He lifted my chin with a gentle hand. "I'm sorry that I ever did. My bitter heart refused to see any Egyptian as guiltless."

"Well, that's good to know," I said. "And I'm very glad for your skill with a knife. Thank you—for saving me from my stupidity."

"I'm glad that I was so helpless to take my eyes off you that day. If I had missed him taking off with you . . ."

My heart stirred at his admission. "But you didn't. You saved me." I held his gaze.

He leaned closer, his voice dropping to an intimate volume. "You will always be protected."

"I will?"

"Yes." A teasing smile played across his lips as he pointed

at the instrument in my lap. "Besides, who would attack you with that weapon in your hands?"

"How can a lyre be a weapon?"

"A beautiful woman playing an alluring song? There is nothing more dangerous." He raised a brow.

My throat was too tight to speak. I could do nothing but watch him watching me, until a thought surfaced through the haze. "What are you training for? Pharaoh's army is at the bottom of the sea."

"We are in Midianite territory. And they are not the only tribes that roam these parts. There have been rumors that a large contingent of Amalekites is moving this way."

"Who are they?"

"A large group from the south, and among the most ruthless tribes around. They move from place to place, claiming any grazing land and livestock they come across. "

I shivered.

"Exactly." He nodded. "They are beyond vicious. And we must be ready. Our crossing at the sea has put us directly in their path northward."

"Why doesn't Mosheh lead us somewhere else? We need to get away from them." Panic rose in my throat. "We can't risk it."

"Do you not believe that Yahweh is protecting us?"

"I don't know . . ." I searched the skyline above the hills for an answer to my doubt. I deliberately kept my glance from the north end of camp, where the blue Cloud glowed relentlessly near Mosheh's tent.

"No one dares attack us, Kiya. I spoke with some traders that came through yesterday. Word has traveled all over the region about our miraculous rescue through the sea."

"It has?"

He nodded. "Every tribe around has heard of it. They are terrified."

"Do the Amalekites fear your god?"

Confusion crossed his face. "Is he not *your* god as well?"

I pursed my lips while considering how to answer and then opted for the truth. "I believe he is a powerful god—perhaps the most powerful. But he frightens me. I am not sure I can submit to a deity who slaughtered my people so wantonly."

"And your Pharaoh did not slaughter *my* people?" His eyes pinned me.

"Yes . . . but . . ."

"Do you not think our freedom was worth the price that was paid? That our murdered sons and fathers, our violated women, did not deserve justice? Blood for blood? A life for a life?" Anger drew his brows together, and he pulled away from me.

"I don't . . . I don't know . . . Must blood always be shed?"

"Yes. Yahweh is the creator of life, and it is his alone to give and take away. Your worthless gods have no such power."

"My worthless—" My lips trembled, and blood crashed through my veins. "Your god cares only for his own people."

"You are here, are you not? Your brother, your mother, they are safe? And many of your countrymen followed us as well. It has always been so—anyone who follows Yahweh is welcome." He lifted his chin, a challenge in his expression. "Even Avraham was not a Hebrew, his father was a maker of idols and he came out of the land of Ur. From our very beginnings, those who answered Yahweh's call were brought close."

"He has not called me. I have not heard some voice out of a burning bush. I came with you to save my brother and to be free. Yahweh cares nothing for me, and I care nothing for him."

He did not respond but leaned forward with his elbows on his knees and hands grasped tightly together. His silence testified to his dissatisfaction with my answer. He hung his head, leaving me unable to see the effects of his contemplation in his expression. Was he regretting the affection he'd shown me?

This time spent with me? Would he turn his back on me now, like my father had?

As tempted as I was to contradict my own words, to profess my belief in Yahweh, to smooth the sharp edges that had come between us in the past few minutes, I held my peace. I could stomach no more lies, and I would not willingly deceive him, even if it meant losing the tenderness I had cherished in his gaze today. Already the wound of the loss throbbed at my core.

Eben stood. He offered me a hand to stand but released me quickly. I followed him back to camp, blinking away tears and clutching the beautiful lyre to my chest as if it could somehow keep me bound to the man I had come to love—in spite of the obvious canyon that once again yawned between us.

36

"Are you certain we are safe here?" Remembering my conversation with Eben about the marauding tribes that called this wilderness home, fear prickled up my neck as I looked up at the sheer cliffs that loomed over us.

Shira pointed farther up the wadi, where a few scattered trees and chest-high grasses choked our view of the stream. "Eben said there are three lookouts up there, and they will alert us to any dangers." She elbowed me with a smile, trying to lighten my mood, which had been at the bottom of a well since Eben and I parted ways yesterday. "There are men stationed all over the place, Kiya. We are fine. Let's wash and then see what we can find."

It was almost a relief that Eben had left after the morning meal, called to a meeting once again. Rumors of spies among the traders were rampant, and a few stragglers had gone missing over the last couple of days as we made our way through rocky canyons, group by group. The air seemed to crackle with anxiety as we waited to move along, nearly as much as it had on the beach by the sea when we waited for Pharaoh.

Zerah had asked us to look for plants for dyes here in this

narrow canyon where a small stream wound a twisted path among the rocks. She hoped we might have a bit of time before the Levites were told to move to the next stage of our journey.

Zerah had promised to teach me to weave. I was fascinated by the swirl of her distaff as she spun and the complicated patterns forming on her looms. Excitement built in me as I considered which plants would create the most vibrant colors. The desert yielded a surprising abundance if one knew where to look—henna, dye-weed, indigo—all useful for making paints for Jumo as well.

My mother walked with Shira and me, saying she was desperate for a wash in the stream after many days of little water. Jumo hobbled along, too, slowly picking his way behind us across the uneven ground, a short sword hanging at his side.

Yesterday evening he and Eben had practiced swordplay before our meal, and I had resisted the urge to protest. His encumbered limbs prevented him from doing much more than basic defense. Yet Eben had encouraged him at every step, and Jumo's smile bore witness to his pleasure at being treated like a man instead of a child.

He found a nearby rock to sit on, his crutches across his lap, and focused on the sun hanging low in the sky. What was going through his mind? If only he were able to express with freedom what was in his heart. I knew him, I could see that he was enjoying the beauty of creation, studying it. The sharp attention to detail that was so evident in his paintings made him aware of every leaf, every flower, every stray ray of sunlight.

Every so often, he pointed out a plant to us as we searched, his keen eyes finding them long before anyone else could see, even while he still sat on his rock.

Shira found some roots, and we used pointed sticks to dig around the edible tubers. My mother ventured farther down the stream to wash. I watched her out of the corner of my eye as we worked. Shira went to find a private place to relieve herself, a constant frustration for all of us. She went back the way we had come and disappeared behind a boulder.

Shira had asked me nothing about my time with Eben yesterday but had fawned over the lyre he had given me, exclaiming that it was one of his finest instruments. The comparison made my heart ache worse, for he had made this exquisite gift for me and offered it to me along with a tender caress—a wordless admission of his attraction to me, and I had repaid him by rejecting his god.

Must I throw away everything in my heritage to love him? Must I submit to a god I feared?

I knew the answer; Shira had told me that they were only to marry other Hebrews, that there had been dire consequences when that direction was not obeyed. Eben could not marry me. He would be forbidden by the elders to do so.

And just like Shefu had reluctantly agreed to marry Tekurah, Eben would marry another. And just like Shefu, I knew that Eben would not fight against the command. His loyalty to his people and to Yahweh was too great. Any affection between us would be sacrificed.

The promise of deep friendship—of love—with Eben that I had glimpsed yesterday afternoon during our lesson had been a mirage, yet my thirst for it was acute.

Had I been wrong? Eben seemed to think Yahweh had called me here into this desert, pulled me along on this journey for some purpose. Jumo had received some sort of dream telling him to come with the Hebrews, but I had come of my own will. Hadn't I?

Even my mother seemed drawn to Yahweh; many times a day I noticed her watching the Cloud, her face a mixture of awe and peace. Did my mother hear the call of Eben's god as well?

The sun was very low in the sky, painting the rocks around us red. I told Jumo we needed to head back to camp, and he agreed.

I called out to my mother and began gathering our plants and tubers into a basket. She did not answer.

I called again.

Only silence returned.

A deep chill shot up my spine. "Jumo, where's Mother?"

Eyes wide, he shook his head.

I walked downstream, my feet in the cool water. It flowed shallow here, bubbling on the many rocks. Twenty paces along, I saw her, facedown in the stream, black hair flowing around her, blood and water staining her white-linen dress crimson.

I tried to scream but no sound came forth, only a strangled cry drowned out by the frantic heartbeat pounding in my ears. I struggled to turn her over. Her body was limp and heavy.

"No. No. No. Mother!"

Her graceful throat was slit. Lips white and parted. Her eyes—so like my own—open and unseeing.

I opened my mouth, a desperate howl forming somewhere near the bottom of my soul, but then someone put an arm around my neck. How did Jumo find me so quickly? The arm tightened, my air supply squeezed. I tore at the arm with my fingernails, but my efforts did nothing to relieve the pressure.

Six men, all with veiled faces, surrounded me with crudely fashioned swords in their hands. One of those swords had killed my mother. One of these men had stolen her from me and from Jumo.

I struggled against the one who held me, kicking at his shins, biting at the hand that covered my mouth. I managed to slide out of his hold for a moment, but he seized me again with an iron grip.

"Quiet, girl, or you will end up like that beauty," a voice rasped into my ear. He spoke my language but with an unfamiliar accent.

When I obeyed, he unwrapped his arm from around my throat, turning me around as he did. I gasped as precious air tore into my lungs.

"My, my. So very lovely." He stroked my cheek, and I closed my eyes against the lurid intimacy of the gesture. Nausea welled in my throat. My fate may very well be worse than my mother's.

One of the men came up behind my captor and spoke quietly into his ear.

"All right, you have a deal. I believe you may have a good point. The other one was wasted. Take her and tie her up—tight. She's a slippery one. We can't let such a delicate flower escape into the desert, now, can we?"

The second man grasped my arm and put a familiar ivory-handled dagger at my throat. "Come."

I pulled against his grip and twisted around to look at him. The man's face was swathed in a dirty woolen scarf, but the eyes that greeted me were blue as the morning sky.

37

There was a commotion behind Sayaad and a yell. *Jumo!* He surprised my attackers and, using Eben's short sword, managed to clip one of the masked men on the shoulder. But since Jumo was unable to aim with much precision, it had little effect. The man turned quickly on him and lashed back with his own sword. The weapon hit my brother flat along the side of his head and he crumpled, unconscious. A small trickle of blood flowed from his ear.

I screamed with all my might.

Sayaad startled and dropped the tip of his—of Eben's—dagger. "Quiet!" The point was back at my throat and his large hand over my mouth and nose, cutting off my cry.

The leader, the one who had grabbed me first, yelled. "We need to go! They will have heard her scream."

"What about the boy?" Jumo's attacker pointed his sword at my fallen brother.

Sayaad dropped a fleeting glance at me. "Leave him. He looks like his legs don't work. He's not going to follow us, even if he does wake from that crack you gave his skull, Taral."

"But I saw another girl," Taral said. "Right before the cripple hit me. I'm going to go—"

"No. Leave her alone!" I yelled, but my protest was muffled behind Sayaad's fingers.

Sayaad pushed the point of the dagger deeper into my skin. I swallowed and shrank back, my mind whirling. If I did not surrender, they would follow after Shira, add her blood to my mother's in the stream, or carry her off. I had already lost one person I loved, and another lay bleeding and possibly dying nearby. I would give up everything to make sure Shira stayed safe.

The fate that awaited me was a grim one, but if I could buy Shira time to run, I would do it. She'd sacrificed herself once for me, and I would return the favor—pay her back for the love and kindness she had shown an unworthy Egyptian.

Yahweh, if you are listening to me, protect her. Let my sacrifice not be in vain.

I twisted around, begging Sayaad with my eyes. He released my mouth enough for me to whisper. "She's halfway back to camp. Please, I'll come with you if we just go. I won't make another sound. I promise."

Sayaad glared at me a moment but gazed back in the direction of camp. "The girl will alert the Hebrews. Let's get out of here."

The leader nodded and gestured. "Bring your prize, Sayaad. And keep her mouth shut."

Their horses were tied up in an acacia grove nearby, near the bodies of three Hebrew guards and the remains of the smashed shofarim, which could have alerted us to the attack.

Sayaad threw me onto the back of his horse and swung himself up behind me. My wrists were bound, and then a linen strip, cut from my own shift, gagged my mouth. Not that I would yell again—Shira needed to get back to camp and gather men to rescue Jumo, if it was not already too late.

Sayaad gripped me about the waist, his hot hand burning

through my dress. "Did you miss me?" he whispered in my ear, his voice smooth and seductive.

I averted my eyes.

"No? I'm wounded. Not long ago, you were ready to run off with me." He clicked his tongue. "Did your little Hebrew slave-dog claim you for himself after I left?"

I stiffened, and he laughed under his breath.

"Didn't take you long, did it? Well . . ." He ran a finger down the side of my neck, causing my stomach to lurch. "No matter, my little dove. I'm your master now. I've promised Ferren half my spoils when the Amalekites attack the Hebrews so I can keep you for myself."

I turned my head and raised my brows. *Amalekites?*

"Yes, my dear, my friends and I met up with a raiding party shortly after we found a boat to take us across the sea. And since I am half Amalekite . . ." He stopped. "Oh yes, I might have left that little bit of information out of my father's history, but your Hebrews were already wary of me—as they should have been—and I felt it was necessary to keep that tidbit to myself."

Sayaad told me how he had filled their leaders' ears with knowledge of all the gold, silver, and other riches the Hebrews were trekking about in their wagons. Like many had suspected, spies had been slipping in among the Hebrews, some disguised as traders.

"It won't be long now," Sayaad said. "We are almost ready to attack. Your little slave friends won't stand a chance. Your men have no idea how to swing a sword or aim a bow."

The sun had laid down to rest beyond the far hills by the time we reached the Amalekites' camp. The sight of it shocked me. I had envisioned a large raiding party—maybe a small contingent of soldiers—but this mass was not preparing for a small skirmish with the Hebrews; they were outfitted for war.

Did the Hebrews have any idea what was about to come

down upon them? Was Mosheh prepared for the army that lay
in wait within an hour's walk? Thousands of tents dotted the
landscape, with tens of thousands of men silhouetted against
the glowing campfires. The elders must have known and were
avoiding a panic by not telling the rest of the Hebrews. Did Eben
know the truth? Was he prepared to fight? Would he, like my
mother, be slaughtered by these ruthless marauders?

Was she truly gone? My beautiful mother? Could I have
missed a sign of life? Perhaps I had only dreamed her vacant
eyes and her limp body in my arms. I shivered in spite of the
heat of Sayaad's body against my back.

Sayaad ignored the blatant stares as we rode through the
camp. I retreated further into my veil to block out their curious
looks, grateful he insisted I cover my head and face before we
came over the ridge. He dismounted and then pulled me off the
horse, dragged me to a tent, and pushed me into its black mouth.

Was I to be violated here, in the middle of this camp, with
hundreds of ears attuned all around? I had seen the lust in
Sayaad's eyes those many days ago on the shore of the great
sea, and the fire of it now was no less.

He pushed me across the tent. "Lay down."

It was so dark inside, only a faint flicker of campfire light
penetrated the heavy animal hide. The reek of death gagged
me. I did not move.

"Lay! Down!"

"Where? I can't see," I shot back.

He forced me down onto a mound of blankets that must
serve as his bed. He began to tie my feet, and a rush of relief
washed over me. He wasn't going to force himself on me—at
least not right now. He must have heard my breath release, for
he leaned down to whisper in my ear.

"No, my dear. Not now. There are too many wolves at the
door. But soon . . ." He ran his hand up the back of my neck,

snarled his fingers in my hair, and none too gently, he pulled my head back so I was forced to look at his face. Firelight seeping through the open tent flap glistened in his greedy eyes.

He drew a ragged breath. "Soon. I've waited far too long. You are my prize now, but I will enjoy my reward without inflaming the others' lusts. That would make it all the more dangerous for both of us."

After he tied my hands, he released me and left the tent but did not go far. I watched through the narrow opening of the tent door as he sat down by the fire directly outside. He was guarding his prize, as he'd said, and for now, he would ensure I was safe—from the Amalekites at least. But how long would I be safe from him? And when he was done with me, what then?

I fell back onto the crumpled blankets. My hands and feet were bound so tightly I could not move to smooth his bed. I kept my face toward the front of the tent and a close eye on his back. At any moment he could change his mind and come back to claim my body.

My mind raced through the time I'd spent with Sayaad. He had seemed only handsome and interesting and perhaps a bit brash when I'd met him. His brazen near-kidnapping on the beach had startled me. Clearly, I had misjudged him from the start. He was a killer, a thief, and cared no more for me than for the horse he had just ridden. At least he had given the horse a drink of water in a stream on the way; my mouth was as dry as the desert.

Now given the chance to lie still, the chill at the center of my body enveloped me, and I trembled, teeth chattering and dizziness disorienting me whenever I attempted to lift my head.

All I could see was the red stream my mother lay in and Jumo unconscious on the ground, probably near death. I would never see them again. I was sure Shira had made it back to camp; she was a fast runner. But whether Jumo lived, I would never know. And Eben would probably die when this army attacked, and then I would have lost everything, everyone that mattered.

I could not even cry. I wanted to. I might feel some relief if I did, but no tears would come. I might as well be in that stream next to my mother . . . my heart was just as dead, my hands just as cold and numb. I could not even summon anger, or fear, or sadness. There was nothing but ice at my core.

Eben was wrong. Yahweh had not called me. And if he had, it was only to bring me to destruction in this wilderness. He cared nothing for an Egyptian slave. He did not want me.

Sleep was long in coming, but I finally succumbed to exhaustion. I awoke only once in the dark of night. Sayaad lay next to me, his heavy arm slung across my shoulders and his sour breath in my face. I was pinned beside him and had no energy to push him away. There was nothing to do but surrender to oblivion.

The next two days I spent shackled inside the tent, enduring the endless darkness and the uncertainty of eternal minutes at the mercy of my blue-eyed captor. Sayaad said he didn't want to chance the men getting too close a look at me, so he brought me food: some stew, warm beer, and bread, which seemed bland after the sweetness of the manna.

He said nothing more about trying to force himself on me, but his impatience was palpable whenever he came near. Both nights he stumbled into the tent drunk, and I fully expected him to abuse me, but he passed out next to me on the pallet and left me alone.

On the third morning after my capture, well before dawn, Sayaad woke me to tell me that the Amalekites were done playing games with the Hebrew throng and that they were going to war.

"You are leaving?"

"Not for long, my little lotus blossom." He stroked my face

with his palm, and I resisted the urge to sink my teeth into his hand. "We will make easy work of your precious Hebrews. I expect I will be back before dark."

"How will I be safe if you go?" My voice pitched high. Already I had heard two arguments between Sayaad and other men outside the tent in a foreign tongue, and I knew they fought over me. What would happen if I was left alone?

The panic in my voice caused a smug smile to tug at his lips. "The women will watch you."

"The women?"

He laughed. "Yes, Kiya. How else do you think we have this lovely stew? Many of the men bring their wives to cook." He winked at me. "And I know you can cook, yes?"

I scowled. "So, I'm to be your wife?"

He threw back his head and laughed loudly. Voices that had been chattering near the tent ceased. All ears must now be tuned to our conversation.

"No, no, no." He laughed again. "I don't need a wife, little Kiya."

My voice came out flat. "I am just your slave."

He tilted his head and moved in close to me. "Doesn't that concern you?"

I shrugged. "It is what it is."

He stroked my cheek again, and my stomach curdled. I knew that it wouldn't be long before he would exert his full rights of ownership.

He saw the question in my eyes. "You wonder why I am waiting?"

I flinched, disturbed that he could read me so well.

"Well . . ." His blue eyes sparkled in the sunlight now creeping through the tent flap. "Perhaps I am under a foolish notion that you might come to want me back." His voice was soft, seductive. "There was, after all, a time not that long ago when I saw desire behind your eyes when you looked at me."

The first flame of emotion in three days began to build inside me. "You. Killed. My. Mother. Any desire I had for you bled into that stream."

"It wasn't me, Kiya. She was dead before I even arrived. I would not have allowed it. And I saved you. If Ferren had kept you, you would have been sold to a dozen men by now. I am not your worst enemy here."

"Perhaps not, but keeping company with them makes you an accomplice to their sins." Nausea welled, and I clenched my hands to prevent their shaking. I jutted out my chin, refusing to let him glimpse my fear. "It doesn't matter if you want me for a wife or a concubine, I'm still a slave. And I will never want you the way you want me. Ever."

He shrugged, all pretense of kindness now gone from his voice and the tease in his blue eyes replaced with darkness. "Perhaps not. It changes nothing." He turned to leave, but then paused and came back to blindfold me with the dirty woolen scarf that had hid his face before.

"The women are watching you, Kiya," he said low in my ear. "And they are under strict orders to keep you in this tent. And if you think the Amalekite men are bloodthirsty . . . they are nothing compared to the women, especially with a beautiful slave like you loose around their men." He barked a sharp laugh and was gone.

38

Shrouded in darkness behind the woolen veil, I shook as the terrifying crashes and screams of battle met my ears. The bray of shofarim rose above the melee. The sounds of the trumpets calling men to meeting were familiar to me, but these cries ripped high and loud throughout the valley, screeching out a fierce call to battle that raised the hair on the back of my neck and pierced me. *Eben is answering that call.*

As the battle raged to the north—much closer than I had expected—the women outside the tent spoke in low, sharp tones in a foreign tongue. *What I wouldn't give to understand what they are saying.*

Eben and the other Hebrew men had been training to fight using Egyptian weapons salvaged from the seashore and donated by Egyptian households, but would it be enough? Half a million men fought alongside Eben, but he had said the Amalekites were known for their ruthless and merciless tactics. How long would it take for the Hebrews to be overcome? Two hours? Three?

No. I refuse to believe it. Yahweh had tossed Pharaoh's army into the depths. He had forged a path through the sea. I had seen it with my own eyes and walked through on dry land. Yahweh had saved his people over and over. He would not—he *could* not—abandon them now. A god who had destroyed a country to rescue his people surely would not let them perish.

My mother, and possibly my brother, had died in the wilderness, and one way or another, I would be destroyed in this tent as well, but Eben, Shira, Zerah, Shoshana, and Zayna hovered under Yahweh's protection. They must live.

My ears strained. The sounds of agony and the crash of swords seemed farther away, as if the battle had ebbed northward again. Was the battle over? Had the Hebrews been overtaken? Did Eben's sightless eyes gaze at the heavens?

Darkness—almost as thick as the three days of night—suddenly seemed to envelop me, weighing me down in oily blackness. The smell of death that lingered in this goat-hide tent burnt my nostrils; I breathed through my mouth to counter the stench.

Then the battle sounds pitched high again. The shofarim jolted me out of my stupor and rattled my bones at their nearness.

Did that mean that the Hebrews had pushed the Amalekites back? Did the blood that surely stained the sand today include Sayaad's? Or would he return at the battle's end to enslave me and rip my soul apart?

Never. I refused to allow Sayaad to place me under subjugation again. I would fight until my last breath. I preferred death. I struggled against the cords that bound me hand and foot, ignoring the sting of their burn against my skin as I fought them. But no matter how hard I twisted or yanked, nothing could free me of the bondage I had willingly accepted for Shira's sake.

The cries of angry men and the wounded echoed around the valley and reverberated off the mountains surrounding the

Amalekite encampment. The Hebrew camp lay only a little to the north. If the Hebrews pushed them farther and farther south, this tent might stand at the center of the battle.

Still blinded by the veil over my eyes and bound by rope, I lay on my side for hours as the tide of fighting rose and fell, recounting the misguided steps that had led me to this dusty floor, waiting for death.

Once before, bound and imprisoned, I had called out to Yahweh and he had not answered. Or had he? Not long after my plea, Shefu had rescued me and set me free. And before that, I had crossed paths with Shira, whose friendship had provided a way to protect Jumo. The echo of Shira's words came back to me from all those months ago. *Perhaps he is preparing you for something, too.*

Had Yahweh been calling to me? Without words? Had he guided my steps to be among his people? To be set free from bondage and to follow him into the wilderness for some purpose I did not yet understand? Perhaps even the dream that had plagued me after the Nile turned red, when the gods themselves bled, was a message that Yahweh would destroy their power.

My heart contracted as I considered the possibilities. Did Yahweh, the Almighty Creator, hear me? An Egyptian slave? Even though I had refused to surrender to him?

During a disconcerting lull in the noise, as my ears searched for the sounds of the shouts of men fighting for their lives, I began to pray. Even though it was still strange praying to nothing, talking to the air, behind my blindfold I closed my eyes and imagined the formless Hebrew God standing in front of me, listening to my pleas. "Please, Yahweh. Deliver your people. Don't let their enemies say that you brought them into the desert to die."

The more I prayed, the less strange it felt to not be prostrate in front of an idol—with nothing to look toward with my eyes, no temple to face, no image to conjure in my mind. Shira had told me many months ago that Yahweh could not be contained in an image, that his glory outweighed all the gold on the earth, that a mere piece of wood or stone carving could never capture the perfection and majesty of his being. Suddenly this made sense. The idols of Egypt were creations of human hands to worship gods that could be controlled and manipulated. I would never again worship such as those.

I did not know how to pray to Yahweh. I tried speaking to him in Hebrew, but the new language stilted and stammered against my tongue. I could not express myself fully, so I lapsed back into Egyptian. Shouldn't an all-knowing God understand me either way? I prayed some of the learned prayers from my childhood, but none conveyed what I needed to say, so I simply asked Yahweh to deliver the Hebrews. I begged until tears took over and I simply lay facedown on the sandy floor of the tent and cried.

When finally the tears were spent and my hoarse prayers stilled from fatigue, I simply chanted his name: *Yahweh, Yahweh, Yahweh, Yahweh,* until it merged with the rhythm of my breath. Inhale-*Yah*, exhale-*weh*, inhale-*Yah*, exhale-*weh*.

A light fragrance met my senses. An unfamiliar smell, but similar to an incense of exotic flowers mixed with unknown spices. I braced for the headache that always followed the stench of the temple incense, but it did not come. Instead, the odor seemed to swirl around me, erasing the death stench of the tent and pushing back the darkness that gripped me.

Could a smell overcome darkness? Yes, even with my eyes still bound, traces of light pierced the blindfold. I felt bathed in light, bathed in love, as if the Cloud had entered this tent and curled itself around my body. I felt the warmth of it wrap around me like my father's hand had encased mine as a little girl. But unlike my father, unlike Shefu, this Father had not turned his back on me—instead he liberated me.

Here I was in bondage again, yet somehow I felt free. It was not Tekurah, or Akhum, or Sayaad who had shackled me. It was the false gods and my refusal to place my trust in Yahweh that had held me captive.

No longer. Calling out to Yahweh in my brokenness had broken the chains.

War cries surged louder and louder, startling me with their ferocity and nearness.

The shofarim sounded again, and my hopeful imagination found victory in the sound. A shout echoed nearby, and the walls of the tent fluttered as someone rode by on a horse and the women outside screamed.

I pushed up to my knees, an awkward movement with my hands and feet bound. My blindfold slipped, and I blinked at the shaft of light spilling through the flap of the tent.

More shouting, then one of the women stuck her head into my prison and screamed something at me in her strange tongue. I only registered black eyes peeking out from between her veils and a large gold hoop dangling from her nose before she disappeared again.

Startled, I cried out, "Come back, what is happening?"

But she was gone.

I gasped at the force of the fear that Sayaad was coming back victorious . . . and then more fear that he was dead and someone else would claim me.

Tempted to steal a look out the tent flap but terrified of what I might see, I stayed locked in place on the floor, ignoring the burn of the ropes against my wrists and ankles.

The tent walls shook again, and then Sayaad stood in front of me, drenched in blood.

"Get up!"

My limbs would not comply.

"Stand up! Now!" He yanked me harshly by the arm and dragged me to my feet.

"What is happening?" My voice was rough from hours of tearful prayer.

Throwing things into a large leather pouch, he did not look at me. "We are leaving."

"Where are we going?"

"Away from here."

"What happened?"

He did not answer but knelt down to cut the rope off my feet with Eben's dagger. He then stood and placed the tip under my chin. Spatters of blood streaked his face. Whose blood? *Oh, Yahweh, please don't let it be Eben's.*

"Somehow the Amalekites lost this battle, and your precious Hebrews are on their way to finish off the rest of us. You and I won't be here when they come. Understand?"

My heart fluttered like a hummingbird. They won? Yahweh had answered my prayer? Joy and victory swelled inside me, giving me a surge of renewed energy to yank against Sayaad's grip and a determination to steel myself and fight for my freedom. I kicked him hard and screamed with my whole being.

He snatched me by the hair, growling and pressing the point of the knife a little harder into my skin. "If you don't get your pretty little backside onto my horse immediately, I will cut you down, here and now."

I believed him. The blood of Hebrews stained his clothes. He would not hesitate to add mine to it.

The door flap flew back, and Eben rushed in, his bloody sword pointed directly at Sayaad's chest. The victory that swelled in my heart overcame the surprise that the man I loved had come to my rescue.

"Take his dagger, Kiya." He did not take his eyes off Sayaad.

"I can't. My hands. He tied me." My words rushed out in a tangle.

"Well then, my friend." He smiled at Sayaad. "Cut her loose, then drop it and kick it to me."

Sayaad complied, but the look of hate that flowed out of him sent shivers up and down my spine.

"All I want is what I came for. I've killed enough men today. I will leave vengeance to my brothers." Eben jerked his head at me. "But you will never touch her again. If you make one move toward her, you will have no hands left to touch any woman. Ever."

He pulled my arm, placing himself in front of me. He then bent to pick up the ivory-handled dagger his father had given him so long ago.

Sayaad drew a short sword from his cloak, swinging it in a wild arc. I cried out and moved to shield Eben.

But before Sayaad's sword connected with my arm, Eben knocked me aside and jabbed upward in one swift move. Once again, the ivory-handled dagger met its mark, this time directly between Sayaad's ribs. Sayaad fell to his knees, eyes wide and mouth gaping, gasping for breath. Eben paused only long enough to retrieve his dagger from the dying man's chest, then grabbed my hand and pulled me behind him as we fled the tent.

Ignoring Sayaad's horse still tied nearby, Eben pointed toward the hills to the east of the Amalekite camp and urged me to run. A few stragglers, mostly women, ran the opposite way, fleeing the enemy camp, carrying what they could and not looking twice at us. None of them wanted to wait around to see the Hebrews claim their victory, or to be claimed as spoils themselves.

We reached the edge of the valley. Eben gripped my hand and led me to a path snaking upward into a hidden wadi between the hills. I slid on the rocks a few times, sending rivers of stone tumbling down behind me, but Eben's strong arm kept me upright until the wadi leveled out.

He slowed his pace, but we kept moving until the hills behind us cradled the sinking sun. My lungs burned, and my feet throbbed. "I have to stop, Eben. Please, I need a break."

He kept moving but slowed his pace. "There are caves nearby. We can catch our breath there."

"How do you know that?"

He pushed back a low desert shrub with his sword to let me pass but did not let go of my hand. "This is the way we came before."

"What do you mean?"

"We watched the Amalekite camp for two days. Somehow their scouts missed this little valley. I've spent the last two nights in the caves."

"Did you know they were planning an attack today?"

"We assumed they were preparing to attack, but we didn't know it would happen so soon. I sent Michael and Desha back to report to the elders last night." He tugged my hand. "Come on, let's get to the cave so you can rest."

He led me up another steep incline, my sandals slipping again and again on the slick rocks, but he caught me each time. His confidence in his destination reassured me. But as dusk fell, I became completely disoriented, my heart pounding as I imagined sharp drop-offs all around my feet.

We stopped in front of a dark opening in the rock. "Here we are. Let me go in first and make sure there are no snakes."

I shivered. *We are going in there?*

He ducked his head into the cave, and I leaned back against the face of the rock. The sun disappeared and a few stars twinkled low on the eastern horizon as his sword clanged around the cave.

"It's all clear—come inside."

I felt my way into the cave, my stomach in knots. *Must he mention snakes?*

"Are you sure this is the place?" My voice quavered.

A low laugh floated out of the blackness in front of me. "I left my pack here this morning. There is a blanket and some food. Where is your hand?" Although there was not a whisper of light in the cave, somehow his warm, callused hand found my cold one.

"Here." He gently pulled me down next to him and put a blanket around my shoulders. "I wish we could set a fire, but I don't know how many Amalekites might be slinking around." He pressed some bread into my hand. "Eat."

The taste of manna exploded on my tongue. Three days without the sweet bread had heightened the sensation of its spiced-honey flavor. He handed me a skin-bag. After being hidden in the cave all day, the water ran cool over my lips. With nothing to drink but warm, stale beer for the last three days, my parched throat and mouth all but sang with pleasure as I satisfied my thirst.

Eben let out a shuddering sigh. "Are you unharmed?"

My heart stuttered at the gentleness of his voice. I nodded and then laughed quietly. *He can't see me.* "I am not injured."

"Are you . . . all right, though?"

He didn't know how to ask what Sayaad had done to me.

"He did not harm me. I was tied in his tent for three days. He only threatened to . . ."

His breath released. "Thank Yahweh."

I didn't know how to ask what I needed to know from him either. "Tell me what happened after I was taken."

"Why don't you rest? We can talk in the morning." His ragged voice jolted me. *What more do I not know?*

"Eben. Please. Tell me."

He exhaled slowly.

"Your—your mother . . ."

"Is dead." Saying the words out loud hammered them deep into my heart. I felt their sharp edges as they took root.

"You knew?"

"I was there. She was gone . . . dead, before I found her in the stream. They took me from her side." If only I could erase the picture of my mother, sightless and pale, from my memory. "And . . . Jumo?" I braced for the truth.

"Jumo is fine, aside from a nasty cut on his head and a broken heart. He is alive."

"He is? Jumo is alive? Praise Yahweh!" I thought my heart would burst through my chest with joy. I grabbed for Eben and hugged him with all my strength.

What am I doing? I pulled back before he could push me away.

Instead he pulled me closer and wrapped me in his arms. I let the wall crumble and sobbed into his chest. He rocked me back and forth until my heart emptied itself; the strength of his embrace and the warm scent of his body infused me with a deep sense of safety I had never felt before.

I sniffed back my tears. "And Shira?"

"Shira is sick with worry over you, as is my mother."

"She is? Your mother is worried about me?"

"Of course. We all have come to love you and your family. My mother is devastated over the loss of your mother. She and Shira would have come looking for you themselves if I would have let them. And Jumo . . ." His voice trailed off.

"What?" I pulled back. *Curse this blackness hiding his face.*

"Jumo is beside himself with grief and anger. Not being able to protect you or your mother . . ."

"But there was nothing he could have done. He did try." The image of my brother hefting that sword, the fury and the grief contorting his expression—I would never forget it.

"Don't you see? A man who cannot protect his own family . . .

doesn't feel like a man at all." Carefully tucked behind his words were the memories of a young boy carrying the burden of protecting his family after his father's murder.

My heart bled for Jumo—and Eben—and my response was for both men. "It was not his fault."

"Still. He blames himself for Nailah's death and your kidnapping."

I dropped my head into my hands. "My poor brother."

"Make sure that you don't say anything to him, though, Kiya. Just grieve with him, all right?"

I nodded my head, forgetting again that he couldn't see me.

"All right?" His words were forceful but gentle.

"Yes."

"Now, please come back." His hands found mine and drew me back into the sanctuary of his embrace. "I've waited too long to have you in my arms. I'd rather not let go."

39

Eben held me close all night, leaning against the back wall of the small cave. I slept tucked under his chin and surrounded by his arms. When I awoke to the red sunrise blazing through the mouth of the cave, I did not move but lay against his chest, listening to the rhythm of his heart until the fiery sky paled to yellow. He stirred. I looked up at his face, but his eyes did not open.

"Are you uncomfortable?" I whispered.

He shook his head.

I attempted to sit up, but he would not release me. His eyes were still closed, but the corners of his mouth lifted.

"What are you doing?" I struggled against his arms.

"I told you: I'm not letting you go." He opened his eyes and looked down at me. "I'm never letting you out of my sight again."

My heart took flight, threatening to flutter right out of my chest and fly around the cave. "Do you promise?"

"I promise." He kissed my forehead. The tip of my nose. And then, feather-soft, my lips.

I couldn't help myself. I laughed.

He furrowed his brow in confusion.

"I'm sorry. It . . . it tickles."

"Excuse me?"

"Your beard. I've never kissed a man with a beard. Egyptian men would never wear such a barbarous thing." I feigned annoyance and pursed my lips to hide my smile.

His eyes went wide for a second, but then a mischievous look stole into them and he tickled my face, my ears, and my neck furiously with his beard. I laughed until my sides ached and I begged him to stop. He did, but he watched me with eyes changed to gold by the pale sunlight. I returned his gaze, drinking in the intensity between us. How could it be that this man who had seemed to hate me with such ferocity now looked at me with equal admiration?

My chest hollowed as a wave of awareness crashed over me, along with a furious undercurrent of guilt. My mother was dead yet here I was, laughing with Eben. How could I be so callous?

He placed his warm hands on either side of my face and traced my cheekbones with his thumbs in a soothing gesture, as if he sensed the sudden shift in my mood. "Why do you not wear kohl anymore?"

I had forgotten to somewhere along the journey—it no longer seemed important. I shrugged, well aware that he was trying to distract me from thoughts of my mother.

He tilted his head to one side. "The first time I saw you I wanted to jump into those puddles of honey-gold and never come up for air."

A shiver ran through me, and my mouth went dry. "The first time?"

"Mmm. I looked up, and there you were, so furious at poor Liat." He dropped a playful frown, but then sobered. "And all I wanted to do was fly over that table and—"

His lips were on mine and his arms around me, pulling me

closer—but it wasn't close enough. He kissed me until I could not breathe, but I wanted more; his touch dulled the shattering grief. I snaked my arms behind his neck and tangled my fingers in his dark hair.

"Here is what I wanted to do since the first time I met you," I said against his lips and twisted my fingers deeper. "But mostly to shake all of that sawdust out of your hair."

He laughed and then kissed me again, softly, and then with a passion to equal my own. My heart thudded wildly, and the heat of his lips kindled a flame in my veins. Everything was Eben, all around me; I clung to him, lost in blissful disorientation.

Suddenly, he pulled back, a reluctant move. "We need to go." He pressed my shoulders gently, his voice hoarse and trembling.

I nodded and dropped my eyes.

He lifted my chin with his finger. "What is it?"

I was not pure. I had given Akhum the part of me that should have belonged to Eben. If I told him, would that look of desire on his face change to disgust?

A thought struck me. "What do you mean, the *first* time you saw me? I thought you hated me, along with every other Egyptian."

Now his eyes fell. "The strength of my attraction to you was—disconcerting, shall we say. What you saw in me was not anger at you but frustration with myself. You have to understand, Kiya, how much I loved my father. He was the greatest man I have ever known, will ever know . . . and I watched him die . . . did Shira tell you that?"

I shook my head.

"I was there in the square that day, when they tied him to that post and whipped him until he could not stand, until he could not breathe from the pain of it. I saw the light go out of his eyes."

My heart throbbed at the agony of his words.

"All I wanted was vengeance. I spent every spare minute I had learning to throw that knife. Planning the day when I would slit an Egyptian throat with it, any Egyptian."

I winced.

"But then you came along, with all your strength and fire and beauty, and I was undone. What you saw was my fight against myself to keep from loving you." He stroked my hair, and I leaned into his hand. "Yahweh brought you to me, and instead of using my knife for vengeance, I used it to protect the woman I love."

My heart leapt at the declaration. *He loves me.*

But again, shame flared in my throat. How could I feel such satisfaction in the face of the overwhelming pain of my mother's loss? Could the two emotions live side by side?

"Three times." I smirked.

"Yes. Three times. Two deadly snakes."

"And thanks to Yahweh for that." I released a deep breath.

"Have you finally decided to believe in our God?" He lifted a brow.

"How could I not? He was with me in that tent. He guarded me until you came. He revealed himself, just like Mosheh told me he would."

Transient emotions crossed Eben's face—disbelief, curiosity, and then confusion.

"I will tell you about it later. But for now, you need to let go. I have to stand up."

He reluctantly released me, and I crept out of the cave to stretch.

The dry wadi around me was breathtaking in the golden morning light. Colors lined the walls of the small canyon, different strata of rock carved and smoothed over time by the rush of early-spring floods, as if a painter had decorated the wadi with stripes of reds, yellows, and oranges with many brushes. Jumo would love it.

Eben packed his bag and joined me out in the sunlight.

"Fascinating, isn't it?" He stretched out his arms.

"Yes, I wonder how it happened."

"Yahweh *is* a master craftsman after all." He gestured wide to the sky and the land all around us.

"Are you saying that Yahweh made this, painted it, like Jumo paints his pots?"

"Yes . . ." He lifted his brows, as though it were obvious. "Has Shira never told you the story of how the earth was made?"

I shook my head. She'd told me many stories of her people but never the beginning.

"I'll tell you as we walk. The camp is not so far from here."

He took my hand, and as we walked back to the Hebrew encampment, he told me the story of how Yahweh made the world. How he spoke it into existence with just a word from his mouth. He also said that HaAdam, the first man, Yahweh had designed with his own hands from the dust of the earth and stirred him to life with his *Ruach*, his divine breath.

"I think"— Eben began—"and this is only an idea out of my own mind, it could be true or not. You may think I am crazy."

His shy, uneven smile and the memory of his kiss warmed me head to toe.

"I love music, as you well know, and our language is a musical one, one that lends itself to poetry and prose, rhythm and rhyme. I believe that Yahweh did not just speak creation into existence. I believe he sang it into existence. Sometimes when I am alone, playing the lyre and singing, I feel as though he is singing with me. I am working together with the One who made the stars to create something new."

"That is beautiful." I squeezed his hand, which was rough and callused from hewing wood and carving instruments. I thrilled at the touch of it; silken skin could not compare. His hands told the story of his gifts and his past, and I wanted to never let go. I lifted his palm, still bearing three small scars from the acacia bush during the flash flood, and kissed each of them. They spoke of his courage and his love for my brother.

"How did you find me? In all that confusion?"

"It was the strangest thing. The Amalekites were ferocious. They were more than prepared for war with us, almost shockingly so. Even though we have a lot of men to fight, none of us is very skilled."

I raised my brows. Eben was more than skilled with a dagger.

"Well, most of us. Anyhow, only a few minutes into the battle and we were losing. They attacked at dawn, and we feared that before the sun even fully rose, we would be crushed. But then Mosheh came."

"You saw Mosheh?" I had never told anyone of my brief encounter with our enigmatic leader, but I kept silent, saving my revelation for another day.

"He was hard to miss up there on the ridge above the battle. When his arms and his staff rose high above his head, all of a sudden the enemy seemed to weaken."

"Why?"

"I'm not sure. But then, whenever his arms seemed to tire and droop, we began losing the battle again. Then a few minutes later, he would regain strength and then we would be stronger, push the Amalekites back even farther."

I was so fascinated by his story that I stopped walking. "But the fighting went on for hours and hours."

"At one point it looked as if Mosheh could not hold up his arms anymore. We were close to defeat. But then, two men—I have no idea who—came to stand beside him. Mosheh sat on a boulder and each of the men held up an arm. We pushed the Amalekites back, almost to their camp, and it was then that I saw Sayaad. When he caught sight of me, he turned and ran, and that's when I knew he had you." He gritted his teeth. "It was as if Yahweh guided me to him."

Eben looked off toward the hills and said nothing for a while. I wondered what images were behind his eyes. It was the first time he had been in battle—who knew how many men he had been forced to kill in hand-to-hand combat yesterday? And then, Sayaad as well.

All of us had lost so much in the past few days. How would any of us ever heal from these wounds? I wrapped my arms around his waist and laid my head on his shoulder.

How could I return to that camp, when my mother was no longer there? Even with the comfort of Eben's arms around me, the pit of my stomach ached. My beautiful mother, buried beneath the sand, her golden eyes closed for all eternity. Panic seized me. All I had ever known about death was from the stories of my people. I knew little of Yahweh, but I suspected that my idea of the afterlife might be as warped as my understanding of the gods had been. I clutched Eben's tunic, my breath coming quickly. *It is my fault she is gone.*

With concern on his brow, he wiped my silent tears. He kissed my lips and then leaned his forehead against mine. "I am here," he said.

Our breath mingled, and his nearness gave me strength. I drank it in like elixir.

Water gushed from an enormous rock on the side of the hill, tumbling down in an inexplicable torrent and creating a gentle river that split the camp in half. Eben explained to me how Mosheh had struck the rock with his staff to provide water for us—a response to the near rebellion that swelled when this valley was found to be completely dry. I wondered if the Ama-

lekite attack had something to do with this miraculous gush
of water in the desert, for surely their people and flocks were
as thirsty as ours.

Even more astounding was the vegetation that had already
sprung to life along the path of the river. The parched ground
had been awakened, long-dormant seeds joyfully pressing ten-
tative shoots of green skyward.

Many wounded men lay on pallets throughout the camps,
and I knew that there were many other men who had met their
end on the battlefield nearby. A rush of gratitude that Eben was
walking next to me, unscathed, flooded through me.

I did not fail to notice, however, some of the looks from the
Hebrews we passed. Some tried to be covert about it, duck-
ing heads down as we passed to whisper in each other's ears.
Many seemed to have no problem at all voicing their opinion
of a Hebrew man escorting an Egyptian woman through camp.

"*Zonah* . . ." accused one woman as I passed.

Another flung the word *traitor* at Eben.

Eben turned to defend us.

"No." I placed a hand on his shoulder. "Let it go. Let's just get
back to our family." Shira, Zerah, the girls—they had become
just as much my family as my own had been. I was as anxious
to see their faces as I was to look into my own brother's eyes.

Shoshana was the first to spot us, perched as usual on the
top of a wagon, her cry of happiness ringing out over the camp.
"Eben! Kiya! They're back!"

A flurry of shouts, fierce hugs, and tears enveloped us. Zerah
pushed everyone aside to wrap her arms around her son, her
face stoic, but palpable relief flowing out of every pore. Then
to my extreme surprise, she released him and turned to me,
grasping me tightly and kissing my cheeks.

"Welcome home." Her eyes pooled, and I realized that she
too grieved my mother.

Shira hugged me so tightly I could hardly breathe, but Jumo was nowhere to be seen. I craned my neck to search him out.

Shira whispered in my ear. "He is in his tent. He's barely been outside in the last three days."

"Does he know I am here?"

She shrugged. "Why don't you take him some food? I tried earlier, but he refused it."

Jumo was sprawled on his back across his bedroll when I entered his tent. His eyes were closed and his arm slung across his forehead, but he was clearly not asleep.

"Brother?"

His eyes fluttered open.

"Ya-ya." His brown eyes glittered with tears. Visible grief weighted his gaze, and I knew my own echoed the sentiment. I put down the bowls of manna I had brought with me and lay down beside him, stretching my arm across his chest.

"I'm home, brother."

Tears trickled down the sides of his face. I pressed my cheek to his, and they washed down my own face as well.

I ached to tell him that it wasn't his fault, but the memory of Eben's warning silenced me. Isolated on the island of pain we were stranded on together, we cried.

The odor of death lingered on the goat hide above me. I shivered. Sayaad's tent had smelled just like this one. I tried to sleep, but memories of my mother gathered like ghosts around me in the howling void.

Everything whispered of her: her empty pallet, her cosmetic box, Shefu's amulet now back around my neck. Jumo had returned the precious treasure to me, and I was grateful that somehow her murderers had not stolen that as well. Yet I almost wished that the symbol of her love for Shefu had been buried with her in the unmarked grave that lay somewhere in this barren wilderness.

Almond oil and frankincense permeated the dress I wore, one of her favorites. I prayed to Yahweh that the fragrance would never fade. I would wrap it inside other linens to preserve it, and place it inside the empty jar of Shefu's wine she kept hidden among her clothing.

I tossed back and forth on my pallet, the image of her unseeing eyes jeering me every time I closed my own.

Why had I not checked on her earlier? Or gone with her upstream? What if the lookouts hadn't been killed and had warned us? Would she now live? Question after question assaulted me, until I could no longer lie on my mat. I sat up, knees pulled to my chest and eyes blinking into the accusing dark.

The tent flap flew open, and the outline of a body slipped inside. My heart pounded so loudly I almost missed the whisper of my name.

"Shira! You startled me."

"I'm sorry." She sat next to me on my mat. "I didn't want you to sleep in this tent all alone."

I released a long, slow breath. "Thank you. I'd rather not."

She stammered. "Do you want to talk about—?"

"No."

I regretted the harsh interruption as soon as it flew past my lips. Even in the darkness, I felt her shrink back.

I cleared my throat. "Not right now."

"I understand."

"Thank you." I found her hand and squeezed it. "You've always been kinder to me than I deserved. And I never apologized after my hateful words on the beach—"

"There is nothing to forgive."

"Yes, there is. I was wrong. Wrong about everything." My voice broke.

"Kiya, I love you as my sister. Nothing you say or do will change that. Your hurt is my own. And . . ." Her voice softened. "I loved Nailah, too."

With nothing more to say, I lay back on my mother's pallet. Breathing in what remained of her beautiful fragrance, I let my tears flow.

Shira grasped my hand until I fell asleep.

40

"Are you coming?"

Eben crouched next to me. His hand brushed down my arm, bringing with it the heat of a lightning bolt across the night sky. His fingers entwined with mine, and I bathed in the indulgence of the obvious delight in his eyes before I answered.

"Where to?"

Mischief cocked his brow, and he pointed his bearded chin at my tent. "Not far, bring your lyre."

Jumo was seated across the Senet game box from me—one of the many gilded treasures given to Eben by Akensouris. We had been playing for hours, both of us trying to ignore our mother's uninhabited seat by the campfire. Jumo was a master of the game, always quick to block me, as if he could predict which move I would play next. I had won only a couple of games so far.

"G-Go." Jumo waved a hand, as if to brush me away.

I narrowed my eyes. "You just want me to go because I am winning."

Jumo unsuccessfully tried to smother a small smile, and a tiny spark of life, one I had not seen in days, glinted in his dark eyes.

To my surprise, he seemed to simply accept Eben and me together, and by the hints he'd dropped all day, he'd known much more than he had let on all along. My brother—always perceiving so much more than he could vocalize. Once again, a pang of regret that he could never truly tell me all he wanted to say, stung my heart. What would my brother say if he had been born with the ability to freely express his deepest thoughts?

I retrieved my precious lyre from the tent, and Eben led me to a place nearby where we could sit in the shade of a large olean-der bush yet still within sight of the camp. The reminder of our last day together, before the attack, was acute, and I hesitated when he asked me to sit, overcome with memories and regrets.

Compassion filled his gray-green eyes; he seemed to under-stand.

I chewed the inside of my cheek to keep tears from forming, wishing there were not witnesses to my grief all around us.

"Tell me." Tenderly, he smoothed a hand down my hair.

"My fault." My voice hitched on gulps and sobs. "If we had not left Egypt . . . or if I had kept her in my sight . . . or . . ."

"No. No. No." His hand gently met my cheek. "Your mother is not gone because of you any more than my father is gone because of me."

Did Eben blame himself? "I thought Egyptians killed your father."

"They did." He blinked slowly and released a shuddering breath. "But I had a hand in it as well."

He gestured for me to sit. I settled the lyre on the ground next to me and waited for Eben to sit as well.

Instead, he stood, half turned away, as if he could not face me.

"My father was the best of men. Twice the musician I am, able to hear and play anything without practice. He told me Elohim sang songs directly into his heart. They poured out of him. His stories were our bread; we lived on them, day to day."

He gazed toward the rock, which still gushed fresh cool water from the depths of the earth. "I loved my father, but I was young and foolish, more interested in running wild with my friends than sitting at his knee. I apprenticed with him but stayed at the shop only as long as was necessary before running off to find mischief with the other boys."

He stopped and smoothed his beard with his knuckles, seeming unsettled by the story he had to tell.

"I was twelve, eager to prove myself as a man and angry with the overseers who took pleasure in humiliating us. Even more so with Hebrews who lightened their load by doing the overseers' bidding."

Thoughts of Latikah flooded back, and again I wished that I had stayed with her that night, forgiven her, instead of leaving her to her fate.

"One man was known to be a well-rewarded traitor and lived at the edge of the Hebrew quarter. My friends and I waited until he was gone and then broke into his home and vandalized it. We ripped his clothes, spilled his food onto the ground, and slashed his linens. And careless as I was, I dropped my knife."

He patted the ivory handle now back in its sheath at his side. "The traitor found it when he returned home and knew immediately whose it was; my father was known to have carried it long before he gifted it to me, and a carved ivory dagger at the hip of a Hebrew drew attention."

I covered a gasp with my hand, anticipating the end of his story.

He nodded. "Yes, you guessed correctly. The Hebrew turned my father over to the Egyptians, and he was imprisoned. It was only two days later that so many of our men were rounded up to be slaughtered, my father among them."

Eben lowered himself to the ground, sorrow in his expression. "In the heat of my reckless twelve-year-old fury, I confronted the traitor the next day. The man was actually remorseful when I told him it was me that had destroyed his belongings. He returned the dagger, vowing that he would not have turned my father in if he had known what would happen."

"So"—he pulled my hand into his—"now you see. Without my destructive choices, my father might be alive now. And as much as I tried to lay the blame at the feet of the Egyptians, at my core my anger was directed at myself. It took friendship with your brother and falling in love with you to face it."

He ran a finger down my cheekbone, and I stifled a sigh.

"When I saw you talking to Sayaad, when your wagon broke down, it was all I could do not to sling you over my shoulder and run off with you."

"Truly, you knew even then?"

His finger moved to caress my lips. "Yes, my love. I was half mad with jealousy."

"No wonder Jumo was smirking at me."

His brow quirked.

"Jumo always knows."

Eben laughed. "Yes. That he does. He teased me mercilessly from that night on. But I am glad he did, because it helped me to admit that it wasn't you I was angry with, or even your people, but myself and my foolishness."

"But you were only a child. You could not have known what would happen."

"That is true; my father may have been rounded up had I not done what I did—evil men do evil things and even Yahweh's people are not immune to suffering. You did not know what would happen to Nailah, either. You were following the path Yahweh made for you, here into the wilderness with me. And your mother loved you; she would not hold you responsible."

I missed my mother so much, ached to hear her voice again. There were so many things I had never told her, questions left unanswered, memories yet to be made. She would never see me married or hold a grandchild in her arms. I longed to tell her of my love for Eben, and of the experience I had on the floor of the tent when Yahweh surrounded me in love. Her face on the morning the manna appeared—*"I asked for bread, and he provided,"* she had said—she must have understood, at least in part. But still, I had only begun to know her, to see her not as some goddess far above my reach but as a fallible and lovely human, weak in some ways and strong in others.

Would this chasm inside me ever be filled?

Eben gazed into my eyes. "Would you like me to play for you?"

I nodded and handed him the lyre, then folded my knees under my chin and wrapped my arms around my legs.

He played the song he had sung at the campfire by the sea, a lament that matched the heaviness pressing against my ribs yet brought with it also the memory of the night I had fallen in love with this fascinating and talented man. If he truly meant what he said, that he would stay by my side, then perhaps the pain might be easier to bear.

Shira had questioned, all those months ago, whether Yahweh was preparing me for something. Now I could see that it was true. Yahweh had brought me here into the wilderness to free me, to show me how to leave my idols behind, and to meet the man I would spend my life with. Yahweh cared enough to bring me out of slavery and ignorance, protect me in the desert, and to reveal himself to me in a tent during the middle of a battle.

The God who parted the sea could surely mend the rift in my heart.

41

We stood at the foot of a mountain. The Mountain of Yahweh, many were calling it. The Cloud that had protected us from the hands of Pharaoh hovered above the summit, larger, darker, and now violently booming and flashing sporadic blue lightning. Shoshana huddled beneath Zerah's arm, and Zayna buried her face in Eben's shoulder. She twitched every time the thunder rolled out from the mountain, shaking the ground and threatening to knock us from our feet. The sound of it was even more bone-rattling than the storms that had plagued Egypt.

Three days had passed since Mosheh had returned to the summit, carrying a promise from the Hebrews and from all of us who chose to be included in a covenant: a promise to Yahweh that we received his offer to be his *Am Segula*—his special people—and follow his instructions, his Torah.

Eben had taken me aside after the elders relayed Mosheh's instructions from Yahweh. He said that Jumo and I, anyone who desired so, regardless of their heritage, would be included in this covenant with the Hebrew God, if we chose to take part.

324

I was Egyptian, my mother and father, both of them born of the Nile, but my heart leapt at the prospect of becoming a part of this nation, the nation that would be called Israel.

From the day I had fallen on my knees and cried out to Yahweh, I had desired to know him better. If I felt his presence there on the sandy floor of an enemy tent, how much more would I know as a part of his chosen people?

Now, after three days of washing, preparing, and making new linen garments, we stood at the foot of the great mountain. All eyes were trained on the path from the top, a white-clad sea of people waiting for the return of Yahweh's messenger, Mosheh.

Midway through the morning, a tide of murmurs and echoes swam through the crowd.

"Mosheh has returned!"

"There, do you see him?"

The silver-blue Cloud roiled above the mountaintop, and a figure appeared at the foot of the path, standing high above the crowd.

Our families were so far back in the multitude, however, that his voice could not reach us.

But the message rolled back through the crowds.

". . . Yahweh will speak."

". . . his own voice."

". . . wonder what it will sound like . . ."

Zayna's little face peeked out from the sanctuary of Eben's chest. "Yahweh is going to speak? With his own voice?"

"It sounds that way," Eben said.

The voice of a god? I had served silent gods—wood, stone, and gold—for eighteen years of my life. And now, this God of the Hebrews would speak? Would we all hear it? Or would the words need to be passed among the multitude?

Jumo's eyes were locked on the summit of the mountain. The flashes of lightning reflected blue in his dark eyes. I reached out and put my hand in his. He squeezed, a reassuring gesture, but did not look my way.

A shofar sounded in the distance. Once again, the eerie sound raised the hair on the back of my neck and sent a mixture of longing and fear through my veins. The sound began to grow and build. It must be moving closer to us. It continued to intensify, coming not from the valley floor but from the summit of the mountain.

This was no ordinary instrument, and no human breath could produce this loud of a tone.

Louder.

Louder.

Ear-splitting.

Many around us covered their ears. Children shrieked at the abuse of their eardrums.

My bones vibrated in rhythm with the complicated patterns of notes echoing off the steep cliffs all around this protective valley. Who—or what—was giving breath to these ethereal instruments?

As the notes grew louder, the Cloud sitting atop the mountain seemed to respond in kind, billowing higher into the sky and blazing brighter as it did. It became a swirling rainbow of color, hues of every shade, some I had never seen before. The sensations were overwhelming—light, colors, and sound.

A Voice emanated from the Cloud, knocking me to my knees. An earthquake shook the valley, rattling the mountains and tossing boulders about like pebbles.

Most everyone was on their knees, or on their faces, many pleading or crying, some screaming in terror. My body instinctively attempted to struggle, to stand, but the weight of the force was immense.

Every horrible thing I had ever said, done, or thought swirled through my mind. Every time I cursed Tekurah, every time I disobeyed my mother, every disrespectful word I had spoken to Salima, every patronizing one to Shira, the nights I had spent with Akhum . . .

And the thoughts—the thoughts were even worse than the words or actions—every dark, violent, or evil imagining that had ever flickered inside my brain bubbled to the surface, ripped and tore its way through my consciousness. My stomach quelled violently at just how depraved I could be. I was black inside, filled with hate and pettiness.

The Voice did this; with only one pure syllable it stripped me bare, and I was undone. I hadn't even discerned the word spoken by Yahweh. The echo of it swirled around the valley, bounced off the cliffs, rose above us, and dissipated into the sky.

As the echo of the word died away, it left me with an emptiness at my core. Vaguely aware of those around me, their faces slowly blurring back into focus, I was not the only one decimated under the scrutiny of the Voice.

Most were sobbing, eyes closed, gripping their stomachs with clenched fists.

Eben was on the ground next to me, his face in the sand, arms outstretched toward the mountain. Shira crouched in front of me, protective arms wrapped around Shoshana, but Shoshana held her chin high, gazing at the face of the mountain. Her head was not bowed.

I peeked at Zayna sitting on the ground next to Eben. Her hand rubbed circles on his back. The precious girl was reassuring her older brother. Her upturned face was so peaceful, so joyful. A stab of envy shot through me. The Voice broke me into a million pieces, but the girls were enraptured. In fact, all of the children were looking up, their faces bright with the same fierce joy. They were not afraid of the Voice; they must hear something in it that I could not understand.

The Voice sent splinters of fear shredding through my veins, but I ached for it at the same time. I could not reconcile the confusing emotions.

The Voice spoke again. This time, the words filled my senses. They hung shimmering, as though written in the air, visible and musical—a song far more beautiful than human words could describe. And the fragrance . . . How could words have a smell? But they did, and it was the sweetest and loveliest smell to ever be imagined. I had smelled a shadow of it before, while I lay on a sandy floor with my hands bound. There was no spice fragrant enough, no breeze sweet enough, no fruit ripe enough to compare to the smell that permeated this valley. I pulled in an open-mouthed breath that melted on my tongue like a luscious delicacy.

The Voice told us that he was Yahweh, the God who had rescued us from Egypt, and there were to be no other gods before him. For hours, maybe days, he told us what he expected of us. He taught us, like little children, everything he wanted us to do, how we should live and treat each other, and most of all, how we should respect him, our God.

And what he promised, if we obeyed him like little children, was so far beyond what I expected. Yes, there were consequences for our disobedience, but the promises far outweighed them. We were to be his *Am Segula*—a special chosen nation, and as his people, we would inherit the promise given to Avraham so long ago, the land specially chosen to bless his family. But even more exciting was that Yahweh promised to be among his people, to reside with us, and teach us, protect us, and guide us. How could that be? A god, walking among humans?

When the last of the precious words shimmered away, I stayed on my knees, wishing the Voice would speak again. I wanted the song to fill my ears and heart forever. I ached long after the echo faded and knew I would do so for all my days. I understood every one of Yahweh's words, but had he spoken in Egyptian?

Or Hebrew? Or something else that my soul understood instinctively? I tried to remember the specific words, but only the meaning rang through me.

Long minutes passed before people began coming to their feet and moving off toward their tents, slow and silent.

I stayed on my knees in the sand, willing the Voice to return. But when Shira finally stood, I did as well. She put her arms around me—her face full of the joy that I had seen on the girls' faces, and I knew mine must be a reflection of that as well.

"Kiya," a voice said.

I glanced at Eben, thinking it was he who spoke my name, but he stared at something behind me, a startled look on his tear-stained face.

I spun around. Jumo was behind me.

"Kiya," he said again.

Shock flooded me, and I blinked hard and fast. "Did you just . . . ?" I whispered.

He nodded.

"Sister, I can speak easily now." Tears streamed down his face, and mine.

"How . . . ?"

"I am healed." He spoke with reverence; an awe filled his new voice that almost brought me to my knees again.

My mouth gaped; no coherent words would form.

"The very first word that Yahweh spoke healed me. I knew instantly that I could speak. And . . ." He stepped back, then turned and walked in a circle. Smooth, effortless movements.

My brother was completely healed. His speech was clear, and his legs were whole—as if he had never been afflicted in the first place.

42

The milky-white spray of stars above us witnessed a barely contained celebration. Hundreds of bulls were sacrificed at the foot of the mountain and the meat shared with all of us. Zerah had skewered our gift on a spit, the fat popping and crackling in the fire, and the mouth-watering scent of beef smoke drifted over the camp.

Between the sweet bread baked with manna, the tender flesh of the bull, and a few sweet onions purchased from traders that Eben and Jumo had encountered in the desert a few days ago, we feasted. However, my overstuffed stomach could not compare to the fullness of my heart.

Eben sang near the campfire until his voice was hoarse. He told me his fingers were numb as well, but he kept on playing, his joy spilling out into the language of music.

Jumo, too, sang in an unfamiliar and clear, sweet voice, in flawless Hebrew. His brilliant mind had absorbed every word in the long, unbroken months of listening as we journeyed toward this mountain.

We had spent the day together, knee to knee, absorbed in precious conversation, sharing stories of our mother, crying, and adjusting to the absence of silence between us. He told me more of how Yahweh had called to him in a series of dreams, promising blessings if he would follow the Hebrews, and I told him of my surrender on the floor of Sayaad's tent and my conversation with Mosheh.

Jumo's heart bubbled over, his thoughts tumbling over themselves like the water from the rock. The exquisite pain of finally understanding the depths of my brother's heartbreak over his inability to protect our mother—and me—dredged up fresh grief. We cried, foreheads pressed together, until the sun passed into the underworld.

Now he played the drum—the one made by his own hands, under Eben's guidance—with freedom and dexterity. Sweat poured down his face and soaked his black curls as he worked out the complicated patterns. Exhilaration was painted all over his face. I laughed until my sides ached and my cheeks were sore and my heart did not feel quite so empty of my mother's presence. She was there in his face, the thickness of his hair, the flicker of his smiles as he enjoyed his own talent.

Although I would grieve for my mother, probably for the rest of my days, I was grateful for the pieces of her that Jumo carried. And after basking in the all-encompassing light from the mountain and grieving with my brother, the sharp edges of pain did not throb as deeply tonight as they had yesterday.

Zayna and Shoshana finally succumbed to sleep, their little bodies exhausted from dancing like butterflies all evening. Shira and I gathered bowls, scrubbed them with sand, and rinsed them with water from the nearby stream.

Jumo sat cross-legged in front of the fire as the remainder of the flames licked at the embers. I wondered what was going through his mind and was tempted to ask him more questions, but for now, I sensed he needed time alone to wonder at the restoration of his limbs and his tongue.

Arms went around my waist, and Eben's low voice tickled my ear. "Come with me."

My pulse took flight. "And where am I going?"

"You'll see." His breath on my neck affected my equilibrium. "I'm stealing Kiya, Sister. Are you finished with her?"

Shira lifted an eyebrow, pursed her full lips, and folded her arms. "Well, there are a couple more pots to clean . . ."

"Hmm . . . I'm sorry to hear that." He pulled me by the hand with a mocking grin, and Shira's musical laugh floated behind us as he led me outside the reach of the firelight.

Shira had taken me aside earlier to tell me of her joy at the connection between Eben and me, and that she hoped she and I would soon be more than sisters of the heart. The thought of such a future lifted my hopes to unimaginable heights yet called attention to the delicate bond that could be broken by the truths in my past. Would Eben turn his back on me when I revealed such things? The burn of anticipation in my chest, and the conviction to tell Eben, grew the farther we moved from the campfire.

I should be fearful, plunging into the night, following Eben up a hillside path with only a small torch to light our way, but with his strong hand wrapped around mine, and the memory of the light of Yahweh's presence, my lifelong fear of the dark had been completely erased.

When we finally stopped climbing, Eben guided me to sit on a flat outcropping high above the valley floor. I caught my breath. The campfires spread out below us were smaller and farther away than I'd expected. Echoes of distant laughter and music floated up to our perch.

Eben secured the torch in a crack in the boulder next to us and then put his arm around my shoulder, pulling me close. I laid my head on his chest and breathed in his warm scent, a mixture of sand, sun, and his skin. No exotic perfume could ever compete.

"It's so quiet up here." I let out a trembling breath.

"Yes, it is."

"Everything seems too quiet now."

He pulled back to look at me, eyebrows raised.

"What?"

"That was exactly what I was thinking."

I laughed and put my head back on his chest. "After hearing the Voice in my head all day, filling my every thought, everything seems so hushed somehow."

He sighed. "When the music stops, we miss the song."

"Yes, exactly."

The rhythm of his heart against my cheek filled a bit of the space, but nothing could ever compare to the euphoria of Yahweh speaking directly to my heart, not even my love for this man who had drawn me in against my will.

"Do you think Yahweh will speak to us again?" I looked up at Eben, and my question echoed across his expression.

He pursed his lips. "I don't know. I hope so. Extraordinary, wasn't it?"

I nodded. "Makes me feel like everything here is just a shadow."

"How so?"

I straightened my back. "It's as if the Voice is the only thing that is real and this"—I gestured to the mountains and the camp below—"this is only an illusion."

"Hmm. Intriguing thought. Yahweh is the creator of all that there is. He is the most real thing, the only eternal thing. Our hearts will stop beating, our eyes will close, the mountains may someday crumble, the trees will wither away, but Yahweh will always be."

I considered that, but my frail human mind could not wrap itself around the concept of a god, a being, that was the beginning and the end of everything. I looked up at the stars, brilliant lights created simply by his words—or perhaps by his song. Did they sing, too? A reflective resonance of the music begun by the God who sang the first note?

No longer under the illusion that their sparkle contained the souls of departed gods, I simply appreciated them for what they were: lights to tell the story of the God who made them and to point ahead to the coming of a Redeemer who would make all things new. Eben had told me that many people thought Mosheh was the One, for he had led us out of slavery in Egypt, but I knew now that only surrender to the pure fragrance and light of Yahweh himself could free my soul from the bondage to the idols I had served and cleanse my heart from the shame of the sins I did not even know I carried. My heart now resonated with the song Yahweh had sung over me.

"Who is Yahweh, Eben?"

He shook his head. "I don't know. I know he is the Creator, Elohim, and the God who took us out of Egypt. We know now what he expects of us, as his people. His instructions give me a glimpse of his character. But there is much left to learn about this God we follow."

"I want to know everything." I gazed up at the mountain. The Cloud of light still hovered there, and a faint remnant of the fragrance, so potent in the valley earlier, wafted by on the breeze.

"We are his people now, and as long as we follow him, cling to him, I think we will learn more."

"Am I truly a part of his people? Even though I am Egyptian?"

He stared into my eyes, the burn of love and sincerity intense in his own. "You stood at the foot of the mountain and entered into a blood covenant with Yahweh. You may have been born Egyptian, but you are part of this nation now. Besides"—he caressed my palm and entwined his fingers with mine—"once I marry you, you will be considered flesh of my flesh and bone of my bone. Every right of my people will be yours."

"You want . . . to . . . me?" My tongue tangled to a halt.

"Did Jumo steal your words and give you his affliction instead?" The sound of his musical laughter echoed off the rocks around us.

"But yes—my beautiful, brave Kiya . . ." He put his finger in the center of my forehead, slowly skimming it down to the tip of my nose. I closed my eyes to savor the sensation of his slightest touch rippling through me. "I want to make you my wife. I have desired it since the moment you told me you would sacrifice yourself for my sister."

I peered at him. "When did I tell you such a thing?"

"You were prepared to offer yourself to the guard to rescue her." He winced and exhaled. "It took every bit of self-control inside me to not pull you into my arms, right then and there. And walking away . . ." He groaned. "The next day was torture, knowing what you were planning. Every moment since then I have regretted that day."

"Nothing happened. Yahweh protected me from myself."

"Yes. He did, but it does not negate my choice to turn away from you. To let you—"

I placed my hand on his cheek, my thumb silencing his lips. "It is in the past. Lay it down."

He met my gaze. "My life was nothing but scattered rhythms and dissonant notes before I met you."

"I think Yahweh is creating something new from our broken pieces." I slid my hand around the back of his neck and drew him close to me. "Perhaps he is writing a new song."

"Yes. And you, my bride-to-be, are the melody." His lips brushed mine with exquisite tenderness, melting every thought but this man who would be my husband.

I pulled back and lifted a playful brow. "And you will of course plead with Jumo for my hand?"

"Already done." He smirked. "It is settled. You are mine."

I narrowed my eyes. "And was the bride-price exorbitant?"

"Oh, terribly. Something about a goat . . ."

Feigning offense, I elbowed him, and he laughed until I joined him. But the conversation my mother and I once had about Eben began to whisper in my thoughts.

"Aren't Hebrews supposed to marry only Hebrews?" The insults that had been hurled at us as we walked through camp seemed to follow us everywhere now. I had been accepted by Yahweh, that much was clear. But would I ever be accepted among his people?

"Yes, but you have chosen to serve our God. The traditions we have to marry our own kind are to protect us from the influence of other gods."

A spark of mischief glinted in his eyes as he grinned and tilted his head to one side. "You aren't going to drag me into your heathen idolatry, are you?"

My mother's amulet was packed among her other belongings; it was no more than a thing to me now. Hathor was an illusion, like everything else I grew up believing. Only one God had ever listened to my prayers, even before I believed.

My answer was emphatic. "No. I serve Yahweh."

"Well then." He raised a brow. "There is no problem now, is there?"

Only one. I sighed. I could not keep it from him any longer. I must surrender it all.

He lifted my chin and looked into my eyes. "What is it?"

My confession spilled out. "I am not pure. Akhum, the man I was betrothed to, we . . ."

He put a finger to my lips. "It does not matter."

"But . . ."

"I already knew, Kiya. I was there, that night in the garden when that—" He paused and swallowed, a fierce expression on his face. "I came to make sure you were safe. I couldn't bear not knowing."

He was there? When Akhum tried to make me his slave? I groaned, covering my face in my hands. How could he even look at me?

Gently, he tugged on my wrists, forcing me to meet his gaze. His beautiful eyes latched onto mine with piercing intensity.

"I was paralyzed, watching you sit there in the moonlight. I could not take my eyes off you . . ." He brushed his hand down my hair. "So when he came, I was trapped in the shadows, and I heard your conversation."

"All of it?" The burn of shame in my throat squelched my voice. It came out in a tortured whisper.

He leaned his forehead against mine, his breath sweet with manna. "Shh. It does not matter. All the darkness the Voice uncovered within me today . . . there is nothing you have done or could do that would rival it."

"You would marry me? Knowing this?" Relief flooded through my veins.

"What I know is that after the shame of being laid bare, when the Voice faded away, I felt as if my black heart had been washed clean. Don't you feel the same?"

I did. Clean. Free. And although I still mourned my mother, the weight of my grief seemed lighter, as if the rift were already healing. What grace I had been shown today—by Eben and by the One True God.

"I do not know how to follow Yahweh," I whispered.

He faced me, the light above the mountain reflecting in his eyes. "Neither do I, my love. We will learn together."

A Note
from
The Author

Many wonderful books have been written about Moses and other main players in the Exodus story. But I am a simple girl; I know little of kings and less of political machinations. My imagination was sparked not by the glittering palaces and the powerful men who walked their halls—however fascinating—but by the inhabitants of the mud-brick homes that have long since washed away, the slaves who toiled beneath the lash of Pharaoh's whip, and most of all by the "mixed multitude" spoken of in Exodus 12:38 who made the choice to walk away from everything they knew to follow an old man and his faceless god into the wilderness. Out of my own personal curiosity into their motivations, Kiya's story was born.

Fascination with the world of Ancient Egypt is nothing new. For hundreds of years, explorers and archeologists have been drawn to divulge its secrets and piece together its mysteries.

When Kiya called to me from that distant land, asking me to tell her story, I knew nothing of Egypt, other than odds and ends from school, church, and popular culture. And as it is with most history, the deeper I delved into Egypt's past, the more I realized how little we truly know. So much of Egyptian culture—especially that of the everyday citizens—has been lost to the harsh climate, tomb robbers, and overzealous amateur archeologists, and confused by exaggerations and misinterpretations over time. Even Sir Alan Gardiner, the famous Oxford Egyptologist, said that what we have of the Egyptians is "merely a collection of rags and tatters." Since it is only these rags and tatters that I had to work with, any imperfections in historical details are due to either conflicts of opinion between historians and Biblical scholars, or my own overactive imagination.

The reader will note that I do not name the Pharaoh anywhere in this book. I have two reasons for doing so. First, I believe, unapologetically, that the Word of God and its histories are true. Because the chronologies, built upon the writings of a third-century Egyptian priest named Manetho and accepted by most secular Egyptologists, do not fit with the Biblical account, I hold them highly suspect. When anything conflicts with the Bible, I will always defer to the Word.

There is, however, exciting new evidence being brought to light by archeologists and scholars that does support the Biblical timeline. I would encourage curious readers to look into the recent documentary called *Patterns of Evidence: Exodus*, which highlights these interesting discoveries.

Secondly, in Ancient Egyptian culture, names were very important. A person's *ka*, or spirit, was symbolized by their name. If that name was chisled off a written account on a tomb or temple wall it, in effect, erased that person from history—thereby destroying their rewards in the afterlife. Many historical figures, such as Akhenaton and Hatshepsut (the famous female

Pharaoh), were treated thus by their enemies, and it has taken hundreds of years for their histories to be rediscovered.

I believe that God purposefully chisled Pharoah's name from the Word, and therefore, history. The names of the kings that Moses interacted with will never be known for sure, so their achievements are unknown as well. But conversely, take a moment and read Exodus 1:15–21. Whose names are written in the Word of God, for all posterity? Shifrah and Puah—the brave midwives who stood against the most powerful man in the world and, out of fear for God, lied to Pharoah's face to protect Hebrew lives. The Pharaohs of the Exodus account are nameless. Yet these courageous women are honored for eternity.

Although I began the journey into Ancient Egypt and Kiya's story alone, there are many people who have traveled with me. I would like to inscribe their names into the "wall" here and acknowledge them for their help along the way.

Thanks go first to my sweet husband for his support and willingness to let me put aside other things to pursue my passion. And to my beautiful children, who are my greatest cheerleaders and put up with their post-late-night-pre-coffee mama on a regular basis. I love you to the moon, my precious family.

I am so grateful for my mother, Jodi Lagrou, for being my endlessly patient sounding board and for her insights and wisdom into the Word. Thank you, Mom, for praying for me, encouraging me, and letting this book-a-holic check out giant stacks of books from the library. I am sure I still owe you lots of late fine money.

Putting a story out into the world is a scary proposition for any aspiring writer. I have been blessed with so many people who read my scribblings and saw potential in them. Without their support and encouragement, this book would not have been published. With her kind words, Adina Schenkenberger, my first reader, gave me the courage to show others my work. After enduring my trembly-voiced readings of my first drafts, Lynne Gentry, Kellie Coates Gilbert, Janice Olsen, and all the rest of the lovely Brainknockers gave me the confidence to pursue publication. Susan May Warren, Rachel Hauck, and everyone with My Book Therapy floored me with their enthusiasm for my story and generosity with their expertise. My awesome agent, Tamela Hancock Murray, took a chance on this newbie and found the exact right home for my stories. Thank you to Charlene Patterson, Raela Schoenherr, and everyone at Bethany House for catching my vision for this story and to Jennifer Parker for crawling into my imagination and designing such a beautiful cover. Juli Williams and her brilliant daughters, Anni and Cassi, were some of my first "fans." Thank you, Juli, for reading my ever-changing drafts, sharing your honest opinions and insight, and being my Personal Image Consultant and a sister of my heart. Ami Trull, my talented friend, made me look all "author-y" with her gorgeous photography. My lovely beta readers, Misty Hunt, Karla Marroquin, Kristen Roberts, Brenda Jeter, and Jennifer Traugott, have helped me immensely with their suggestions and support. And finally, thanks to all the prayer warriors, including Melissa Tabor, Heather Hardin, Heidi Thedford, Aamanda Bragg, Laura Kanaykina, and my Remedy Church family, who faithfully keep me and my writing before the Throne. If I have forgotten anyone, please forgive me—but know that your names are written on my heart forever.

QUESTIONS
for
CONVERSATION

1. Kiya's life changes drastically at the beginning of this book, due to the consequences of someone else's actions. When have you found yourself at the mercy of another person's poor decisions? What good, if any, came out of that situation?

2. Kiya's love for her family determines her choices in many ways, to the point of sacrificing her own freedom. When have you chosen to place someone else's needs above your own? What sacrifice was required? When has someone done the same for you?

3. From the time she was a young girl, Kiya was terrified of the dark. When Egypt is struck with plagues, she is forced to endure three days without light. Have you ever had to

conquer a phobia? Which of the plagues do you think would have been the most frightening?

4. Kiya was intrigued by the way Shira responded to her circumstances. How did the way she lived draw Kiya toward Shira's God? How can we live winsomely so that others will desire to know our God?

5. Kiya comes to realize why Tekurah is such a bitter woman. When have you struggled with bitterness? How does bitterness affect your relationships? What do you imagine happened to Tekurah after this story?

6. As someone who grew up believing in many gods, Kiya struggles with changing her worldview to one that acknowledges Yahweh as the One True God. How is your worldview different from the culture in which you live? How does your faith impact the way you live your daily life?

7. The plagues and miracles of Exodus have been depicted in various ways in popular culture (books, movies, etc.). Which ones, if any, did you visualize differently than the author? What new insights did you gain from the author's descriptions of the plagues and miracles?

8. Idol worship was commonplace in the ancient world. What are some things in our culture that have been elevated to the status of idols? In your own heart, what are some idols that you struggle to leave behind as you move toward Christ?

9. Egypt was the most powerful and wealthy nation in the world at the time of this story. What similarities do you

see between Ancient Egyptian culture and our own? What lessons can we learn from the demise of Egypt?

10. The story of the Exodus is a beautiful foreshadowing, or prefiguration, of Jesus's death and resurrection, and the sacrifice he made to purchase our freedom from sin (Exodus 12, Hebrews 11:23–29). What similarities can you see between Moses and Jesus? How does Kiya's journey echo your own spiritual journey?

11. When Kiya arrives at Shira's home the night the firstborns of Egypt are killed, she is confused by the blood on the doorway and the other "strange" Hebrew rituals. For thousands of years, the Jewish people, and many Christians, have memorialized that night by celebrating Passover. Have you ever attended a Passover celebration? If so, how did it enrich your perception of Jesus?

12. The next book in this series follows the story of Shira. What do you imagine will happen? What themes from this story do you think will be further explored? Which characters are you curious to know more about?

When she is not homeschooling her two sweet kids (with a full pot of coffee at hand), **Connilyn Cossette** is scribbling notes on spare paper, mumbling about her imaginary friends, and reading obscure, out-of-print history books. There is nothing she likes better than digging into the rich, ancient world of the Bible and uncovering buried gems of grace that point toward Jesus. Her novel *Counted With the Stars* won the 2013 Frasier Contest and was a semifinalist in the 2013 ACFW Genesis Contest. Although a Pacific Northwest native, she now lives near Dallas, Texas. Connect with her at www.connilyncossette.com.

More Biblical Fiction

When King David forces himself on Bathsheba, a loyal soldier's wife, she loses the husband—and the life— she's always known. Now, pregnant with the king's child, she struggles to protect her son and navigate the dangers of the king's household.

Bathsheba: Reluctant Beauty by Angela Hunt
A DANGEROUS BEAUTY NOVEL
angelahuntbooks.com

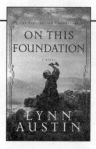

When news reaches him that Jerusalem's wall is shattered, a distraught Nehemiah seeks God's guidance. As soon as he is granted leave from his duties to the King of Persia, Nehemiah sets out for Jerusalem to rebuild the wall—never anticipating the challenges that lie ahead.

On This Foundation by Lynn Austin
THE RESTORATION CHRONICLES #3
lynnaustin.org

Only two men were brave enough to tell the truth about what awaited the Hebrews in Canaan: Caleb and Joshua. This is their thrilling story, from the toil of slavery in Egypt through the trials of the wilderness to the epic battles for the Promised Land.

Shadow of the Mountain: Exodus by Cliff Graham
SHADOW OF THE MOUNTAIN #1
cliffgraham.com

BETHANYHOUSE

Stay up-to-date on your favorite books and authors with our free e-newsletters. Sign up today at bethanyhouse.com.

Find us on Facebook. facebook.com/bethanyhousepublishers

an open book

Free exclusive resources for your book group! bethanyhouse.com/anopenbook